CLEAR
TO THE
HORIZON

Dave Warner is an author, musician and screenwriter. His first novel *City of Light* won the Western Australian Premier's Book Award for Fiction, and *Before it Breaks* (2015) the Ned Kelly Award for best Australian crime fiction. Once nominated by Bob Dylan as his favourite Australian music artist, Dave Warner originally came to national prominence with his gold album *Mug's Game*. In 2017 he released his tenth album *When*. He has been named a Western Australian State Living Treasure and has been inducted into the WAMi Rock'n'Roll of Renown.

www.davewarner.com.au
@suburbanwarner

DAVE WARNER
CLEAR
TO THE
HORIZON

 FREMANTLE PRESS

To those who wait and those who work tirelessly to help them

PART ONE

CHAPTER 1

I remember the 22nd of October 1999 better than I remember most days. Most are a jumble. Hell, nowadays most years are like rubber bands left too long in a drawer. When you're not looking, they mutate into one sticky glob. Ninety-nine stood out partly because of the Prince song, 'Tonight I'm going to party like it's nineteen ninety-nine'. But here was '99 and there was very little partying to be had in the domain of Snowy Lane. There was a lot of shit going down in Timor. Pro-Indonesian militants from the west side of the island were raiding the recently autonomous east. They wanted things how they used to be. Don't we all? I crave for the body of my football days when I could run and twist and turn but twenty years on this was my exercise: floating on my back in the Indian Ocean, a stone's throw from the Ocean Beach Hotel, looking up at a timeless sky and the belly of the occasional big transport heading out to sea. I would right myself and gaze towards Rottnest Island. The silhouette of warships had grown more frequent these last few months. In my youth I might have found it exciting but now I didn't want war, I didn't want anything messing up my life which was – apart from being unable to twist and turn with my youthful exuberance – better than it had ever been. Business was good. There was just the right amount of employees stealing from their work and just the right amount of suspicious spouses to keep a private detective employed, with enough free hours to kick back. This was me relaxing, salt water licking my ears, the smell of seaweed close and fresh. There was a bunch of us, probably fifteen all up but usually around six to eight, mainly guys, one or two women, who would find ourselves half-asleep at the beach when the sun was still pale. We'd swim from North Cottesloe down to Cottesloe around the pylon and back, maybe two to three k,

I suppose. After that we'd dry off and trudge up the stairs to the café above, share a coffee and toast before taking off back to our real lives.

Most mornings I made the ritual. When I had a job on I sometimes had to skip but there's nothing like a swim to get me going. The reason I remember this day, it was a Friday, was because on Sunday, there would be – as Prince predicted – a party: Grace's first birthday. We weren't planning anything fancy, just a play in the local park with other kids and parents from the playgroup Natasha had clubbed in with. My job was to blow up balloons and cook sausages, Tash would bake cupcakes. After Grace was born, Tash had taken five weeks off full-time work. A smart move because that took her into Christmas and New Year, which all Australians know, is a virtual holiday. Goannas shut down in winter, for us it's summer – aestivate, I think is the word I remember from sweaty classrooms when a single ceiling fan did its best to push our collective BO around while a male teacher in short-sleeved nylon shirt, long socks and comb-over tried to teach science. From the Melbourne Cup in November till Australia Day at the end of January, we're occupying space but the only work being done is planning the Christmas party. Tash's workload was thin enough to manage from home while taking care of the baby, so in that regard I was off the hook most of the time. Tash does some editorial thing with a style magazine called, wait for it ... *Swysh*. Yes, that's how it's spelled. There's a lot of drivel about which coverings are in this year, a lot of recipes, a lot of stuff on weight loss. The two biggest interests for her generation seem to be food and how to make it look like you've never eaten it. I should have sold up my detective agency, bought a pizza parlour and a gym.

On October 22, 1999, Natasha's thirtieth birthday was around the corner but she hadn't aged in all the years I'd known her: not back then, not now. For a long time it was like that for me. Every day I'd stare in the mirror to shave, and my face looked no different than it had ten years earlier. Then Grace was born, and overnight I had character lines and my whole take on the world changed and ships on the horizon and low-flying transports were no longer exciting or interesting but disturbing.

Perth's October is as reliable as your parents' old Holden. This one was no exception. The sun was warm, not fierce, the flowers smelled good, tiny creatures hummed, the final field was almost decided for the Cup, and the bacon sandwich they made at the café, while overpriced, was good quality. I often idly wondered what it would be like to live around here instead of where I did, inner-city north among retired market gardeners and Vietnamese. Very pleasant, I guessed, but knew, even on our combined income, I was dreaming. Former leviathan businessman Barry Dunn was said to inhabit an expensive apartment across the road and to frequent the café but our paths hadn't crossed for years. In fact I'd only seen him once since the funeral of his mistress, my former lover. A psycho rich kid had cut off her head; I'd wound up with broken ribs and become a five-minute hero exposing corrupt police and the wealthy they protected. Then I'd slipped back to anonymity. Dunn had taken a dunking on some big international plays, his ex-wife got the mansion, his racehorses had to be sold. The upstart Dunn would never get back to where he had been; the captains of industry were determined to keep him a cabin boy.

The grass isn't always greener. I had Tash and Grace, enough money to pay the bills, the ocean and a tasty bacon sandwich, so whatever envy came my way was fleeting. That day I sat back and sipped my coffee, grabbed an abandoned *West* off the table next to me. The headlines were all Timor. Was Indonesia going to become more involved, send troops back over the border? Consensus was it was covertly already provisioning the militia and this might escalate. There was an article about how our computers were going to stop working on New Years Day – I could only hope – and another about the Olympics. In a year's time they would be on in Sydney. Sports journos were tipping record medal counts, naysayers were claiming stadiums wouldn't be adequate. This is what I remember of October 22, 1999. Later the date would be burned into my brain because it was the last time I swam without a shadow looming over me, and I don't mean a troop transport.

About forty hours on, Emily Virtue, a twenty-year-old woman, said goodbye to her friends at a Claremont nightclub, went out to get a taxi home, and disappeared. Claremont was one suburb inland from where I sat that morning. It was the heartland of the city's rich and powerful whose kids carried on charmed lives around private schools and the university, a few Dolce & Gabbana clip-clops south of where twenty years earlier Mr Gruesome snatched the young female victim I later found.

In 1979, I was a young cop. That was an epoch away, before mobile phones and CDs, when there were still drive-ins and bands like Loaded Dice filled the pubs six nights a week. But nobody was thinking about that precedent, even though Emily's disappearance was out of character. The family were beside themselves; the police, I knew, would be taking it very seriously. They'd be looking at boyfriends, perverts, anybody who might have held a grudge but these dreadful things happen not infrequently and Emily's disappearance just buzzed in the background of my life, another nasty piece of news that bobbed up on the TV during sessions while I tried to feed Grace yoghurt.

...

Things changed just after Australia Day as Perth grudgingly went back to work disappointed to find the computers hadn't stopped.

I'd headed into the office. A year earlier I'd finally shelled out for an air conditioner but otherwise it was just a slightly cooler version of the same crappy upstairs space I'd rented for fourteen years. I was writing up a report on an unfaithful husband. The wife was sure he was having an affair. She'd paid me to tail him over Christmas because she knew he'd bought a bracelet and suspected it wasn't for her. She'd even offered me triple rates for Christmas Day. Tash told me to work, she wasn't up to much anyway and the money would be useful. I advised the wife to wait and see if he gave her the bracelet. He ran a printing operation out Osborne Park way and for the nine days I'd be on his case he was flat out, working even Christmas Eve, long after all his employees had gone home. I ticked each one off as they departed. None came back, no dalliance there. He finally shut up shop around 10.00. I followed him home, no stop-offs. I was starting to think the wife was mistaken. She rang me at 9.30 Christmas morning to say he'd given her a basket full of beauty products but no bracelet. He'd also warned her he'd have to head into work right after the extended family Christmas lunch. This, she was sure, was when he'd give the lover the present he'd bought. I grabbed a couple of prawns from what was to have been our lunch platter, then roasted in my car in downtown Dianella imagining those along the street enjoying turkey, sparkling wine and traditional plum pudding. Around 2.00 in the afternoon I watched the target head out and followed.

There was little cover Christmas Day but it's not the day you're going to be looking for a tail either. He didn't go to his work. Instead he drove to a house in Yokine, got out and let himself in. There were no other vehicles in the place. About twenty minutes later a familiar car pulled into the driveway. The car was one that had been at the extended family gathering. A woman got out. At first I thought it was my client, same age, same slim build and, from a distance, same features. It crossed my mind she was going to confront him and something horrible could happen. But as I was about to jump out and stop her I saw it wasn't my client at all but her sister. Instead of getting out, I took photos. After she'd keyed herself in I crossed over to the house and scanned for a clear window shot but there was nowhere that was not covered by a blind. I went back to my car and waited. Seventy minutes later he emerged. There was no kiss on the doorstep unfortunately. I followed him home and reported my findings next day to the anxious wife. Of course she was beside herself: her sister was a slut, her husband an arsehole. She was going to take him for everything he was worth. I handed her the photos and promised her a report in due course. My fee was paid by cheque six days later but there had been no further communication from her. That isn't unusual. Clients often don't want to be reminded of such humiliation. Then last week she'd called me out of the blue.

'How are things?' I asked, cautious. 'I was a bit worried.'

'Things are fine. It was all a mistake.'

That pricked my interest. I asked her how so.

'Tony told me he knew I'd hired you.'

'What? I never ...'

'He said he followed me to your office and guessed what I was up to. He decided to teach me a lesson. He had my sister get involved. She'd picked the bracelet out for me and he was going to give it to me but was angry I didn't trust him, so he made out like something was going on. I was stupid. You told me he worked all that week, right?'

You had to hand it to the guy. 'And your sister backed him up?'

'Yes. But it's all fixed. I even got the bracelet.'

'Okay. I'm glad it all worked out.' What else could I say? 'I still need to write up a report.'

'That's fine, I don't need it.'

'I'll do it anyway, fulfil my part of the contract. You can burn it or toss it in a bin.'

'Whatever. Don't bust a gut.'

And she'd hung up. So here I was in the early days of the new millennium doing useless work in a crappy office. My phone rang. I answered, still writing.

'Lane.'

'Snowy Lane?'

Not many people call me that any more – footballers, cops I used to work with. His voice sounded too young to be somebody from my past.

'Who is this?'

'Snowy, it's Dan Husson from *The West Australian*.'

Doubtful he was a potential client. Almost certainly some young journo wanting to quiz me about the Gruesome case. Every few years somebody rings me. They always get the same answer: I have nothing to say.

'This is about Gruesome?'

'Yes. You're certain you got the right guy?'

This was a new tack.

'Goodbye, Dan.'

'Wait. Have the police spoken to you yet?'

My brain was entirely on the phone conversation now.

'About what?'

'You know about Emily Virtue?'

'Yes.'

'Another young woman has just gone missing. She's eighteen. Caitlin O'Grady. She was at the same nightclub, Autostrada, left to get a taxi.'

I felt numb. 'When?' I said.

'Saturday night, early Sunday. You see why I'm asking?'

Yes, I saw. The Mr Gruesome killings had been perpetrated by two young psychos, Steve Compton and Joey Johnson. I'd been told Compton killed Johnson and I had no reason to doubt it because the person who told me that was Compton's father, before he shot his own son dead and turned the gun on himself.

'These murders aren't the work of Gruesome. Compton and Johnson were responsible and they're dead.'

'Johnson's body was never recovered.'

'Listen, mate, you write whatever story you like but this isn't Gruesome. That ended years ago.'

'Maybe there was somebody else? A third party?'

'Run your theory by the police, I'm sure they'll be glad for the insight.'

When you are touched by evil, it leaves deep within you a trace like some dormant virus waiting to be reactivated into full-blown dread. That phone call was all it had taken. I felt sick. I didn't know enough to guess whether this was some copycat, or another psycho striking out on his own. I was certain however that I had nailed Gruesome, that Johnson and Compton were dead and that they were the only people responsible. I wanted to leave the whole thing, to go back to my mundane case of the unfaithful printer. I wanted to forget that the world could be this ugly, even in the little nook in which I had chosen to live. In the blink of an eye, Grace would be one of these young women, out there enjoying herself with friends. I wanted the world to be safe for her to do that. My heart bled for the parents of the missing girls. Somehow I felt a failure all over again. Early in the Gruesome case I thought I'd helped catch the killer, only to find I'd been deceived. I'd regrouped, gone back, caught the real Gruesome. But you can't slay the darkness of the human soul. Victories are only reprieves before the next battle.

I reached for the phone. George Tacich was my link. He was now the top Homicide dog. I guessed he would be running the case. Funny, I hadn't even thought of him before in connection with Emily Virtue. We'd got on well in the Gruesome case and I'd lined him up a good job as an investigator with the corruption team investigating political skulduggery but he'd decided to go back to Homicide. From time to time I'd seen him on TV but it had been about four years since we'd spoken. That had been at his bowling club. I'd happened by while he was at the bar and we jawed on for a good hour or so without feeling obliged to follow up. Now I called the main switchboard and asked to be put through to Homicide but the woman on the other end was having none of that. I left my name and contacts, told her I was personal friend of Inspector Tacich and asked her to get a message to him to call me when he was able. I was guessing that could be a long while. Assuming the police were called about Caitlin's disappearance sometime on the Monday morning, it meant they would be just over the forty-eight-hour window now. Everybody would have pedal to the metal, the adrenalin stinking up the case room. Most wouldn't have slept more than an hour or two. I finished the report but it was even more meaningless now. I stuck it out in the office for just under an hour then drove home because I wanted to see my wife and hold my daughter and protect her forever from those who would do her harm.

...

Grace was driving her mother nuts. Tash was trying to eke out the last few days she had free to get anything meaningful done at home before work roared back to life, so I was welcomed with open arms. I put Grace in a papoose and walked to the local park. She sat in the sandpit and played with rubber Disney figurines. It helped.

Caitlin's disappearance led the evening news. The assistant commissioner took the questions. No sign of George Tacich, too busy I guessed. I dropped any expectation of him calling. Then around 10.15, the phone rang and it was him. Natasha had long hit the sheets, exhausted.

'I won't ask how it's going,' I said.

'Good, because we've got sweet FA.'

George knew me well enough to know that anything he said was staying zipped. I told him about Husson's call. He knew right off why I'd wanted to talk.

'Don't worry, Snow. For a start, if they are dead, he's not dumping the bodies. I don't see anything similar in the MO, not to mention it's been twenty years with no activity in-between.'

Perth's population had grown by probably twenty percent since those days. This was a psycho for the next generation. I asked one question to reassure myself.

'You spoken to Listach?'

'Yeah. He runs a restaurant in Bali now.' Franz Listach had been the celebrity shrink who had been treating and hiding Steve Compton. 'He confirmed what he told us twenty years ago. Steve Compton killed Joey Johnson and there was nobody else involved.' There had never been any benefit in Listach lying about Johnson. In fact the opposite was true. I breathed a little easier.

'How's Natasha?'

'She's great. We've got a little girl, Grace.'

'Best times. Don't waste them. Sorry mate, I have to go.'

'Good luck.'

'Thanks, we need it.'

That night I slept soundly. I didn't even hear Natasha get up to feed the baby. Next morning I swam, went to work and posted the report on the philandering printer. Like everybody else, I followed the case of the missing young women through the news. Husson's piece came out and created a brief flurry but I'd already lit out of town. Tash had given me the green light and I'd driven up to Geraldton to stay with an old footy teammate who ran a cray-boat. George Tacich was on the news a couple of times, eerily reminiscent of a coach whose team was welded to the bottom of the ladder, talking up inconsequential 'positives'. The case was stalled. They had no body. That was a huge problem. I ended my short vacation, went back to work, nobody bothered me about the case, Grace settled into a better sleeping pattern. By the time winter crept into our beds, life in Perth was almost normal. Women were still careful about waiting for taxis alone; Claremont's night scene was skinnier than it had been but not anorexic.

And then Jessica Scanlan disappeared after drinking with friends in the same area. Australia-wide the story went ballistic. My phone rang constantly, reporters wanting a comment. In his rare TV appearances Tacich looked strained. Three young women, who all had attended the same school, vanished without a trace, a modern-day Hanging Rock. The city was petrified. The lack of any bodies stymied the press from dubbing these serial killings. Husson tried valiantly to tag the unknown perpetrator Ghost of Gruesome. Those seeking to spin the events as evidence of white slavery had even less success. But we all knew this was real and that unpleasant truth covered the city like invisible smog.

Yet, not quite a year on from when it had all started, here I was, seemingly unchanged, sitting on the terrace of my regular North Cott café with a view clear out to the horizon chatting with my swimming mates about the Olympic Games opening ceremony that we would all be watching that night. The women were excited about the prospect of Farnsy and Livvy. Living vicariously through Grace, my viewing highlight promised to be the Bananas in Pyjamas. One by one people drifted away but I had a light day ahead and was studying the paper and the chances of gold medals for our swimmers when Craig Drummond loomed alongside me. Craig was around fifty, slightly paunchy, pretty quiet. Even though he'd been swimming in our group for close on two years, I didn't know him very well. I believed he was an accountant or something in finance. We'd exchanged morning pleasantries many times, the temperature of the water, footy results but not much more.

'Mind if I join you?'

'Sure.'

I pulled out a chair. He looked slightly uncomfortable and even before he sat I had the awful premonition he was going to ask me something about discovering whether his wife was unfaithful. I would have to beg off. This was my one grotto.

'You're a private detective.'

Here it came.

'Yes, mate, but if this is about work ...'

'I know it's not the right situation but my friend is out of his brain.

Gerry O'Grady. His daughter Caitlin is one of the missing girls.'

He didn't have to tell me which missing girls. 'Oh. It's my worst fear. And mine's not two yet.'

'He's worried there's no advance in the case. He and his wife, Michelle, they're like ghosts. They can't work, they can't think of anything of else.'

'It'd be the worst thing. The worst thing. But I know the cop heading up the case. He's as good as they come.'

'That's the worry. If he can't find anything, what other cop's going to? Gerry wants somebody else to take a look. In case there's anything the police missed. You cracked Gruesome. You're the obvious choice.'

I could have said it was impossible, that I'd been out of the loop too long, that George Tacich was a friend and this would jeopardise that friendship. But all I could think of was, what if it was my Grace and I was the one asking.

'Okay. I'll meet with them, see if I think I can offer anything. I don't need money.'

'I know what your fee is. There's a group of us who'll pay. I don't want you out of pocket.'

'It's not necessary.'

'I'm his friend. I want to do this for him. And you might need assistance. I've got staff, office space, vehicles. They're at your disposal. Thanks, Snowy.'

He held out his hand and I shook it.

'You want another coffee?'

I suspected I was going to need a lot more than one.

CHAPTER 2

The O'Grady house was modest by the standards of some in Dalkeith, a pretty Californian bungalow, leadlight windows, neat rose bushes and lawn. A Mercedes nestled in the driveway alongside an older Corolla, P-plates attached as they would have been back when Caitlin had set out on that weekend after Australia Day. Drummond had told me Caitlin's only sibling was a younger sister, Nellie, but she was too young to drive. Drummond had offered to come with me but I thought it was better I did this alone. His job was simply to set up the meet. By the time I'd finished my coffee I was on for 11.00. I went home, showered, and caught Natasha as she was about to head out. Fortunately it had already been agreed Grace would spend the day with Natasha's mum, Sue. It had taken a long time but Sue had finally forgiven me for taking up with Tash. Mind you, Grace had helped.

'You think I'm doing the right thing?' I asked Tash. She held me tight.

'You've got a gift.'

Maybe I'd had a gift. I wasn't sure of its currency. It had been a long time since I'd investigated anything like this. A couple of disappearances, yes, but right off I'd nailed those as businessmen skipping out on wives and debt. This was different. My brain knew it the way it knew pi was 22/7. Sitting there looking over at Caitlin's car, I knew it now in my heart too. I felt crushed in. This was probably the lawn she'd tumbled over as a toddler, these were the flowers she'd smelled, the magpies she'd heard call. It was all intact, a perfect shell, but without her it may as well have been a painted set. It wasn't going to get easier no matter how long I sat there. I got out of the car and started up the slightly faded red concrete path. I was about to insert myself in somebody else's tragedy. Some stern objective voice inside told me to turn back but I shut it down and knocked. Gerry O'Grady opened the door. He was a fairly big man, six two maybe, balding, broad across the chest. He wore a diamond pattern pastel vest over a white shirt, slacks, brogues. Drummond told me he had a business supplying glassware and crockery to restaurants and hotels.

'Please come in.'

I walked down a Persian runner, over polished jarrah, past an oil painting of men with beards chopping down what looked like an Australian rainforest circa the days of W.G. Grace bowling underarm. It was an oddly masculine touch and I wondered if O'Grady dominated the house the way a lot of men in this suburb did. The sitting room was right off the entrance hall. It was high-ceilinged, quite light for winter, the light entering via glass doors that led out to the back. The furniture was good quality but comfortable and lived-in. I imagined happier times when they all sat around the telly to cheer the Eagles or Han Solo. Michelle O'Grady stood to welcome me. She was petite, had dark brown hair, attractive without being a beauty. I put her around my age, a couple of years south of her husband. She had prepared tea and coffee, cake and biscuits, the pots sitting on a little serving trolley.

'Thank you so much for seeing us,' she said. There was strength in her, resolve but fragility too. O'Grady moved beside his wife. In my game you make snap judgements. I made one now. The self-blame, pity and anger these two would have had in the aftermath of the disappearance flashed by on fast forward. I could almost smell the tears in this room and taste the dregs of wine drank for comfort in lonely hours but I sensed a unity. This was a couple who would stand together, defying pain and darkness.

'Please.' Gerry O'Grady indicated I sit. I chose a comfortable armchair.

'Tea or coffee?' asked his wife.

'Thank you, white coffee no sugar.'

In truth I didn't need another coffee but she'd gone to trouble and when people have something to do they relax. I wanted them to relax because I wasn't sure how much I could. When she'd poured me a coffee and I'd selected a biscuit, they sat opposite on the sofa. Neither of them took beverage or food. I started straight in.

'I feel very deeply for you guys. I want to help if I can but I have to be straight up about some things. I've worked with George Tacich and I believe he's a good detective. The chance I'll find something they've missed is remote. I haven't done this kind of work for a long time.'

Gerry O'Grady leaned forward, his hands clasped between his knees.

'We understand that. We're not expecting miracles.'

'Also,' I hesitated, 'you must not get your hopes up about a happy outcome.'

This time it was Michelle who spoke.

'Believe me, we've thought of every scenario. We still hope. But we won't abandon her, alive or dead.'

I sipped my coffee and glanced at the walls, family portraits, Caitlin around fourteen in the biggest. A pleasant open teenager, she had the broad face of her father rather than the delicate features of her Mum. Those seemed to have passed to her younger sister.

'We have these photo albums of her,' said Michelle tapping what looked like three big volumes next to her.

'We also have family films and videos.' O'Grady gestured at a stack of videos on a bureau.

'Whatever you want from us, we'll do.' Michelle offered me another biscuit. I wasn't aware I'd eaten the first. This time I declined.

'I suggest I work on this for a month, see if I can find anything at all they might have missed. If something breaks before then you won't need me anyway.'

They sought consensus from one another's faces.

'Sure.' Michelle O'Grady's vulnerability was more obvious in her voice.

'Have the police given you any indication they've made progress?'

They shook their heads in unison.

'From time to time Tacich has said they are following leads ...'

'... but nothing seems to happen.'

They were tag teaming. He'd gone first. 'Following leads' sounded ominously vague. I guessed the police had some tips, nothing concrete.

'I'm going to have to go over ground the police have already covered. I apologise but there's no other way.'

They understood that, they said.

'Have you been in touch with the parents of the other girls?'

Michelle revealed that via George they had been given details on the Virtues and about a month after Caitlin's disappearance the four parents had got together here.

'They live in Peppermint Grove,' she added. That was a couple of suburbs away. They had called each other a few times after the meet but contact had faded.

'Even reaching out can be hard.' Gerry looked at his brogues.

When Jessica Scanlan disappeared, George Tacich had asked them if it was alright to pass their details on to her parents. Michelle had been happy to offer support but apart from one call with the mother they'd never spoken.

'She thanked me but said they wanted to deal with it by themselves.' She shrugged, what could she do?

'Had any of you known one another or had any contact prior to this?'

Michelle spoke. 'We talked about that with the Virtues. Emily was two years ahead of Caitlin at St Therese's but so far as we know they didn't mix. Emily was a sporty girl, Caitlin did debating and drama. Emily started at the school year eight, Caitlin year seven.'

'No doubt they would have crossed paths but nothing close so far as we can ascertain.'

Gerry O'Grady put his arm around his wife.

'And Jessica?'

'Gerry knew of Dave Scanlan but we'd never met. As far as I know the Virtues don't know them either. Jessica is three years older than Emily and only attended St Therese's for her last two years so she wasn't there when they were.'

A weary old lab staggered in on shaky legs, sniffed the biscuits and implored with big eyes.

'No, Soupy.' Michelle waved him off. Soupy stood his ground, the eyes almost tearing up.

'Soupy!'

Gerry O'Grady's voice was more commanding. Soupy slowly headed out of the room. My eyes found more photos on the wall. Caitlin about twelve with Soupy. Cher was right: if only we could turn back time. Gerry spoke.

'Both the Virtues and us are members of the tennis club.'

'We hardly ever use it.'

'We don't remember them there. Apparently Emily used to be pretty good in her school days and still played a fair bit in summer.'

I nodded, considering the massive task of collating the lifestyles of three families to see if there was any common ground. Already I was considering my pitch to George to get his data and save time. Then again, if they'd missed something and I relied on them, I might miss it too.

'What about boys?'

Gerry deferred to his wife.

'Caitlin only had one real boyfriend, Adam Reynolds. They lasted about a year. It finished around ten months before ...' she caught herself. 'They were still friends, I think. He has another girlfriend now. He was in Bali that Australia Day and for the next week.'

'How old is Adam?'

They said he was a year older than Caitlin. He had gone to Scotch College and was now at university. He seemed like a normal, pretty sensible young man and his friends seemed of a similar ilk. They gave me the names of two who had been around to the house regularly. Caitlin had held her seventeenth birthday here. They had photos and lists of those who had attended. I was pretty sure that whoever had abducted the girls was going to seem nice and normal.

'Who might Caitlin have accepted a lift from?'

Gerry said, 'Very old family friends, girlfriends, friends she knew well from university, some of the boys she felt she knew very well. We're talking Adam and his closest friends.'

Michelle said her daughter was a very sensible girl. When Emily's disappearance had been made public, she and Gerry had reminded Caitlin and her sister of not trusting people you did not know extremely well.

'She would never accept a lift from an acquaintance, let alone a stranger,' Gerry said emphatically.

'Teacher? Somebody like that?'

They wouldn't consider that possibility. She was either forcibly abducted or somebody she knew very well, somebody she trusted, offered her a lift home. I asked them to take me through the last day they had seen her, Saturday the 29th of January. Gerry had been back at work for two weeks but things were still slow. Michelle, a housewife, was enjoying having the girls around. Nellie had another week before school started. Caitlin had weeks before she needed to go back to uni. She had just finished her first year of Economics at UWA. Her marks were good, not outstanding, pretty much where she'd always been academically. Gerry and Nellie had gone for a morning swim at Cottesloe. Caitlin had got up, taken Soupy for a walk, then noodled around the house. Michelle had shopped. They'd had sandwiches for lunch. Gerry watched cricket, Australia cruising to a win over the Windies. Caitlin had washed her hair, played a board game with Nellie and then picked up her friend Hanna and driven to the OBH for drinks with friends. This was around 3.00 pm. They'd stayed there till around 5.00 pm. Caitlin had dropped Hanna home, she lived not far away. Because she was driving, Caitlin had not had any alcohol. I interrupted.

'Who were the friends at the OBH?'

'Girls she and Hanna knew from school and uni. There were a couple of boys. One is the boyfriend of one of the other girls. The others were boys he knew or the other girls knew.'

Caitlin's plan that evening was to go to Claremont, dance, hang out with friends, and no doubt scout boys. Hanna begged off, she'd consumed a few wines at the OBH and was going to sit home and watch a video. Caitlin spent a while on the phone confirming which friends she would meet and where.

'I'd made a chicken salad. She loves that kind of thing. We all ate it here. She got ready. Girls that age ... she watched some television with us. She wanted to have a drink and dance so she decided not to take her car. Gerry dropped her off.'

The club strip was only a ten-minute drive, if that, from the house.

'We left here about nine-thirty. She kissed her mum goodbye.'

I looked over at Michelle fighting emotion. Gerry continued.

'In our day the pubs closed at ten, right? Nowadays it's just getting going. I dropped her right around from the Sheaf by the bottle shop at a quarter to ten. I made sure she had a taxi fare. We're usually in bed by eleven-thirty and I knew she wouldn't be home till at least one. They all take taxis. I told her to have a good time.'

For some hours the night had gone according to plan. Caitlin had met up with three girlfriends at the hotel. They had drinks there and chatted till around 11.30 then took themselves across the road to Autostrada, which was pumping but not yet packed. Around 1.00 am on what was now Sunday, one of the girls had peeled off with a boy she knew. By 1.30, Caitlin was ready to head home. She'd danced, and according to her friends had consumed a daiquiri and a single vodka. At the hotel earlier she'd had only one vodka, so three spirits all up. Many people saw her and spoke with her. All backed up her friends' account that she was not drunk but she was happy, a little buzzed with the alcohol. Caitlin's friends wanted to stay on – one of them was hopeful a boy she knew might make a play for her, the other was staying as backup – so Caitlin said goodbye. There was CCTV footage of her leaving the club at 1.36 am and that was it. From that moment she had disappeared.

At the time, Emily Virtue's disappearance was only vaguely on the radar of young women in the area and heading to a taxi was not something to cause alarm. If Caitlin had stuck to her plan she would have crossed back to the pub side of the street and walked a hundred metres down Bay View Terrace towards Stirling Highway and the taxi rank. Which side of Bay View Terrace she'd taken wasn't known, despite extensive questioning. There were still plenty of people in the area but no definitive sightings. A band had played the hotel earlier and a roadie was out front loading the truck at that time but had not seen her. A taxi had arrived at the rank at 1.40 am but the rank had been empty. At 1.47 the driver had left with a fare. According to the O'Gradys, the police had been unable to establish whether there had been a taxi at the rank between 1.36 and 1.40. The previous taxi to have left the rank estimated the time to be 1.32. Four minutes: that was the critical window. It could not be ruled out that Caitlin had still been in the area, talking to someone, and had simply not made the rank. If that were the case then the person she'd been talking with almost certainly had to be her abductor.

'She had no enemies you know of?'

No. Caitlin was a popular girl but conservative.

'You've had no break-ins, no calls where someone just hangs up? Nothing like that?'

They had not.

'What was she wearing at the time?'

Michelle O'Grady ran through in detail what Caitlin had on. They had no photo of the frock she was wearing but they had collated other photos showing the shoes, the thin watch and plain gold necklace she had stepped out in. The police, I knew, would have put out an Australia-wide notice for the jewellery. I figured for now I had everything I needed to make a start. I stood to go.

'If I could ask you to do something for me? Call George Tacich. Let him know you have asked me to investigate privately. Then I'll call him.'

They promised they would.

'Nellie is home when?'

'I pick her up from school at three-thirty.' Gerry didn't have to explain why he was doing the pick-up these days. I said I would make a convenient time to speak to her. I also made sure I had details of Hanna Bates, the friend, and Adam Reynolds, the ex-boyfriend.

I'm ashamed to admit I felt relief when I stepped out of the house. For me the visit had been an interlude. I was able to return to a normal world.

There was no prospect of that for the O'Gradys. They were trapped in a different dimension. I opened the door to the old Magna I drove. No fancy remote like some of the new cars had, just a key. As I stood on the road looking back over at the house I made a promise to myself I would do everything I could to find Caitlin. Even then, I knew, if I achieved my goal, she would likely be found dead.

...

The first thing I did was drive over to Autostrada. It took nine minutes with daytime traffic but then I had to figure that the traffic in the precinct was a lot less now than it might have been back then. This part of town, even the cleaners were expected to wear designer. A cappuccino could set you back more than a new thermos but that had never troubled the regulars. Today though, the shopping strip was less populated than the Simpson Desert. A couple of elderly folk doddered from the newsagency clutching scratchies, elegant women in dark skivvies looked tense and tended counters in near-deserted boutiques. The atmosphere was reminiscent of the clubrooms of a losing grand finalist but there was another layer: fear, invisible, tangible. I parked at the rear of shops near Leura Avenue, on the east side of Bay View Terrace, and took a short, narrow lane through to it, quite aware this could have been the very lane used by the abductor. When I emerged, Autostrada was immediately on my left in an old brick building almost directly opposite the pub. It was painted black and purple and was closed at this hour. The post office was on my right and occupied the entire corner. Bay View Terrace is not a long street. I reckoned you could walk from the railway end where I was to the highway at the other end in less time than it took Shane Warne to bowl an over. I checked my watch and walked south at normal pace past Autostrada. There followed the newsagent, a gift and homeware store, a shoe shop, a bank and a garden place. Here there was another lane, another possible abduction hotspot. I continued, passing a boutique and another homeware shop and then reached a third lane. Directly opposite on the other side of the street was the taxi rank. It had taken me ninety-five seconds. I continued to the bottom of the street, passing another boutique, a home loans office and a vet on the corner of the highway. The shops all had areas above them; one was a dentist, one advertised tax returns, the rest I guessed were used as storage areas. I crossed over the street and walked back up a slight incline past a bar-restaurant, which I knew closed by midnight. Then there was another homeware shop, a shoe boutique and one of those stores that sells storage items. The taxi rank was out front of it. Then came a travel agent, a jeweller and eventually St Quentin Avenue, the 'avenue' being some town planner's April Fool's Day fun because it was little more than a wide lane. Unlike the lanes on the opposite side of Bay View Terrace, which fed directly into a carpark, this street ran west straight down to the next block, a good half k away. Halfway along on the southern side was an entrance to a Hungry Jacks restaurant and carpark. The northern side gave directly onto a footpath which itself bordered the rear of shops and a couple of private parking areas sealed by roller doors. Headlights from vehicles entering or exiting the Hungry Jacks carpark would potentially illuminate anybody all the way to the junction at Bay View Terrace. The extra width here and the length made it more exposed. If Caitlin had been snatched here, the abductor had either a car idling or access to the rear of those buildings on the north side. Crossing St Quentin and heading north on Bay View Terrace, I passed a jeweller, a small Italian restaurant and then the pub, which ran clear to the next corner. I was beginning to see why there had been so much focus on taxi drivers or people who may have been known to the girls. While there were areas where simple snatch-off-the-street crimes of opportunity could take place, it would be very high risk. On the other hand, if somebody the girls trusted had cruised past – 'Hi Caitlin, hop in, I'll drop you home ...' – ten seconds into a car, gone. I crossed the road and walked back to my car through the lane beside Autostrada, checking the rear of the nightclub. There was a single door downstairs, locked. A narrow iron staircase led to a door on the first floor, an emergency escape, I supposed. There was also a small carpark behind the post office, cut off from this separate carpark by high kerbing and a screen of small bushes. Yet another place where the abductor could lie in wait. I sauntered south down the carpark, towards the highway again past the rear of the shops I'd already traversed via their frontages. Faint traces of salt wafted from the ocean, mingling with the fresh smell of pine, the kind of day that carried with it echoes of a shrill whistle of an umpire in white, the excitement of footy finals and kids in team jumpers despite the warmth. The hardware store actually had a customer access door here too, and a loading bay where tradies could reverse their utes to load in supplies directly. I walked all the way to the third lane. Already I was thinking that if it were a straight snatch, this was the most likely point, as the third lane was more isolated than the other two. An abductor could have a vehicle ready in this carpark. They could then exit via Leura Avenue at the rear, turn down towards Stirling Highway or up towards the railway line with no one the wiser. I continued to the rear of the vet clinic. It had four designated bays, two for staff and two for visitors. I would need to come back at night and check the lighting but I could see three poles with high lamps that would offer quite good coverage.

By now hunger was kicking in but I wasn't going to eat here where a ham and salad roll would cost the best part of six bucks. I avoided the highway, following the railway line past Karrakatta Cemetery, heading towards the city, careful not to speed because there was always some mobile camera here. The government had sublet the cameras to private individuals and it was not uncommon to find these unattended revenue-raisers smashed, or blocked by wheelie bins some good Samaritan had shoved in place to help his fellow drivers. My mobile phone rang as I was approaching the Shenton Park subway. These mobile things were still foreign to Snowy Lane. I picked up, with no idea who was on the other end.

'Hang on.'

I turned through the subway and took the first quiet side street. I left the engine running, noted I'd need more fuel soon and kept my answer short.

'Yep?'

'Snowy, it's George.'

'George, thanks for calling.'

'Can you hear me alright?'

'Yeah.'

'You're a bit faint.' My mobile was a Sagem. Not the cheapest but nor was it was the Maserati of mobiles.

I said, 'The O'Gradys called you.'

'Yes.'

'I didn't tout for this, George ...'

'Understand. Why don't you come in Tuesday arvo. Say two?'

'Great.'

'I'll make an official introduction. Can't speak.'

'Gotcha.'

I hung up, dwelling on George's last words. His tone indicated there were others around. I could imagine what they might be thinking, having somebody like me nosing in on their territory. It was a positive start and the timing was perfect; a good three days plus to get my own house in order.

As I started driving back towards my office, I clicked on the radio. All the talk was whether Cathy would win gold. Everybody expected her to. I felt sorry for her. I'd just been reminded what it was like to carry others' expectations. By the time I sat down in front of my iMac, I'd eaten lunch, filled the car and made a courtesy call to Craig Drummond to say I was on the case. He told me a cheque for five hundred dollars was on the way. I thanked him. The first thing I did was create a spreadsheet to cover Caitlin O'Grady's life. This wasn't one of those fancy computer program things, I didn't know how to do that, I just hand wrote a table of headings and then copied that onto the computer in a simple word program. First was Family. Normally with a murder or missing person case you're going to start and end here but this was different. We already had two other missing young women and, sure, it's theoretically possible somebody could have snatched two girls to mask the real target but I wasn't buying that. All the same, people who knew the family well would engender more trust than strangers and if there was a common intersection between all three girls then we were in business. Of course, I was certain Tacich would have thoroughly checked all that but for now I had to run my own case. My question would be simple: Name the people from whom Caitlin would conceivably accept a lift, or with whom she would at least drop her guard. Next, Education. I divided that into primary school, high school and uni. My starting question would be: Who were her teachers and close friends? But ultimately, I'd want a class list of everybody she'd been to school with. After that, Friends. This was likely to be the biggest area I'd need to investigate. I made a subheading, Romance. I added Entertainment – where did she hang out? What movies did she like and where did she watch them? What videos did she hire, what store? The same with Hobbies. Did she play sport? Who was on her team? Transport next. Where was her car serviced? Where did she regularly get petrol? Who taught her to drive? Did she catch a regular bus? Under Leisure: what shops did she frequent? Did she shop a lot along the Bay View strip? How about Employment? What jobs had she worked? Had she ever worked around that Claremont block from Leura Avenue to Stirling Road? She probably babysat for somebody as a younger girl. Who were her clients? Where did she bank? What pharmacy did she frequent? Who was her doctor? Had she ever been hospitalised? What church did she attend, if any? I wrote down everything I could think of that might bring her into regular contact with somebody, somebody with whom she might feel comfortable enough to drop her guard.

I made a special section for the twelve hours preceding her disappearance. I'd seen TV shows of FBI profilers talking about how serial killers would cruise around looking for potential victims and then bingo: something would just set them off. So I wanted to especially know all her movements in that time. If it were possible to trace every single person with whom she crossed paths, I'd do that. Of course that was highly unlikely but I could try. Easiest to check would be staff of the hotels and club, and they might be able to tell me who else was in the venue at the time. If she stopped for a burger I wanted to know who was in the queue with her, who served her. I'd only scratched the surface on this. It was going to be a massive job but I was resolved to do my best.

It was close to 5.00 pm by the time I finished constructing my web in which I hoped to catch all the facts of Caitlin's young life. I called the O'Grady house and got Michelle. I explained I'd made a start and would see the police Tuesday.

'I'd like to come over to your house tomorrow morning, first thing, say seven.'

The next day was Saturday. I explained that I wanted to follow as exactly as I could Caitlin's routine on the day she disappeared. It would have made more sense to follow Emily Virtue's routine, as she had gone missing much closer 'seasonally'. Caitlin had disappeared in the height of summer but I had to work with what I had. If the O'Gradys didn't want me nosing around, I had to respect that, but Michelle was pleased.

'It makes us feel like we're doing something,' she said.

...

'You're looking for a guy in his twenties, early thirties.'

Natasha nibbled on a corn chip as I dished up tacos. I only cooked twice a week and my fare pretty much ensured it would stay that way.

'Or a teacher. Or the mayor. Or a TV newsreader, somebody who seems safe,' I said thinking I was successfully following her drift. Natasha shook her head.

'Forget them. Maybe for Jessica, the newsreader. But Caitlin's eighteen. That age, anybody over thirty is old.'

'You were about that when you threw yourself at me. I was thirty plus.'

'It was your cooking.' She can cut when she wants. She started in on the taco. 'Seriously, if Bill Clinton drives up, they're not getting in that car.' Before I could say anything, she held up her hand. 'Okay, not the best example but I'm saying: with Emily and Caitlin you need somebody they know, somebody they know is local, like a boy in the same street. Or somebody heading their way that they know is heading their way so they know it's not taking him out of his way.'

'Why? Why not somebody who says "No trouble, really"?'

'No.'

This time her head shake was firmer than the front row chests on Oscar night. Up until about four years ago she'd had long hair. She'd worn it short for a couple of years but now it was almost back to its old length. I loved her hair any way, any length, but if she changed, I always told her I liked it.

'Why not?'

'Because you don't believe him. If you get into that car, you're figuring you owe him. He puts a move on you, you don't want to feel obliged, you want to say "Fuck off, Jason".'

'Jason?'

'They're all Jason these days. Or Justin.'

I went with her train. 'But if you know he lives down the street ...'

'... and you've ridden your bicycles around when you were kids, or caught the bus together, sure, you believe he's genuine.'

'What if the guy's really sexy?'

'Especially not then. Unless you think you're really hot. But I don't think these girls thought they were really hot.'

'So if you don't think you're really hot but a really hot guy takes the trouble to chat ...'

'Either he's a slime or you want him to ask you on a proper date. Or maybe if the girls are dumb, but these girls aren't dumb. Anyway, if he's hot, he's not cruising for girls.'

'Psychologically damaged: Ted Bundy.'

She shrugged, indicating the possibility was about the same as a stray asteroid hitting earth.

I pushed. 'There's no factual basis for your theories.'

'Life experience. If the guy is that hot, believe me, somebody notices him hanging around.'

I weighed what Tash had said. I couldn't use my wife's intuition or 'life experience' as a tool to narrow my search but I wouldn't discount it either.

...

When I arrived at the O'Grady house just after seven next morning, they were dressed and waiting for me, which wasn't really the point of the exercise but I understood them not wanting to be in their pyjamas with a stranger hanging around. As the family portrait had suggested, Nellie was more finely featured than her older sister. She was sixteen and had grown tall like her dad. I told them to go about their routine as well as they remembered it, and over breakfast chatted with Nellie about her sister.

'I'm three years younger. She's never really told me all that much about her friends but I know most of them.' She ran through them. I jotted notes.

'Anybody creepy?'

She couldn't recall Caitlin mentioning anybody. She was sure she would remember something like that.

'What about school? Anybody who stood out?'

'Teachers or girls?'

'Both.'

Caitlin didn't seem to have trouble with anybody. She was an easygoing person. On the day of the disappearance, Gerry and Nellie had gone for a swim, leaving the house around 8.30. Today it was still a bit cool for an ocean dip but I encouraged them to head out anyway and come back the same time as they had done the day of the disappearance. I'd never tried this process before and it wasn't like I was expecting anything from it but sometimes there's something you overlook when you're just running a scenario in your head. They left the house and it was just me and Michelle. I helped her clear the dishes.

'That morning she was still here in her bed. I probably grumbled to myself about her sleeping in, leaving mess around. But I knew she was here.' She threw a glance down the hallway. 'Now, when they go, it's so lonely.' She looked as flimsy as tracing paper. I asked to see Caitlin's room.

'You just do what you did that day. I'll be fine,' I assured Michelle. She went off to do whatever that was.

Like most Perth houses of its era, the bedrooms were high ceilinged and spacious. Caitlin's had been left more or less as it had been that day. I knew the police had been through it looking for clues. Obviously they hadn't found anything earth-shattering. The bed was a single, the spread blue with gold patterns. Once more I was hit by a wave of sadness. Caitlin had her whole adult life ahead of her. She'd barely left childhood behind. There was an Apple computer on a desk against the wall, textbooks and magazines neatly stacked. On her wall was a poster of Friends' star David

Schwimmer. Interesting choice. From the look it had been there since her school days. There were a handful of CDs on a shelf, artists I'd never heard of. I sat down on the bed and imagined her next to me.

Help me. I didn't say it aloud but I thought it. Caitlin had her mobile with her when she disappeared. It was a Nokia 1998 model. I hoped George Tacich would give me a list of all her calls. I sat there for a time trying to think like Caitlin. I was guessing her mind would be occupied by trivial things: what to wear, who would drive, what time they'd leave, a troubling pimple. Soupy the dog wandered in and checked me out. Then he slowly took himself out again. Maybe he'd heard the noise, hoped Caitlin was back.

I found Michelle in the back garden, on her knees weeding.

'This is when the weeds start,' she said by way of explanation.

'Did Caitlin use her mobile for calls?'

'Too expensive. She always used the home phone unless she was out. She called Hanna about this time. They planned their day.'

'Then?'

'I went shopping. She took Soupy for a walk.'

...

Initially Soupy had stayed snug in his large dog bed near the back door, unbudging as an England opener on a flat track. But after I'd wiggled his lead in front of his faraway eyes and made breathless little exhortations, 'Come on, Soupy, time for a nice walk,' he finally raised himself on old legs and tottered with me to the door. Michelle had given me the route Caitlin had taken that morning, Soupy's usual one, up the street to the north, around the block, clockwise. Once outside Soupy shed the years. He trotted and sniffed and cocked his leg from the edge of the driveway all along the street. I just hoped he wouldn't poo but I had the bag ready in case. Outwardly I was just a man walking his dog but I was studying the houses, the cars, and wondering if a serial killer lived in one of them. After I turned east, Soupy encountered a miniature poodle. They sniffed each other. The poodle's owner was an attractive woman my age in a designer tracksuit who looked like she'd seen much more of Umbria than I ever would.

'Labs are gorgeous.' She had dark wavy hair and smile lines. 'How old is he?'

'I'm guessing about ten. I'm walking him for a friend.'

'She's nine next year.' She indicated the poodle.

'Smart dogs, poodles.'

'She knows how to get round me that's for sure.'

The dogs seemed to have lost interest so we smiled and went our separate ways. Pets, I thought. That was one heading I'd left off my spreadsheet of Caitlin. For some reason women always think they can trust a man with a dog, and Caitlin walked Soupy. Maybe she'd see somebody regularly when she walked Soupy? You pass them in the street even late at night, you smile, of course you do. I wondered which vet the family used – the one up on the corner of the street where she disappeared? Something to check out. The only other dog walkers I passed showed little interest in getting to know me or Soupy. One was an old boy coughing and spluttering and tending it with a handkerchief. He had a Jack Russell trotting obediently behind. The other was an elderly woman who crossed to the other side of the street before I got too close. She had one of those yappy silkies.

I got back to the house with the poo bag still unused. Nellie and her father had returned. They'd gone for a walk along the beach. Gerry was giving his car a quick vacuum. I asked about Soupy's vet and he confirmed using the one at Bay View Terrace. I followed him into the house.

'Listen, we rang Hanna's parents and asked if she would mind coming over to speak with you. Is that okay?'

'No, of course.'

Michelle O'Grady pulled into the driveway with shopping. Everything is different I thought, she's shopping for three now, not four, and she must sense that every time she scans the shelves of the supermarket. There was no cricket to watch but some Games soccer was underway even before the opening. Gerry and Nellie sipped at it as they went about their separate business. Half an hour later Hanna arrived and we were introduced. She was a good-looking girl, brown shiny hair, slim, confident. She accepted the juice Michelle offered. I went with tea. We sat on the back veranda, the smell of spring rising with the heat of the morning.

'Are you best friends?'

'Kind of. I mean we used to travel to uni together and have lunch together.'

Hanna was an arts student. She ran through their close group of friends. No weirdos, no creeps.

'If I'd gone with her that night, none of this would have happened.'

'No, it probably would have happened, maybe not to Caitlin but to some other girl. Do you know Emily or Jessica?'

Hanna knew of Emily through friends of friends but she'd never met either of the other missing girls. She'd gone to PLC so hadn't known them from school. I asked her to tell me about Caitlin. Her description was near identical to everybody else's. A nice girl, friendly, smart but liked to socialise, loyal to her friends, open, not duplicitous, not into drugs.

'Was she loud?'

'No. I'm the loud one.'

'Were you guys together the night before?'

'On the Friday I started in Fremantle and then moved on, to The Sheaf actually, with other friends. That's why I didn't really want to go out the Saturday. Caitlin went to a movie with friends and then came home for an early night.'

'Could I ask you a favour?'

'Anything to help.'

I asked if she was free this afternoon to take me through things as they had been that day.

'I was going to get my hair done but I can cancel.'

'We could do it another time.'

'No. No I want to help.'

'I appreciate that.'

She finished her juice. I was aware of the O'Gradys hovering, understandable, but I wanted Hanna to be as free as possible with me. Other questions could wait.

'So, three at the OBH lounge,' I said. 'Do you want me to pick you up?'

'No, I'll meet you there.' She picked her glass up, put it down, staring at it because she couldn't meet my eyes. 'But please make sure you're there first. I don't want to be by myself. It's still scary. I don't go out anywhere nearly so much, and always with a friend.'

...

The Ocean Beach Hotel was an institution. Generations had revived themselves with a glass of cold beer after a swim in the Indian Ocean. It was particularly popular with imports. In my pub-going days, most locals had preferred the Cottesloe Hotel and its beer garden up the road but I didn't know if that still held. The OBH was about three quarters full. Noisy chatter fuelled by beer and amplified by open space and the sound of aluminium furniture being shuffled gave it a sense of urgency. The set now seemed younger than I remembered but I guessed that was just because I was a middle-aged married man. I'd made sure I was there fifteen minutes early. Just as well it wasn't longer – the price of a glass of beer was higher than a reggae bass-player. I'd have to pace myself. I wandered through the main bar and out to the pool room, which was as packed as I remembered. The best players on the coast hustled here, and more often than not brawls used to break out over somebody skipping the queue. At the table nearest me a couple of surfer dudes were taking on a pair of crew-cut, muscular guys, likely SAS whose barracks were just down the road. I checked my watch and made my way back to the entrance by 2.55. Hanna arrived ten minutes later and was relieved to find me. I felt guys turning to watch as she came towards me.

'If anybody asks, I'm your uncle from Sydney and you are showing me around. Would you like a drink?'

'Orange juice will be fine.'

I settled for a light beer to look the part.

'Can you show me where you guys were that day?'

She led me over to a section near the heart of the room, which was relatively free compared to the bar.

'Was it busy that day?'

'Busier. We'd just had Australia Day, it was kind of the last fling of summer, you know?'

'How long were you here for?'

'About two hours. I had a few ciders. Caitlin didn't drink alcohol that day. She was driving.'

I gazed about me. There were plenty of vantage points where somebody could have watched the girls over that time: from the bar, nearby tables, even near the gents, which serviced the adjoining pool room. If the girls had been engaged in conversation they wouldn't have noticed.

'There was nobody that day you felt was staring at you? Or came over to bum a smoke?'

'If there was, I don't remember.'

There'd been three other female friends, and they had been with two boys, one a boyfriend. The boys' friends and other girls had dropped over from time to time to say hello. All in all, Hanna thought there could have been close to twenty people circulating directly by Caitlin's table.

At the table closest to us were three young women, well gone on vodka or tequila, one of those clear drinks that makes everything unclear. They were quite raucous and I could hear lots of what they said. One was leaving for Bali the next week. It would have been easily possible for somebody to overhear where Caitlin was going that night.

'Suppose Caitlin had bumped into one of the guys she'd met here that day. You think she'd have accepted a lift?'

'She didn't know any of them well enough.'

'Not even the guys directly at the table?'

'No. I really don't think so.'

'Had you girls talked much about Emily Virtue?'

'A little bit. I mean, we knew she had disappeared but we weren't like ...' She didn't know how to finish the sentence. I tried to help.

'You thought it might have been a personal thing?'

'Yeah, I guess.'

Young people didn't go to bars these days to drink. They hadn't for a long time. You wanted to drink, you'd go to a bottle shop and get three times as much alcohol for the same price. People came here to meet somebody that at some time in the future they might have sex with. I watched the constant circulation of guys in tank tops and tees moving to tables of girls and other guys, edging in on the perimeter, trying to find a niche. I was relieved I didn't have to do that anymore.

'Was Caitlin a regular at Autostrada?'

'Over summer, for sure, I mean, it's close, you know? We'd go there or The Sheaf probably two weekends out of three.'

'So you get to see the same faces?'

'Sure.'

'Would she trust any of them enough to accept a lift?'

She thought about it.

'Guys she knew really well, that she'd known from school days or who were part of our group. But not guys she'd just danced with or bar staff.'

I asked her about herself, her family, how she'd found uni. All the time I was taking in the dynamics of the place. The guys were always checking out the girls between shouting rounds at the bar, or wandering in from the pool room. The girls were also checking out the guys. After about forty minutes I said, 'Well, that's probably enough.' I offered to walk her to her car.

'I'm fine.'

'I'll do it anyway.'

After Hanna had driven away I walked across the street and gazed out over the ocean. It was still sunny, dusk only now shuffling towards its carriage. The blue water rippled in a moderate breeze. How could wickedness live in the heart of something this peaceful?

CHAPTER 3

A young uniform cop laden with files kept trying to not stare at me as we rode in the lift to the Homicide Division at Police HQ. By now, I had pretty much mapped out all the areas of Caitlin's life I would have to investigate. Some things I'd followed up with the O'Gradys but whatever I might try and do, I knew it was fairly hopeless without deeper knowledge on the other missing young women. So far I'd not checked out Autostrada or The Sheaf firsthand, reasoning it would be better to wait until after this meeting. For instance I was sure George Tacich would have run the microscope over all the staff and I didn't want to blunder in on some train of inquiry that might be in progress. The door opened and the uniform waited for me to exit first. A mainly open-plan space with various individual offices at the far wall, the room didn't look that different to how it had twenty years earlier, except for the computers. There was one on almost every desk. At first glance I counted three young women and six or seven men but I couldn't say who was a cop and who was civilian. I caught sight of George in an alcove, figured it was the kitchenette and started towards him. He was in the company of an older man in a suit. The uniform who had gone on ahead of me handed him the files he'd been carrying. He must have mentioned me, for I saw George look up quickly in my direction. But before I could offer a friendly wave, I had jammed in front of me the face of a guy bitter with what life hadn't handed him.

'Excuse me?'

'Richard Lane ...'

'I know who you are.'

He flexed on his toes ever so slightly. Had to be a cop. I guessed he was a shade older than me. He struck me as the kind of guy whose weekend highlight would be washing and polishing his car. I could hear him on the sidelines at soccer criticising his kid's teammates.

'I'm here to see the Inspector.' I indicated George, who was starting over. My guy wasn't aware and was not shifting his ground. A short blonde with a sizeable backside moved in to support him. She looked like she'd offer some mean wing defence Saturdays at Matthews Netball Centre. George's voice climbed over their shoulders.

'It's alright, Collins. This man is a legend: Snowy Lane.'

Collins didn't tell his boss he knew who I was. By now they were all watching me. I could almost hear the laughter in their heads. Legend? This guy?

One of the policewomen, fine features, dark hair, lighted on my name and whispered to the guy beside her. Put it this way, it wasn't exactly a cheer squad but after Collins, it felt like one.

'G'day Snow.'

George put out his hand and I shook it. The older man he'd been talking with had followed him and was at his shoulder. For the benefit of the others, George added, 'This man is one of the best detectives I ever worked with. He's been engaged in a private capacity by the O'Grady family on Caitlin's disappearance. Snowy, this is Michael Unwin, he's our media officer on the Autostrada Task Force.'

The task force had been named after Caitlin's disappearance but before Jessica's. I shook his hand. We both eyed each other carefully but without judgement.

George said, 'DS Garry Collins.'

Collins didn't offer his hand and I didn't offer mine. Somewhere a phone rang. One of the crew went to it.

'I won't introduce the others because you won't remember the names anyway. You want a tea or coffee?'

'I'm fine.'

George addressed the wing defence. 'Jill, you hold the fort.' He turned to the uniform who had ridden up with me. 'Daniel, thank Roy and ask if he could go back as far as ninety-six. Snowy, come through.' George indicated a door on the other side of the room. I trailed in his wake. He gestured the others follow. This surprised me. I'd assumed that some of them at least would be assigned to other homicides or major crimes. George opened the door marked with a sign AUTOSTRADA TF and ushered us into a large windowless space that was clearly the engine room of the investigation. At its centre was a long trestle table – on closer inspection two trestle tables, joined, with what must have been twenty chairs. I could see only two desktop computers, one at each end of the room at separate workstations but laptops littered the table like napkins after bridal cake. There were two large whiteboards, one to my left at the short end of the rectangular room, the other behind me as I walked in. They'd been flipped so any writing was hidden but the maps of Bay View Terrace, photos of the missing women and various printed time lines and facts on the three women were displayed on the wall ahead of me. I noted red string had been used to cross-correlate items underneath each of the women's photos. At a guess there were nine or ten strands. A large empty space on one wall marked with blu-tack suggested some display recently removed. My guess: photos of persons of interest taken down prior to my arrival.

'Please, Snowy, sit.'

I picked out a chair and the others settled in around me. George read my thoughts.

'There are more than twenty of us all up. Five work the night shift.'

'Other cases?'

'We manage okay most of the time. If something major comes up we have to hive off some of these guys.'

Unwin spoke for the first time. 'Naturally we don't want any specifics of manpower being made public.'

What Unwin and his bosses actually didn't want was some opposition politician claiming the task force was under-resourced.

George addressed the room. 'You guys don't know Snowy. I do. He will not leak anything or compromise our investigation in any way. Right?'

'Absolutely,' I said. Collins was picking his nails.

George carried on. 'We want to help the O'Gradys, all our victims' families but we can't have the investigation compromised. These young women may still be alive. If we mess up, we could cause their deaths.'

I said I understood. Already I'd picked up on the formality in George's manner.

'We can't give you access to any of our investigation on any persons of interest. For your own sake, it's probably better you sift through the facts anyway, a virgin. That way, you never know, you may find something we missed.'

Unwin interjected. 'Of course that's unlikely but if you did, you would bring that information to us before making it public.'

Time I put him in his place. 'I will simply pass it on to my clients. You need to ask them for their cooperation but I have explained to them my absolute confidence in Inspector Tacich and his team.' George, I reckoned, suffered this guy the way a bus-driver suffers piles.

'Good.' George pointed at the wall where the girls' eight-by-ten photos had been placed. 'This is what we can give you. Precise time lines of each of the girls on the day of their disappearance, also any common areas in their lives we have been able to establish.'

'How about access to your tips?'

George looked to Unwin first before stonewalling me.

'I'm sorry, that is confidential. As are interviews we may have done. We can only give you the raw data, mate, otherwise you are on your own.'

It was skinnier than a greyhound on Pritikin. It would save me a couple of weeks, sure, but it left a monster slab to chip away at.

'What about criminal records of abductions and sex crimes going back say three years, solved and unsolved?'

Unwin threw to George who ignored him. 'We can do that. What else?'

'You interviewed a lot of taxi drivers, other people in the area at the time ...'

'Sorry, Snow, we'd like to help but it's a legal minefield. You will have access to any witness statements concerning the time of disappearance: what they saw, didn't see, so forth. That's not bad. Anything else?'

'If I want to look into anybody, can you help on any criminal record?'

Unwin seized the cudgel. 'Absolutely not. You'll have to pursue other avenues.'

'You can hand us the information, we'll take it from there,' said George, softening the blow.

I felt all eyes on me, sensed their resentment. I was yesterday's man and I had no right to sneak in and plunder their hard work looking for some flaw that would trip them up.

I wasn't done yet though. 'The O'Gradys feel like there has been no progress. Can you tell me if there are any strong leads you are following?'

Again Unwin and George exchanged glances.

George said, 'Snowy, you know what it's like. Sometimes eliminating a lead can be progress, it might not look like it from outside but we can concentrate our focus.'

'So, no, you don't have any real leads.'

Collins looked like he wanted to strap me into one of those carnival whirly rides, put the speed up full and then just walk away leaving me screaming. Unwin spoke.

'Inspector Tacich has been most gracious to you, Mr Lane. The O'Gradys should know everything possible is being done. We have the largest investigative team ever assembled in the state working on this around the clock.'

I told him I appreciated that but on behalf of my clients I was obliged to try and get as clear a picture as possible.

'What about staff at The Sheaf and Autostrada? You must have investigated them thoroughly?'

George said, 'We've checked and rechecked. All staff who were working on the nights in question, all staff who weren't on duty those nights and every former staff member we could find going back two years. We didn't find anything to give us grounds to suspect any of them. Now, I'm sorry, Snowy, but we have to keep moving. If you come up with anything, rest assured we'll treat it very seriously.'

The kiss-off. 'Right. Thank you.' I stood.

Unwin said, 'We would appreciate you explaining to the O'Gradys how we have given as much assistance as we possibly can.'

I looked him in the eye. 'I'll give them an accurate report, Michael.'

'I'll see Snowy out.'

George opened the door for me. I followed him back through the main room to the lifts. As we reached the elevator he whispered, 'The zoo, quarter to five.'

I shook his hand. 'I'm partial to the polar bears.'

He nodded that he understood and walked back to his team. I felt their eyes on my back all the way until the steel door of the lift closed them off.

...

It had been many years since I'd wandered around the zoo and I'd forgotten how calming it could be. This time of day it was near deserted. A few mothers pushed toddlers around, one or two Asian tourists took snaps of peacocks strutting by but, all in all, you'd find more action at a wharf on Labour Day. I was already looking forward to another year from now when it would be opportune to bring Grace through. That led me to thinking about Caitlin O'Grady. No doubt her parents would have held her little hand and walked her past the exotic lions and tigers, the penguins, the hyena compound. I felt angry about what had happened. And impotent.

George Tacich and his task force had got nowhere; who did I think I was to do any better? I'd arrived early but try as I might I couldn't find the polar bears. As a kid I'd always been fascinated looking down the concrete walls into the green water pool on those hot January days where the big white bears would swim backwards before lumbering out into their dark concrete cave. Ten minutes walking, I was back where I'd started. The Freo Doctor was blowing strong now, leaves were rustling. George would be here soon. I spied a keeper exiting the crocodile compound and asked her where I might find the polar bears.

'Try the Arctic Circle. The last bear we had died around twenty years ago.'

I couldn't believe it. I suppose in these days of enlightenment it was felt that it was too cruel to keep polar bears in this climate. Or maybe there just weren't enough of them. Sure there were big cats on offer here but nothing beats a bear. I checked my watch: right on 4.45. Hopefully George was running late. I sprinted back to the entrance, my quads protesting. Apart from my lazy swims, the last exercise they'd tasted had been indoor cricket going back three or four months. After the polar bears I was rapidly losing confidence in whether I still had any viable place on the planet. George's arrival ripped me out of my funk.

'No polar bears,' I explained.

'No polar bears?' He was as surprised as me.

'Not for twenty years.'

I remembered that in the early '70s a young man who was either on drugs or having some psychotic episode had jumped into the pit and been torn to shreds by the two bears. I supposed my disappointment might not be universal. George and I started walking away from the entrance. The zoo closed at 5.00 pm and what few people were still there were coming in the opposite direction.

'They'll give us about fifteen minutes before they shoo us out,' he said.

If he wanted to be away from prying eyes it would be hard to think of a better place.

'Sorry about earlier. I didn't know how else to play it,' he said. The smell of guinea pigs overpowered frangipani as we turned up one of the avenues.

'I was hoping that was it.'

'My guess is I haven't got much longer on the task force. We've turned up nothing concrete. There's a new commissioner, Cosgrove, Pom, and he's going to want a head. That will be mine.'

George was a good solid cop but I didn't dispute his reading of the tea-leaves.

'I'm sorry to hear that.'

'I'll be okay. They're talking a superintendent job for me. Might be Kalgoorlie but it'll work out. Don't expect any help once I'm out. Unwin's there to save the Minister's arse but you probably guessed that.'

I told him I had.

'DS Collins didn't go me much.'

'Thick as. Workhorse, no analysis. Most of the others are in the same category. Well, not thick like Collins, just inclined to stay in the box instead of looking outside. Sutton, the pretty brunette, she's good, especially from the girls' angle. Piper's a young bloke we picked up from Fraud who has smarts. Truth is, Snow, I haven't managed to get us closer, so it's probably for the best. But I hate it. I want this bastard.' He stopped, looked around. Nobody else was in sight. 'You got a computer?'

'Yeah. When it freezes, I turn it off and back on. If that doesn't work I'm fucked till Natasha can help.'

'The advantage of younger staff.' He reached under his jacket, pulled out a manila envelope and pressed it on me. 'Floppy disks. They've got all the relevant stuff: all the persons of interest, criminal records, basically everything that's not complete chaff.'

'They could sack you. Take your pension.'

'You're not gonna tell them. Just be careful. I want to help those families but you can't let them know about this.'

I promised complete discretion. A call came over the PA saying the zoo was closing in five minutes and would anybody still in the grounds make their way to the exit.

'What do you think, George, in your gut?'

He sighed, pushed out his bottom lip. 'I believe we're up against somebody very efficient. I think they're dead. All of them. I hope I'm wrong.'

'Somebody they know?'

'I think so. You know the area?'

'Checked it daytime.'

'Very open except for those laneways, a lot of pedestrian traffic, vehicles cruising slow looking for parks. I mean, Emily Virtue, okay, nobody knows there's an abductor out there, so maybe she could be snatched. But after that, people are aware. After Caitlin everybody was looking at everybody. Jessica was on high alert.'

'Alcohol might dull their danger detection.'

'True. But none of them had been drinking heavily. And from the week after Caitlin, I had undercover people, male and female, inside the venues and out. They didn't see anybody who rang bells. We didn't get reports from other girls saying somebody followed them. I had people in those carparks night after night taking number plates. Nothing stacked up.'

I heard what he was saying. If these were simple crimes of opportunity the perpetrator was going at a one hundred percent success rate.

'So, more likely somebody they know or trust.' I was drawing the inference he'd thrown out.

He shrugged, turned, heading back to the exit. 'What you don't know is what you don't know. We found some cross-correlations, school, tennis club, friends. We also looked at all those shops nearby. Who lives there, who cleans, who has keys.' He tapped the bag. 'It's in there. Hope you find something I missed.'

We both stopped instinctively a good hundred metres from the exit.

'Good luck, Snow. I mean it.' He slapped me on the back and headed out. I waited a moment, the weight of evidence in my hand.

Only time would tell if it was gold or sand. I took a last look at the zoo and thought about Caitlin once again. She'd been in a zoo of a different kind. Strutting peacocks, chirping birds, and somewhere in the shadows a predator who could sniff her out. I vaguely recalled a high tower here at the zoo where kids would queue to ride elephants. Or was it giraffes? No, surely had to be an elephant. Gone like the polar bear pit, a different time. We were more humane now. We cared for and protected animals so much better. It was our fellow humans who suffered our thirst for cruel entertainment.

CHAPTER 4

Grant Hackett was up against the great Kieren Perkins in the fifteen hundred metre freestyle final, an event that we Aussies considered our birthright. Susie O'Neill and Ian Thorpe had already won gold but as a nation we were nowhere near sated. Like the conquistadors of old we craved more gold. From time to time you hear about other 'sport-loving' countries. Really? I just laugh. Okay, maybe in Sydney where multinational millionaires suck crayfish off their fingers while staring across at the Opera House, the need for sporting glory is a softer pang, but that's the only place in this wide brown land. Melbourne footy teams can pull more people to training in finals week than most English Premier League teams get to a match. Heather McKay pretty much never lost a squash game from the time of the first Queen Elizabeth till when the current one became a grandmother. For Babe Ruth to have been as dominant a player as Bradman, he would have had to hit around two hundred homers a year. The greatest tragedy in Australia wasn't being born into poverty but into a family that followed North Sydney Bears or St Kilda. What I'm saying is, this was a big deal: two great Aussie swimmers and only one could win gold. Natasha settled in beside me on the sofa. The guys trooped out to their blocks. And suddenly I was hit with this thought: was he watching this too? Right now. In a family lounge room or a pub with beer flowing, or in an apartment reeking of unaired bedclothes and pizza. Of course I had no clue whether the abductions were the work of one or more people but one was easier to picture.

I'd been on the case a week now and every minute I felt further away from any end point. George Tacich had given me nine disks in all, each one crammed with information. There was one disk for each of the girls, every aspect of their lives broken down into headings and subheadings, just like I'd done for Caitlin. There was a disk which covered those who lived or worked in the main Claremont commercial block, a disk relating to all cases of sexual assault solved or unsolved going back eight years, a disk relating to tips – hundreds and hundreds of them – the good people of Perth suggesting everybody from star footballers to fictional TV characters. Two disks were dedicated to people who knew or were known to have come into contact with two or more of the girls. The last disk was the summary disk. The one that narrowed the focus to what they hoped would be manageable proportions and included all reliable witness statements. This was the disk with the critical time lines as well as the main persons of interest. The only thing I had not been afforded by George was direct interview transcripts. So what I had was extensive. That was the good part. But the task ahead made Hannibal's Alps seem like sugar cubes. I felt exhausted before I started, and when I did start I felt overwhelmed. I had crammed the lives of all these people into a sack and been dragging it with me from dawn till the early hours. Tonight, for an hour, I got to place it on the floor and snuggle into Natasha.

Hackett jumped out early and we waited for Perkins to apply pressure. It never happened. Thirty laps of the pool, Grant Hackett wrote his name in history, Perkins the bridesmaid. Natasha had made us a stir-fry. I gobbled it down.

'You're not going to call ahead?'

The way she asked made it sound like it was stupid not to.

'No.'

'They're all going to think you're the guy. You'll creep people out.'

'An old guy like me at Autostrada.'

'Yes.'

'That's why I want you to come.'

'An old guy with a mother reeking of breast milk?'

'It would be an improvement.'

She'd tried to get her mother to mind Grace but it was Sue's bootscooting night.

'What are you hoping to find?' She scooped up my empty plate before I could think of seconds.

'I have no idea. I just want to see the place, get the feel.'

...

The doormen at The Sheaf looked me up and down. I was wearing my best sports coat, Country Road slacks and a decent shirt. A year earlier when business was booming they would have advised me to look elsewhere. Eventually the tall Tongan nodded and I stepped into the pub, a classic old-timer with a '90s makeover, the pub I mean, though the description was as apt for me. It was still quite crowded, most eighteen to twenty-five, a dozen up to early thirties. My only peers were a couple of well-dressed guys and their wives who'd been to dinner or a show and popped in to make use of the babysitter's last half-hour. In this main room a female DJ was pumping out poppy music. I had no idea whether it was current. The last stuff I'd listened to in this mode was Bananarama. I liked them. They had a sense of humour. A lot of people were dancing, an ecstasy and water crowd, I guessed. I ordered a Heineken off a barman. Early thirties, he might just remember vinyl.

'Wasn't there a band here?' I had to shout.

'Thursdays and Sunday Sessions. Used to have a band early on Saturday but not any more.'

I sipped, felt eyes on me. I drank half my beer, checking out the place. The abductor couldn't be drunk and gesturing like this young guy fresh out of private school I was looking at right now. Too much precision required. He might be talking with mates but not really engaged, all the time watching. I caught a young woman looking at me from the side of the room. The guy with her wasn't quite right. Not western suburbs enough somehow, not relaxed like he was on his own turf. He had the clothes but this wasn't his scene. My guess: George Tacich's undercover crew. I took myself up the old wooden staircase, had to turn sideways as two young women squeezed back down. The phantom I was seeking might have done this, felt a little charge as the girls squeezed past, followed them with his eyes, told them in his mind he'd be arranging a little more one-on-one time later. The top floor was more of the same, music, dancing, a smaller bar. Darker though, easier for him to glide through and watch.

...

George Tacich and his task force had narrowed the field considerably. They'd examined the lives of all three young women across virtually the same areas I had split Caitlin's life into: School, Church, Work/Uni, Entertainment and so on. They had also looked in detail through phone records of the girls and their families. The points where two of the girls intersected on something were many: Royal Perth Yacht Club, St Brigid's Church, Highway One Motor Mechanics, and so on. Emily and Jessica had attended the same ballet school when in primary school, Emily and Caitlin had both at some point held holiday jobs at The Grove Shopping Centre in Cottesloe. Jessica and Caitlin had both spent holidays as younger women grooming horses at the Claremont Showground. Jessica and Emily both had pictures on their walls from the same picture framer in Mosman Park. The Scanlans and O'Gradys had once used the same reticulation firm. There were hundreds of these points of intersection. Fortunately the areas where all three of them intersected were much less, though still substantial. The one the press had focussed on was they had all at one time or another been students of St Therese's, a high-end Catholic all-girl school, which had been a convent run by nuns until lay staff gradually took over in the 1970s. That they had once been students there should have led to some other lines of investigation, and indeed the obvious ones were covered – teachers, fellow students, non-academic school staff who were common to the girls. All the same, some things had been missed or at least weren't covered in the summary. How did they get to school? Did they all catch the bus, were they dropped by parents, or did they ride or walk? This was the kind of detail I'd been noting as I combed the disks all week. If they all rode the same bus maybe some psycho rode the same bus, year in and out, to his job. As I had nowhere near enough resources I hoped the police had winnowed out the chaff, saving the good stuff for the summary disk. Here I was focussed on two simple areas: was there anybody who all the girls trusted sufficiently to get close?; and, what similarities had there been in the girls' movements on the days they disappeared?

Looking at the second question first, there was a striking similarity between Caitlin and Emily: both had spent Saturday afternoon drinking at the OBH with friends, both had finished around 5.00, then gone home to get ready for a night out. Once in Claremont, both first had drinks at The Sheaf before moving on to Autostrada. Emily had left the club at 1.48 Sunday morning saying she was going to get a taxi. A taxi had arrived at the rank at about 1.53 but there was no sign of her. One witness reported seeing a young woman fitting her description very close to 1.50 standing at the rank. She thought she saw the young woman start towards Stirling Highway a hundred metres or so south down the hill. This was common practice because often it was quicker to find a taxi cruising past on the highway than at the rank. The police had put out public requests for anybody in the area at the time to come forward. Nobody else had presented to say they were the young woman the witness had seen. No passing drivers – and several had contacted police – reported seeing a young woman near the intersection of Bay View Terrace and Stirling Highway around that time. If it was Emily at that rank, she had vanished between 1.50 and 1.53. A note in the file cautioned however that the witness may be out on her time line by as much as twelve minutes.

Unlike the other girls, who had gone missing after a Saturday night out, Jessica had disappeared late Friday night, early Saturday morning. She had not gone to the OBH beforehand but had been in the city where she worked for a stockbroking firm. She had caught the bus to Claremont where she had joined her friends for an Italian meal. When they left she'd dropped in to the adjacent Sheaf alone and had stayed at the pub drinking and chatting with acquaintances. The last confirmed conversation was 12.20. Then she'd pulled up stumps and left without advising anyone. Why Jessica would do this being quite cognisant of the abductions – her dinner companions had said it had been touched on that very night in their conversations – was in itself a mystery. Alcohol can give a false sense of security and, while by no means drunk, she'd had two wines over dinner and another at the pub. I was yet to be convinced that was enough for her to drop her guard. Unlike Autostrada, The Sheaf had no video surveillance on the doorway, something I found unbelievable after what had already happened. The doormen had been busy with patrons entering and exiting and, though she was very attractive and wore distinctive jewellery, they couldn't give confirmation of when she left. Three witnesses claimed to have seen Jessica walking towards Stirling Highway just past St Quentin Avenue on The Sheaf side of Bay View Terrace. This would be where she would go for a taxi.

And then she too had vanished.

The area at the time had quite a volume of pedestrian traffic. It was earlier than when Caitlin or Emily had left Autostrada, more people were heading to and fro. Bay View Terrace itself was well lit, additional lighting having been provided by the council since Caitlin's disappearance. Maybe these were contributing factors and Jessica had felt safe. Tacich had two people in Autostrada and two circulating the area on foot but none of them had made visual contact with Jessica, although they had been able to confirm seeing two of the witnesses who claimed to have seen her. One theory was that she had encountered her abductor at The Sheaf, maybe an acquaintance, they'd chatted and then she'd left, either with him or having arranged to be picked up by him. Everybody felt it had to be somebody who did not stand out. The police had run background checks on the proprietors, staff and cleaners of all the businesses in the block between Leura Avenue to the east and Stirling Road to the west. Bay View Terrace bisected this area. There were not many residential dwellings in the block but they doorknocked and checked those too. They also doorknocked and checked the businesses and dwellings on the river side of Stirling Highway. They had a couple of minor hits but in both cases the persons had credible alibis.

I left The Sheaf just as Jessica had done, at 12.20, feeling the eyes of Tacich's undercover people on me. Glancing up as I left the venue, I saw the telltale dome of a surveillance camera. Too late for Jessica but it might identify the abductor if he was crazy or bold enough to try again. I crossed the road to Autostrada. The girls and guys hanging near the doorway smoking looked at me like I had to be guilty of something. Again there was no queue. The door bitch checked me out. She was about thirty and didn't recoil. She took my money, the bouncer stamped me and I stepped into fluoro and pumping music, guessing this would have been pretty much how it would have been for Caitlin, only busier. It was still maybe a little early but the place was only half full. The main dance floor was right up front but there was an adjoining side bar where it was less frenetic, though still viable only for shouted conversations. This time there was nobody around my age. I made my way to this bar and ordered a Pernod and lemonade. Like the upstairs bar of The Sheaf, the whole place provided plenty of darkness and shadows for somebody to observe.

Two major persons of interest had been identified by George as having potentially been in contact with all three young women. Ian Bontillo was the drama teacher at St Therese's and had taught all three young women. In his early thirties, he lived alone in a flat in Swanbourne not five minutes' drive from the area and had no solid alibi. Bontillo claimed to have not been in The Sheaf or Autostrada on any of the nights in question, though he had occasionally drunk at The Sheaf and OBH. Nothing weird there, they were virtually his locals and it would have been more suspicious if he denied it. He was alibied by his sister for the Caitlin disappearance. She said he had been at her place for an Australia Day weekend party up until nearly 3.00 am. Bontillo admitted having spoken to Emily since she had left school – they'd bumped into one another a couple of times around the Claremont shops – but not within six months of her disappearance.

Tacich had liked the look of Bontillo as a suspect even though the teacher had attempted to lessen interest in himself by stating he was gay. Inquiries had confirmed this but opinions commissioned by psychiatrists stated this was no leave pass for Bontillo. Indeed, he could still have deep-seated misogynist feelings. Tacich's notes on Bontillo were: 'smart, organised, trusted, lives nearby'. This however had not been enough for a search warrant although Bontillo had invited police into his flat when they had called after Jessica's disappearance.

The Pernod was gone and I wasn't prepared to fork out for another. The money for my fee had arrived but I had better things to spend it on. It was too dark in here to spy George's people but I was sure they would be here, probably alerted to me by The Sheaf crowd. The place was gradually filling but not even close to being crowded. From what I could see this was still very much a venue where clumps of kids who knew one another hung together, had a drink, maybe danced. You were going to have to be part of the scene, friend of a friend, to get together with somebody you didn't already know. Forty minutes was enough for me. I bailed before 1.00 am.

It was chilly now, though you could still get by with a short-sleeved shirt. The breeze had picked up, blowing in from the ocean across the open spaces of Claremont Oval on the other side of the railway tracks, where I'd gone to battle wearing blue and white against the Tigers under the reign of Graham Moss. There'd been many a great game played there in my day, the likes of Doug Green, Ken Judge and Tony Buhagiar up against Moss and the Krakouer brothers. I'd even booted three goals myself – albeit half an hour before the main game in the reserves. Reserves was always trailing at my heels like a faithful dog. No matter how fast I ran towards the bright lights of league, it would rarely let me get away. If I did give it the slip, it would soon pull me back. I think the most league games I played in a row were nine.

The Terrace wasn't exactly deserted but it wasn't humming, and people moved the way they do when trying to reach a connecting flight, quick of stride and focussed. Every woman I saw was in company. I set out south towards Stirling Highway just as I had during the day the week before. When Emily had left Autostrada there had been a truck parked opposite at The Sheaf. Loading out the band's gear had been Gavan 'Party Pig' Partigan, the second main POI for the task force. Partigan was the last person who claimed to have seen Emily and as such he had to be looked at anyway. The fact he was actually at his truck made him doubly interesting. Okay, in theory he would have had to get her into the truck without being seen and then subdue her, but it was right there on the spot. The same went for Caitlin although Partigan made no claim of having seen her, saying he was busy inside packing up band equipment. But without a camera on The Sheaf, no exact time line could be established. Nobody in The Sheaf could be found who would verify he was there the entire time. In fact some people remembered not seeing him there after the band finished. Partigan claimed he must have been behind the large speakers – entirely possible. The doormen were off by then so he could have slipped out for a few minutes and come back. On the Friday when Jessica had disappeared, Partigan had been working a walk-in gig in Northbridge. He'd finished by 10.30 pm and there were witnesses placing him at an eatery not long after. He claimed he then returned to the house in Bayswater he shared with his girlfriend and she backed him up, saying he'd arrived back around midnight, but somebody had noted she was a 'junkie and unreliable, could be lying'.

By now I was standing at the third laneway, just across the road from the taxi rank. I'd observed how people passing had kept to the far kerb away from the short lane. I looked into the lane myself; it was shadowy but not pitch dark, illuminated by the street lights on this side and lighting from the other end in the adjoining carpark. I didn't shiver but my skin prickled as I entered the space and walked through the ten metres into the adjoining carpark. I knew Tacich had the area under surveillance and wondered if anybody would approach me. There were fewer than twenty cars in the carpark, and almost as many empty spaces, but last October and January, I bet it would have been jammed. Was there enough time for somebody to have snatched Caitlin, dragged her back through this lane and bundled her into a waiting car? I supposed so but she would have had to have been taken by surprise and subdued quickly. Then he would have had to drag her back, get a door open and heave her into the car, confident she could not escape. I was about to head back out when I noted that there was a vehicle parked in the Staff Only bay right next to a rear door of the vet's. I wondered if somebody might be working there at this hour. After all, there were plenty of free spaces, it seemed unlikely a random would choose that spot. I walked over and saw light under the door. A bell was clearly marked After Hours. There was also an emergency phone number. I rang the bell, looking back at the carpark, thought I spied movement in a Falcon halfway along. I considered ringing the bell again, decided not to, was about to head off when the wooden door opened. A strong, steel grill door remained shut. A woman with a few flecks of grey in her hair stood on the other side. She wore a kind of lab coat, was short and had glasses on a chain hanging down around her neck.

'You have an emergency?' she asked suspiciously, eyeing me up and down. Given the circumstances, I didn't blame her.

'Not exactly. I'm very sorry to trouble you. My name is Richard Lane. I actually rang a couple of days ago and left a message on your machine.'

This was in fact the truth. One of the headings the task force had not replicated from my breakdown was Pets.

'You're working for the O'Gradys?'

'That's correct. I'm here tonight just taking a look around. I saw the car ... Look if it's not convenient I can return during the day.'

'Can I see some ID?'

I fumbled for my wallet, showed her my driver's licence. That did the trick. She opened the steel door and let me into a room stacked with bags of various pet foods. A small mesh cabinet and the small fridge beside it were both padlocked. Some kind of drugs I guessed. At the doorway to a corridor was a small wooden table with two chairs. The smell of dog and cat was potent. On my right was a sink and above it a small set of shelves where a tin of coffee and tea bags jostled with rows of worming tablets and vitamins. I followed her through into a dim corridor with cages each side, floor to ceiling. I thought I made out cats in some of the higher cages.

'I'm only in tonight because we have Walter the Weimaraner recovering from a fairly big operation.' The dog was on bedding in a large cage. The other, lower cages were empty apart from a small white dog who gave a ruff as we passed.

'It's alright, Chewbacca. Chewbacca's boarding with us for a few days.'

We emerged into the reception area, which was dark until she clicked on the light. She indicated a comfortable sofa and I sat. She wheeled the receptionist's adjustable chair around for herself.

'The police have interviewed me. All of us. I wasn't around on any of those nights so I can't help. I wish I could.'

'Are you the only one in the practice?'

'I have another vet, Gillian, and two nurses who double as receptionists. They each do three days a week. When Caitlin disappeared we were all away, except for Gillian. She and I take it in turns. The police interviewed all of us. Even my cleaner and a master's student who was doing his thesis.'

'I'm sorry if the police have already asked you this stuff.'

'That's alright. Anything to help them.'

'You're Soupy's vet.'

'Yes, I've been tending darling Soupy for years.'

'Are the Virtues or Scanlans clients?'

'No. Neither of those families.'

Which would be why there was no cross-correlation mentioned on the disks.

'Do you know the O'Gradys socially?'

'No. I'm originally from south of the river. My daughter went to Penrhos and my son to Wesley.' South-side private schools. 'I only know them as clients.'

'So you haven't had much to do with Caitlin?'

'She'd come in with her mum and Soupy. She's a very sweet girl. I keep hoping.'

We both knew what she meant. Sometimes you just try a shot in the dark.

'Ian Bontillo, is he a client?'

She shook her head. I dug out a list of names the task force had made of suspects who cross-correlated with at least two of the missing girls.

'How about any of these people,' I began reading names. 'Rick Harvey, Terry Gorman, Simon Glendale, Shane Crossland ...'

Instant recognition.

'I've looked after their pets for years. You see them growing up, on and off. His sister, Bekky, she's settled down. I've seen Shane around here, stoned on pot or something else.'

She wasn't stupid. She knew why I was asking. 'I've never seen him with Caitlin. He was always nice with their dog, though: Mimi, a toy poodle.'

I made a note and read another raft of names. None of them rang a bell. I had a thought.

'Would it be hard for you to check for me the dates when Soupy's been in for treatment and when Mimi has been in?'

'Not with computers.' She looked at ease firing up the desktop. 'How is Michelle doing?'

I mumbled the requisite, 'As good as could be expected.'

She found her client list and scrolled through, first one then the other.

'May thirteenth, nineteen ninety-eight, Soupy was in for an infected paw and May eighteenth, Mimi was in overnight having put her back out.'

Okay, it wasn't the exact same day but it was the same week and at least theoretically possible that the paths of Shane Crossland and Caitlin O'Grady could have crossed. I handed her my card and thanked her. I also asked her to keep our discussions confidential.

'You understand I'm running around shaking every tree I can. I'm going to be looking at a lot of innocent people.'

'I understand. I won't be blabbing.' She saw me out. 'I don't like coming here by myself now,' she confided. 'Even at my age.'

I was walking back through the carpark trying to follow my own advice and not think about Shane Crossland when a sedan swung in and cut me off.

'What are you up to, Lane?'

The very friendly DS Collins, alone.

'Walking the scene. You know the drill. What about you?'

'Got a report of a dickhead with tags on himself.'

So it was going to be like that.

'Sorry you wasted your time, Sergeant. And your guy in The Sheaf? He doesn't fit. He's too Dianella.'

Collins didn't answer. He simply swung back out. The car where I'd seen movement was still in place halfway up the carpark. I was betting task force.

...

Back home, mother and daughter were both asleep. I fired up the computer and searched for Shane Crossland to refresh my memory. While I'd read through all the disks, in truth, not that much had stuck. I found him under a list headed Access All, Knew Two, No Alibi. Shane Crossland was a twenty-one-year-old labourer, brother of Lucy Crossland, a good friend of Emily Virtue. Shane Crossland had been one of the group of friends who had been drinking with Emily at the OBH on the afternoon of the day she disappeared. Crossland had spent two hours on and off with Emily's group and playing pool. On the night of Emily's disappearance, Crossland claimed to have gone back 'pissed' to the flat he shared with one James Killeaton, and crashed for the rest of the night. Killeaton himself had left the flat around 9.30 and gone clubbing in the city until the early hours and was unable to confirm whether Crossland had been even in his bed when he'd gotten home. The night Caitlin had disappeared, Crossland admitted to being at Autostrada. He claimed not to know her or to have spoken with her. Cameras showed him leaving thirty minutes before her. Crossland claimed to have gone straight home. His flatmate was staying with a girl that night and couldn't confirm this. James Killeaton was able to confirm however that on the night Jessica Scanlan had disappeared, Crossland was not at the flat until around 1.30 am. Crossland had witnesses to support his claim he'd gone drinking after work and then into Fremantle to 'cruise'. He had been able to produce a witness who put him in Fremantle at midnight. That left very little time for him to get to Claremont but it was possible. Crossland claimed to have slept in his car for an hour or so before heading home. It would have been extremely cold in the car and the story was not highly credible. Crossland, I noted, had a conviction for pot possession and had been described as a low-grade dealer. His connection with Jessica was that she had known his older brother Mitchell quite well. They had friends at uni in common. Mitchell had done an Ag. Science course. Jessica had met Shane Crossland in company with his brother at Steve's Hotel near the uni at least twice, two years earlier. Mitchell Crossland had since completed his degree and was living in Northam.

Trying to tamp down excitement, I sat back and mused on Shane Crossland. He was the right age and he'd been on the spot the day two of the girls disappeared. It was possible he had known Caitlin. The address given was a flat in Mosman Park. I wondered how long he'd been living there. Before that, had he lived at home? I grabbed the White Pages and searched for Crossland. There was a Crossland with a Dalkeith number. I was jumping a little – okay a lot – but *if* he was living at home and *if* the house wasn't too far from Caitlin's, maybe they did cross one another's paths, in the park say or on the street. That night in Autostrada, he recognises her. Maybe they have a quick chat. He leaves and waits ...

No way would that kind of thing stand up in court. For the barest moment I considered passing on this lead to Tacich. But what compelling info did I have? They shared a vet. Not enough, nowhere near enough. I clicked off the computer and made my way to bed. Natasha was out to it completely. I hugged her and tried to make my mind blank.

...

I'm guessing a lot of guitar cases in a lot of dressing rooms smelled like Shane Crossland's 1993 Holden Commodore: sweat and stale pot. Being a cop had a lot of advantages over being private: all those lab technicians you could call on, superannuation. Being private had advantages too. Like you didn't need a search warrant to be standing in the underground garage of a block of Mosman Park flats at 3.30 am with a torch. I was gloved, of course, and wearing a non-descript cap just in case there was surveillance somewhere. Whatever I might have been expecting to find wasn't announcing itself. There was a windcheater, turned inside out in a jumble on the back seat, a few CDs in front. Lots of old receipts, parking and shops, just scattered about. I scooped them up, you never know, might find something. I pulled the boot, nothing but a pair of flippers, no obvious blood spatter, gaffer tape, that kind of thing. I'd come prepared, a bottle of luminol acquired from an old Forensic mate. I sprayed evenly, pulled out the ultraviolet light from my bag and switched it on but there was no illumination to tell me blood had been present. Gently, I closed the boot. George Tacich wouldn't have let me see those names if he didn't want me checking them out. At least that's what I told myself.

I'd been surveilling Crossland four nights. During the day I'd checked his bin: baked beans, eggshells, bacon rind, empty beer bottles. I was angry with Shane Crossland. Thanks to him I'd missed watching a great moment in Australian sporting history: Cathy Freeman winning the 400. I'd been tempted to give Crossland a miss that evening, the Monday. I thought of the whole nation cheering, glued to their televisions. The final was on a little after 6.00, so I told myself I could catch the race and then head over to Mosman Park. Heck, I could even sit up at the Mossie Park Bowling Club and watch it there. Crossland's place was a few streets away and I'd be in place by half-six. But then I thought of the O'Gradys and the giant hole there would have been in that room at that moment. So I made do with listening to the radio as I sat outside Crossland's flat. He didn't come out. Just as he hadn't come out Sunday after heading back from drinks at the Cottesloe around 6.30. The next two nights I'd followed him from his work site to the bottle shop. He'd bought sixpacks, driven back to the flat and not been out until tonight when he'd driven off around 9.00. I'd followed him a few blocks where he'd picked up a mate and they'd cruised over to the headland south of Cottesloe Beach, parked and lit up joints over two hours, drunk a few beers. Then he'd cruised back, dropped his mate and returned to his flat in one of the smaller blocks. I'd given him about an hour to pass out. I moved back to the front of the car, and sprayed the luminol. When I clicked on the ultraviolet, I felt a jolt through my whole body. The car was lit up like a showroom.

CHAPTER 5

'You gotta be kidding me.'

A moment earlier I'd been a kestrel hovering in anticipation. I was in my kitchen. George had rung from a public phone somewhere. I'd geared myself for what he was about to tell me, for the back slaps, the praise but his words were still stumbling in my brain, like players after Mad Monday. How was it possible?

'No blood?'

'None.'

Maybe the receipts I took had tipped Crossland off and before the police arrived he'd cleaned up.

'He must have bleached it.'

'No, the car lit up for our guys too.'

After my visit to Crossland's vehicle I'd made contact with George and given him a heads up. He'd been as excited as me. Task force cops had turned up the next day at the building site Crossland was working on and asked if they could test his car. They had a warrant in train anyway but wanted to check his reaction. Fine, he'd told them. But now I was confused.

George said, 'You mentioned him smoking joints in his car down the beach.'

'Yes.'

'Did you smell them? Did he have the windows down?'

'No, he's not stupid. I've got these great infra-red binocs. I saw clear as day.'

George explained patiently, 'People smoking in a confined space like a car can give a false reading on the luminol test. It's the tobacco or something.'

Shit.

He obviously picked up on my silence. 'Mate, don't feel bad, we've had a dozen of these kind of false dawns.'

'It could still be him. He could have used another vehicle.'

'He won't be off the radar any time soon.' He added, 'I got the chop last night. I'm off the case.'

'Because of Crossland?'

'No. I told you it was already in train.'

I felt hollow. I'd let him down. 'I can't have helped.'

'It made no difference at all. They're giving me three weeks break then I'm off to Kalgoorlie.'

'Who's taking over?'

'Dean Tregilgas. He's the wonder boy out of Fraudy. He's cracked some big cases. He's smart but thinks he knows it all. If you're ever in Kal ...'

'Wouldn't miss it.'

I hung up, flatter than a farmer's vowel. I was sorry for George and for myself too. He'd been my conduit into the case. I didn't want to let go of Crossland. Okay, it would have been hard for him to get Jessica but not impossible. He could have left Freo in his own car, had another standing by in Claremont. He could have had an accomplice. Could have, might have, might not have: not a place that was going to prove productive.

...

Tacich's removal as task force head was announced two days later. There was talk of 'fresh eyes' and the investigation moving into a 'new phase'. He was perfunctorily thanked by the Pommy Commissioner who was keen to put a positive spin on Inspector Tregilgas and his 'elite crime solving capability'. The next day Gerry O'Grady called me to inform me that Tregilgas had made an introductory phone call to him and Michelle O'Grady in which he suggested they might be wasting good money on a private detective.

'Look, I have no problem if you think I'm not achieving anything here.'

'No, we want you to keep going.'

I had to be honest with him. I explained the police cooperation I got from here on might be much more limited.

'That doesn't matter. We want you to keep looking. That's what we told Tregilgas.'

I thanked him for the vote of confidence but in truth I had a queasiness in my stomach that I was wasting everybody's time. Much as I might not wish to, I figured I had better try and make contact with Tregilgas. I dug out the number of the spin doctor, Unwin.

'Yes, Lane.' As pompous as ever.

I explained that I did not want Tacich's leaving to alter the relationship between the police and my investigation.

'There is no relationship. We were merely offering a courtesy to you on the instructions of the task force commander.' The past tense had crept in like an intruder with a tomahawk. I asked if he might pass on my wish to meet with Tregilgas.

'He's a very busy man. But I will pass on your request.'

He must not have been that busy because my phone rang about forty minutes later.

'Inspector Dean Tregilgas. You wanted to speak with me?'

I thanked him for his prompt call knowing how busy he was.

'Exactly, I am busy, so I'll be blunt. Your help is not needed by this task force. You wasted time and resources on the Crossland business and I have suspicions as to how you obtained that information. We will continue to pass information direct to the O'Gradys as we see fit and proper. What they do with it is up to them.'

'So if I were to find anything ...'

'You're not going to. The world has moved on. Is that all?'

'Good luck, Inspector.'

It could have gone better. Question was, could it have gone worse? I was on my own from here on in. That much was clear.

...

By Grace's second birthday I'd achieved bugger all. Nor did I have any instinct that it might be about to change. After the Tregilgas call I'd determined to take a look at the two prime persons of interest: the teacher, Bontillo, and the roadie, Party Pig. They were about as different as you could get. If Bontillo, the self-confessed gay teacher, was responsible he would have used very different tactics to the roadie. He would have engaged the girls in conversation, acted solicitous of their welfare, offered a lift. In the case of Jessica, alerted to a predator, he might have been insistent: you can't wait around here, I'm safe, I bat for the other team. Party Pig Partigan on the other hand would have relied on being part of the furniture: a guy loading the band truck, you walk past him without looking. The police report said Partigan had called the information line around a week after Emily had disappeared. They had paid a visit to Rock Solid, the sound company that owned the PA and truck and employed Partigan. Party Pig claimed he simply didn't hear anything about Emily's disappearance until the next gig at The Sheaf. He thought about what he'd seen and told the police right away.

But the truck had not been tested until the Wednesday after Caitlin went missing. No blood, no DNA matching the girls but by then various crew had been traipsing through loading and unloading. The police found it suspicious Partigan had cleaned his car on the Sunday afternoon after Caitlin went missing. The car had been parked at the Osborne Park factory where Rock Solid was located and Partigan used it to get to and from work. The roadie claimed he had been thinking of selling the car and had vacuumed it and cleaned it for that purpose. He said he had not seen Caitlin at all on the night she had disappeared, and did not even recognise her by sight. When asked by the police why he had not gone ahead and put the car up for sale, Partigan replied he changed his mind.

I had a few gay male friends, some I'd made way back on the Gruesome case. I asked those I was closest to for help, told them I needed information on Ian Bontillo: people who knew him, ex-lovers, whatever. Was he bi? Did he like rough trade? One of my contacts, a PR guy, came good with 'Simon', a guy who had spent some time with Bontillo and was prepared to sit down. We met at a café in Subiaco, a suburb one grade down from Dalkeith with its company directors and old money. There were plenty of BMWs to be found in Subi but it tended to be the domicile of realtors, accountants, successful small-business people, with more than a few doctors from the nearby hospitals. Simon was younger than me and wore an open-neck white shirt better than I could. He lay back in his chair with his legs casually crossed in a manner that suggested tanning and powerboats. His loafers were elegant and at home in the aroma of fresh coffee. We made a little small talk. I knew he was in the IT business and was originally from Sydney. This was a big advantage for me. Perth was a village and those who had grown up here never wanted to get the elders and witchdoctors offside. He knew I was a private detective but I'd promised a hundred dollars for his time.

'You were Ian Bontillo's boyfriend, is that right?'

'Not exactly *boyfriend*.'

'You were intimate for a time?'

'Yes. Is this about those girls? Are you working for a newspaper or something?' Far from being concerned, his eyes twinkled.

'Which girls?'

'Those three girls that are missing. Ian taught them all. The police spent ages interviewing him. I thought that's what this was about.'

'It might be. I can't tell you who my client is but I absolutely guarantee you anonymity.'

He waved that away.

'How long have you known Ian for?' I asked.

Simon had seen him at clubs going back eighteen months. They'd hooked up between the previous November and carried on casually till around April.

'Does he have any attraction to women that you are aware of?'

Simon smiled and sipped his coffee. 'He likes dresses but his tastes are strictly left fork.'

'Did he ever mention the girls to you?'

'He could hardly avoid it. The cops came to see him after the second girl disappeared.'

'How would you characterise his reaction?'

'He was upset. He remembered the girls, like, not that well but a bit. He wanted to help however he could. Ian's a nice guy. Can be a bit of a nanna but he hasn't got a malicious bone in his body.'

'Not misogynistic in any way?'

A pause. 'Well, a couple of times the kids got to him. Fooling around, you know. He said, "I could strangle those little bitches" – but it was just a teacher blowing off steam, seriously. He wouldn't hurt a fly: I know. I've seen him shoo them out windows.'

'What's his relationship with his family, any idea?'

'He didn't talk about them much. I got the impression there was some problem between him and his mum over him being a poof. He wouldn't be the first. They live in Melbourne somewhere.'

'Did you ever engage in, or did he ever suggest anything ... bondage ..?'

'Who hasn't?'

A cheeky grin. Then he rocked forward, looked me in the eye.

'I don't know your sexual history but let's put it this way: nothing we did or he suggested was that far off the path that it made me think he'd hurt those girls. If you're trying to paint him as a psycho-killer, forget it.'

Simon was prepared to give me some details of their sex games. The most extreme involved bondage, candle wax, pinching. No cutting, slapping, threatening, nothing that made Simon feel Bontillo had changed when in the moment.

'Play acting, games really, that's all.'

I pushed on for another forty minutes but wasn't getting any more juice.

'When the third girl disappeared –'

He cut me off. 'We'd run our course by then. I mean we weren't boyfriends anyway. But I haven't seen him around. I'm guessing it would have really knocked Ian hard.'

'You didn't call him?'

He shifted uneasily. 'I didn't want him to try and start anything up again. I broke it up between us, whatever there was. I mean, I didn't feel anything for Ian, to me it was casual. He, I think, wanted something more but to be honest he's a bit ... boring for me, and I don't want to run him down, because he's a perfectly nice guy. He's not your guy.'

...

'Please, come in.'

Ian Bontillo was shorter than me, around five-nine, fair and slim, though his hips were like a luncheon drinks bill – larger than you expected when you took a close look. He ushered me into his flat, a large art-deco number in a Swanbourne side street south of the railway line. Simon had spoken in his favour but I wanted to meet the man myself. I called him, explained who I was and how I was working for the O'Gradys. When I asked if I might visit him he'd suggested a Saturday afternoon. So here I was, sinking into a '50s armchair replete with a rest where civilised folk would perch a martini on a coaster while listening to big band albums. He sat on the sofa opposite. Light spread in under the blind, highlighted his hair, traces of red. Behind him the lower half of a bronze female nude balanced balls on the mantelpiece. Given the recent Olympics, my mind went that way and suggested she came into being around the time Jesse Owens was tormenting Hitler. No coffee on offer. Nonetheless, I thanked him for seeing me.

'I feel for the parents. I didn't know them. But, anything I can do.' There was a pause, he wriggled ever so slightly. 'Obviously I'm somebody the police are going to look at.'

I was relieved he'd got straight down to it. 'You taught all three girls?'

'I didn't abduct them. I'm gay by the way.'

I raised an eyebrow, as if that might have escaped my attention. 'Please, don't take this personally,' I said, 'but it would be great if I could ask you some questions. I'm sure the police have done this but Caitlin's parents feel they are in the dark.'

'I barely remember Caitlin. I did not abduct her.'

I nodded solicitously but went on my way regardless. 'I've spoken to Beth Springer, asked if it was alright to interview staff. She said it was fine if they were willing.'

Beth Springer was headmistress of St Therese's and what I was saying was the truth. I did not want Ian Bontillo thinking he was a prime suspect, and I'd already had a chat with an English teacher, Jenny Clohessy, the only other teacher as it turned out who had taught all three girls, though several other staff had held tenure across the girls' student years. They could wait.

'So, is it okay to proceed?'

He opened his palms as if to say 'sure'. I produced a mini tape-recorder. 'Do you mind if I record us? I never keep up if I'm writing.'

'That's fine.'

'Please don't think I'm targeting you in any way other than to establish facts. The questions I ask you will be the same as I asked Jenny Clohessy.'

'You've spoken to Jenny?'

'Yes. Do you remember the girls well?'

He was relaxing slightly now, edging back more comfortably into his seat. 'The only one I remember very well is Jessica. She was one of the leads in *Guys and Dolls* that I did as the school play. She was a natural. Emily I don't recall very well. I think she did drama only for a couple of years and she wasn't in the passionate core group of kids you tend to find. Caitlin … I said I hardly remembered her, that's not accurate, I meant, when it first happened I couldn't place her. But then I saw her photo and of course I remembered her. She was one of those kids who … drama wasn't her thing especially but she'd put up her hand to be a spear holder.'

'Do you recall any time or instance the three girls might have been together?'

He was shaking his head. 'I've thought about that. Jessica was finishing when Emily was starting. I can't think of anything.'

We talked about the girls for a good half-hour, their personalities, friends.

'Did you ever see any of the girls outside school?'

'Jessica, who I had most to do with. I saw her up the shops a couple of times. Once when she was at uni, then a few months ago we chatted briefly. She was in the city, law ... no stockbroking.'

'What about other staff at school. Academic or cleaners, anyone you thought ...?' I left it to him to fill in the gap.

'No. I can't believe it of anybody. Look, whoever did this, I don't think they give off the vibe, they must fit in.'

'I know the police would have asked you this but I have no access to their material ...' okay that was a lie, '... could you tell me where you were when each of the girls went missing? You know I need to ask this.'

'Emily went missing in October. I was at the school preparing for the school play, which we always do in November. I worked there with one of the music teachers who was MD and one of my set designers, our tech teacher, till about eleven. They left. I stayed for a while, maybe forty minutes, then came back here to bed. That Saturday after Australia Day when Caitlin disappeared, I was at my sister's for a party. Everybody except her and me flaked about midnight. I stayed and helped her clean up till around two. The night Jessica disappeared, that was a Friday. I was worn out. I came back here, cooked myself a meal, surfed the net, watched TV. My team St Kilda was playing Collingwood. We lost.'

'St Kilda,' I said with sympathy.

'Born in nineteen sixty-six.' Chagrin is the word I think that describes how he said it. The Saints had won one premiership in their history, and that by the lowest possible margin, one point, back in '66. Maybe it was a calculated tactic on his part to win me over. If so, it worked pretty well. One minute I'm stalking him like he's a duplicitous monster, next it's like he's a dolphin I'm trying to protect from ritual slaughter. I delved into his background. He'd wanted to be an actor but realised early on he wouldn't be elite enough to crack the big companies so he pursued teaching. He'd come to Perth in '91, having landed the job at St Therese's.

By the time I'd left I was no wiser on what had happened to Caitlin. Did I think it was Bontillo? I never rule anything out, but no. Quite apart from the St Kilda thing and the gay thing, and the fact he was alibied, I just didn't get a sense that this guy was anything more than a coincidence. Frankly, Jenny Clohessy was scarier. If she'd have been teaching me English I would have read Jane Austen cover to cover. She was alibied, so was her husband and her seventeen-year-old son; hey, I'm thorough if nothing else.

...

While checking up on the designated persons of interest was a main focus, it wasn't my only line of investigation. I was especially interested in prior criminal or deviant behaviour: rape, sexual assault of course, but even snowdropping and flashing. Too often people dismiss some teenage kid stealing his neighbour's panties off the line as nothing more than a quirk. To me it was a big warning arrow – cliff edge approaching – and over that edge lay violent behaviour spurred on by long-held sexual fantasies. Flashing, even more so. Some creep hangs out in the sandhills and bares his wares at a passer-by, one day he's going to go further. The task force was onto it too. There were twenty plus convictions related to these more minor crimes, going back three years. Thing was, there'd be double that number unreported, and as many unsolved. Also with this kind of behaviour you might have to go back ten years. The serious sexual assaults and rapes were well documented. Thankfully, over the last three years there'd only been one serial rapist and he'd been caught and was behind bars. The task force had done a good job of listing all those convicted of serious sex crimes, and anything related to deprivation of liberty, going back thirty years, not just in WA but nationally. They had clearly spent a lot of hours sifting through each and every entry but none of those previously convicted had stood up as a strong suspect. I ran through the list of names and their crimes, wishing I could transport them to an island and nuke it. This was not going to be a line of inquiry I could fruitfully pursue, too much ground to cover, too many resources needed and much better left to the task force.

But it was while trawling through unsolved rape cases that I finally felt a jolt.

Back in January '98, Carmel Younger, a twenty-two-year-old sales assistant, was walking past Karrakatta Cemetery around 2.00 in the morning when she was grabbed from behind, dragged into a dark part of the cemetery and raped. Younger had been drinking from late afternoon at the Cottesloe Hotel until about 11.00 pm. She had then cadged a lift to Shenton Park with some of her fellow drinkers where an impromptu party had ensued. About 1.40 in the morning, alcohol affected, she had decided to walk the five kilometres to her home in Nedlands. The people who had given her a lift to the party were too drunk to drive and she had thought she'd probably hail a taxi if she saw one but she wasn't especially concerned.

She didn't own a car herself and often walked to the beach and back. After crossing Aberdare Road, the city side of the cemetery, she walked down the hill past the cemetery and had traversed about a quarter of the block to the next cross-street, Loch Street, when she suddenly felt herself lifted up in the air and carried away from the road into the cemetery itself. A hand clamped her mouth, an arm pinned her right arm. It was too dark to see her attacker's features but she saw the knife he brandished under her eye before turning her over, pulling down her pants and taking her from behind. Too terrified to scream, she had half expected her throat to be cut. Even after her attacker had satisfied himself she expected the blade and remained kneeling, sobbing to herself. She felt him move back but that was all. After what might have been a minute or two she gathered the courage to turn around but there was nobody in sight.

He had vanished. She did not recall hearing any vehicle but by then she was likely too distraught anyway. She did not possess a mobile phone at that time and had done her best to battle her way back to the road where she had stumbled on in a daze in the direction of her home, too terrified to flag down the few passing cars. She had eventually made it home and woken her housemate. The housemate had called the police. The subsequent police investigation had focussed first on those at the Shenton Park party. It was sound enough strategy: that the rapist was one of the guests who had seen Younger getting progressively drunk and had followed her, waiting until the cover of the cemetery. They had two potential suspects but both cleared on DNA and it was back to square one with time having elapsed. The next stage had been looking for witnesses who might have been driving by. They checked the speed camera inevitably set up at the cemetery, followed up on a couple of infringements roughly around the time of the rape but got nothing. One motorist remembered seeing a young woman, most likely Younger, walking unsteadily south near Aberdare Road. It was a dead end. Nobody was ever charged. I left the file open on my desk. I wasn't finished with it. Maybe it wasn't somebody known to Emily, Caitlin and Jessica who had abducted them. On the other hand, maybe it was.

...

'It's not fun having the cops accuse you of being a serial killer.' Party Pig Partigan slid the speaker box off his broad shoulders and placed it down at the back of the truck.

I offered a correction. 'We don't know the girls are dead.'

He pursed his lips. Partigan was only around five-eight but built like a bull. 'That's how they acted. That Sergeant Collins, he was … he was fucking heavy.'

I could imagine. Partigan had been on a north-west tour with a band for the last week and a half and this had been my first chance to get to him. It was already November, Grace was officially a year older and my investigations had stalled. Soon as he was back from tour, I called Partigan at work and he'd agreed to talk while he loaded up for a gig that night.

'I mean, look at me,' he was sweating through his singlet, hair sprouted from his shoulders. 'You think those girls are going to jump in the truck with me?'

I didn't want to rub him up the wrong way but I felt obliged to point out the cops may have thought he just grabbed them.

'Right out the front of The Sheaf? With people coming and going all the time? Besides, like I told Collins, "Where do you think I put them?"' He gestured through the open back door of the truck. It was jammed tight with sound gear. The only space left was for this last speaker box.

'Did you know the girls?'

'Not personally, no.'

'Did you recognise them though?'

'Not really. They were a type, you know? Those rich chicks. I mean, there's a few girls always would dance down the front of the stage trying to catch the band's eye. You get to know them after a while. The others just give you a hard time when you politely ask them to take their drinks off the mixing desk.'

Partigan sounded like he might have a chip on his shoulder. That could be the sort of guy who would abduct these girls. I baited.

'Like you're the one in the wrong?'

'Exactly. I'm just doing my job.'

He heaved the box into the truck. It fitted snugly.

'You saw Emily leave Autostrada.'

'Yes, I did.' He slammed the doors shut and bolted them.

'How did you know it was her?'

'I recognised her when they put her photo on the news.'

Earlier he'd indicated these girls were a 'type'.

'This was a week or so later?'

'Yeah. I remembered. I was out there loading the truck. People were coming and going and then it was one of those lulls. There's nobody there and I saw her walk out of Autostrada and turn towards Stirling Highway.'

'You know why you remember her?'

'Just did.'

He was fiddling with his keys, giving me a signal he wanted to get going. I refrained from asking about Caitlin or Jessica at this point.

'Did you notice anybody lurking about? Any vehicles?'

'Just the station wagon.'

My ears pricked up. I'd been over and over the reports. There'd been no mention of a station wagon.

'What wagon was this?'

Partigan explained that for a gig at The Sheaf he would pull up in the loading zone out front and drop all the gear in. He would then move off and park the truck in one of the carparks for the duration of the gig to clear the loading zone for other deliveries.

'After the gig, I'd go get the truck. When I went to get the truck that night it was pretty deserted. Few pedestrians heading to Autostrada. Where I parked the truck there was a station wagon, engine running, but no headlights. It was a bit odd. I forgot about it at first but when I was trying to remember stuff, it came back to me.'

'You didn't see who was in it?'

'No. It was parked next to my truck on the left facing the wall so I couldn't see in the window. And when I was in the cab, I was too high. When I reversed, I was too busy making sure I didn't run into anybody.'

'Where exactly did you park that night?'

'There's a little carpark behind the post office, just four or five spaces. You back out onto Railway Parade or whatever it's called.'

He meant Gugeri Street on the railway end of Bayview Terrace. I remembered the small carpark, hidden away.

'What time was this?'

'About twenty minutes, half an hour, before I saw Emily. I'd packed all the gear up ready just inside the front door of The Sheaf, so I just had to load it in the truck when I parked back there. I reckon I was halfway through when I saw her leave. So, yeah, twenty minutes, I reckon.'

'Anything else you remember about the car? Make, model, colour?'

'I think it might have been a Holden. It was dark; dark red I think. There was no light, so I'm not sure.'

He didn't recall stickers, an aerial or obvious dent. He checked his watch. 'Man, I want to help, but I gotta go.'

'You told the police all this?'

'Yeah.'

He climbed into the truck and drove out of the warehouse. I supposed the detail of the car was contained in his interview and therefore not available to me on the police record. The police report summarising what Partigan had claimed to have seen was quite long and detailed as it was and maybe whoever was doing it figured this wasn't critical to go in. Or it could simply have been some lazy police work. Then again, maybe I was the sloppy one; there was a file marked VEHICLES containing close to two hundred vehicles the police wanted to track in relation to the case. I'd only skimmed through this. Maybe I would find it in there?

···

I did not find any mention of Partigan's account but I did find a report of a dark-coloured station wagon in reference to the disappearance of Jessica Scanlan. According to that, the day Jessica's disappearance was made public there was an anonymous call to police of such a car being seen at the highway end of Bay View Terrace at 1.05 Saturday morning. Somebody had noted in the margin this was forty-five minutes after Jessica had left The Sheaf and was therefore 'unlikely'. But the caller could have got the time wrong. Okay, two sightings in the vicinity of the disappearances around the time wasn't remarkable but it was more than interesting. There was also a sighting of a silver Camry for the time and nights Jessica and Caitlin disappeared and for this vehicle the timing was more exact with the last known time they had been seen. Trouble was, silver Camrys were a dime a dozen. There were also multiple sightings of a light-coloured Ford Falcon in the area on the night of all three disappearances but again there were thousands of these cars. I was working off my home computer. The hard copy I'd printed was at the office. With Grace on the scene I found I was splitting myself more frequently between the two locations and even though it was a five-minute drive to the office, it was a pain in the arse to be shuffling around.

I'd come straight back from the PA factory to the house to relieve Sue, who had been holding the fort. I was still dwelling on Partigan and barely took in what my mother-in-law was explaining about Grace's eating and pooing. In terms of assessing his credentials as a killer, my interview with the roadie had been no more illuminating than that with Bontillo. It was like trying to sightsee the Colosseum at night with a single match.

I heard the key in the lock and unmistakable footsteps up the hall. I turned to Grace who was on the floor on a rug fiddling with building blocks.

'Mummy's home.'

Tash entered in her work clothes and her eyes went straight to her daughter. Grace gurgled, delighted, and her arms reached out. Tash scooped her up.

'I never get that reaction.' It was true. I might as well have been a guy measuring curtains as far as my daughter was concerned.

'When she's older, you'll be the favourite.' Tash gave me a consolation kiss.

I guess we'd have to wait a while to see if that was true.

...

Before dinner, Tash and I popped Grace in her stroller and walked to Hyde Park. It felt good having Tash on my arm, her body pressed into me. Simple things in life, eh. It was one of those cool, breezy November evenings that pop their heads up for a little guerrilla rear-guard action after spring had lulled you with warm, peppery-scented days suggesting the battle was over and summer was about to roll in, the conqueror, a column of scorchers in tow.

'You think it's possible they could still be alive?' Tash shuddered as she spoke. I wasn't sure if it was the night air or the idea.

'I didn't at first but the longer no bodies turn up, you have to think it's possible.'

'They make TV shows about that stuff. Some psycho with girls chained in a cellar. You don't think it could happen here.'

I didn't contradict her but after Gruesome nothing surprised me. The universe had shrunk, evil was but a mouse click away and little ol' Perth could be every bit as malevolent as LA or Adelaide. Even though Grace was too young to understand, I had an aversion talking about the case anywhere near her, like it could contaminate our family too.

'I don't really feel like talking about this right now,' I said.

'Sorry, I just ... it's so unreal.'

'It's not your fault, it's me, I'm ...'

How do you express how every minute on the case choked the life out of me?

'It's like smog that I'm surrounded by all day and I just need a little fresh air.' I wanted to assure her my lack of communication was temporary so added, 'When we get back.'

'Smog?' she raised her eyebrows, chipping me, but I knew she got it. She always got it.

...

As it turned out we never got around to further discussion. Tash went to put Grace down and I warmed the stove with Van Morrison as background. Back in the early '70s, I used to go and see a band called Roadband. They were the ones who turned me onto Van the Man. He made cooking easier too. My culinary capability had all the range of my cheap mobile in a concrete tunnel, but what I did, I did really well ... fifty percent of the time. I opened the fridge, saw eggs and decided I'd fix us an omelette. As I cracked an egg, my mobile phone rang. Only clients rang it. I answered, reaching for a knife to slice cheese.

'Yes?'

'It's Craig Drummond.'

In my game you read the tone in a voice quicker than the short acceptance speech you pray they'll give and never do. You can pick anger, fear, envy, and so on in a breath. In Drummond's voice I heard anxiety.

'Do you know anything?'

Yep, there it was, high anxiety.

'About what?'

'You haven't seen the news?'

I turned down the stove, picked up the remote and sent the magic beam to the new flat screen I'd bought specially for the Olympics but barely watched. The screen ignited on bushland, police in forensic gear. Even without the big type that scrawled over the screen – REMAINS OF YOUNG WOMAN FOUND – I would have guessed what was going on. Drummond was back in my ear.

'Do you know if it's Caitlin? Have you heard anything? Gerry rang me. They're beside themselves.'

'I haven't heard anything. Tregilgas will call the family. I'm persona non grata, he's made that clear.' I wanted to concentrate on the news item. 'Listen, I better watch this, I'll call you if I hear anything.'

He thanked me and rang off. I sat on our cheap sofa and leaned closer to the screen. I recognised the netballer cop and Collins in the background.

The body had been found in a shallow grave in bush near Jarrahdale, an hour south-east of Fremantle. They switched back to their reporter on the scene, a young woman pretty enough to be in an ice-cream ad. Her long brown hair was flailing in the wind as she pitched a stream of excited words into her microphone. Apparently the remains had been found early that morning and police had been on the scene all day processing it. It was too early to say if it was one of the missing young women but police had said the state of the remains suggested the time frame was consistent. Tash entered the room and sat silently beside me. At some point she rested her hand in mine. I suppose there were people all over the city doing the same thing, all imagining what it was like to be the parents. A lot of times we fervently hope for something in life but this time I prayed for something to not happen: I did not want to find myself in the situation of those parents, ever.

I knew the police would be looking for something distinctive to identify the body. In Caitlin's case the thin watch and gold necklace. Jessica Scanlan had been wearing a gold bluebird necklet when she disappeared, Emily had three gold bangles. An Australia-wide search had failed to turn up these items in pawn shops or anywhere else for that matter, leaving the possibility they were still with the girls or their abductor. Neither Tash nor I had much appetite after that. I think we had some toast, it was a blur.

CHAPTER 6

That night I couldn't sleep. Eventually I got up, turned on the computer and started looking again at the reported rape of Carmel Younger. In the whole pile of facts and conjecture it was the one thing that had given me that slight tingle: maybe. The assault had taken place one suburb north of Autostrada. Five minutes by car. Younger was of a similar type to the other girls but had been dressed more casually, which made sense as she'd basically gone out for the afternoon and partied on till the early hours of the next morning. I thought of Partigan's story of the station wagon with the engine running and looked to see if there was any mention of such a vehicle in the rape investigation.

Nothing close. The police had identified a white van that had been parked on the side of the road about a hundred metres south of the assault area but inquiries revealed it was owned by the operator of the speed camera and had been unattended. I made a note of the operator's name. Maybe they still had negatives or whatever and I could get a look at the photos of the cars that had been speeding. The task force had not bothered to include any of that on the disks. Apparently it took up a lot of disk space or something, so the only photos in the floppy disks were of the missing girls and Bay View Terrace and its carparks. I checked the address of Carmel Younger against the phone book but couldn't find her name. I wondered if she was still around. I had a contact at the RTA who could help. I went back through the other crimes that might have been a precursor: trouble was, snowdropping, for example, usually went unreported, and I figured anyway I'd have to go back to maybe 1980 because often it's some bent teenager taking the first steps to a major crime they'll commit a decade later. There was nothing around Dalkeith, Claremont, Swanbourne,

Cottesloe that really clicked, apart from a pervert in Cottesloe who had been peering in bedroom windows. The cops had got him but they had checked on him for the Autostrada abductions and he was confirmed to have been in Sydney at the time of the disappearances.

By 4.00, I was tired enough to go to bed. Grace was sleeping through now till around 5.00; great timing on my part.

...

It wasn't until midafternoon the following day that I got the call from Gerry O'Grady. I'd been less focussed than the photos in a retirement home newsletter but had managed to get a call through to my RTA pal. As of yet I hadn't heard back with an address for Carmel Younger.

'Yes, Gerry.'

My voice tightened. If I was assessing myself, I'd register as high on dread.

'Tregilgas just called. It's Jessica Scanlan.'

I can't describe my emotional condition. It wasn't any sort of relief. Perhaps if it had been none of the girls I might have been able to think they were all still alive somewhere.

'Did they say how they identified her?' Really I was just looking for words to keep the world around me real.

'No they didn't. He warned us they are conducting a search over the entire area.'

The area was massive, nearly all thick bush. They could be weeks, months combing it.

'How are you guys doing?' It was a dumb question but to not ask it would be even more insensitive.

He took a deep breath, his voice quavered a fraction. 'Not so bad. We need resolution.'

'I understand. I'll keep going.'

'Have you found anything at all?' There was a grain of hope in his voice. That made me especially careful.

'There's a couple of things I'm looking at. They might be a dead end but then again they might not. If you like I could brief you on what I've done so far but I think it might be better if we wait a while, see what might eventuate.'

'Okay.'

I asked him to hang in there and then we ended the call. The only positive to come out of the finding of Jessica's remains was that it opened up some more space to investigate. They might well be able to tell how she died, how long her body had been there, how she had been transported. A time frame would allow them to look for witnesses who may have seen something in the area. And they might get DNA from the killer off it. I didn't think there was any point me heading out there, I'd just be making a nuisance of myself. Coldly I analysed what I'd avoided with Gerry O'Grady on the other end of the line: the chances of Caitlin being still alive. They were very, very poor. In some ways if it had been Emily's body there in the bush it would have been better news. That sounds terrible but dealing with murder is. You had to figure that if the first girl abducted was the first to turn up dead, there might still be time. But Jessica was the most recent. On the other hand maybe the scientists could get more information from her remains because she was the last abducted. I was swirling in black. My phone rang.

'It's Nipper.' My contact at the RTA.

'Yes, Nipper.'

'I have an address and phone number.'

'Thanks, mate.' I copied it down, hung up and debated whether to ring or call around. I rang. The prefix told me Melville.

'Younger residence.' A woman's voice.

'My name is Richard Lane. I'm wondering if I might speak with Carmel Younger.'

'She's not here.' Curt, not rude though. 'I'm her mother. May I ask what it's in relation to?'

'I'm a private detective employed by the family of the missing girl, Caitlin O'Grady. My investigation turned up the assault on your daughter. No suspect was ever arrested. I thought Carmel might be prepared to talk with me.'

'She's overseas.'

'Oh. For how long?'

'At least another six months. I'm happy to talk with you though, if I can help.'

'That would be much appreciated, Mrs Younger.'

She asked when I would like to drop by. I told her as soon as possible, I already had her address.

'I'll see you in an hour,' she said, and gave me directions.

...

An hour later I was parked outside of a Californian bungalow–style home in a street running parallel to Canning Highway but about a kilometre south. There was a newish Mazda in the driveway, the garden was well kept. Could equally be the home of a welder or an accountant. The coolness of the previous day had been replaced by humidity and droplets from a neighbour's sprinkler scented the air with that distinctive Perth smell of bore water and latent heat. As I drew closer on the neat path, the door opened. With the light in my eyes and shadow from the alcove I couldn't see Mrs Younger clearly behind the flyscreen but her shape was detectable.

'Richard Lane,' I called out as I took the first of three steps to a low porch.

A well-groomed woman, mid-fifties in a casual floral dress, stepped out and ushered me in.

The entranceway was carpet not board. She showed me to a lounge room on the right. It was clean and fresh, some flowers in a vase on a highly polished dining room table that looked rarely used. There were photos of the family on display. I made out a brother, sister, two parents combo. It might have been the O'Grady's place except smaller and with slightly older taste. A family portrait photo I dated as being about six years ago showed a smiling round-faced man with not much hair. I guessed Mr Younger, more tradie than accountant, but I still couldn't be sure. Carmel would have been around eighteen. She had slightly dull eyes but then so did the brother, the family portrait not exactly a highpoint in a teenager's busy schedule.

'Please.' Mrs Younger indicated a low white sofa. She sat at the other end and asked if I'd like a tea or coffee. I told her I was fine. Her manner on the phone had not been one of a woman who beats around the bush. I dived right in.

'I appreciate you seeing me. I've been looking at anything I can, anything the police might have missed, to help identify the person who abducted these young women.'

'They said on the news it was looking like it was one of them they found.'

'It's likely.'

'As soon as it happened, the first girl, Emily? I said to my husband this could be the same man as attacked Carmel.'

'How is Carmel?'

'Slowly getting better. She was a fun-loving girl. She's lost that. She's travelling around England with a girlfriend.'

'When did she go?'

'August.'

'Did the police interview her again?'

'Yes. A policewoman came and asked if there was anything else she could remember about her attack. She couldn't. We all wish she could do something to identify the bastard.'

'How about at the time of the attack? Did you feel they were thorough in their investigation?'

She pulled a face. 'They were thorough with everybody who was at the party she'd been at. They obviously thought it was somebody from there but they didn't find anything.'

'What does Carmel think?'

'She doesn't think it was anybody from there. She thinks she was just the wrong person at the wrong time.'

I told her that I had access to a summarised report of the crime and asked if she would mind if I read it out. 'If there's anything missing, it will help me to know.'

'Go ahead.'

I read through the summary verbatim.

'No, that sounds right.'

'The attacker had no particular odour, like cigarette smoke...'

She was shaking her head.

'Carmel had no idea anybody was about. One moment she was walking then she was just yanked off her feet. He didn't speak the whole time, just showed the knife.'

I got her to describe the knife. It was what was commonly called a hunting knife.

'It took her a long time to be able to talk to me about it. She couldn't even face her father. He wasn't blaming her, you understand, his heart was breaking. She just couldn't do it.'

I didn't think I was going to get any more from Mrs Younger about the attack. I doubted I'd get anything new from Carmel from the sounds of it.

'Did Carmel have any problems with any male friends before this: ex-boyfriends, would-be boyfriends, strangers?'

'No. She'd had three steady boyfriends, didn't have any real break-up problems. It's not like she walked that route every night. It was just shocking bad luck.'

I thanked her for her time. She showed me out. The breeze had woken up, carrying a faint sound of highway traffic that had previously been inaudible.

'I pray you find him. I think there's every chance it's the same man.'

I didn't quite know how to end this interview. 'It must be very difficult.' It was stock but from the heart.

'I feel for those other parents. We still have Carmel.'

...

Back at the office, the full weight of my failure bore down. The discovery of Jessica's body was a game changer. Sure, I could plough on with my investigation but some of the things I'd be chasing might be redundant. Without knowing if the remains gave any new clues, I was firing blind. So did I wait, try Tregilgas again, hope he'd share? Or did I look for some angle that wouldn't be affected by what they might find now with the remains?

I lifted the phone and tried the guy with the traffic camera.

'Vince Santich.' Reasonably thick accent suggesting peppers and cold cuts.

'Mr Santich, this is Richard Lane. I called and left a message.'

'Sorry, you were on my list to call back.'

I explained I was a private detective and interested in the case where a young woman was raped in the cemetery.

'I remember. Awful thing.'

It sounded like he was eating something. For the first time in hours I felt a pang of hunger myself.

'I don't suppose you would have a copy of the shots the camera took that evening.'

'Police property. I pass all that along.'

As I expected. I would have to go back to the task force and see if I could access the stills somehow.

'Your van was parked nearby all night, is that right? Did you visit it at all?'

'Not until the next day to collect the speed camera and check the video.'

I nearly fell out of my chair.

...

'We were having lots of problems with the cameras: outright vandalism, to some smart-arse taping something over the lens. One of the other operators, his camera, they wiped human poo over it.'

Vince Santich was close to fifty, with cropped hair, mainly brown. He wasn't as tall as me and didn't have to stoop quite so low to get under the roller door of his factory unit somewhere out the back of Dianella, where the sand was fine and the grey of school shorts, and blackboys still grew. It was not yet 8.30 am. When he'd called the day before it had been too late in the day for him to see me but he'd be happy to see me first thing in the morning, he said. I gave the ocean a miss, swam a few laps at Beatty Park and headed on out with a kiss from Natasha, who had managed to negotiate a late start to work. Grace seemed to wave goodbye with an egg-smeared hand but maybe it was wishful thinking.

Santich wore a dark blue body-shirt stretched over his chest, and dress-shorts with a belt, tennis socks and sneakers. The floor of the steel and brick unit was concrete. I relayed back to him what he'd told me over the phone, making sure I had it right.

'So you had people wrecking your speed camera, or blocking it, and you set up another camera to catch them.'

'That's right, a video camera running the whole time. We put it in a van see?'

'But the police never checked it.'

'Never.'

'Did they know about it?'

'I thought so but ...' He was leading me through shelving towards a back area. 'What must have happened was ... it was January, from memory. I always go on holidays just before Australia Day for three weeks. The cops didn't contact us right away. I mean they would have had the camera film anyway. But I get a call from my assistant, Don, not the sharpest tool in the shed.' We had swung into what was a kind of office area with a desk, filing cabinets and a small sink. 'Don emails me and says the cops contacted us about our van. Could I give them a call. I was in fucking Thailand. I had to work out international dialling and all that shit. Anyway I call, get this policewoman and I tell her, yes that's our van, what's it about? She says they are looking into an incident and asks when I was at the van. I tell her I parked it there about 7.30 pm and set up the camera and went straight to my niece's twenty-first and I give her a number where they can confirm that. I didn't even think about the surveillance video. I was on holiday. I mean, the traffic camera wasn't damaged so I'm not thinking about it. If I did think about it I probably thought Don would have mentioned it.'

We stopped by the desk where he rooted around in a large cardboard box and emerged with two videos.

'I knew where they were,' he said.

'When you got back you didn't contact the police.'

'Like I said. I wasn't thinking about it. I was only thinking about damage to my traffic camera. I mean I really don't think you're going to find anything on there. I'm sorry but I just thought Don would have told them. It's funny, though, normally I record over them unless we get something. These two ...' He drifted, contemplating things that can't be explained by rational thought, then shrugged. 'There's probably nothing on it.'

'You never checked the video you had running?'

'My speed camera hadn't been touched, so no need. After you rang I dug around and found them and popped them in the monitor to make sure they weren't blank. They're still good. Eight hours' worth, eight pm to four am. We'll be in and out. There's a toilet back there, tea and coffee. You might be out of luck with the biscuits, I'm not sure. Just call me when you're finished, I'll come and lock up.'

'You're okay with me here?'

'Anything goes missing, I know where to look.'

I slid the tape into the player. The usual grainy black and white video came up with a time code in the bottom corner and the date 17-01-98. The lens had been set up somewhere behind the middle of the front seat so it shot through the windscreen, pointing at the speed camera itself which was off to the side of the cemetery, that is the east side of the road, about thirty to fifty metres north. The speed camera was placed in clear view under a pool of amber light. Even from this distance there would be a good chance of identifying a culprit. Carmel had been attacked another fifty metres north of the speed camera, out of range of this covert surveillance. I could have fast-forwarded till 10.00 pm but figured it wasn't beyond the realms of possibility the attacker could have arrived five or six hours before Carmel walked past, just biding his time, waiting for the right mark. Within ten minutes it was obvious I was probably only going to get a rear view of anybody approaching from the south, that is, as they passed the van. Anybody crossing the road between the van and the camera would offer a better chance for identification. Time crawled. A couple of young guys, Santich's employees I guess, maybe one the highly recommended Don, came into the warehouse around forty minutes in. They waved a greeting, loaded up with a camera and shuffled out. By 9.30 pm tape time I'd seen only one group of pedestrians – teenagers, a girl and two young guys – walk past the van heading north, and two cyclists who did not appear to slow, heading south. Later a couple of young guys walked north, past the van on the hard shoulder. They seemed to be in conversation, beach towels slung over their shoulders. I paused the tape and grabbed myself a coffee. I thought of calling Tash but decided against it. The rates were just too high on mobiles.

I returned to my post. The minutes moved like they held a grudge. More than once I was tempted to fast-forward the tape but I hung in there. Finally I got to the time around when Carmel Younger had been attacked. There'd been no pedestrian traffic visible within an hour, the last being a young guy and girl walking carrying skateboards heading south. The camera wasn't angled to the road but slats of passing light designated vehicles on the road. I was convinced by now the attacker had not come in this way. Either he had come from the north, or through the cemetery. It was unnerving knowing that at this point as the camera rolled, just out of its range Carmel was being dragged away at knifepoint. If only the camera had a longer range.

And then, at 2.26 am, in the dark fathoms of background behind the speed camera, there was movement. I literally gasped. Something was heading towards me on the very rim of where light became dark on the border of the cemetery, a hunched figure moving steadily but not running, a man wearing a cap, long pants, face tucked down near his chest. He wore a t-shirt. He got steadily closer to the van until he was walking right past it. You couldn't see his face but you could see part of his upper arm and a tatt with a pattern. I paused the video and tried to make out the pattern, the shape seeming familiar. It took maybe twenty minutes of staring at it before I got it: it was a dagger wrapped in wings, the logo of the SAS.

CHAPTER 7

'You think it could be an SAS guy who raped Carmel?'

Straight back from work to more work, Natasha was folding baby clothes. I was still buzzing, getting in her way.

'Not only that ...'

'Autostrada?' She pushed past me. Grace was asleep in her cot. We'd tried to make her room comfortable but she wouldn't be growing up noticing a pea under her mattress. I cramped Tash even more.

'We've all been wracking our brains about who would they trust enough to accept a lift? You said they wouldn't.'

'Good memory.'

She reached up high, right in front of me to put the clothes away. I held her waist. She kissed me, broke off, started clearing up toys left on the floor. I joined in, haphazard.

'We all thought it was too hard for somebody to abduct three different girls but what if that's exactly what you were trained to do?'

She reasoned quickly. 'Their barracks is about ten minutes away, right?'

'Exactly. And SAS guys play pool in the OBH. A soldier with that training, he could manage any one of those girls.'

She looked at me and sighed, already mapping out my investigation and the problems ahead. 'Where are you going to start? The police would have a hard time getting to interview SAS personnel, let alone some private eye.'

She was right, going through official channels would be a nightmare but I didn't have to go through official channels.

...

A friend of a friend from the North Cott surf club knew a woman whose sister was married to a recently retired SAS sergeant, Tom Cornelius. Cornelius looked more like a surfer than a soldier, broad across the shoulders, sandy-haired, a coloured plastic necklet of some sort.

'I grew up around Cobram in Vic,' he told me over the top of his can of xxxx. We were on his balcony up Mullaloo way, the ocean visible in the distance, rippled, dark blue. It was around 3.00 in the afternoon but the sun hadn't lost its punch and I found myself squinting with the glare. 'I was stationed at Swanbourne for a while. Fell in love with the place. Met Lill.' Aussie men admit to falling in love with places but rarely with their partner. I guess that goes without saying. We'd already had some small talk so I knew he now had a job working for an international company that supplied defence materials to the army.

'You left about six months ago?'

'February.' He offered me another beer and I accepted. xxxx isn't my favourite brew but I grew up on Swan, and anything, South Australian lagers aside, was exotic. 'After Timor I'd had enough. Time to settle down.'

Via Lill, a delicate brunette who was somewhere indoors, he knew why I was here. It was time to get to it.

'Tom, do you think it's feasible an SAS-trained soldier could abduct these girls?'

'Absolutely. I mean, I don't think they'd be wearing camouflage paint and pants, they'd want to draw as little attention as possible but, as for the physical thing, yes, they could subdue a girl, and get her to a vehicle.'

'Would they need help?'

'No. We're trained under very difficult conditions to infiltrate, negate, extract ...' he gestured with his hand to indicate numerous capabilities.

'Please, I don't mean to cause offence, but do you believe there would be somebody in the unit who would do such a thing?'

'Mathew Carter.' He hit me with the speed of a blackjack dealer, saw my surprise. 'Ever since Lill mentioned what you wanted to talk about I've been thinking about it. He's the one who came to mind first, and pretty much is the only one.'

'Why do you think Mathew Carter could be the guy?'

'I heard some stuff, rumours, nothing official, about his conduct in Timor with village women.'

'Rape?'

'Nothing so bald as that. You hear things, they dribble down.'

'Like what?'

'Nothing specific. "Carter was giving the women a hard time", "Carter got his rocks off". Look, you make the SAS, you're good, you have to be. You do a lot of tests, psych stuff not just some obstacle courses. You have to be able to depend on every guy out there. They have to be able to depend on you. You don't have to all like one another.'

'You didn't like Carter?'

'We didn't socialise a lot. He can be good company but there is something about him, an edge of craziness. He's not the only guy who has that, mind you. It can be an asset, but Carter, he's always looking at women and going like, "That one I'd fuck from behind over the washing machine", "Imagine those lips around your cock". And there's a look in his eyes when he says it.'

'You know if he has a tattoo on his right arm?'

'He's got a few tattoos.'

'One with the SAS logo, here?' I pointed at the spot.

'Yeah but I'm not sure which arm.'

...

It was the right arm. I knew because I was staring straight at it only ten metres away, sipping beer at the Swanbourne Hotel in the tin shed–like structure they'd tacked onto the Art Deco façade, probably back in the '60s. This was the games room: darts, pool tables, concrete floor. For about thirty years this room had hosted a Sunday afternoon jazz session, then the music got retrenched. Word was the whole place was being knocked down for yet another retirement village but I wasn't thinking about any of that, I was wondering if this was the guy who had raped Carmel Younger and abducted three young women. Carter would have been six foot, maybe six one, wiry. The guys he was playing pool with were housemates Dean Heaton and Stuart Filbert, also SAS, all twenty-five, give or take a year. They rented in Mount Claremont about ten minutes away, a modern white brick townhouse, small patchy lawn, a carport offering an old Corolla and slightly more recent Holden sedan, stacked surfboards and wetsuits left to dry.

Tom Cornelius had located Carter for me but had declined to get further involved. How could you blame him? If Carter was the man responsible, you didn't want to give him cause to seek you out. At least not till he was locked up. I asked Cornelius if he thought the other two would be involved in anything criminal.

'Heaton's a bit of a puppet but I don't see him getting into hurting women. Not willingly. Filbert's new, transferred from Darwin about three months ago. You could speak to Luke Whitmore or James Feruggi, they used to be close with Carter. Whitmore shared a place with Carter but moved out. He was my Timor source. He's still in Perth. Feruggi transferred out.'

'Why didn't these guys make an official complaint?'

'Carter's a good soldier. He's got your back. And when you spend time facing live rounds together, you're mates whether you like somebody or not.'

I understood what he was saying. I'd felt the same thing when I was a cop.

He continued. 'Besides, you make some allegation, it doesn't stick, you're up shit creek.'

...

I'd tailed Carter and his mates from the house, Heaton driving the Corolla, no need yet to take a look around inside. About five hundred metres out, I guessed their destination as the Swanbourne. I gave them twenty minutes, then wandered into the bar. What Cornelius had said played out. Carter perved on the barmaid's chest and when unaccompanied girls strayed in, he would turn to his friends and make some comment about their 'tits', audible even to me. The others offered embarrassed grins but shunned him with body language. I wasn't convinced yet that this was the guy who had abducted Caitlin but I was more positive his DNA would match Carmel Younger's rapist. After about forty minutes, I'd seen all I needed. They'd been going an hour, which I figured gave me at least another hour free and clear.

I finished my beer and then drove back towards their townhouse, parking two blocks away, walking past sprinklers and the sound of basketballs on concrete driveways. When I reached their place I walked straight to the front door like I lived there. I was conscious of a woman watering her lawn on the other side of the street but nobody close. There was one wooden front door, no screen, which made my job easier. I carried a set of master keys that opened most locks. This one didn't prove too challenging.

The room I stepped into was an open-plan lounge–dining room, separated from the kitchen by the servery. There was a smell of recent toast, trademark to most shared male houses, but overall it was surprisingly tidy. Maybe the discipline of the army helped. I was on my guard but not expecting to find any girls captured or dead here. I slipped on latex gloves, checked the laundry and took myself up the short staircase. There was a bedroom at the front facing the street, one in the middle, one at the back. The one in the middle was the smallest and I reckoned that would be Heaton's. Carter would pick whichever one he wanted, probably the front. I walked into a neat room and well-made bed. On the dressing table was an ANZ bank statement to Dean Filbert. Other than that and some small change, the dressing table was clear but there was a desktop computer and printer sitting at a small workstation. No office chair, just a kitchen chair.

I left the room and walked across tired but still thick carpet to the back bedroom. About the same size as the front room it was darker and smelled of BO. The bed was rumpled, a few socks and some running shoes, higgledy-piggledy on the floor, but relatively tidy. I carefully opened the walk-in robe. The doors slid easily. I guess that was the only time I'd tensed up. I don't know whether I thought I might find a body or at very least a scary balaclava but all that greeted me were uniforms and a few casual clothes, shirts, body-shirts, one pair of Country Road slacks, and jeans. I dared not contaminate this scene. I carefully pulled the clothes apart, looked in the back of the wardrobe: no knife, roll of gaffer tape, anything like that.

That left the smallish dressing table topped by a digital clock, aftershave and hairbrush.

I slid open the top drawer first. There was some cash, a bank book plus a few bills, not the phone bill, though, which might have been of some interest. The second drawer was almost empty, old batteries, the small sizes, a Walkman and earphones, a pack of cards. The third drawer was way more interesting. At the bottom under a jumble of developed photos still in their wallets was a metal cashbox protected by a small padlock. The urge I had to take it and break it open then and there was almost irresistible. But I couldn't do that. Inside could be evidence, jewellery from the missing girls or other trophies. I picked up a photo wallet, started flicking through. The first couple were recent and uninformative, showing Carter and various guys, including his housemates, at the beach, playing park cricket and drinking with young women at a beer garden. None of the young women looked familiar. I couldn't place the pub offhand.

It was a tight shot, not much to go on. I slipped one of the prints into my pocket. The next wallet I dug for revealed army shots, Timor I was guessing. While I hadn't been to Timor, it had the look of Darwin, a town I had. Carter was no Max Dupain. The shots were pedestrian, mainly the guys hanging around camp. A couple of guys were in a lot of the photos, I guessed Whitmore and Feruggi. One snap showed Carter posing with grinning village girls. I kept it, picked up another wallet, started thumbing and froze.

I was staring at Carter in t-shirt and shorts leaning back against a maroon Commodore station wagon with one of the guys from the Timor shots – Whitmore or Feruggi? There was no station wagon at the house now. Had he sold it? The shot seemed to be around the same vintage as the Timor photos.

I must have been too engrossed in my discovery to hear the car arrive. The door downstairs opened and low voices swirled in. Shit. I dropped the photos into my back pocket with the other two and slid the drawer closed as quietly as I could. There was no way I would make it down the stairs. I pulled back the dull brown curtain covering the rear window. Below was a small backyard, devoid of cover. A picket fence separated the neighbours, back and either side. To my left was a gum tree that rose up beyond the back roof. Maybe I could make it from the window? The windows were aluminium, sliding but clipped shut. The voices below bubbled for a moment then I heard somebody take the stairs. By now I was not worrying about finesse, just escape. I unclipped the window, slid it open – thankfully it moved easily – and was about to climb out onto the narrow sill when I saw the hairbrush sitting on the dresser. I pulled one of the small plastic bags I'd shoved in my pocket, just in case and pulled a clump of hair from the brush. I shoved it into the bag and sealed. Whoever was coming was already at the landing. I climbed up onto the sill. The closest branch was maybe five feet away. Normally I could make that but here I was crouched, my body twisted to the left. I'd have bugger-all momentum.

I stood up on the outside of the window, my toes pointing inwards to the room. I tried to reach the tree with my right leg. Nope. No alternative now.

I pushed off hard.

I didn't so much sail through the air as slowly arc down. My eyes were locked on the looming trunk. For a split second I thought I'd make it.

Then again, as a kid I'd thought Dawn Wells off *Gilligan's Island* was going to meet me and fall in love with me. Where this might have happened I hadn't thought through: the fish and chip shop, I guess, because that was the only place I ever experienced social interaction. What I'm saying is I'm an optimist: I was aiming for the trunk, I was dreaming. My nails brushed against it briefly as I plummeted. I got lucky, kind of. A wedge of branches forked out beneath me. My shin, then my groin, hit solid wood. I slid back towards the trunk and got jammed like a footy you have to bring down, shying rocks and half-bricks. Even as the pain in my leg competed with the pain in my balls, I kept looking up at the window. No face appeared. I wondered if I'd made too much noise, if somebody was going to appear in the backyard. Nothing. Carefully and painfully I extricated myself, putting my body as far as I could to the south side of the trunk, thereby camouflaging myself from anybody who happened to be looking out the back window of the ground floor. I tried to ease down but fell faster than an Italian striker milking a penalty. The grass offered some shock absorption but the landing still jarred. I thought I heard the back door open and hobbled for cover at the side of the house. A waft of music found its way from the lounge room. Finding myself in a narrow brick walkway confined by the wall of the house on one side and the picket fence on the other I pushed forward towards the street. A toilet flushed on the other side of the wall and scared the shit out of me. I squeezed past a pair of bins and emerged in the carport. Having memorised the number plates of the two cars, I then did my best to saunter casually out to the road though my ripped palms were burning and my joints throbbing.

Only when I made my own car did I partly relax, keeping an eye out as I recorded the number plates. Then I started up and pulled out, fighting the impulse to toot the horn and shout to the heavens: finally I had something.

CHAPTER 8

Luke Whitmore, who it turned out was the guy in the photo with the station wagon and Carter, sipped an orange juice as he stared out towards the ocean, hunching in his fleecy top. It was around 6.30. The sun had dropped faster than Eddie the Eagle and caught me by surprise in my short-sleeved birthday present, a check shirt I didn't like all that much but wore for Tash's sake. After putting me in touch with Whitmore, Tom Cornelius had generously offered his deck as a meeting ground and after a quick social brew had discretely withdrawn indoors to leave us to it. Whitmore was about my height, like Carter, sinewy, but with hair that looked like drawn waves on the artwork wall of a kindy class. He seemed naturally quiet, and took time to weigh up his answers. As a favour to Cornelius he had agreed to meet me to talk about his colleague, Carter. I had not revealed why exactly I wanted the information but had sworn I was private, not from any government department.

'Most of the time he's a great guy. But he can turn quick, and nasty.'

'With women?'

Whitmore studied me curiously.

'With anybody. Even his friends. That's why I got out. I'd had enough. Plus I've got a girlfriend and ... well, to be honest I wasn't comfortable her staying over there.'

'You think he might try something?'

'Not so much that. But he can be crude, you know? He thinks the world is one big wet canteen.'

If being boorish was a punishable offence, Australian sports TV would barely have a newscaster left.

'What about in Timor? With the women. You didn't like how he treated them.'

Whitmore weighed how much he should say. 'No, I didn't. I'm not saying he raped any women, I didn't witness that, and even if I had I probably wouldn't tell you. No offence.'

'None taken. But he disturbed you, right?'

Another long pause, another sip. 'There was one occasion, this village on the border we thought might be sympathisers with the pro-Indonesian militia. We came on them one day, all the men were out. That was suspicious in itself. Carter took one of the women into the hut he said "for interrogation". When she came out she was crying. The way she held her clothes ... it was suspicious. Other times he was more just ... inappropriate.'

'You never reported him.'

He shook his head. 'Carter is the kind of guy who saves your arse every second day. I didn't have anything to go on. You're sure you're not government?'

I gave him my word. I wanted to go back over something he'd said.

'You said you didn't think he would try anything with your girlfriend. Is that because you're his friend?'

Finally a smirk. 'That wouldn't stop him. More because he knows I would beat him to a pulp.'

'What about if he came across a girl who didn't have somebody to protect her?'

Whitmore's eyes bore into me for what seemed a very long time. Finally they broke away. 'If you're asking me if I think he could pressure or intimidate a woman, I'd say it was possible. I can't say any more than that but if, for example, some woman has complained about what he might have done to her, well, I wouldn't dismiss her story.'

'Carter used to drive a Commodore station wagon, right?'

'Yeah. He might still have it.'

'No, he traded in for a sedan. Any problems with it?'

'Usual: leaked a bit of water. Why?'

In hindsight I shouldn't have mentioned the wagon. I didn't want to point Whitmore in the direction I was looking, wanted to obscure my real intentions, act like I might be working for some potential employer Carter might have applied to.

'The sedan is newer. Somebody mentioned he had money troubles.'

'Not that I knew of. Mind you, he would always slug you for a loan, forget to pay it back.'

I thought I'd extricated myself okay. There was little else I was going to get from Whitmore. By what he had left out, he'd more or less told me that Carter was capable of some form of sexual assault. I thanked him for his time and left him to catch up with Tom Cornelius who had been briefed by me to act dumb on what my real motives might be.

...

Queens Gardens, the location of choice for wedding photos in the '60s and '70s, was a little haven at the border of the CBD's eastern flank, right opposite the back of police headquarters. Adjacent to the better-known WACA, it was the place my dad would head into with a Gladstone bag of Swan lager chocolate soldiers and plastic cups when it hit lunchtime in the Sheffield Shield games. I'd sit there and sip my lemonade as he furtively drank from the bottles wrapped in brown paper bags. Nowadays, for all but the tests, cricket crowds were thinner than the skin of a doctor's receptionist. The place, even at lunchtime on a late November afternoon, was deserted except for me and a brace of brave Japanese tourists. Maybe that was because the day was unseasonably cold again and the frigate grey sky gave you the impression of being in a highway underpass, or maybe it was because Perth had moved on from homemade sarnies and a thermos. I glanced around the place and imagined office workers of bygone years with their thin ties, *Daily News* and packets of B&H passing the lunch hour and squeezing a few extra minutes from their government pay packets. These days they'd be at cafés twirling pesto pasta on a fork and sipping bottled water. I was a man whose generation was fast finding it was more familiar with what used to be than what is.

After my discovery at the Carter townhouse, my next move had been to check with my RTA contact on Carter's vehicle ownership history. Sure enough he'd had a Commodore wagon from '97 till three months ago when he'd traded for a sedan. The suspicious Snowy Lane wondered whether he was obscuring any evidence trail. The circumstantial evidence was growing but it needed cops from here on. Tregilgas didn't want a bar of me. And I couldn't very well go and say I'd broken into the guy's house. But if Carter was our man, every second meant some other young woman was in unnecessary danger. Tash offered to call in with an anonymous tip but you never knew who they'd send to follow it up. George Tacich hadn't been overly impressed with what he had going for him on the Autostrada

Task Force but I called him anyway to see if he could put anything in train.

'I go to them, it'll be worse than if you do,' he'd said down the phone. For my own protection and his, I hadn't told him how I'd found out what I'd learned. He wasn't stupid though, he would have guessed. 'Your best chance is Nikky Sutton. She's smart and I can call her, set something up.'

And that's what he'd done and why I was here now checking my watch, waiting for DC Sutton, the scent of flowers whose names I didn't know telling me I should be thinking about Christmas shopping. She walked through the gate right on time. I moved out of the shadows and waved. She headed my way. She was shorter than I'd remembered but her eyes were sparkling. I went to introduce myself again.

'Don't worry, you're famous. Or infamous,' she said with a smile.

'I hope you meeting with me isn't a career-ending move.' I was only half joking.

She waved that away. 'I can handle myself. Besides, they don't know. George gave me a brief run-down on your person of interest.'

I started walking and she settled in beside me. I began with the fact that I had somebody who was worth looking at. As soon as I mentioned the rape of Carmel Younger, her eyes drove into me like needles.

'At Karrakatta?'

'Yes.'

She nodded slowly. 'That's why George got you onto me. I worked that case, Sex Crimes. That's what I was doing when I was seconded to the Autostrada TF. We never made an arrest. Go on.'

I was unsure now, the ground had shifted, she might not like what she was about to hear. I told her anyway.

'There was another camera?' Her voice was hushed with a chill that conjured images of shocked rabbits emerging from a burrow into bracing winter.

I explained the situation.

'Oh my God. I missed it.'

'These things happen, somebody thinks somebody told somebody. Miscommunication.'

'But you found it.'

Not wanting to seem like I thought I was hot shit, I said nothing. I was glad she added, 'I'm glad you did, for Carmel's sake.'

From there I took her through my meeting with Cornelius and my surveillance of suspect Mathew Carter who had a tattoo in the right place and had recently disposed of a station wagon that fitted the description given by Gavan Partigan of a vehicle parked behind Autostrada. I told her Carter had a strongbox in his drawer.

She looked me straight in the eye. 'How do you know this?'

'I saw it.'

'Did you touch anything?'

'I wore latex gloves: didn't plant anything, didn't open the box, but I did find these in Carter's hairbrush.' I handed over the plastic bag. 'I believe you can get DNA from these?'

'Sometimes.' She wouldn't take it yet. 'You couldn't use it in court.'

'I'm not suggesting that. But if the DNA matches the swab in the Carmel Younger rape kit you can go back in with a warrant based on the other stuff, get an official sample.'

She thought for a long moment. Her hand snaked out and the bag disappeared into her pocket. I showed her the photos. She told me to keep them myself and asked if I had told the O'Gradys.

'The only people I've told anything to are George and my wife. She will speak to nobody.'

Nikki Sutton sighed. 'It's good but there's one big problem. Tregilgas believes he is closing in.'

'You've got a suspect?'

'Yes. Some things have come to light about a previous person of interest.'

'Crossland?'

'Bontillo.'

She didn't have to tell me I was not to mention this to a soul. It was in her look, and even if it hadn't been, it was understood.

'I spoke to him. I got no vibe off him.'

'We followed up all his previous jobs. There was scuttlebutt at a boys school in Melbourne, nothing official. Unofficially there was an allegation that he drove some boys home from soccer training and made one of the boys uncomfortable.'

'How?'

'The boy says Bontillo put his hand on his thigh, started talking about the wonderful birds you could see in the bush.'

'How old?'

'Sixteen.'

Even if it were true, it didn't make him a killer. I said as much.

'That's not all.' We'd started walking again. 'His sister contacted us and admitted the night Caitlin went missing, Bontillo was gone just after midnight. Her husband pressured her to tell the truth.'

'So now Bontillo has no alibi for any of the nights the girls went missing?'

'That's right. The boss is hot for him: he's lied to us and he has a history of sexual misconduct with students.'

'Allegations, not proven, and a male at that.'

She shrugged. 'I'm giving it the way the DI sees it.'

Which I understood. She told me they were watching him very closely now.

'All of which is going to make it hard to get the boss to look at your theory.'

'Not if the DNA matches.'

'There might be no usable DNA. As it is, it'll take weeks to get this back from the lab. It's not like the TV shows.'

I must have presented as a hot bottle of Coke shaken and ready to explode. She carefully eased the seal.

'We can class him as a suspect in Carmen's rape. If the video plays out like you say that might give us a warrant, certainly an interview.'

'I've done some rudimentary checks: Carter's squad was in Perth the night each of the girls went missing.' This was something Cornelius had steered me through. I explained I hadn't wanted to do any further digging in case it leaked and scared Carter off.

'What about the housemates? Could they be involved?'

'Filbert's only been here a few months. What I've been told of Heaton would suggest not. And neither of them were with him at the time of Carmel Younger.'

She digested it. 'Whatever I do, your involvement has to be redacted.'

She was right, the info needed to be quarantined from the source. I couldn't care less about bragging rights. Let her present it as her theory.

'Fine with me.' I handed her the video I'd had copied. My mind was running angles now. 'What would be the chances of getting a search warrant?'

'Unless this video clearly shows his face –'

'It doesn't.'

'– then not strong. We can interview him though, ask him to show us around, ask for DNA but he's under no obligation to give it.'

'You do that, he'll be on his guard. At the very least he'll have time to dispose of evidence.'

She could see I was scheming. 'What's your plan?'

'If there was a break-in nearby and somebody reported a car that looked a lot like his ...'

She stared at me like I was an extinct form of reptile.

'I just make up a false report?'

'Maybe it won't be false.' My turn to shrug. She shook her head but I could tell she was warming to my antediluvian ways. I know that word because Tash uses it to describe me all the time.

'I'd better be getting back. I'll try and pull a favour on the DNA but don't expect it any time soon.'

'Let me know if Tregilgas is prepared to investigate. We'll take it from there.'

'I will, Snowy.' She allowed herself a smile the way somebody on a diet allows themselves a single jelly bean. 'George really didn't do you justice.' Then she turned on her heel.

...

For the next few hours I actually relaxed. Tash had taken Grace into work with her so I slipped by and picked her up. She howled for a good ten minutes when we drove away. Then, as quickly as she'd started, she stopped. I drove to Crawley and let her run around on the foreshore. The wind was up and the river frothed. A lone sailboat battled the elements and I felt a kinship with the invisible helmsman. I'll be honest, I felt good about myself. Much as I pretended to talk it down with everybody else, I was convinced Carter was the guy. This led me to debate whether I should say anything yet to the O'Gradys. I was walking a fine line, wanting to give them hope, just not false hope. Ultimately I chose to wait until I at least knew Tregilgas had given Sutton the all clear to further investigate. In the meantime, there was Grace.

If you've ever had to change a nappy in the teeth of a Perth wind, you'll know that the skill required leaves running huskies through the Arctic for dead. Grace was almost beyond nappies now but given it had been a long stint away from base, we'd gone with the precaution. Good thing too.

I drove back home, fed Grace and myself and started to get anxious that I hadn't heard anything. For a distraction I began odd jobs I'd been putting off since Vlamingh landed here. Thanks to Grace, my efficiency was impaired but I told myself when I got her down for her nap I'd pick up. That proved optimistic. Put it this way: I was marginally more efficient than Telstra. I still couldn't concentrate and kept downing tools in case the noise masked the ringing phone. When Sutton finally rang I was on the bathroom floor engaged in home plumbing. She was to the point.

'I've got the green light on Carter. I watched the video; I'm still kicking myself. The boss doesn't think it's going to amount to anything on our case but he's not stopping me from looking.'

'What did you tell him?'

'Said I got a tip from an informant that sent me back over my old files, then realised I hadn't spoken to the principal of the traffic camera business. He thought it was good work. I owe you.'

'How about the DNA?'

'I got that to an old friend in Sex Crimes, asked them to run it against the Carmel Younger kit. They didn't ask too many questions.'

'We could just wait,' I said, though my heart wasn't in it.

'I'm thinking about every young woman out there in this city. We don't have time to wait.'

My kind of girl.

'Okay, sit tight and expect a call.'

'There better not be any blowback, Snowy.'

'There won't be.'

...

Three years earlier Peter Hrovios had been a client. Now he was a friend, playing the odd round of bad golf with me, sharing an occasional lunch. His family-owned clothing factory had been losing five leather jackets a week, regular as clockwork. The manager had tumbled to it about a month before Peter contacted me but after I suggested a full stocktake Peter was able to estimate it might have been going on a year or more. There was no sign of forced entry. Besides Peter, the manager was the only person who had the code to open the office and then the roller door to the factory. Naturally I looked at the manager but he rang no bells. He was an older guy, proud of his work and pissed off somebody was stealing from the place he'd worked nearly thirty years. The first thing I had Peter do was institute a full bag search on all seventeen employees whenever they left the building. Nothing. But the jackets kept disappearing. I'd set up surveillance cameras outside and in. These ran twenty-four seven and I would laboriously go through video tapes, checking to see if anybody was breaking in late at night. Nothing, nothing, nothing. It had to be an inside job but I couldn't see anything suspicious. I kept checking the video. I was missing something. I started to think the guard had to be in on it even though I'd interviewed him and hadn't sensed anything off. I studied the tape of the employee security gate and watched the guard searching employees on the way out. He seemed to do a thorough job. I told Peter I wanted to put one of my people in for a couple of days as guard. My guy, a uni student who was smart, sharp-eyed and motivated, stood in for three days. He searched every employee as they left, lunchtime and end of the day. Still nothing but another jacket was stolen. We were stymied and shared a beer in silence at my local pub, which is almost directly under my office.

'You've shaved your beard off,' I said.

'Shaved it off a week ago.'

I hadn't noticed. And bam. There it was. We see what we expect to see, what our memory of something is, not how it actually is. I almost ran out of the pub and back up to my office and started rechecking the video surveillance. An idea was taking shape. Despite the cameras we'd put up, you could take a jacket from lots of places inside the factory without being seen. The thing was, that didn't do you much good because you had to get it out of the factory and we had cameras all around the perimeter and at the gate, as well as the physical search. Bags were searched on the way out, even at lunchtime.

It wasn't the guard, my guy had missed it too, but now armed with my new insight I went back and looked at every worker coming and going.

It took about thirty minutes for me to spot him: a young guy, general dogsbody. Every morning he arrived on foot in his own leather jacket, one of the factory ones the employees could buy for a discount. Every lunchtime he left the factory to get his ham and salad roll. Wearing a leather jacket. When he returns, nobody is thinking to check what he's wearing. Genius in its simplicity. He arrives at work in his own jacket. Before lunch he steals a new one from the rack and replaces it with his older one so nobody will notice the rack is one short. Bold as brass he slips on the new jacket and walks out. He's not carrying anything to be searched. The guard 'sees' him in his original jacket. Nobody is looking at him when he comes back from lunch without a jacket, all the focus is on the heading out part of the equation. So now all he has to do is retrieve his original jacket and walk back out at day's end. Again, the guard sees him in his own jacket and this reinforces the guard's memory.

We busted him the next day.

'No hard feelings, boss,' he'd said when I marched him into Pete's office.

'No hard feelings! I mean he's ripped me off about thirty thousand dollars.'

Pete shook his large head and laughed as he swizzled Diet Coke and ice. He drank a big gulp and placed the heavy tumbler on the glass coffee table that separated our sofas.

'So what is it you want me to do for you, Snowy?'

'Let me break your window. I'll pay of course.'

'You better.'

But he was curious not angry. We were alone, his wife and daughters out putting his credit card through its paces.

'So why am I letting you break my window?'

'Cops need a reason to hassle a guy who is likely a real arsehole. You're going to say that as you arrived home from a short drive to the beach, you saw a car, this car,' – I showed him a photo of Carter's Holden Commodore – 'pulling out of your driveway and heading down the street. This gives them a reason to check on similar cars in the area.'

He grabbed a handful of salted peanuts from a plastic dish he'd found at the bottom of a kitchen drawer after much rummaging. I had the impression Pete didn't know his way all that well around the working side of his kitchen. He gave a slight shrug of his shoulders. 'Go for it.'

I asked him to point to the window furthest from any neighbours. He suggested the window in the spare room on the ground floor.

'One more thing,' I told him as I hefted the half-brick I had brought with me in anticipation. 'When you returned you found the window broken and jewellery missing. Not a lot, just a few pieces: diamond earrings, a gold bangle, a Rolex.'

'You've been through our drawers already!' He slapped his thigh at his joke. 'I guess I don't get to claim insurance?'

'Prefer you didn't.'

'Okay, Snowy, go ahead, rob me.'

I walked around the side of the house, aimed and hurled the brick. It broke the window with a satisfying thwack. Then I dialled Nikky Sutton.

Carter was in play.

CHAPTER 9

'They were all home when we turned up.'

'We', Sutton explained, was her and Detective Roylan. Detective Constable Sutton sat in a chair in my office sipping a glass of red I'd poured. I was pacing, occasionally glancing out my window at the bored hoons of North Perth squealing rubber. It was close to 10.00 pm. This was the first chance she'd had to communicate with me. Earlier we'd agreed my office was the best place to meet. She'd told Tregilgas there had been a break-in near Carter's place and wanted to use it as a pretext. As long as he didn't know how she knew about this break-in, he gave her the green light to investigate. He still didn't buy Carter as a suspect for Autostrada but was happy to nail a rapist as a by-product. Sutton continued now.

'I told Carter and his pals there had been a burglary and we had been given a partial number plate consistent with Carter's.'

This is what we'd worked out: a good reason for the police to visit but not so much as to put Carter on his guard.

'How'd Carter and his mates react?'

'No problem. Carter said he owned the car but hadn't been out for a few hours. He explained he was in the SAS, as were his housemates. I empathised, said I understood but we still had to follow up. Then I asked if we could take a look around as there had been some things stolen and it would help us greatly if we could clear them of any suspicion then and there.'

Time for me to pour myself a drink.

'That set off any alarms?'

'Carter was sanguine enough.' You had to admire a cop with that kind of vocab. 'Filbert wasn't rapt. He thought it was going a bit far. I said fine:

why don't you just let us take a quick look over your dressing tables or drawers? They agreed.'

'And?'

'The metal box was there as you'd suggested. We got Carter to open it. It contained a pistol and a small amount of bullets. Turns out he belongs to a gun club. He has a licence, all in order.' My disappointment at there being no serial killer "trophies" was counterbalanced. He could have used the gun in the abductions. I mentioned that.

'Same thing crossed my mind.'

'Nothing else?' I hoped maybe she was holding out on the good stuff for dramatic effect.

'Nothing. No knife, no jewellery. I glanced through the photos. They were standing there watching.'

My deflation must have been obvious.

'Hey, we still have the DNA. I'm also waiting for the army to get back to me with movements of his squadron on the nights in question.'

'What can I tell the O'Gradys?'

'Absolutely nothing.'

Which of course I knew but the sadist in me needed it confirmed. I really wanted to give them some sense that we were progressing.

'Can you get eyes on Carter?'

'The boss won't go for that. But I've circulated his photo and description to all our task force and the patrolling uniforms in Claremont. Also his car and rego. Of course, if somebody else wanted to put eyes on him ...'

Sutton stood, found my pathetic basin and rinsed her wineglass.

'Thanks for the vino. I'm thinking overall it's positive, the gun especially. I'm running down the station wagon, will let you know when I've tracked where it is now.'

Once people have imparted what they need to, my office rarely tempts them to stay. She was already at the door by the time I spoke.

'What did you think of Carter?'

'Arrogant, smug. I don't know about Claremont, but I think you're right about Carmel Younger. If the DNA agrees, party-time.'

After Sutton left, I sat and moped. Halfway through another slug of red I told myself not to be despondent, my expectations had been too high. Soon the police could point to Carter as the man who assaulted Carmel Younger. Then they'd be able to bring real pressure to bear. In the meantime, starting tomorrow, I'd be devoting more of my attention to

Mr Carter. If he was the Autostrada guy I'd need to check him in the dark hours. Eventually I settled on this routine: surveillance 5.00 pm to 3.00 am, home for a sleep till 8.00 am, time with Grace and Tash before she left for work, after which I'd do all the domestic stuff I had to do and any more research into the case I could before grabbing another hour of sleep between 3.00 and 4.00 pm, which was when Sue would come over to hold the fort with Grace until her daughter returned. Carter was at the barracks till 5.00 pm, so I'd try and pick him back up as he left. If he was keeping the girls or their bodies somewhere, maybe he'd go straight there before heading back home?

...

Three days into my surveillance of Mathew Carter I had nothing to show but bad eating and sleeping habits, and developing piles. I wished I had the power of the police department at my disposal and could check on whether Carter had ever been involved in any training or bivouacs in Jarrahdale where Jessica Scanlan's body had been dumped. I wished I could trace the station wagon myself and run forensics on it. As it was, my resources were a surveillance van fitted out like a plumber's, my old Magna, a Sony Walkman and a bunch of old cassettes. Sure everybody else now had portable CD players but I came from a tradition where furniture was varnished, verandas oiled and tyres retreaded. The old man had drummed into me that you looked after and maintained, wringing every last drop of service before discarding or contemplating replacement. I'd only bought a CD player four years ago, a decade after almost everybody else, still had my vinyl and still played it. Unlike my record collection – which consisted of some albums I'd saved for as a teen, others I'd bought through the '70s and '80s but each carefully chosen – my cassette library was physical evidence of the haphazard, the unplanned, the whim. Prince rubbed shoulders with a *Reader's Digest* Bill Haley & His Comets I'd bought at a garage sale, Linda Ronstadt found herself in a Dugites cover, Loaded Dice was sandwiched between *Honky Château* and *Born Sandy Devotional*.

The plumber's van I had parked in advance on the street opposite Carter's. My routine was to tail Carter from the barracks in my car. If he did drive off somewhere, the car was far less conspicuous than the van. So far that hadn't happened, he'd driven straight home. I would then park the car in a nearby street and walk back to the van. The van's only bonus was neighbours couldn't see you camped in the front seat like they could with a sedan. In a place like Perth with its low-traffic streets, you'd arouse immediate suspicion. The first night, Carter emerged with the other guys around seven. I tailed them in the van to the Swanbourne Hotel where they had a counter meal before returning home. I parked the van on the other side of the street. Lights were all out by midnight. I spent the night with my cassettes, beginning to hate every last one. At 3.00 am I called it quits, locked up the van and walked back to my car.

Day two was a carbon copy of day one except this time they drove to the Captain Stirling Hotel on Stirling Highway, under ten minutes by car from Autostrada. Once again, however, they all returned.

The morning of day three, Nikky Sutton rang to tell me the latest.

'The army got back to me. Carter's squadron was free and in Perth on the dates Carmen Younger was raped, and Emily Virtue and Caitlin O'Grady disappeared.' I restrained my excitement, I felt a 'however' coming on. 'However ...' – there it was – '... the night Jessica Scanlan disappeared the squadron was in Northam on a training exercise.'

It was a blow but not fatal.

'Maybe he was able to get back? Northam's what, an hour or so away. It would be the perfect alibi.'

She had considered the same thing. 'I haven't been able to speak to anybody in person yet, this just came through as a fax.' She would keep trying, she assured me, as she would for the station wagon. It had been located but from now on it was a logistics matter as the wagon was in Esperance, hundreds of ks away, and a tech had to be peeled off to examine it thoroughly. I told her about my surveillance and she was grateful. We agreed to talk if either of us had any news.

...

The rest of the day panned out pretty much like its predecessors. It was 9.00 pm, and I was in the back of the van listening to Johnny Warman's only hit so far as I was aware, 'Screaming Jets', when my phone rang.

It was Gerry O'Grady. He sounded agitated but I wasn't sure if it was excitement or anxiety.

'We just had a call from Tregilgas. Did you know about this suspect?'

I was about to say 'I'm watching his house as we speak' but Gerry ran on. 'Ian Bontillo.'

My heart sank. I was surprised Tregilgas would have mentioned Bontillo.

'I interviewed Bontillo. He was cooperative. He didn't ring any bells.'

Gerry was keen to get it all out. 'The police took him in for questioning. Apparently a reporter got wind of it so they wanted to call us to warn us. They told us he had lied about his alibi. They said a history of sexual misconduct with students had come to light.'

'That's gilding the lily.' I set him straight on what I knew. But for the first time in months they had some hope.

'Snowy, he lied. He has no alibi for any of the nights the girls went missing and he taught them all.'

It was a strong point of course, and I wasn't sure I ought to dissuade him just because I had my own hobbyhorse.

'I'm following up on something else. It's promising. I think I should keep going but it's up to you if you want me to stop.' I knew when I said that I was putting myself between a boulder and a canyon wall.

'What is it? You've got a lead?' You could taste the eagerness in his voice.

I told them I'd come right over.

···

'So, this Mathew Carter could be involved in the other rape?'

Michelle O'Grady spoke for both of them. We were sitting in the lounge room that now felt almost as familiar to me as my own. Nellie was in her room doing homework. In deep slumber, Soupy lay side-on, his flank rising and falling. I'd laid out everything with the care of a mother packing for junior's first school camp.

'Yes. That will give the police a much stronger reason to check everything about him.'

Michelle bit her lip. Gerry leaned forward. 'Is there any evidence he might have known the girls? Other than playing pool at the OBH?'

'No, but I don't think that's critical. We're talking SAS here.'

I could sense his reservations.

'Look, I'm not saying it's not Bontillo, only that I didn't get that vibe. But maybe that's why he has gone undetected. I honestly don't know. But I don't think there's anything to lose following Carter.'

They looked at one another, then turned to me.

'You better get back.' It was Gerry who spoke. I reminded them that it would be better for everybody if they didn't mention all this to Tregilgas.

'He's not obstructing the line of inquiry,' I hastened to point out. 'But he might if he knew I was involved.'

We agreed to communicate the next day. I stepped back out and, even in the dark, felt the hot breath of summer on my neck. Bill Hayley and I drove back to Carter's house and I resumed my vigil. The car was still in the driveway. I watched until around 2.00 am before calling it a night.

Tash was fast asleep when I got home. I made myself a toasted sandwich, showered and climbed into bed beside her. Lately I'd spent no time with her and I missed her company. For a long time I couldn't sleep. My brain kept picking back through images of Caitlin, the dark station wagon, a figure approaching out of the dark. It stuck Bontillo's head on the shoulders of the figure, then Carter's. Finally I fell asleep.

...

When the phone woke me there was no sign of Tash next to me. The clock radio showed 9.07. The house was too quiet for Grace to be around. Tash had gone to work and taken Grace with her to drop at her mum's; that's what my brain was somehow churning through as I fumbled for the phone.

'It's me.'

'Snowy? It's Nicole Sutton.'

I sat up. 'Any news?'

'Yes, not good, I'm afraid. The DNA isn't a match.'

My brain wouldn't register what my ears were being told. 'What? Sorry, say that again?'

'Carter's not your guy. He didn't rape Carmel Younger.' The words were like knuckles, driving my hope down. My innards were crushed.

'You're sure?'

Of all the lame lines to come out with – but I couldn't help myself. I'd been so wedded to the idea that I had cracked not just Carmel Younger's case but the whole Autostrada thing.

'Yes, I'm sure. I double-checked with the lab. If that is Carter on the tape he's probably going to say he was simply out walking.'

'So, what's going to happen?'

'Nothing. I'm up to my neck here – a neck I stuck out to have this thing checked.'

My brain was finally warmed up. 'He might have seen something.'

'The tape and notes have been passed over to the Sex Crimes unit. They can follow that up but I'm telling you there's nothing to go on. I'm sorry, Snowy, you did good work but you know what it's like, ninety-nine percent pans out empty.'

I tried to keep her engaged, to ask if they had acquired the station wagon but she cut me off.

'I really have to go. It's all hands on.'

'Bontillo?'

'You do the maths.'

I'd sometimes wondered what it must be like for those climbers who are stuck dangling over the crevasse, threatening to bring down the rest of the team till somebody does what has to be done and cuts the rope. When Sutton hung up and disconnected me from Autostrada, I got a fair idea. I sat there, my back to the wall, a swirl of sheets over my body. I felt worthless, guilty. I'd wasted Sutton's time, given false hope to the O'Gradys, made Tash carry the burden of the house. She didn't care about that because she wanted to support me, Snowy Lane, the great murder investigator. I'd confused pride with skill, deluded myself into thinking I could find leads others weren't smart enough to see.

I forced myself out of bed and boiled the kettle. My scrambled ego tried to pull itself back together. There must be some logic that said it could still be Carter. But Sutton was right. All I had was a grainy video that proved nothing. I would have to call the O'Gradys, kill any false hope that I might be onto something.

That's what I should have done.

···

Instead, that evening I found myself back at the Swanbourne Hotel having followed Carter and Heaton from the barracks. They were in the games room playing pool with half-a-dozen other patrons, young guys who wouldn't have known if the Alien rocked up and started chalking a cue.

'Mathew Carter?'

I tried to use a neutral tone: like I could be a doctor calling out to the waiting room, not quite sure who was going to step forward. He looked me up and down, no more than curious at this stage.

'My name's Richard Lane. I'm a private detective.'

'If I've been rooting some married sheila, that's news to me. I don't do that.' He looked with a smile to Heaton who grinned, resting on his pool cue.

'But single women are fair game?'

'I'm not gay if that's what you're asking.'

'What about if they don't give consent?'

The good humour was gone. He narrowed his eyes. 'What the fuck are you on about?'

'January before last a young woman was raped at Karrakatta Cemetery. There was a camera, caught this image.'

I showed him a still I'd had done of the video frame and then had blown up. He seemed rocked. I didn't offer him an out.

'Care to explain what you were doing there? I mean, that's you, right?'

Now he was definitely over any courtesy. 'Fuck off.' He shoved the photo back at me.

'Of course. I was just asking.'

Heaton chipped in. 'You can't even see the face. Lots of guys have tatts.'

My eyes hadn't left Carter's. 'You gotta admit that looks a lot like you, Mathew.'

'I guess. I like to walk a lot. That a crime? Anyway, you're not a cop, right?'

'That's right.'

'Just a private dick-head.' Carter's witty repartee set Heaton giggling. This encouraged Carter. 'So, dickhead, take a walk.'

There was a real coldness in Carter's eyes. I guess that's what I wanted to see up close and personal, that look that said he could have done it. Maybe the hairbrush I'd picked up was somebody else's, left by mistake? Or somebody else had used it? I wondered if Nikky Sutton had considered that, if she might give it one last go and get Carter's DNA.

'Thank you for your time, gentlemen.'

...

I left the bar and made for my car, which I'd parked on the other side of the narrow road beside some pine trees. I'd reached the boot when I heard footsteps. I turned. A fist blurred towards my head. I pulled away instinctively, and even in the dimness of the overhead railway lights saw the surprise in Carter's eyes as his punch barely grazed me. Heaton stood behind him. I took all of this in in a blink as I retaliated with a left that caught Carter somewhere on the neck. It was a hit but nowhere near good enough to finish him with one punch and that was what I needed. His left caught me in the ribs and as I doubled over, he hit me on the chin with the hard base of his palm, a short, sharp karate blow that snapped me back with a sound like a new deck of cards being broken. Heaton didn't intervene, he didn't need to. I was down in broken bitumen, my ear resting on pine needles. Carter seemed a long way up, even as he bent towards me.

'You harassed me and swung at me. I was defending myself. This man is my witness. You go to the cops, you'll wind up paying me.'

With that he turned on his heel and strode back to the pub.

Four hours later my ribs were still delicate as a ballerina's bow but I hadn't let on to Tash, not even when we made quick love while pasta boiled on the stove and Grace in her cot dreamed of Teletubbies. I'd told Tash about the DNA but that was all the failure I could own up to for now. If she knew of the altercation she'd either want to drive to Carter's with a baseball bat or oh so gently let me know I wasn't in the kind of shape I once was, both of which were worth avoiding. So instead I kissed her and folded into her and turned all my disappointment and disintegrating self-belief into a low hum of rising blood pressure and carnal absolution.

...

Over the next few days I gradually built myself back up. My call to Sutton asking her to reconsider getting Carter's DNA was not returned, my convictions wavered and I accepted that in all likelihood Carter was just an arsehole in the wrong place at the right time. Whether he might have helped me before, I really doubted, but I was sure he wouldn't be offering me any help now about what he might have seen. I still believed the nature of Carmel's rape and the proximity to Bay View Terrace was worth investigating further. I called her mother again and asked if I could call Carmel in the UK. She said she would pass the request on next time they spoke. The next morning when I was up the park pushing Grace in a swing, my mobile rang.

'This is Adele Younger.'

I pictured the woman in her neat suburban lounge room.

'I just got off the phone to Carmel. You can call her now, she'll wait for it.'

I thanked her profusely and memorised the phone number she gave. Then I bundled up Grace and scooted back home, speaking the number over and over again. Once inside my own house I scrawled the number on the back of an envelope, placed Grace in front of a *Bananas in Pyjamas* video and dialled.

Carmel answered right away. The intercontinental delay was annoying but we blundered our way through the polite stuff. She was in Kent. It was cold but quite sunny. I explained how I had been hired by the O'Grady family to look into Caitlin's disappearance.

'It's possible it's the same person,' I said, though I was sure she had been able to join the dots herself, if she hadn't already done so during conversation with her mother. 'Could we talk about that night?'

I kept looking over at Grace who still seemed entertained by Rat in a Hat. Carmel did all that could be expected, she went back over the rape, her breath halting in parts. At one point she stopped altogether.

'I'm sorry to put you through this,' I said, wishing I had something more adequate to offer.

'No, it's okay.' But I knew it wasn't. Her voice was teetering more now than when we'd started but she hung in there. There was nothing new in the story from the account I had read in the police report.

'There was no particular smell; no accent, no tattoo?'

'All I remember,' she said, suddenly stronger, 'is the taste of my tears.'

When I was convinced there was nothing more to be gained I took her back through the earlier part of the evening. I asked who she recalled from the pub, then from the party. She gave me a list of names, people who were there, two girlfriends who might be useful. We'd run through more than twenty minutes.

'Thank you for your help, Carmel.'

'Whatever I can do.'

...

I followed up each and every name she had given me. Like the cops, I focussed on those at the party. There were five guys of interest, one had moved interstate, the other four were scattered over the metro area. I checked them at their work. I followed them and watched them in parks, pubs and clubs. I didn't see anything that raised suspicions. One of them worked at a garden supply place in East Vic Park. When he went to lunch at a nearby hotel, I followed. It was one of those old places that had been spruced up along the lines of sophisticated bars in faraway places without quite getting it right. It was open, the furniture lighter than the pepper grinder, the grill hood like something off an aircraft carrier. The clientele, mainly young guys in tradies shirts and shorts, enjoyed their burgers and salt and pepper squid with the aid of cold beer while the till rang cheerfully. I was keeping light surveillance, shovelling my counter meal of penne pasta into my gob and sitting directly across from the wall-mounted plasma when a banner scrawled across it: PERSON OF INTEREST IN AUTOSTRADA CASE FOUND DEAD. I paused mid-spoonful, let the gist of the reporter's spiel lick me: a man known to the deceased Jessica Scanlan and the missing young women Emily Virtue and Caitlin O'Grady had been found dead in his Claremont apartment after a relative went to investigate why he hadn't been answering his phone. The camera panned to the block of flats in question. It wasn't Claremont, it was Swanbourne. I knew the building where an Art Deco nude waited quietly on a mantlepiece: Ian Bontillo's flat.

...

'Are you sure it was suicide?'

I trusted George Tacich. We'd both worked with corrupt cops. Tash's father, Dave Holland, was one of them but I still believed he was essentially a good man who did a very bad thing for what he thought was the right reason.

'Yes, Snow, I'm sure. He overdosed on sleeping tablets. Tregilgas may not be your cup of coffee but he's thorough. There's nothing suspicious.'

The note Bontillo left for his sister had said 'I'm sorry for all the hurt I have caused'.

I pointed out that was ambiguous, hardly a confession to being a serial killer. Tacich did not disagree. I pressed. 'Come on, if he was the Autostrada guy and he did this because he felt guilt, why not say where the girls are buried? Why not say he's sorry to the O'Grady family and so on?'

'What you're saying is valid but Tregilgas is confident he got his man.'

'It might have been "his man" but there's nothing I've seen says Bontillo was a murderer. The worst we have of him is possibly hitting on a pupil. Tregilgas hounded him, got him sacked ...'

'Suspended.'

'... which was going to lead to a sacking. He took away the guy's reason to live.'

Tacich let that pass and said calmly, 'What are you going to do? Tregilgas will close the file with this.'

With no active police support – and, let's face it, even without Bontillo I was about as welcome at HQ as a white ant at a home inspection – the task of breaking the case was impossible. If I worked hard for six months I might turn up a suspect or two but ultimately I was going to have to hand what I had over to police who had the resources to go deeper. Tregilgas had no intention of going deeper. The case was over.

Later that day I called the O'Gradys and told them there was no point going on. They had reached the same conclusion, I think, and were optimistic that Tregilgas would eventually find the remains of Caitlin, though I knew there was no way they had foregone all hope of her being alive. The Police Commissioner told the people of Western Australia that the task force would continue until all the girls were accounted for. What he didn't say was that the task force was sure it had its man, and that it was going to require some bolt from the blue, at worst another abduction, before it would focus on anybody other than the dead Bontillo.

Sure it hurt, failure always does, but I didn't skip a beat going straight back to work for a chain of motels with a pile of suspicious insurance claims from guests who'd slipped in showers or fallen down stairs. Craig Drummond paid me in full and thanked me for my efforts. I told him I wished I'd produced a better result.

...

Christmas passed: Teletubbie costumes, games to enhance a toddler's brain, a load of picture books. Eventually summer caught a long wave in. The nights got colder but more beautiful with a sky cleared of bushfire smoke and Tash's cheek pressed against mine as we dozed on the sofa to the hum of inane television. No more young women disappeared. Autostrada was quietly scaled back with assurances the police would continue to search for Emily and Caitlin. Bay View Terrace was a chronic patient; people still didn't feel comfortable sitting at its bedside but taxi drivers fared better, custom gradually improving, though women tried to make sure a friend was there to watch them go. Sometimes at night I'd drive there and sit in the car, the window down, the swish of wet tyres an urban lullaby. I would stare through a dappled windscreen and wonder: is he out there? I'd imagine Caitlin walking away from Autostrada towards me, her head filled with nothing more than the relief of getting off her shoes once she got home and what time she would need to walk Soupy in the morning. I'd imagine her looking at me with her young, soft face, the hint of a dimple as she turned just a fraction more my way before continuing. And then I'd check the rear vision mirror and of course there was nothing but a few fat drops of rain on a rear windshield and a fleeing headlight from the black highway beyond.

PART TWO: THE PRESENT

CHAPTER 10

Shepherd's arms were pumping, his quads stretching out. He was in prime condition, footy finals approaching but, damn, this guy was quick. The hare jinked left down a lane, his figure silhouetted in moon-glow. 'I can do it, I can get him,' Shepherd told himself even as his hamstring yelled for him to take it easy. So hard was he breathing, and so loud the slap of his big feet on the pavement, that the sound of footsteps ahead was already gone, burley in an ocean. Shepherd broke right, his big frame on an angle making him skid, leather-soled shoes a handicap, but then he hadn't exactly expected to find himself involved in a pursuit at 2.00 am on the way back from cards.

He stopped abruptly.

He had powered down the short lane and reached the T-junction onto the road but there was no sign of the arsehole, left or right. He'd vanished. Okay, he was quick but not that quick, surely. Shepherd's chest burned, he gulped air, bending over, resting his palms on his knees. His brain, never lightning fast, continuing to chug: no vehicle sound so either his quarry was hiding in the lane and he'd run straight past him, or else ...

Shepherd swung around and looked up to the roof. Bastard! Just a glimpse heading north but that was him up there. Shepherd charged north down the middle of the deserted street. This wasn't New York and an endless roof-scape; the prick only had twenty metres and he'd have to drop. Headlights. A car swung into the street heading towards Shepherd, forcing him back towards the footpath, buggering up the angle to maintain a visual.

'Get off the road, ya dickhead!' Voices slung at him from the open window of the passing car.

As Shepherd reached the end of the building he angled back out again and, looking up, was frustrated to see his target had doubled back south while he had been momentarily forced inboard. He grunted and started back and saw the figure on the roof suddenly turn to his left. Bastard was going to jump down the other side. Shepherd angled back through the short lane, the pre-season grind standing him in good stead. He was just in time to see a dark shape flutter through the sky and land in the street with the agility of a cat. Shepherd continued his chase, confident he'd get him now, stamina was his strong point. But blow him down if the hare didn't duck back into the shadows by the wall, and next thing he was zipping out heading south down Carnarvon Street on a bicycle that he must have had stashed there. Shepherd told himself, 'I can do this. I can get him.'

Fifty metres on he was forced to acknowledge that was bullshit. He couldn't do it. No matter how hard he strained, the distance increased until ahead there was only a hint of a bike rider, a dim shape ... nothing.

The slippery little bugger had got away with it.

...

'I'm telling you I had him, if that car hadn't come at me.'

As Dan Clement arrived at the office, he saw Josh Shepherd was well into some story. Shepherd's stories could go on. They usually concluded with Shepherd as a hero or should-have-been hero if only fate hadn't intervened. This sounded like one of the latter. Graeme Earle and Jo di Rivi were listening with morning starter coffees in their fists. Earle held his usual current bun from the bakery hostage in its white paper bag. Clement wasn't going to ask Shepherd what he was on about but Shepherd gave him no choice.

'Our B&E friend. I almost had him.'

Now Clement pulled the strands together. 'When?'

'Last night, after poker with the boys.'

Earle's interest was waning already. Clement saw him ferreting in his paper bag. The late dream that eventually had woken Clement had left him out of sorts, as if he had shoes on the wrong feet.

'You didn't see his face?' Even as he asked it, Clement was aware his question was a conscious effort to bring his body and soul together rather than being organically swept up in Shepherd's tale.

'Not his face. But he had to be Indigenous.'

''Cause he'd broken into the dive shop?'

Clement knew di Rivi was having a dig. Shepherd was prone to snap judgements. But maybe Shepherd's shrewdness was growing. He didn't giving her the satisfaction of biting.

'No, because no white bloke's that nimble. I wish we had him playing for Townies. We need some outside pace.'

The remnants of his dream once again wrapped themselves around Clement like some stubborn mist. He'd been on an airplane, a big jet – though the spatial dimensions didn't make sense because there was a small swimming pool and a kitchen eerily reminiscent of the one at the first house Marilyn and he lived in. Even so, it had been a jet with seatbelts, tray tables. Marilyn had been beside him. They were going somewhere, a vacation maybe? He seemed to remember she was in a summer frock, white with coloured patterns. Where had they been going? It was elusive but there was that budding excitement that coincides with a holiday. Phoebe wasn't in the dream. It was just them, like way back when.

'So you were walking back from your mates' place?' Clement forced himself back to the subject at hand even though the image of the jet was as real as those hard paper coffee cups.

'Yeah. I won, bluffed them on a pair of queens. And I heard something over in the shops there and I'm looking up at the back of the shops when this bloody shape jumps out the fucking window. Probably the toilet, because it was tiny, narrow ...'

'Yeah, it was the toilet.' It was di Rivi. She was the uniform who had followed up the job after Shepherd called it in.

'And I yell out "stop!" and he keeps running, so I chase.'

'What'd he get?' Earle took his first mouthful of bun, directing the question at di Rivi.

'Three dive watches.'

'Went for what was light and valuable.' Shepherd was still smarting.

Clement was thinking this was the third of these shop break-ins the last month – probably a meth addict – but the dream was still at his shoulder, in particular the horrible moment when he'd looked at the seat next to him to find Marilyn no longer there. There was an instant of dread, of panic that he'd lost her, followed by the sudden command to himself: 'Don't worry it's a dream, it's not real', in turn followed by a counter-warning: 'No it's very real. You've lost her, for good this time.' And that's when he'd woken.

'We have any idea who it might be?' For once he was grateful for the distraction of local crime.

Earle shook his head, the bun already half-devoured.

'Nothing on the street,' added Shepherd.

Clement suppressed a smile at the cop-show parlance. In Broome, 'on the street' was pretty well literally on the one street.

'Usain?' Clement speculated. Usain, real name Simon Mifflin, was a shoplifter whose modus operandi was to pinch stuff in plain sight and then run like the clappers. Earle swallowed the last of the bun.

'Still in hospital.'

Usain's career had come unstuck when he sprinted out of the news-agency, unaware that its sliding glass door, open when he'd entered, had since shut. He'd been travelling too fast for it to reopen in time and had cut himself to pieces.

Clement looked up to see his boss Scott Risely gesturing at him from his doorway.

'When you got a minute.'

'Now's good.' Clement addressed the trio. 'Stay on it. He's probably swapping the stolen goods for meth. The watches'll turn up. Then we can find the dealer and our thief.' The tragedy was that if the thief got away with it for much longer, any chance of saving his life would be down the toilet of meth addiction. He'd be better off being caught.

Clement stepped into Risely's sparse office and shut the door. Risely looked up from his computer and gestured Clement should sit.

'How's it going?'

'Apart from our B&E specialist, pretty quiet.'

'I meant how are you going?' The emphasis on 'you'. 'When's the wedding?'

'Six weeks.'

Clement had never had a deep and meaningful with his boss about how he felt about Marilyn and her impending marriage. It was irritating that Risely discerned it was affecting him. If it turned out Risely had been alerted by Graeme Earle or the others, well, that would be even more galling. Clement hated being the subject of office gossip but he was resigned to it as a fact of life.

'How do you feel about it?' Risely's demeanour was surprisingly neutral, not unlike the psych he'd had to visit after the big murder case the summer before last.

'I don't know: pissed off, happy for her, all at the same time.' Surprisingly, before this, he'd never got close enough to the question to look for an answer. He'd just accepted his emotions were confused, unruly. There was something that hurt about the finality of it but the worst part – that she was no longer his, that somebody else had her love – well, that ache he'd long grown accustomed to.

'They staying here?'

'Far as I know. Phoebe tells me they are planning a lot of travelling.' Which was the best part. There was talk of him getting Phoebe for something like three weeks while they honeymooned before she joined them overseas. It wouldn't be all that long, maybe eighteen months, before she'd be going to Perth for her schooling and maybe lost to him forever. He had expected Risely to ask another question as if this had been leading to something about the way he was doing his job but Risely just nodded sympathetically and looked back at his computer.

'You ever heard of Ingrid Feister?'

Half joking, Clement said, 'Any relation to Nelson Feister?'

'His daughter.'

The reclusive Nelson Feister was the richest man in Western Australia, one of the richest in the world. His company controlled the largest iron ore deposits on the planet. Risely continued.

'Two weeks ago Ingrid left Perth to head north with her boyfriend. Ten days ago they were in Port Hedland. That's the last communication from them. Normally she posts on Instagram but there's been nothing. There've been no calls from either her phone or her boyfriend's. The AC called me to ask us to check around. I spoke to Richo in Hedland and he's looking into it that end.'

'How old is she?'

'Ingrid is twenty, the boyfriend twenty-one. No criminal record but the AC says they called him a druggy-musician-loser.'

'Who is "they"?'

'The half-brother and sister. Apparently they don't want to upset the old man too much, he's getting on.'

I remembered now that Feister had divorced wife one and married a much younger woman, a caterer or something like that. Could that be twenty-odd years ago?

'So Ingrid is his daughter by the second wife?'

'That's right.'

Clement asked why Ingrid's mother had left it to the siblings to call.

'No idea.'

'We've got car rego? Photos?'

Risely hit a key on his computer and the printer began sputtering. He jerked his thumb at it and added, 'Contact numbers for the brother and sister are included.'

'What was the purpose of the trip?'

'The AC didn't ask them.'

Clement's guess was that if you were the daughter of a billionaire it was hardly looking for work.

'I'll get onto it. Is HQ trying to get a bead on the phones?'

Risely stood with him, collected the printout and handed it to him. 'Trying. But up here ...'

He didn't need to tell Clement about the difficulty of tracking a phone not in use in this remote part of the world. 'Why don't you come to dinner this week?'

'Sure. Wednesday?'

'Wednesday's good.'

Neither man referenced the fact the invite was obviously to offer Clement support in his time of 'need'. Clement was not used to being a welfare recipient. He didn't like it one bit.

...

Clement sat at his desk in his office and studied the photos of Ingrid Feister and boyfriend Max Coldwell. They looked the kind who would search for dolphins while strumming guitars and smoking pot. Coldwell had long straggly hair with a goatee. His eyes were soft. They didn't scream intelligence. Ingrid had a spark about her but she also had the unadorned look of somebody who has rejected reticulation, swimming pools and pinstripes. The siblings were Kate Hayward (nee Feister), forty-five, and Simon Feister, forty-one, both of Dalkeith. Clement decided he would call Peter Richardson, his Pilbara equivalent, before he contacted them.

Richardson answered swiftly. He knew why Dan was calling.

'I've just got back from the Kookaburra. They booked into one of the motel units Thursday seventeenth of August and left Friday eighteenth. Got a maid who saw the car leaving. I thought I'd try the local office of Giant Iron, see if by any chance the boss's daughter had called in and, bingo, she had. The kids' old Landcruiser was losing water,' Richardson said, 'so Ingrid asked if a mechanic could check it out. They put in a new radiator and gave it a service.'

So Ingrid wasn't beyond using the family connection.

'That's where we're at. Unless they stuffed up the service we're not talking breakdown. I figure the next step is checking roadhouse cameras.'

Richardson was deftly handballing into Clement's court. If the couple had headed north towards Broome – given the way they looked in their photos a near certainty – then they'd almost certainly call in for petrol at Sandfire. This was Clement's bailiwick. Truth was, he didn't care.

'Don't worry, I'll check that out, call you soon as I know anything.'

'Appreciate that.'

The Sandfire Roadhouse was around three hundred k north of Hedland and the same south of Broome. About three hours. The beauty of this part of the world was that, despite its vastness, there was still only one main road, the Great Northern Highway, and one main stop. It shouldn't take too long to locate them on CCTV if they had gone via Sandfire. Besides, Clement could do with a long drive.

Graeme Earle looked up from his desk, more curious than anxious as Clement emerged. 'Everything okay?'

'Rich kid gone missing. Mal,' Clement called out and waved the paperwork.

Sergeant Mal Gross edged over, paint chart in hand. Clement indicated the chart.

'Renovating?'

'I caved in on Laura's demand: a new look for the house. It's bought me time on her other ultimatum: a new look for me.'

'He's weighing whether to cut down on beer or fish and chips,' joked Earle.

'I've been weighing that for five years. I'm starting to think light beer and keep the chips, or full strength and just the fish.' Gross scanned the paperwork and raised an eyebrow at the name.

Clement said. 'We need everybody looking for the vehicle. Graeme, you take the accom, see if they booked in anywhere.'

'You want me to send a car to Sandfire?' asked Gross.

'No. I'm going.'

'Who are we talking about?' Shepherd grabbed the papers off Mal Gross, read. 'Is she ...?'

'Yep.'

Clement knew Shepherd would be trying to factor in the chances of a reward.

'So what's my role?'

Shepherd liked to think of them as a footy team, each with a designated role.

'Your role is to find our B&E specialist who gave you the slip last night.'

'He was lucky he had a bike.'

...

The weather this time of year was about as clear as it got, temperature around thirty in the day, a bit under twenty at night. The skies were blue, cyclone build up a month or two away. You could even swim in the water off Cable Beach without being stung to death by jellyfish. Yet Clement was aware that to match his mood the skies should have been gloomy and threatening, full of rolling cumulonimbus. He would have stuck on Leonard Cohen but he'd left it in the deck of his CD player at home after giving it a heavy bash last night. What was she thinking? Brian wasn't up to her speed. He wasn't a bad guy, he earned better money than Clement, bought Margaret River reds and took painstaking photos with a heavy camera; pretty good shots, Clement had to admit. Clement had scrolled through Phoebe's Facebook for glimpses of Marilyn – there were a few – and then tried to read her expression, the secret codes he was convinced only he would ever really know. Mostly he read tolerance, as in, okay, I'll let you photograph me even though I really don't want to be displayed like some butterfly on a leaf – a favourite subject of Brian's. So, a guy who takes nice photos of butterflies on leaves, sells plastics or buys plastics or something from China and thinks it's a big deal to drink the same red wine as his rich business cronies. Is that really the guy she should be marrying?

Of course not. She shouldn't be marrying anybody. She had her independence, which was what she claimed she was after when they split. Now she was giving it up.

Clement blotted her out, splat, like the bug on his windscreen. Only now did he yield to the veracity of his senses, the sky was clear and blue. He fumbled through his CDs. Beach Boys, yes, perfect desert music: blue sky and sand. At the first chords he realised his mistake. She'd been the one who had introduced him to The Beach Boys. All he'd known of them was the snappy 'Kokomo', which he'd first heard up here, under the hot bronze gong, while riding his bicycle, or sprinting across burning sand to protect the soles of his bare feet. But then when he was all grown up, or thought he was, he met Marilyn and at night on her single bed while traffic sizzled past underneath her first floor window, he held her, smelled her hair and hushed when she commanded, to 'God Only Knows' or 'Surf's Up'. He smelled her hair now.

He managed to fight the impulse to eject the disc. If he had to give up Marilyn, he wasn't going to throw Brian Wilson into the deal.

Too much time to think: that was the trouble with living up here, a vastness that seemed prehistoric. You could look clear to the horizon both sides of the car and see nothing but low scrub, and Clement couldn't help but think that one time way, way back, the whole world would have been like this. Okay, there might have been rainforest or mountains, but no glass and steel environmentally observant skyscrapers, no houses, bridges, no man-made landmark. Which he supposed was why the people who lived here got to know every dip in the red earth, every drooping branch, every slight incline.

The other Wilson Brothers were dead. Only Brian was left. Don't talk, put your head on my shoulder ... listen ... listen ... let me hear your heart beat.

Clement thought of that morning dream again, of the one bedroom apartment where he held Marilyn. What had been Them was now only Him, and a vacant road that stretched who knew where.

...

The CCTV footage revealed the Landcruiser arriving at Sandfire just after 11.30 on the same morning it had left Port Hedland. The registration papers showed the car belonged to Ingrid Feister but it was the boyfriend Max Coldwell who was driving. On the tape Ingrid stepped out, alive and unrestricted. The resolution wasn't crystal clear but it was much better than it had been in days of yore when you found yourself dealing with old VCRs, the heads clogged with grime.

Clement watched in the manager's office, a sweat box without the comfort of air-conditioning. A desk fan and standard fan did their best to circulate air but it was difficult. The desk was a jumble: lever-arch files, computer, printer, phone, an empty glass. A broken till, an old freezer and other detritus injured in the service of hosting weary travellers, straddled the floor like a rugby scrum On the desktop computer screen, Clement watched Coldwell pop the fuel tank and pump petrol while Ingrid headed off screen to the loo or the shop.

The interior camera picked them up a few minutes later. You couldn't see their faces all that well but you could recognise Ingrid as she paid for a couple of soft drinks from the fridge. Coldwell joined her, hair unkempt in the fashion of star AFL footballers. Ingrid pulled a wad of notes from her jeans, peeled off cash and paid the cashier. Not wise to be flashing a big roll of cash like that, not with hungry eyes about. Clement instinctively checked out other customers. A guy in a cap at the soft-drink fridge didn't appear to be looking but could have caught the reflection, Clement supposed. Thing was, it might not have been here somebody saw the cash. Could be Broome, or wherever they would wind up. He watched Ingrid and Coldwell peel away. Then, almost out of camera, they stopped and faced each other and there was a desperate hug. What was that about? Just hippie types showing their emotions? They clung for quite a while, then broke apart and left. The body language pinged Clement's brain but it was too murky in there to say what it might be sensing. Him and Marilyn perhaps, one of those times when she was a trainee teacher up the country and it was agony to part after a wonderful city weekend.

Wouldn't it be nice to be together ...

Too late now.

CHAPTER 11

There was nothing out of the ordinary about this particular morning. It was a Wednesday and the colour of the sky matched my grey Toshiba laptop, which was six or seven years old and still ran Windows 7 because I tried Tash's once, which ran on 8, and couldn't manage it at all. I hate updating anything but especially computer stuff because everything you finally figured out counts for nix with the snap of a keystroke. That's what was great about swimming. It's the same Indian Ocean, same sky, same distance from North Cott to Cott and back. All that changes is the price of the coffee afterwards. Seventeen years before, at the beginning of the new millennium, my cappuccino cost me three bucks. It had gone up fifty percent. The group I swim with had probably changed by fifty percent too over the period but you don't notice. It's not like everybody disappears at once. But one day somebody brings in an old photo, the kind you used to get in little wallets from the chemist, and that's like a frypan in the face. You hope you haven't aged as badly as the rest and then realise that half of those in the snap have moved out of your life without you even noticing.

Anyway, it wasn't actually overcast, it was just early morning mid-August, spring was dusting itself off and so was I after three big glasses of red the night before. I'd reached the point in my life where I drank less than your average pensioner after an expired Happy Hour. Tash and Grace were in Spain, however, so for the first time in twenty years I'd been left to my own devices and the cheap red had caught my eye right around the same time I'd been salivating over my takeaway Tibetan. Goodness knows what was in the dish I'd ordered. I doubted yak, it was too cheap, they'd have to import but it tasted fine and the rice was excellent. Naturally I hadn't bothered to turn on the dishwasher after eating, figuring I may as well wait till breakfast. Such indulgences of the single man had become as foreign to me as available street parking. I think it was probably goat in the dish, something I'd never be able to eat with Tash who considers herself pretty much vegetarian because she only eats chicken, fish, and sausages at the netball. Unfortunately there'd not been much of that lately. Grace, who showed a bit of sporting potential in that area, had recently broken her father's heart by saying she was concentrating on her Spanish. I sat back on the couch and cracked the red. Skype had been a disaster – like Control's Cone of Silence in *Get Smart*. Either the girls couldn't hear me or I couldn't hear them, and we'd resorted to phone calls in the end. Barcelona was brilliant apparently. Tash was doing some work thing that involved photographing stylish ideas and eating at exciting restaurants, while Grace studied at some special class. I could have bought a case of the red for the price of the twelve minutes we talked about nothing in particular, so I made rectifying the Skype problem my highest priority. They'd be gone another ten weeks and the way it was heading it would have been cheaper for me to have gone with them and let the adulterers and petty thieves of my great metropolis get away with their misdemeanours.

Yes, I missed the girls, a lot, but the bachelor life had compensations: stacking the dishwasher half as often, not having to watch gym bodies on TV in some lame reality show, leaving clothes in the dryer till I needed them, playing vinyl albums on the old stereo – not even Grace got Toots and the Maytals. I retained some self-discipline though, hauling my arse out of bed and down to the ocean to join the pack of like-minded swimmers. There were about ten of us today. Somebody, usually Camo, who had a few years on me but was a better swimmer, would wade in and start off and the rest of us would casually follow. Our only competition was against our personal times and I knew in my condition I would be challenging my worst rather than my best, so I lobbed along and let my mind drift to everything from digging up the roots that kept blocking our sewage pipe, to football, to renewing my car insurance. The water and my even breathing relaxed me. Before I knew it North Cott loomed on the return leg and I managed a token sprint over the last fifty metres, then began to wade in to shore.

I was contemplating how much extra my car insurance would be with Grace driving, when a scream of 'Shark!' gatecrashed its way in. I don't know who yelled it but now I was looking at bodies charging towards the shore, dimly aware that there was something thrashing, churning water just to the right of the evacuees. Like one of the many horses I had backed, I stood flat-footed, my obstinate brain not wanting to admit the reality. Turk Stanbridge also hadn't moved and was still in thigh-high water near the spume. My brain was trying to sort packages on a too-fast conveyor belt but my body was inert. Then Camo, who had been drying himself off, dropped his towel and charged back into the water. My muscles came alive. I ran back out behind Camo, fearing Turk had been attacked until he began screaming, 'It's Craig, it's Craig!'

By now I could see dark ink in the water and a bare torso, Turk's body blocking a full view. The shark must have already run. Camo joined Turk who I now saw was supporting Craig Drummond's head and shoulders. Camo screamed to shore to call an ambulance but Barbara was already onto it. By the time I reached Camo and Turk, they had already started in, walking backwards carrying Craig Drummond whose face was waxen with shock. I helped lift him out of the water, and saw that his right leg was severed below the knee. Somebody else, one of the women, joined in, and Murray Hurst splashed into the ocean with a towel and tried to tie it as a tourniquet but there was so much blood it was sodden in the blink of an eye.

Carrying him, we ran halfway up the beach towards the steps. Swimmers swarmed with towels and their own windcheaters to wrap around Craig. Somebody ripped their towel into strips for a better tourniquet. It was too early for the lifeguards but people were calling on phones and yelling to the restaurant up above the steps. I was looking at Craig Drummond's face, the skin grey now, the light in his eyes faded. I had stood there when a man put a gun to his head and killed himself: the digital experience, life–no-life with the flick of a switch. But I had never seen this, the cliché of life draining away from somebody before my eyes. And for the first time I understood the trauma of those soldiers who came back from the battlefield, and of survivors of train wrecks and bus crashes who sat with fatally injured passengers as they slowly left for another realm. Camo started CPR. He worked furiously. His face was red, he was sweating. He exhorted Craig to hang in. But Craig was gone.

...

A fortnight later I stared out over the same patch of sand that had been soaked rust red with Craig Drummond's blood. I was sitting at the café above sipping tea. I hadn't ventured anywhere near the area for a week, not till after the funeral, but the last week I'd managed to sit myself here and stare out at the shiny ocean, running the same dumb thoughts over and over again like a coach uselessly trying to improve a team that actually belonged in a lower division. If I had not made that last stupid sprint attempt, would I have been the one taken? Could I have reacted quicker, got back out to Turk a little faster, or thought to tear strips for a tourniquet there and then so the rescue might have been successful. If Camo hadn't raced past me back into the water, would I have dared? Did I only act out of a blind shame and, if I did, was that more stupid than staying safe on the beach? Until something like this happens you don't have to ever assess your action or inaction. But it was real. One part of me said I owed it to Tash and Grace to be here for them for as long as I could; another said that's a coward's excuse – that the only true question is what would I expect one of my cronies to do for me if I'd have been the one attacked. When I could face that question, which wasn't too often, I honestly couldn't answer it. I liked to think that I'd be magnanimous and say, it's just bad luck, it's just fate, you can't risk your life to protect me. But then I would imagine the terror of knowing for an instant that a savage wild creature had, from all the humans on the planet, targeted me, and in that instant, as I began to shut down and go into shock, would not my silent plea be 'Somebody, help'?

Truthfully, I was grateful that Tash and Grace were away. It wasn't something I could share, not because I might have felt tainted as scared, but because it was a sacred moment I had shared. Scared, sacred … the realignment of one letter changed everything, just like that day, that hour, that minute. The only people I could open up with were the others who had been with me, and even then it was a case of feeling my way along a reef in bare feet. Camo wore his heart on his sleeve. He was a big, bluff open guy. He cried at the funeral but then he was released, over it. Turk was a mess, he'd not made it down here at all. Helen, who it turned out was the woman who had helped me carry Craig up onto the beach, was the most like me, confused, upset, guilty.

The funeral was a large affair held at the Christ Church chapel. Craig had been an old boy of the school and many of his former schoolmates, now pushing sixty, turned up. Among the mourners mingling on the green lawn outside the chapel beside Stirling Highway was the O'Grady family – well, Gerry and Michelle. Apart from an odd news grab on TV, I hadn't seen them since the death of Ian Bontillo, prime suspect in the

Autostrada abductions. The significance was not lost on me. We were standing within a kilometre of where their daughter had disappeared. Bontillo's flat, where he had been found dead, could have been reached with a wind-assisted torpedo punt. I made my way over. Gerry grasped my hand firmly. Michelle smiled and clasped my hand in hers. The years had glanced off her like a zephyr. Sometimes you say somebody doesn't look a day older. In her case it was true. Later it occurred to me that her grief back then had accelerated her ageing and since then things had balanced out. Gerry was more typical. He still looked fit but he was broader in all zones except his hair, which was thinning noticeably. We exchanged the usual stuff you do in this kind of situation. I asked after Nellie, Caitlin's younger sister, then for a terrible moment dreaded something tragic might have happened to her too. Thankfully Nellie was fine, now working in New York. While I knew that officially Caitlin's case remained open, unofficially the police considered it closed with Bontillo's death. The fact there'd been no similar series of abductions or murders since, not just in Perth but the whole country, reinforced this notion. Even I, sceptic that I am, had to admit I had probably been wrong but that doesn't mean Bontillo's guilt sat comfortably with me. There had to be a chance the real guy was simply smart enough and strong enough to quit while he was ahead, or he was dead or in jail for something else. But I wasn't going to raise any of this with the O'Gradys. If they'd finally discovered a measure of acceptance about their daughter's fate, then who was I to stir it up? And so we talked briefly of Craig Drummond, their friend who had personally paid my fees when I'd been on the case. I'd swum with the guy many mornings for a couple of decades but I didn't really know him. I had never met his wife or family, nor he mine, but we'd floated in the same salty water and dried off under the same clinical sun. Gerry knew him from school and told me Craig had been a really good squash player. We avoided talk of Caitlin. I wished the O'Gradys all the best and went off to express my condolences to the Drummond family. I left, with an emptiness in my stomach that reminded me of that emotion on a long flight home after an extended absence when you have abandoned your past but not yet attained a future.

...

The weird sense of dislocation had persisted. I was steaming through my fifties in a mundane job, in a world that was more foreign to me by the day. They no longer played the football I'd grown up with; now it was all corporate boxes and prepaid memberships and footballers on every channel who fancied themselves as personalities as they fed us the same dull chaff as every other professional sportsperson. If a player gave somebody a whack on the field he was treated like a child molester – and those predators too seemed be to growing in number by the hour, to such an extent that if a little kid fell off their bike and you helped them up, you had a dozen fingers poised to dial 000. Nobody went to church anymore. The closest that people got to organised worship was when they gushed over the release of new Apple products. There were no dark cool pubs either, everywhere was open and noisy, the sound of cutlery reverberating through atriums like a twenty-one-gun salute. My mechanic's workshop was quieter than most restaurants. And in the middle of this world sat Snowy Lane who couldn't do a thing to save his friend from bleeding to death on a beach and whose last contribution to making this state a better place had been thirty-five years ago. I sipped tea, staring out an implacable ocean, brooding.

'G'day Snowy.'

Smile lines creased his face. It was weathered but women might still dub it rugged. There was the odd bit of pigmentation too and his hair was thinner but only a little, and still sandy. Barry Dunn was a good fifteen years older than me but seemed only one or two years my senior. Even with the collapse of his empire he'd obviously still had enough collateral to invest in a fountain of youth. He pulled up a chair and sat opposite. He was wearing a polo shirt and shorts with sandals.

'How you doing?' I asked to be polite.

'Ah, I long for the time PSA meant Public Schools Association and not a gloved finger up my date, but it's alright. You?'

'Getting by.'

A coffee arrived for him, macchiato by the looks. The young dark-haired waitress smiled at him and vice versa. I doubted he had to place an order. In Perth's Jurassic age, Barry Dunn had been the T. rex, and that still carried clout. He sipped his coffee.

'Married? Kids?'

I gave him bare facts on a wafer: wife, eighteen-year-old daughter.

'I never married again.' He gazed wistfully over to Rottnest as if thinking about where his mistress had met her demise. If he harboured a grudge because I'd been sleeping with her too, he never showed it. 'I've recommended you to a friend.'

Hard on the heels of my surprise came suspicion. He read it.

'You're still in the PI game?' Asking it like he wasn't sure.

'Of course. But I have a few things in train.'

This amounted to an exaggeration. I had one case, a simple adultery.

'Drop it or hand it off. I've quoted two thousand dollars a day plus expenses on your behalf, which is what he pays his legal counsel. If you think I've underquoted you can take it up with my friend.'

I didn't think he'd underquoted. I'd never earned that kind of money.

'I draw the line at shooting someone.'

The eyes crinkled and his chuckle seemed forced. 'I'm serious, Snowy. His daughter is missing.'

'The police ...'

'Waste of fucking space. I told him he needed you. You in?'

What was I going to say? 'On the face of it, sure.'

'It's Nelson Feister's daughter, Ingrid.'

This rocked me. Feister was rich as Croesus. I looked around to see if anybody was listening in. There was an elderly couple – from the long socks on the husband, I guessed English visitors. A trio of young mothers with bored children strapped in strollers, and a Brazilian beach bum fiddling with his phone, made up the balance of the clientele. No obvious threat but I lowered my voice. 'I haven't heard anything about that.'

'Course not. You got a phone?' He gestured for it.

As it happened, I did. I handed it over. He popped on some glasses that had been hanging on his shirt, grunted in disapproval at my low-tech appliance and dialled. It must have been answered quickly.

'Nelson, Barry. I'm with the guy now. He's in. When do you want to see him?' He looked over his glasses at me. 'Twenty minutes?' I wasn't sure which of us he was asking but I nodded. 'Text your address to this phone. Yep, no worries, China.' He ended the call and slid my phone back to me. 'Done.' He sat back, proud he could still make a deal talk.

'How long she been missing?'

'Not sure. Two or three weeks. Ingrid's the wild child from the second marriage, so they weren't worried. But there's a loser boyfriend. Anyway he can fill you in. Good to see you again, Snowy.' Delicately he placed his empty cup on its saucer and stood up. My phone pinged with a text.

'Thanks, Barry.' I reckoned it was the first time I'd called him by his first name.

Dunn had taken a step but paused and some part of me wondered if he was about to take me to task for the familiarity. 'Watch out for the daughter.'

'Ingrid?'

'The older one from the first model.' He could have been speaking literally or figuratively, I wasn't sure what line of employment the two Mrs Feisters were in prior to marriage. The family had always been exceedingly private and I wasn't one to follow the movers and shakers of Perth society. 'She likes older men.' He winked and exited with a wave to the waitress, who smiled generously.

I studied my phone. The address was premium: Jutland Parade, Dalkeith. I was in shorts and t-shirt, underdressed. I had to hope it lent me some kind of cache.

...

If somebody were to ask me what I wanted to come back as in the next life I'd answer: a lawn on Jutland Parade. The houses varied. A few Californian bungalows remained but there were also the kind you see on American TV shows, belonging to Beverly Hills personalities, or plantation owners, with long driveways usually ending in white stone columns. The lawns though were always pristine, superior to your average public golf green. The parade was on the crest of a hill so the backs of the houses sloped down to the Swan River. Over the years, lots had been sold and houses developed on the hill slope but a few properties had maintained land all the way down to the river, ending there with boatsheds and private jetties. My guess was the Feisters' property might be one of these. The front of the house was fenced and gated. Trees ran down both sides, pencil pines, in close formation. I presumed they hid fences to the neighbouring properties. I pulled up the short entrance way and pressed the intercom.

A woman's voice answered. 'Yes?'

'My name is Richard Lane. Mr Feister is expecting me.'

There was a click and the gates began to swing inward. Clearly whoever was on the other end of the intercom already knew about me. The driveway was a good sixty metres and ended in a circle. A separate garage to the right was open and the rear ends of twin Mercedes gleamed like the teeth of a cartoon villain. I left my car as close as I could to the front door and climbed out in my shorts with the guilt of a dog owner whose pooch had just left a steaming turd on the footpath. The house itself was more modest than I had expected. Tudor in style, it ran only a third wider than your average stockbroker's, but gables hinted at height and depth to the rear. Waiting for me at the door was a woman, thirty-five to forty, with the kind of sexy haircut, expensive suit and shoes that suggested a bottle of Pol Roger in a fridge stocked with yogurt and greens and little else. No ring on her hand. I wondered if this was the elder daughter.

'Dee Verleuwin. I'm Mr Feister's private secretary.'

She extended her hand and I shook it. There was a time that slender arm and delicate hand would have had me thinking all kind of things but I was married and my flirting days as ancient and foreign to me as cuneiform. I followed Ms Verleuwin into a cool entrance hall and tracked her pert backside along parquet into a wide-open area with marble tiles and three sets of staircases. We avoided all of these and continued along a narrow wood-panelled corridor that made you think you were on a ship. We passed three closed rooms, two on the right, one on the left. The corridor ended in a massive sunken open living room with a bar and kitchen area and copious views of the Swan below. It seemed the Feister block didn't extend all the way down for I could see rooftops angling down the hill to the river. To my surprise we did not enter the room but turned sharp right, the narrow and panelled corridor continuing to a large jarrah door which had been left ajar. Ms Verleuwin preceded me to push the door open further, then stood back and announced me to those assembled in what I guess was the den but was exactly how I imagined one of those posh gentlemen's club's reading rooms would look: dark wood, green leather sofas and armchairs, a large desk, a hint of brass and some discrete technology.

'Mr Lane: Mr Nelson Feister, Mrs Kate Hayward, and Simon Feister.'

We mumbled greetings. Dee Verleuwin asked if I would like a refreshment of any sort.

'Thanks, I'm good.'

She withdrew. Feister was standing at the side of his desk. The other two were seated on one of two sofas. I'd been hoping Feister might have been in some casual man-about-the-house clobber so I wouldn't feel quite so out of place but he wore a dark suit with an ochre tie. He was trim, the kind of man who thinks exercise a virtue. I put him around twelve years older than me. There was something in her eyes that made Kate Hayward a Feister. I presumed she was the elder daughter and bore her married name now. She was carrying a kilo or two more than optimal but had the curves to compensate and a posture that spoke of years competing in high-grade equestrian events. Unlike his dad, Simon Feister didn't emanate authority. His chin was slightly weak and his forehead high but he was closest to me in dress sense with slacks and a short-sleeved shirt worn out, not tucked.

'Take a seat, please.' Nelson Feister had a deep voice. I sat on the same sofa as his daughter. 'How much do you know?'

'Basically nothing. I was having a cup of tea at the beach and Barry Dunn approached me. He told me your daughter, Ingrid, is missing. He thought for about two weeks.'

'Two weeks exactly.' It was Kate who spoke. There was a rasp to her voice and I wondered if she smoked.

'Ingrid left Perth with her boyfriend to go for a holiday up north,' her father said. 'They stayed at Port Hedland. The police tracked them as far as the Sandfire Roadhouse. Then they just disappeared.'

I knew the Sandfire Roadhouse from forty years ago. It used to be run by a one-armed misanthrope who worked whatever hours he pleased. You could be stuck for hours waiting for the place to open to get fuel. The first time I ever pulled into the roadhouse a truck driver was upending the servo bin. 'Serves the prick, right,' was all he offered before climbing into his truck and driving off. At that time I had no idea who he was talking about but I quickly came to learn.

I looked over all three of them. 'No word from them at all?'

'Typical of Ingrid.' Like the rest of him, Simon Feister's highish voice measured badly against his father's.

'I'm still not certain there's a problem but her sister and brother convinced me to look into it.' There was something almost more machine than human about Feister. It put me in mind of a locomotive slowly rolling away from a platform, barely tapping latent power.

Kate said, 'Ingrid took six thousand dollars out of her bank account before they left. Max is a no-hoper.'

'Max?'

'Coldwell, her boyfriend.'

I was regretting having come straight here. My habit was to tape and take notes. I asked if I might borrow pad and pen. Nelson Feister handed me a document with plastic binding.

'We did up this to help.'

By 'we' I intuited he meant Dee Verleuwin. I accepted the dossier and flipped it open on a large photo of Ingrid Feister. I knew this because it had her name in large print with salient details beneath, like her birthday, passport number, Facebook, Instagram, car registration, driver's licence and favourite foods. A quick calculation told me she would be twenty-one in a couple of months. If I had to sum up in one word what the photo told me about the subject, I would say defiant. Physically, Ingrid resembled the inevitable model girlfriend of a rock star, a mane of unruly hair and the Fuk U attitude unable to camouflage the aesthetic beauty of her high cheekbones and slender neck. She was wearing a t-shirt with writing on it. It might have said Pussy Riot, which I think was the name of the female Russian punk band that got arrested for slipping Putin the finger. I flipped the next page and there was a photo of Max Coldwell. It was blown up from the cover of his CD and showed a young guy with requisite goatee beard, long black hair and soulful but not intelligent eyes. Okay, I know you can't tell all this from a photo but if we were playing that game where you describe a person as an animal, Max would be a cow. Again Kate pitched in.

'He produced the CD himself.' With the inference that no record label would be dumb enough. 'There's a copy at the back.'

Which there was. Her brother waded in. 'We'll email you the electronic files of all this.'

I was feeling my way with all the information. 'When did you notify the police?'

Kate was now defined as the spokesperson. 'Three days ago.'

'That's not an awful long time.'

'There was no sign of them having reached Broome,' Nelson said with the kind of detached air that he probably employed negotiating with the Japanese. 'They had a four-wheel drive so they could have gone off-road. We have some mining operations in the area and it's even possible they might have gone for a look.' His son's derisive snort gave this option as much credence as making razor blades sharper by sticking them under a glass pyramid. His father ignored him. 'We put up a couple of light planes and they've been searching but have come up with nothing so far.'

'Is there any history of violence from Coldwell?'

'He's an inveterate drug user.' Kate Hayward made it sound as inevitable as night following day.

'Hard drugs?'

She shrugged. 'Probably.'

Her father shot her a look that said 'steady on'. He turned to me, measured. 'He was arrested for marijuana four years ago.'

'They do one, they do the other,' his daughter snapped back at him.

I didn't want to be involved in a family spat. 'Okay, so the way I see it, this is not a kidnap for ransom or you'd have long heard from any kidnappers.'

'The police said the same thing,' said Simon Feister.

'So there's four possibilities. They both met with foul play, Ingrid has met with foul play at the hands of Max, they've had an accident, or else they've gone to ground for whatever reason.' I was thinking of the attitude in Ingrid's photo. I addressed Simon Feister directly. 'From how you've reacted, I take it the last possibility isn't out of the question.'

'Two years ago she flew to the Philippines and cut off all contact with us. Four months later she turned up here as if nothing had happened.'

His sister qualified. 'Yes, but she kept posting on Facebook and used her credit cards. This time she's just vanished.'

'If she had six thousand dollars in cash she wouldn't need her cards for some time.' I was trying to be even about all this. There was an odd vibe in the room I couldn't quite put my finger on. Kate seemed extremely anxious about her half-sister's fate, yet dismissive of her at the same time.

'Has Coldwell contacted his family?'

Nelson Feister said, 'The police say his mother has heard nothing.'

'Probably too drunk to remember.' Kate with that cutting tone. I wondered how her husband coped.

I trod carefully with my next question and directed it straight at Nelson. 'Has her mother heard from her?'

'No. She's visiting family in Sweden. We haven't let on yet that Ingrid is missing. I don't want her worrying.'

'How long since you spoke with Mrs Feister?'

'Yesterday.'

'I suggest you inform her of the situation. It's possible Ingrid will contact her.'

'It's possible pigs might wear parachutes.' Kate checking her watch like each second was costing her a kidney. I expected Nelson Feister to make some comment but he let it go and I was forced to ask if there was any problem between Ingrid and her mother.

Feister shook his head. 'No, they could be closer but it's just a phase she's going through.'

I asked if Ingrid lived on the property. I thought it would be important to check her room.

'She has a flat in Fremantle. There's a key in the folder.' Simon Feister pointed.

'In that case I think I'm done for now. I'll go home, get changed, and start work.'

I stood. Nelson Feister had not yet extended his hand to me and still did not. I understood I was a hireling, no more.

'Dee will take care of you. She'll be your point of contact.'

Dee Verleuwin appeared at the door as if she had some telepathic link to her employer. Maybe she'd been waiting outside the whole time or maybe the room was miked. I nodded a farewell and exited, following at her heel. She turned and handed me a cheque without stopping. I saw it was for three thousand dollars.

'I hope a cheque is acceptable. Mr Feister still prefers cheques and paper invoices. He says one day some computer bug will erase everything.'

In that regard, at least, Nelson Feister was a man after my own heart. We came from an older generation that had seen too many astonishingly bad things happen to place our trust in a remote server and a satellite. We reached the front door. Ms Verleuwin unbolted it. I went out on a slim limb.

'I wonder if you can help me?'

She ushered me out into a glorious spring day and walked to the end of the porch. In for a penny ...

'I couldn't help detecting some vibe in the room.'

'You mean with Kate and Simon?'

'Partly. It's like they are pushing their father ...'

'If Ingrid dies, they split her share of the family trust. Nelson would probably have waited a bit longer. Ingrid is a wild kid, she's disappeared before.'

No wonder they were interested to know what might have happened. If their sister were dead they'd be even richer. We'd reached the end of the porch.

'You know Ingrid, what do you think?'

'I'm not paid to think.'

'I am. Is this like the other times?'

She seemed to give it great consideration. 'I think it's fifty-fifty. They could be meditating in the middle of the desert smoking pot, or they could have been taken by crocodiles. I think Ingrid and Max are both stoned most of the time. You know if you ever repeat this to anybody Mr Feister will sue the white ants where your house once stood?'

'Of course. That's why you hired me, because Dunn told you I'm a vault. So you don't think Max is violent?'

The way she checked me out hinted at how she evaluated shoes: as if she was attracted but was weighing the downside. 'I wouldn't have thought so. Not like some men.'

And I just knew she was talking of me but I couldn't tell if that excited or repelled her. I lifted my folder as a farewell. 'I'll be in touch.'

'I've texted my details to your phone,' she said before turning on her heel. Yes, a younger Snowy Lane might have got into considerable strife there.

CHAPTER 12

'Detective Inspector Daniel Clement, Broome. I'm after Mr Angus Duncan.'
Clement hated working the phones himself but it wasn't fair to leave it to
the others when he had nothing else on his plate but the elusive thief. He'd
put a call through to Feister's Giant Iron HQ in Port Hedland.

'Sorry, mate, Angus isn't here.'

Only in the north-west could your rank be so easily reduced to 'mate'.

'Do you know when he'll be back?'

'Probably this arvo. He's gone to Tenacity Hill.'

In his fifteen months back in the Kimberley, Clement had come to
know all the major mine sites. Tenacity Hill didn't ring a bell.

'What's Tenacity Hill and where?'

'Hundred and fifty k north-east of Marble Bar, give or take. It's a camp.'

By which Clement guessed his 'mate' meant an exploration camp.

'Who am I speaking to?'

'Terry Northcott. I'm a production super. I dunno why they put you
through to me.'

'Would you know if Miss Ingrid Feister might have called in to any of
the company operations?'

'I wouldn't have a clue. She the boss's daughter? You'd best speak to
Angus. He could be back before the end of the day.'

That hardly seemed likely. 'That's a couple of hundred k, right?'

'He flies a Cessna.'

Smart guy. Clement left Terry his number and requested Angus Duncan
call him as soon as possible. He crossed the squad room to Scott Risely's
office.

Chin resting on his hand, Risely was staring at a computer screen.

'Tell me how can I save money *and* put more personnel on the street?'

Of course Risely didn't expect an answer. He was just relaying the misery of being between a rock and a hard place: politicians' promises to their constituents and the resources they made available to those entrusted to ensure they were kept.

'There's no sign of the girl, the boyfriend or her vehicle since Sandfire. I've got my lot going through all the CCTV they can get a hold of, here and at the roadhouses. Course a couple of them have cameras down.' Clement didn't bother to hide his frustration. The Kimberley region was about the size of the US state of Ohio but most of it was serviced by only a few surfaced roads with roadhouses dotted every couple of hundred k. Theoretically anybody you were tracking, even in an off-road vehicle, should turn up at one of these sooner or later looking for fuel. But without cameras you were relying on ID from a human source and those working outback roadhouses in forty-degree heat were almost a different species.

Risely understood the problem better than anyone. 'I'm told Feister had planes checking the desert.'

'There's no indication they ever made it here. We should have been able to find something. But there's no CCTV of them anywhere. Not so far anyway.'

Risely looked up at his wall map even though he had the geography photocopied into his memory. 'Could have gone off-road to the Gibb or be anywhere along Eighty Mile Beach.' Which, translated, meant they could have headed east through the desert, then north to link up with the Gibb River Road, a six hundred and fifty k stretch of tar and dirt that took you to the gorges of the East Kimberley, or alternatively they might have turned west to the desolate coast. Either way, if they'd gone off-road you needed aerial help or keen eyes among the few on the ground. Risely switched back to him. 'Parks and Wildlife?'

'Of course. They're keeping a lookout too.'

Risely sat back in his chair, contemplative. 'Say we rule out foul play, for now at least. If they came up here to sightsee, my money would be on the Bungle Bungles or the gorges but, gee, they could be anywhere.' He picked up a pen and gestured vaguely at the map on the wall. 'Worst scenario is they went inland, struck trouble.' People had perished in the desert before. Their vehicle breaks down, they foolishly leave it and try to walk. They become dehydrated, delirious and die. As if answering his own thoughts he said, 'I'll get more air patrols.'

Clement sidled back to his desk, checking the clock. It was now ominously close to 5.00. Unlike the others, he had nothing to look forward to once the workday ended. Dinner at Scott Risely's would actually have been a welcome way to soak up time but that was tomorrow night. He sent a text off to his old school friend, Bill Seratono, the only friend he had here outside of work colleagues, asking if he wanted to catch up for a drink. His phone buzzed almost immediately: **Anglers 5.30**. He felt good about that and annoyed with himself at the same time for being so pathetic. Marilyn was always going to remarry, get over it.

Graeme Earle was getting ready to leave. 'There's still no sign of the Feister girl or her vehicle here, Fitzroy Crossing, Derby or Kununurra. They could be camping. It would be so much easier if we could go public.'

'Ain't that the truth. But it is what it is. Keep chasing.'

'I've got court tomorrow.'

Of course: The ice addict who had attacked two of the nurses at Derby Hospital. Clement's brain was bogged. Normally he would never forget a court case. Earle was looking at him like he had something on his mind.

'What?'

'You seen Louise again?'

'No.'

What was it with everybody? All trying to pair him up. Earle was unrelenting.

'Come on it's been over a week. You have to move faster than that. She'll think you're not interested.'

'What makes you think I am?'

Earle made some sound through the top of his nose, then he enumerated. 'She's gorgeous. She's smart, she earns good money and she's in a job that means she understands our world.'

It was true that Louise Albertini was a very attractive young woman. She was a lawyer, so presumably earned good money too. More often than not she appeared in court, which was where they had met, acting for people Clement was trying to put away. Despite this, they seemed to get on and Clement had invited her to lunch on the basis of some popular belief that the best way to forget an ex was in the arms of somebody new. Halfway through the chicken chilli salad he'd been aware that he wasn't ready for anything more than conversation but at least he'd not been so hopeless as to talk endlessly about Marilyn. The lunch had ended pleasantly enough.

Earle remained stubbornly waiting for his justification.

On the defensive Clement fended with, 'It's not like she doesn't have a phone.' It was lame and he knew it. Earle hauled a case full of files off his desk and rolled to the back door with a parting quip.

'Man up, Inspector.'

...

Clearly Tuesday was not a popular day at the Anglers Club; it boasted six customers of which he was now one. Concrete floor, cheap furnishing, air-conditioning; the club was a functional bar – its function to sell cheap grog. Faded photos of fishermen with a prize catch dotted the walls. The photos had not been sharply focussed in the first place but by now they had about them a bland uniformity. Like soldiers too long at the front, all their individuality and vitality had leached into their surroundings. Bill was waiting for him at the most distant of the tall tables, a full beer at the ready. He inclined his head towards it.

'Thanks.'

They raised glasses and sipped. Bill said, 'How's tricks?'

'Got a missing couple.' Clement laid out the bones of the story without mentioning names. 'If you could ask your mates to keep an eye out?' Bill's network of fishermen, boar hunters, camel drivers and long haul truckies, acquired over his lifetime in the Kimberley, was likely to be more effective than any police bulletin.

Bill said he would pass the word around. With his eyes fixed at some point on the far wall he said. 'You gotta forget Marilyn.'

'I don't recall mentioning her.'

'Didn't need to. Look, it's like when you have that most beautiful barra hooked, ready to land. Or landed, and woosh, it gets off the hook, out of the boat, back in the water. It galls you. You keep thinking: what if? And then you start thinking: maybe I can catch it back? That's pointless. It's gone and if you set your sights just on it, you're in for a very frustrated life. But dangle your line, you'll land another very tasty fish.'

'Thanks Bill, your poetic language knows no bounds.'

Seratono chuckled. 'What I'm saying is, the reason you wanted that fish was pride. It was so beautiful and you wanted to show it off to everybody. You wanted having it, to make you feel good. That shouldn't be why you fish.'

The worst part was, Clement knew they were right. Bill, Graeme Earle, the others who didn't say anything to his face.

'Alright. Can we stop with the metaphor?'

They clinked glasses and drank. The beer was cold and he felt good that he could lose himself in this simple pleasure. At the same time it could never be sufficient. He knew too many for whom these kind of spaces became the normal landscape of their lives. Female companionship and sex were not something he was yet prepared to do without. While he had felt no need to get back into a dating world, and certainly no self-consciousness about how he might go with a new woman, he understood that the longer he left it, the harder it would be.

Bill put down his empty glass. 'Your buy, I believe.'

Clement finished his own beer and headed to the bar with the empties. He put them on the counter, pulled out his phone and located Louise's number in the contacts list. Should he? Could he?

His phone sprang into life. If it was her calling him, that had to be a sign.

But it wasn't her name on the display, just a number he didn't recognise.

'Dan Clement.'

'It's Angus Duncan from Giant. I got a message to call you.'

'Thanks for getting back to me.' Automatically Clement moved away from the bar out of earshot. 'You saw Ingrid Feister and Max Coldwell on Thursday the seventeenth. That right?'

Duncan confirmed it was correct. He was showing a Chinese client around when he learned Ingrid and Coldwell were in Hedland having their car repaired. He invited them to dinner at the pub and they accepted.

'I was a bit surprised actually. They were hippie sorts, you know. I didn't think they'd be bothered with us but ... free feed I guess.'

They had eaten in the dining room but then gone outside to see what the big crowd was cheering on. 'Tits and arse show. Chicks in skimpy, see-through stuff, miming. My client liked it. Some of the girls invited Ingrid and her boyfriend for a party afterwards, and they invited us.'

The party was actually nothing more than drinks up on the first floor of the hotel where the girls had their rooms. There were a couple of people from the hotel there, the girls' crew and manager.

'We stayed for about an hour and then my client said he was tired so I said we were going. Ingrid said she'd come too, and her boyfriend ... well, he seemed to do what she wanted. We all walked out pretty much together about one. We saw them to their motel unit and then I drove my client over to his accommodation at Finucane.'

'Were there problems with anybody?'

'No. Everybody was fine.'

'Coldwell and Ingrid? Between them?'

'He's a quiet guy. My guess he was a bit stoned, he smelled of weed. She seemed more the party type. But they weren't arguing or anything. I honestly think they're probably just zoning out somewhere.'

'They say where they were going next?'

They had mentioned Broome but only in a vague sense. They were talking about sightseeing and heading to East Kimberley and the gorges.

'So they could have gone inland?'

'Yeah. Or they could have changed their minds and split for the coast. It wasn't like they had a schedule. Well, not that I gathered.'

'Any chance of talking to your client?'

'Not here. For one he hardly speaks English but by now he's back in China.'

Clement thanked him.

'I'm sure they're going to be okay. They're just, you know, Pilates types.'

Ending the call, Clement looked up to see two fresh beers in Bill Seratono's fist.

'Man could die of thirst. I told Jill you'd fix her up.' Bill nodded at the barmaid.

Clement weighed the phone in his palm then slipped it back into his pocket. The easy reassurance of the mining guy should have reduced his anxiety. It didn't. He had a high-profile missing person in an area the size of Scandinavia. Up here a young woman carrying six thousand dollars was like a beacon attracting all the wrong kinds of animals. He'd better savour this beer while he could.

CHAPTER 13

I hadn't been to the Pilbara since the mid-'80s. I was doing a bit of hack work for my old boss at Fremantle CIB who had gone out into security and private inquiry. It was a credit company situation. Branko Ludovic had driven out of Leederville in his 1983 Holden Commodore owing two months rent. We weren't acting for the landlord, who was probably glad to be rid of him, but for the credit company that had loaned him the bucks for the Commodore. Squaring the payments had slipped Branko's mind. No doubt he thought he was far enough away for any action to be taken but I was at a loose end and happy to dawdle up the coast with a mate who'd played footy with me. A hot tongue of Australian air licked us for a thousand ks of low scrub while we rotated Robert Palmer, Rod Stewart and The Wailers, along with an old tape of local blues band The Elks who I'd seen many times at The Charles Hotel. Those were days when time seemed to plant itself and not blink – no mobile phones, texts, Facebook, wireless internet – just a piece of hot metal on endless road. Branko had found a job at Paraburdoo in the desert and the prospect of heading into the oven did not entice me. Especially as there might be no cops to back us up if Branko and a few mates got stroppy. Fortunately we'd learned he drove into Hedland every other Friday and blew half his week's wages. We timed our arrival for the Thursday. I don't remember much about the place except that we had to wait at a crossing for the longest train in the world to roll past. I think it took pretty much the entire side of a cassette, definitely the whole of 'The Killing of Georgie' and then some, wagon after wagon after wagon. I guess it was iron ore being sent out to the wharf for loading. I'm not one for detailed economics or infrastructure. What I remember is that infinite train with the sun turning the sea and the air and everything else silver – like a Boney M jumpsuit had been pulled over it. It must have been evening, I'm thinking, because the next day I woke up in our car and the sea was pea green, the sky a brilliant pale blue and the earth orange-red. We spent the day eating seafood and playing pool in an air-conditioned pub. Branko arrived about 8.00. I let him settle in, then fronted him and asked for his keys. He was a big guy, six two maybe, mean, and I could see he might want to go at it. 'Look,' I said, 'Branko, you've won. You've had three free months with the car, you've clocked up thousands of extra k, so your resale value is shit. If we tangle about this you'll wind up on some assault charge. It's not worth it.' I saw his big hand flexing around the beer glass on the bar. I could imagine the jagged shards cutting my skin, and my right hand was reaching behind me for the pool cue lying on the felt. Then he relaxed, reached in his pocket, pulled out the keys and tossed them to me.

'It's a heap of shit anyway,' he said and turned back to his beer. I walked out and drove his car back to Perth. My mate drove mine. Branko's music taste was predictably hard rock, too hard for me, but solitude and repetition can be a powerful combination and by the time I hit Geraldton I'd almost come to enjoy Motörhead.

I hoped for a similar productive result this time in Hedland but was resigned to being disappointed. Knowing I might have to travel off-road, I'd rented a Toyota Landcruiser. It chewed the petrol but I wasn't paying. After the Feister meeting I'd checked out Ingrid's flat, found nothing illuminating, then spent the rest of the weekend revising and planning and expecting a call to say Ingrid had turned up. No call came. First day, Monday, I'd spent close to ten hours on the road and stopped the night in Carnarvon at a caravan park. That took me back thirty years. I'd left at 6.00 this morning and spent another nine hours staring at bitumen. Most of the way I thought of Grace and her mother enjoying fine tapas, art and culture in Barcelona. Before I left Perth I emailed, informing them I was heading north on a job and not to worry if I wasn't in touch for a while. So far I hadn't bothered to check for a reply. I come from an era where you might not hear word from overseas for a month. In my opinion it helped you think about whatever it was you were meant to be thinking about, and for me right now that was the best way of tracking down Ingrid Feister and Max Coldwell. As I crossed the railway tracks, I caught a view of the port. It was vast now, iron lattice, giant wheels, cranes and, where I recalled one or two ships being serviced, today there was a flock of them hovering like sheep at a trough. I wondered how many billions of dollars I was looking at. The irony that most of them had likely been made from the very ore they were shipping wasn't lost on me. Australia had always been the lucky country: first with wheat and sheep, then with minerals; and that bounty had bred a profligacy. We were like those characters in a P.G. Wodehouse book, burning off the family fortune without ever planning for the day when it ran out, selling parts of the manor when things got tight. Well things were already getting tight. We were exporting five times as much ore to get the same return yet simultaneously closing down any industry that used a hammer, drill, skill – except for construction. And construction was no lifetime industry anymore where a man could sit back with pride and eat with the very utensils he'd made, or dine off the table whose wood had been grown, cut and shaped by his fellow Australians. Construction was a temporary shelter for the unskilled who would blow their hard-earned in Bali or Phuket or on buying stuff on the internet, dollars that would never find their way back.

I passed a truck with Giant Ore stencilled across its flank. That cut the switch on my philosophising. I was here to find Ingrid.

...

As requested, Dee Verleuwin had booked me into the Kookaburra, the same establishment where Ingrid and her boyfriend had stayed. The Kookaburra incorporated the original large hotel with sprawling veranda, offering a beer garden, a big sports bar and dining area on the ground floor level plus accommodation on its first floor level. At some stage in the '80s or '90s, a motel had been added in what had probably been a gravel carpark. It looked like the motel contained around fifteen units. I pulled up near reception. I swear my body creaked when I climbed out. My right hip was aching, so was my calf. Maybe I'd been deluding myself that thirty years hadn't left their mark.

By the time I let myself into my small room it was nearly 4.00 pm. I had a quick shower and changed into a clean short-sleeved shirt. I swapped my shorts for long pants, though at a shade under thirty degrees Celsius it was well and truly warm enough to stay in shorts. This was probably the best time of the year to be up here. The humidity wasn't too sapping and the heat was tolerable. Verleuwin had called ahead so the police should be expecting me. I opened my folder and found a direct number for Detective Inspector Peter Richardson. I doubted I or anybody else in my circles would have been afforded such contact. The power of wealth.

'Richardson.' He answered like a man whose team had just had a dubious free kick awarded against them. I explained who I was.

'Where are you?'

'At the Kookaburra.'

'I'll be there in ten, Sportsman's bar.'

I resisted the urge to put on the air conditioner. My wife and daughter were always on about saving the planet yet I've never known anybody to use more unnecessary lighting or air conditioning than they do. It's nice to arrive in a cool room but I preferred a little martyrdom and self-congratulation.

...

The bar was open and cool – clinker brick with some hanging pots to soften the wide-screens and tubular aluminium. There were about a dozen drinkers, most of them workmen and women in shorts. This was only a Tuesday, I guessed things pumped on the weekend. True to his word, Richardson arrived in ten minutes. At first I didn't realise it was him. Much younger than I'd anticipated, maybe just into his forties, he was dressed like me in slacks and short sleeves. Unlike a lot of cops he didn't have that straight back and broad shoulders, more a distance runner than a weights man, thin and slightly stooped, with thick black hair. I saw him check his phone and then he made a beeline for me, so I guessed the efficient Dee Vee had furnished him with my photo. We shook hands and he joined me in a lemon squash.

'We don't have anything further. Broome hasn't found any trace of them there yet.' He explained the implications. How they could have gone off-road towards the coast or inland and north as a more direct access to the gorges. 'So far as we know, they left here in good health with the vehicle in good order and made it as far as Sandfire.'

'Any chance they may have doubled back?'

He curled his lip. 'Don't know why they would do that.'

'Any problems between the two of them?'

'Not that we could find. I interviewed the people staying either side of the motel unit. No arguments.'

'No problems with anybody here?'

'None we could dig up. They had dinner here with one of the Giant people, Angus Duncan, and a Chinese client. It was a big night. We had a lingerie revue from Perth. Place was packed.'

'I thought they'd been banned.'

'Skimpy costumes, they mime the songs, no stripping. Let's face it, these days the singers are wearing less than strippers anyway. Duncan says he and his guest had a few drinks with Ingrid, Coldwell and the revue people after their show. They all left around one am. He said goodbye to Ingrid and Coldwell at their unit. They were fine, going to leave for Broome the next day.'

'They said they were going to Broome?"

'They mentioned it but didn't indicate if that was their final destination.'

'What was the name of the revue?'

'I don't remember offhand.'

'You didn't interview the revue people?'

'They moved on right away to the next gig. But there was no need. We had a confirmed sighting of Ingrid and the boyfriend leaving the unit the next morning. And since then we know they made Sandfire. Whatever happened, happened after that.'

'Drugs? You check the unit?'

For the first time he seemed ill-at-ease. 'We ran a couple of simple checks, bathroom, dressing table. Didn't find anything except some pot residue.'

That squared with what we'd been told of Coldwell. And I was pretty certain if he was smoking dope, so was his girlfriend. I needed to speak to the maid and already had her name in my file.

'Am I likely to find the maid who saw them leave?'

'Not till tomorrow morning. She was a good witness, gave an accurate description. It was them, and the Sandfire video confirms it.'

I thanked him for his time.

'Hopefully Dan Clement up in Broome will have turned up something by the time you get there. We've got our eyes and ears open. If we see or hear anything we'll let the family know. It's always a worry when people go missing but from what I hear it's not out of character and there are plenty of places you can disappear for weeks at a time. If they hadn't had that service I'd be more worried, but I spoke to the mechanic and he says they went over the car very closely. They knew whose daughter it was.'

We shook hands and Richardson took himself off, telling me not to hesitate to call if I found anything or needed help. Everything he'd said made sense but I wasn't Richardson. I liked to nail down every tiny piece of information. Did they speak to anybody else in the pub, or at this party? Somebody who might have followed them? I approached the barmaid, a slim girl with red hair and fair complexion. She'd need a lot of sunscreen in this climate.

'Hi, my name is Richard Lane. I'm looking for these guys. Their parents are concerned.'

I showed her a photo of Ingrid Feister and Max Coldwell.

'The police spoke to us about them. Apparently they were here the night we had the strippers, couple of weeks back, but I didn't see them. Or I don't remember them. I always work the Sporty.'

'And where was the show?'

'In the beer garden. You should speak to Dougal. He hung out with them a bit.'

'Is he here?'

She checked the clock, pouted as she considered. 'His shift starts six-thirty.'

...

The trouble with Hedland is apart from drinking and pool, there's not a lot to do to kill an hour. It's marginally more stroll-friendly than Aleppo. You drive everywhere. I remember a story, which may have been apocryphal, about the man who had designed Hedland. He was from the UK or the US, somewhere the sun was much weaker. He'd wanted to create a place with a sense of community and had consequently created many cul-de-sacs and circles so that people would be encouraged to leave cars behind and walk instead. When it's hot enough to fry an egg on the bonnet of your car, however, nobody is inclined to walk. Supposedly the guy was so horrified with what he'd done that he killed himself. Even if the rest of the story was true I wasn't putting too much store in the dramatic finale. Ever since C.Y. O'Connor, the great pioneering engineer of Western Australia, had topped himself, we'd shown a penchant for stories that ended in outsiders suiciding because they'd misunderstood the harshness of our climate. This simultaneously made us feel tough and superior. All of which meant I could get in the car and drive aimlessly, sit here and drink, or go back to my unit and catch a few zeds. I settled on the last of these.

After clicking on the air conditioner and sending through a text to Dee Vee that I had arrived in Hedland, I lay back on the single bed and stared at the ceiling. I was glad to have a decent job to help me soak up the time without my girls. I missed them both; there was only so much positive spin-off from bachelorhood. I read the local rag that was supplied. Front page was about Giant's big new iron ore mine and accompanying infrastructure worth many billions. Construction was due to start in a month. The Chinese were putting up the money. A different world, but maybe germane to my case. If some loser realised who Ingrid was, maybe they did kidnap her. Things might have gone wrong, they never got a chance to issue a demand. But I was getting ahead of myself and my muscles were still protesting. I stretched out and cocooned myself in the low hum of the air-conditioner.

...

I don't know when I dropped off. It must have been quick because the next thing I knew my eyes were flicking open and the digital clock told me it was the auspicious time of 7.11. I got up, threw some water in my face, brushed my hair and straightened my clothes. I turned off the air con on my way out. Outside it was already dark and, surprisingly for a place that seemed nearly all gravel and red earth, sweetly scented, particularly with jasmine.

The beer garden offered that soothing tranquillity only truly appreciated in these climates where by day even your clothes feel sunburned. The night sky was a balm. Around twenty people were dotted at tables, sipping drinks and laughing. I located Dougal on my second attempt, reconciling an electronic till. He was your classic waiter-barista: twenties, small-boned, dark features with a goatee. I introduced myself and got to the point of why I was there.

'Yeah, sure, the sExcitation night.' At least he remembered the name of the troupe. I let him tell me how he'd already spoken to the police.

'You partied with the girls, and this girl and guy afterwards.'

'In the rooms upstairs.' He jerked a thumb.

'Who else was there?'

'The roadie, the girls' manager, Bevan from the bottle shop, couple of guys and chicks, a Chinese dude and this older guy who I've seen around before.'

That, I was guessing, would be Angus Duncan.

'Good vibe? No fights?'

'No, everybody was chilled. Girls had a great show, we made good bucks. I threw in a couple of bottles of champers and a case of beer.'

'See anybody talking to the girl or guy in the photo?'

He shrugged. 'It was a party, man. I don't remember any problems, that's what I told the detective.' A short blonde carrying weight on her hips lobbed up and bought a fresh bottle of wine. He placed it in the ice bucket for her, came back to me, seemingly trawling his brain afresh.

'Actually, I think the girl was mainly speaking to one of the strippers, sorry, entertainers, and the Chinese guy.'

'No arguments?'

'No, just, you know, chatting, doing the translation thing.' He indicated plenty of hand gestures.

'You see if she was carrying any cash?'

He made an O with his lips. 'No idea.'

At least it didn't sound like Ingrid had been drunk and flashing a roll about.

'How did the guy seem?'

'Quiet.'

'Any drugs?'

He was like a kid playing in a field who just spotted a bee. I reassured him. 'I'm not a cop. Just want to know what was going down.'

'Somebody had a joint going. Could've been the dude.' He indicated the photo. 'Couple of the girls had a few lines of speed. Not in the party room, though. I saw them when I went to the loo up there. They offered me, but it's more than my job's worth. Honestly man, I've had school formals where there was more shit going down.'

As father of an eighteen-year-old, I wished he hadn't told me that. I thanked him for his time and left him to deal with a man in a very bright shirt with the look of a 1970s full-back, almost bald but no-nonsense tough, who was after a chardonnay. The world had changed a lot in thirty years.

Bottleshop Bevan wasn't working tonight but I bought a couple of stubbies anyway and retreated to my room to cogitate. Okay, there'd been a few drugs at this party. No surprise. Nobody had mentioned Ingrid flashing rolls of cash. Max Coldwell seemed a quiet hippie type. My phone rang. Just for an instant I went to default, expecting to see Tash's name but it was Dee Vee again. I told her what I'd learned, or rather hadn't. She didn't comment. I guess to her I could have been a gardener relaying information about aphids in the Feister rose garden. Her job was purely to organise.

'I had you down to see Angus Duncan at nine am but something's come up and he has to fly out to one of our tenements at seven-thirty. He said he could see you at the airport at six-thirty tomorrow in the morning. Is there a problem?'

I threw a glance at my two small, lonely beers.

'No problem. I wasn't planning a big night. Still no activity on her Facebook or Instagram?'

'Nothing.'

Obviously she would have told me if Ingrid's phone or bank account had been accessed.

'Sweet dreams, Richard,' she said as she rang off, tantalising me with a forbidden image of her in a sheer night-garment. Slipping off my shoes I lay on my bed in the low air con and cast my mind back to a time when women found me attractive enough to sleep with, but not successful enough to stay with. Not that there were too many. Barry Dunn's ex-squeeze, the sexy Wendy Smith was always fun, even though she was hiding secrets darker than a block of Jamaican Gold. But Wendy always played understudy. In my deepest emotional trench, that one way down where fish have eyes on stalks, where your soul hides even from yourself, there was only one body, one image, one ghost: Celeste Magnello. A lifetime on, and I could still smell the soap that oozed from her skin when we made love. Her betrayals were unblunted by thirty-five years of icy currents; they could tear into me like a stingray barb if I let them. I no longer lusted after her. I did not want her in my life. I loved my wife wholly, without reserve. Tash had carried me off to a place of sweetness, light and satisfaction. I thanked God for providing her, and then, aware that God was hardly likely to help this little shit, I tipped my hat to Lady Luck for her assistance – a bet each way if you like. And yet, alone, when the blackness of night was as tangible as fear and at its most seductive, it was Celeste whose image floated from the soft silt of the day's decay and her lips that whispered my name.

CHAPTER 14

Whatever sucked him from sleep was with such fierce magnetic pull that he found himself sitting upright. Disoriented, Clement realised he was shirtless but couldn't think where. Then consciousness flooded: the naked woman beside him, the man's voice outside the window yelling 'Thief!' Louise stirred.

'Stay here,' he said, and jumped from bed. Even after sex he would put back on jocks or shorts just so as to never be fumbling in the dark in an emergency. Perhaps it was a neurosis that would have proved fertile ground for a psych but tonight it was fortuitous forward planning. He yanked open the door of the motel room. A fat guy, naked, was standing on the first floor balcony yelling down into shadows. 'Bastard!' He turned to Clement. 'Fucker took my wallet.'

Clement spied fractured light beneath them, a running figure. Without thinking he vaulted the railing. After momentary elevation he found himself on the arc's downward slope with only his grip on the iron rail to argue gravity. At the nadir his shoulder socket demanded he let go – now! – but he resisted, confirmed the vehicle directly beneath him was his own car and, a scintilla of a second after calculating likely damage to a government vehicle and its consequences, let go. Allowing his legs to collapse upon landing, the way they'd taught him at some long-forgotten parachute drill, he rolled so his hip seemed to take the brunt of the impact, the momentum instantly propelling him through the air like a kid reaching the foot of a water slide. His bare feet landed on smooth concrete but he stumbled and almost fell as he attempted to start running before he had his balance. Up ahead his quarry swung wide, dodging a parked Volvo. Clement was sprinting smoothly now. The catapult effect of the car had narrowed the gap and when he turned the corner of the rear of the motel he expected to be almost able to reach out and seize the thief. To his dismay, he saw that he had made no ground at all and in the course of the next few seconds felt himself slipping back further. Unlike Josh Shepherd, Clement had no pre-season training to help him sustain his effort. His stomach churned and burned and his lungs shut down. The thief, a school satchel slung over his back, a cap on his head, became fainter and vanished. Clement shuddered to a halt and gulped for oxygen.

...

The interior of Clement's car replicated the atmosphere of a hung jury room, a breath between stasis and action, a pause, a neutral point between on and off, yes and no. Clement held Louise's gaze, knowing the past could not be regained now, that by sleeping together they had created an array of possible futures most of which would be complicated, fraught. He guessed the same things were going through her mind.

Of course she was the one who acted. 'Thanks for the entertainment,' she said, and leaned over and kissed him. Then she let herself out of the car and moved elegantly up her small path, doing something with her hair. Inside him an emotion he could barely recognise stirred: pride that he'd had sex with an incredibly desirable woman. Not the boasting, swelling, egomania of the stud but an affirmation that such a thing was possible for him. To be brutally honest with himself, he felt relief in equal measure to pride. Despite the false start in the Anglers, he had summoned the courage to call her and ask her to dinner. By the time he was waiting out front of her place, a little after 7.00 pm, he was affirming to himself there was nothing on the line here, intercourse would be social only. He silently reiterated that when she sat beside him in the car and he smelled her perfume and saw in her eyes the positive vibes she was sending him, this stirring up a faint reminder of what it felt like to be an object of desire. As they finished off something in black bean sauce while she told him yet another colourful tale of representing the accused of the Kimberley, he was still assuring himself there would be no physical culmination. And then it was clear that the meal was over, the wine was drained and it was time to go home or do what he'd been avoiding pretty much since Marilyn had walked out of his life.

'I'd ask you back to my place but it's hopelessly poky.' Even before he finished the sentence he wanted to take it back. It sounded like an excuse.

'I'd ask you back to mine but Mum's up from Perth, staying in my bed. How about a motel? I've always wanted to have a tryst in a motel.'

It was the word tryst that won him over completely. 'Sex' might have been just a bit sharp for where he was at, 'tryst' was playful yet still sexy. And so she'd called her mum and told her not to worry, she was staying with her friend, and he'd driven them around the corner to the Pearl, a respectable two-storey motel with green lighting highlighting a palm by the entrance and a sign that said Foxtel was available. More signs in the small foyer offered highchairs and a fax machine on request but even they couldn't dampen the pleasant tension he'd begun to feel in his loins. Their room was on the first floor. It was clean, neat, with a bar fridge and a thick wallet that offered motel services and sightseeing suggestions. Clement only noticed those items because that's where he placed his keys. When he turned, Louise had already stepped out of the pretty red dress that suited her dark hair and suntanned skin. Her stomach was flat and muscled like she worked out and he should have felt intimidated that what he had to offer was less but it was too late. Lust and desire were working up a furious Grappelli–Django soundtrack in his head. Next he knew they were locked on the bed and after that there was no recorded history, like the waves had washed away whatever his senses had at the time scrawled in sand.

Dawn was lifting itself on creaking knees as he drove through still-slumbering streets back to his flat perched above the chandler, a trace of her perfume lingering. He'd not showered at the motel. By the time he'd got back after his fruitless pursuit, a couple of the night-shift uniforms, Lalor and Hodgkiss, had arrived. They had the good sense not to draw attention to an inspector in his underwear. He told them to take the name of the man next door who sounded the alarm and check whether anybody else had been robbed, then to pass everything onto DC Shepherd.

Yes, he could have taken charge of the whole thing then and there but he did not wish to. It was 2.20 am.

'You sure know how to show a girl a good time,' Louise had cracked. She was back in her red dress sitting on the bed. He locked the door and slid on the chain but had not bothered to put on his clothes. He unzipped her dress and she lay in his arms.

'Think you could get back to sleep?' he asked.

'Maybe.' Banging and voices outside intruded. 'Probably not.' She did a good line in dry humour. On their first date she'd told him her father was a musician who used to play piano bars. That's where she got it from, she'd said, the humour. He told her about the cat-burglar who'd been giving them the run-around.

'He was too fast. I don't have the stamina these days.'

She looked up at him, smiled. Her hand rested between his legs. 'Sure about that?'

...

There hadn't even been a public terminal at Port Hedland last time I'd been there. Mind you there wasn't the internet either. And sure, these were no longer the heady days when iron ore was a hundred and thirty bucks a tonne and a day's work in the Pilbara paid a month's mortgage in Gosford or Townsville but, even in the boom's slim tail, there was enough flick to generate plenty of fly-in fly-outs. The smaller aircraft were hived off to their own adjacent field where I could see a couple of planes and a chopper sitting as I drove in. The sun was still only flexing, the air crisp as a cracker from a freshly opened packet. I parked by a chain-link fence and strode towards a prefab hut that housed toilets and a small waiting room. It was deserted. I caught sight of a figure on the field about a hundred metres away, checking the undercarriage of a Cessna, and guessed this might be Duncan. When I was about twenty metres off, he swung out of shadow and took a couple of steps in my direction, hands on hips. It was already a few degrees hotter here than the perimeter.

'Snowy Lane?'

I was a little surprised he used that moniker. With the Feisters I tried to maintain the veneer of professionalism. Duncan was probably forty or a tick over.

'That's me,' I admitted. 'Angus?'

He stuck out a hand. 'My old man was a big East Freo supporter. Sorry for the change of plan but we have some samples they need picked up.'

'You fly yourself?'

'These days. Iron ore price goes south, everything gets cut back. Officially though, my title is Head of Exploration and Future Development, Pilbara.'

Duncan was not a tall man. Maybe five nine, solid build, fit; sandy, curly hair. He wore shorts. His calves suggested cycling or swimming. He had an open face and the confidence of a man in territory where he knew he belonged.

'Ingrid still hasn't surfaced?' he asked.

'Not to my knowledge.'

'The Broome police called me last night.' He ran me through his conversation with the detective whose name he had forgotten. From his questions, the guy seemed more thorough than his Hedland counterpart.

'So you met up with Ingrid and Max Coldwell ...'

'At the office. Well, at the workshop next door to be exact. I'd just flown in from the exploration camp with our Chinese client. I saw these two ... alternate types hanging around. Dave, one of the mechanics, let me know who she was before I made any kind of scene. I went over and introduced myself and asked where they were staying and so on. I thought it was polite to ask them to join us for dinner and they accepted. Ingrid seemed really keen to ask Shaun about China, even though he speaks little English.'

'Shaun is your client?'

'His Chinese name starts with an X but he knows it's easier for us to anglicise it, so I call him Shaun. Shaun Li. He's the middle son of the Li family. They own one of China's biggest steel companies.'

I remembered the article I'd read. I thought the name Li had cropped up there.

'They're involved in this new billion-dollar mine.'

'More like twelve billion but yes. They're the keystone investor. Shaun was out to look at some other prospects with me.'

'Ingrid is interested in business?'

Duncan stifled a chortle. 'Didn't seem to be. She wanted to know about Buddhism and tai chi and feng shui. I mean she was totally barking up the wrong tree. Shaun is all about his Ferrari and the family business. But, as it turned out, they got on fine.'

'Was Ingrid flashing cash? Did she have an argument with anybody?'

Not that he recalled. They'd had an enjoyable meal. The company had picked up the tab. Then they saw everybody heading out to the beer garden and went out to watch the show. 'The girls were good-lookers. Shaun was a bit smitten so I sent them a couple of bottles of champers and asked what they were doing afterwards. They invited us all to a party upstairs. A bit of fun.'

Duncan had seen no incidents. No fights, no drugs.

'I heard Coldwell had a joint going?'

'He might have. I didn't notice. I was sticking close to Shaun but there was no trouble. About one, Shaun indicated he'd had enough, so we split. Ingrid and Max said they'd come too. We walked them to their motel unit.'

'How did Max Coldwell strike you?'

'Quiet, a bit out of his depth. Like, you know he'd be more at home in a youth hostel with an out-of-tune guitar, but nothing untoward. I can't believe he would do Ingrid any harm. He seemed pretty into her.' He repeated that he had every confidence the car was mechanically sound. 'We've had two planes up checking inland, just in case, but we haven't spotted anything.'

I'd exhausted my questions. He jerked his thumb at the Cessna. 'You want to take a ride out to the camp? I'd be happy for the company.'

'Can't. Gotta get up to Sandfire. You have an airstrip or something?'

He smirked. 'Don't know if you'd quite call it that. We've compacted some dirt. It's hard enough to land and take off.'

I was glad I had work offering me an excuse to avoid his offer. We told each other to take care.

...

'Somebody knows this guy. His dealer, his fence, his girlfriend.'

Clement was addressing the squad – detectives and a smattering of uniforms who weren't out on the job that minute. Finding the sprinting burglar had become personal. 'Maybe he's going to get smart and pull up stumps. Let's get him before then.' Even as he talked, he was experiencing the odd random flashback to Louise. It was as off-putting as it was exciting.

'I think if he was a local, we'd have heard something.' Mal Gross had the longest tenure of any of them and his contacts ran artesian deep.

'Seems to know his way around though.' Graeme Earle stroked his chin.

'Maybe he's like you, boss. Grew up here, went away, came back.' It was Jo di Rivi. In Clement's estimation she was the smartest of the uniforms. He thought she should try for detective.

'Whoever he is, he's not on our books or we'd know him. Not with that kind of speed.'

'Told you he was fast,' smirked Shepherd.

'Graeme, I want you to join Josh on this. Shake down dealers, anybody who might buy the phones and cameras off him. Same with you guys.' He was referring to the uniforms. 'Mal, if this guy is local or was local at some point, guaranteed there's a school teacher or coach who'll remember. We might be looking for somebody recently returned.'

'What was his haul from the motel?' Manners the IT guy had just joined them.

Shepherd checked his notepad. 'He did over six rooms. We got five wallets, three purses, two cameras, seven phones reported missing.'

'Get me the numbers. I'll try and trace them.'

Shepherd lifted a page from his file and handed it across.

'How's the pooch?' asked Manners of di Rivi.

'Not sure, the vet's checking her out.'

It was the first Clement had heard of it. He felt an obligation with that dog. Not long after he'd arrived back in Broome the wild dog had attacked him. He thought he had it killed with a brick but it had survived and di Rivi had adopted it.

'What's up with the pooch?'

It had never been officially named but 'the pooch' was its generally accepted moniker.

'I found a lump under its front leg.'

Clement hoped it would be okay. The dog was living proof of redemption. 'I'm sure it will be fine. It's a tough mutt to kill. Alright guys, get to it.'

Most of them split as they were told. Graeme Earle lingered and followed him to his office. 'You were there? Two am?'

'Yes.'

Earle allowed himself a grin. 'Hope you did more than play Scrabble.'

Clement withheld any answer but allowed the hint of a smile. He entered his office, checked the clock. Not yet midday. Everything seemed to be going so slow today. Was it too soon to call Louise? Of course it was. He sat down at his desk and filled in paperwork. At 12.06 he picked up his mobile and dialled.

'Brandon and Albertini.'

'Is that Louise?' She sounded a bit different.

'No, this is Karla, her PA. She's in court at the moment.'

'Oh.' It was a dumb thing to say but it was out before he could stop.

'Would you like to leave a message?'

He hesitated. What kind of message could he leave? 'No, that's okay. I'll call back.'

'No problem.'

Too soon, he chided himself for not waiting. Now when he called back he'd either have to admit that he'd already called – too desperate – or lie. There was a knock on his door and Scott Risely stuck in his head.

'You eat anything, right?'

For a moment he was lost. Then he remembered tonight was dinner at the Riselys' house.

'I'm not crazy on offal.'

'Me either, you'll be safe. Seven?'

'Sure.'

That gave him an out for tonight at least, although he wasn't sure if he wanted one.

Complications. He shrugged off the baggage of his personal life and made a few calls to his contacts around the East Kimberley to see if there was any sign of the Feister girl. Still nothing. What had been an annoying chore was beginning to grate. Okay, the area was enormous but, unless they were deliberately keeping away from prying eyes, they should have crossed somebody's path by now. The potential they'd met with foul play was increasing. What a shit-storm that would bring. His mobile rang. He snatched for it hoping to see Louise's number. It wasn't.

'Marilyn?'

'You got a minute?'

There was a tone to her voice, fraught.

'Sure. Phoebe okay?'

'She's fine. It's me.'

'What's up?'

She was disturbing him. Marilyn never sounded anxious.

'I'd rather see you. I'm across the road at the Honky Nut.' She added swiftly, 'I don't want to interrupt you.'

'It's fine. I'm on my way.'

...

The café wasn't literally across the road but close enough. He spied her immediately at one of the outside tables in a pale blue dress that set off her unblemished skin. She wore a straw hat yet made it stylish as only women of great beauty can. Marilyn possessed an elegance of line, symmetry in all her features, that made her almost a natural element of whatever setting she was in. Like a leaf on a tree, or the ripple of a wave. He couldn't think of any other way of describing it. She was never an addition but part of the whole. With every second his concern was growing but – and he was trying to step around this truth – there was also some tiny bud of hope that the wedding plans had crashed and burned. Yet as soon as he allowed himself this illicit sensation, it was countered by the fear she might have cancer or some other terrible disease. He was not yet halfway across the road when her eyes met his. They could still make his breath skip. He joined her and pulled up a chair. She had ordered tea. The teapots here were a feature, with gum nuts, kookaburras in relief.

'I ordered the pot. Would you like to share?'

'I'm fine. Are you?'

She gazed at him then shook her head before looking up again, this time right into his eyes. They must have betrayed his fear.

'I'm not sick or anything. It's this wedding. I'm a mess.'

Had she and Brian fought? Had she come to her senses? Clement battled the urge to open that door.

'Are we talking table settings? Main course?'

'Don't be disingenuous. Should I do it? It's not too late. Everybody else is going to tell me what I want to hear.' She massaged that. 'What *they* want to hear.'

Clement couldn't help thinking by 'everyone' she meant her mother, Geraldine.

She continued. 'You're biased, I know that, but you're the only one who will tell me absolutely what you think: am I doing the right thing?'

Should he feel flattered or insulted? 'You said yourself I'm biased.'

'I think you can be objective, because you still care about me. I know that. We still love one another, in our way.'

Why did she have to say that? All this time denying ...

'No, you shouldn't marry him.'

It burst out spontaneously. She looked like she was going to snap back at him but took a deep breath and poured them both tea. For a moment there was no sound but the trickle of liquid on china.

'Tell me why I shouldn't. And saying because you love me is not a reason.'

'It's my reason.'

'We're not going to happen.' She sat the teapot back down. 'We don't work. Love doesn't have anything to do with it. You and me: it's a pitched battle for control. It exhausts us both.'

'Whereas Brian rolls over for you?'

She raised her eyebrows, sipped, bled out a single word. 'Really?' Like that was beneath him.

'I don't understand what you want from me.' He wasn't being obtuse.

'And that has always been the problem.'

He would not be caught that easily. He resisted anger. 'If you're after somebody steady, a man who wants to make your life easy, will be faithful, will book the two of you into a little whitewashed stone cottage in Sicily and in the evening under a string of coloured globes eat the day's fresh catch at a tiny restaurant where they drizzle the olive oil on home-baked bread, I guess Brian is the guy for you.'

'You could have been a travel writer.'

'Thing is you could do that anyway. You have the money.'

'I don't want to do that by myself. I want to share that piece of bread. So far you're making it sound pretty tempting.'

'But you're not sure. Otherwise you wouldn't have asked me.'

He recognised the hat now. It was Nick's, her father's.

'And I'm still waiting to be convinced.'

'There's nothing wrong with Brian. He's solid. But there are a thousand Brians out there and I think, personally, the one you marry should be that, The One. You want the man who lies beside you at night while you sleep and for him every breath is a coastline he patiently comes to know in every detail, every little rock pool, he's immersed himself in.' Encouraged that she seemed to be listening, he blundered on. 'You don't need a man who can peel a couple of hundred bucks for a Leonard Cohen ticket because he's suddenly discovered him with his chums in the wine club; you want the guy who trawled the second-hand shops six years ago and picked up an unloved *Songs of Love and Hate* for two bucks because he understood why it was special. You want a man who knows why you think white doesn't suit you when it does, and why Steve Martin is a great straight man, and when you make love with this guy you want to be flying over Mayan ruins, and feeling the spray from the Nile in Cleopatra's barge, all at the same time. And you want a man who recognises you're wearing your father's old hat with a feather of a dove in the band that he placed there the day his grandchild was born, for luck. That's why you shouldn't go through with this.'

Clement did not know why he spoke these thoughts now when any other day he would have choked them in their crib. Whether it was he was beyond caring, or because he cared too much. Still she had said nothing; no gibes or comebacks, no mocking handclap even. Numb, he got up from his chair and quietly tucked it back in.

He did not look back when he walked away.

CHAPTER 15

It had been risky hitting the motel but it had worked. One haul had brought him as much as four or five individual scores, the weed and eccies an unexpected bonus. It was taking all his willpower to resist sampling but he knew, even as his windows of reason and sanity shrank, that he must. Mongoose would take them in lieu of payment. With the phones and camera and the other shit he'd scored in the morning, that would keep Mongoose off his back. Maybe he could get half the crystal he would normally ask for which would mean ... shit, it was confusing ... he retraced the thought, grabbed it like a goanna's tail before it could get it into the scrub ... yes, if he got half the crystal, he would actually be paying off a little of the debt. Then next time if he took even less crystal he could pay off a little more. He didn't want to disappoint Mongoose. He saw what happened to Dana, and she was a chick. But, here was the thing, how long before the cops caught him? What he should do is get out of here but that was ... shit, if he split Mongoose would hurt him real bad. But he'd have to catch him. Okay, he could never come back but so what? He'd miss Aunty but then he didn't have many choices did he? So, he'd lay this stuff off on Mongoose, maybe take just a little crystal, lull him, then split. Yeah, that was a good plan.

He turned into Mongoose's street and hit his brake pedal. There was a big guy standing on Mongoose's porch talking to somebody inside. He was sure this was the same guy who had chased him. The fit fucker. He'd had to take to the roof. His gaze strayed to the car at the kerb. Yep, one them unmarked sedans. Shit. He turned quickly and pedalled back the way he had come, his brain a buzzing hive. Did they know who he was? Is that why they were there?

No, if they knew who he was they would go to Aunty's place. Mongoose was a drug dealer, that's why they were there. Might be nothing to do with him. He was lucky he hadn't just rocked up though. He had everything on him. A new idea was forming in the small territory of his brain still working. Maybe the police were going to arrest Mongoose? And then Mongoose wouldn't be able to punish him for not paying him back, would he? If he was going to split he may as well do it now. There had to be at least fifty pingers. He could trade those, smoke the weed. Didn't matter really where he went, south, east, up north. He'd hitch a ride and go wherever.

...

'Spoke to Mongoose Cole. He claims he had no idea what I was talking about.'

Josh Shepherd ate an apple as he delivered his news. Clement found this profoundly irritating. He hadn't tried Louise again. The meeting with Marilyn had thrown him. He felt like a ball spinning in an uneven roulette wheel. One of Shepherd's informants had suggested Mongoose was the new ice heavy in town. He'd not previously been on their radar.

'How'd he get the name Mongoose?'

Shepherd took one final big bite and pitched the core into the wastepaper basket across the room. He spoke with his mouth full. 'You'll like this.' He swallowed. 'The previous go-to guy was Sammy "The Snake" Carlisle.'

Clement could see where this was going. 'Cole got rid of Snake, hence Mongoose.'

'You got it. Rumour is he took to him with a cricket bat. Snake fled back to Fitzroy Crossing.'

It showed how fast things moved in drug-land these days. Clement had assumed Snake was still one of the town's three main dealers. Graeme Earle had already struck out with the others. That was not unexpected. The only way the dealers would cop to knowing the identity of Speedy Gonzales would be if the cops had leverage, which they did not.

Mal Gross strode in, looking pleased with himself. 'Sidney Turner, nineteen. Spoke to Jammo from the Wanderers Hockey Club. Sidney's from around Moore River. Went to school here for about three years from when he was fourteen. Jammo says he's never seen anybody so quick. Kid stayed here with his great-aunt when his mum went off the rails. Quite a nice kid, did okay at school but then left to go live with his older brother. Jammo didn't even know he was back but saw him running down the beach about a week ago. Said something had changed. Kid still looked fit but his wiring wasn't quite right.'

Clement was already gathering his sunglasses. He didn't have to ask Gross for the contact details, the sergeant was a step ahead.

'Olive Pickering, eight McMillan.'

'Text Graeme to meet us there. Is di Rivi still around?' Clement wanted at least four of them.

'Think she's at the vet's,' said Shepherd.

'I'll grab her. You meet me there. Park up the street.'

Shepherd went immediately.

Clement picked up his own keys. 'Mal, get a description out.'

Gross gave a thumbs up.

...

Of course Clement should have got Shepherd to pick up Jo di Rivi but that damn dog was worrying him. He retrieved his car and drove the three minutes to the vet, which was located in a newish short strip between a cake shop and dive hire place. There were no spaces out front so he drove around the block, down the back lane. He was lucky, a glazier's van was just pulling out and he was able to park in the one free staff bay. Yes, he knew he shouldn't, but he wasn't going to be long. He got out of the car and walked back around to the front of the building. The day passed as mild for up here. Probably not yet thirty and a breeze was trickling down the street. A lump could mean anything: cancer, a cyst, an infection. He pushed into the vet's waiting room. Despite a standard fan in the back corner and one on the desk, it was considerably warmer in here than outside and stuffy with the thick odour of dog. Di Rivi was nowhere in sight, nor was anybody else for that matter. He should have called first but he wanted to come in the flesh, maybe catch a glimpse of the pooch. He was about to press the desk buzzer when the door behind the counter swung open and di Rivi emerged with the guy he guessed was the vet, fair hair receding, a short white coat smeared with hair and a little blood. They were in mid-conversation but di Rivi was surprised to see Clement and stopped.

'We've got a break on Speedy Gonzales,' he said, aware he was shading the real reason he was standing there. 'You can come with me.'

'Sure. Thanks, Robert.'

'We'll know more after the biopsy.'

Clement said, 'How is she?'

The vet took it on himself. 'We excised the lump. It looks suspicious but it was very contained.'

'Pooch is fine. She's sleeping,' added the policewoman.

Clement's phone rang. Earle. 'Yes, mate?'

'Eight or eighteen? I can't read the bloody screen properly in this light.'

And you might need glasses, thought Clement. 'Eight, McMillan.'

'I'm at the top of Orr.'

'Shep will be there in a minute. I'm bringing di Rivi.'

'How's the pooch?'

'We'll know more later.'

...

Under ten minutes they were assembled just up the road, di Rivi behind the wheel, the three men at the side of Clement's car.

Clement gave the run-down. 'Graeme and I will go to the front door. Shep, I want you around the back.' He looked at di Rivi. 'When we're about to go in I'll radio to start ...'

He never got any further. A cyclist swung by them, a slim fellow. He took one look at them and his eyes bugged.

'Turner!' yelled Shepherd after him.

The cyclist drove his feet into the pedals but in that lag before the wheels spun faster, Shepherd made quick ground. He lunged for the bike, which accelerated just as he was about to lay a hand on Sidney Turner's leg. Shepherd got the slimmest tag on Turner's ankle then cursed as he fell onto the road. Without waiting to be told, di Rivi gunned the car along the inside of the cyclist who looked panicked, stranded in the middle of the road. He might have been okay except for the small sedan that chose that moment to reverse from its driveway into his path. He tried to brake and swing right but he was travelling too fast and slid into the side of the car at a fair clip. He seemed to bounce and roll but miraculously sprang up. Josh Shepherd was on all fours making grunting sounds. Earle was a statue, more used to catching his prey with a fishing line. Clement charged. Sidney Turner ran towards Clement and went to dummy by him but this time Clement did not commit too soon. He kept his feet ready for the change of direction and when Sidney broke to his right, Clement dived to his left and wrapped his big arms around Turner's slim waist, pulling them both to the road.

'Calm down, Sidney. You're going nowhere.'

The boy, for that's what he seemed like to Clement, appeared to comprehend it was done. He stopped wriggling. Graeme Earle arrived and cuffed him. Di Rivi cruised back. Shepherd had regained his feet but was gingerly rolling his shoulder.

'Better not have done a bloody ACL,' he muttered.

Clement's phone rang. Louise. He ignored it and told himself he would call back later.

The woman who had been driving the car involved in the collision was still in her seat behind the wheel. 'I checked. He came out of nowhere,' she said.

'I know. We're your witnesses,' said Clement. 'But you'll still need to blow into the whistle.'

'Really?' She looked worried. Di Rivi was heading over with a fresh kit. Again Clement was impressed by her foresight.

'Have you been drinking?' he asked as he pulled away the buckled bicycle that was pressing against the driver side of the Hyundai. Underneath it was a satchel. He carefully picked it out.

'One glass. I was just going to get some milk.'

Clement felt sorry for her. The car had sustained damage. 'You insured?'

'Third party only,' she said.

Di Rivi asked her to blow into the whistle. A few people had begun to emerge from houses like rock crabs at low tide. Josh Shepherd had headed off to get his car. Graeme Earle remained with Turner and patted him down.

'Inspector,' he called over.

Clement looked up to see a fat roll of cash in Earle's hand. Then he opened the satchel: phones, cameras, some jewellery. Di Rivi sidled over to him and discretely showed him the reading from the woman driver. It was a tad over the limit. He felt like his shoulders were being weighed down a brick at a time. Normally he could turn a blind eye, advise her to park her car and go walk for her milk.

'You'll have to book her,' he whispered to di Rivi. 'Take my car.'

Shepherd arrived back with his vehicle. Clement had one ear on di Rivi as he called out to the cuffed suspect.

'We're taking you back to the station, Sidney. First though, hospital, have you checked out.'

'I'm fine. I don't need hospital. You got the wrong guy. She's the one you oughta arrest.'

'Well, we'll discuss that later.' With a jerk of the head he indicated Shepherd should take him away.

'I'm the one needs to get checked out,' mumbled Shepherd to Graeme Earle as he placed Turner in the car.

...

'Sidney is a good boy. That bag probably isn't even his.'

He guessed Olive Pickering was in her late sixties. She stood with her arms folded in front of a rich, dark-wood dresser topped with a cluster of photos. Several showed her with a beaming young Sidney in his school uniform. The pride burst from her as much as from him. Another black and white photo from around the late '60s or early '70s showed two young Indigenous women in check blouses smiling shyly at the camera. Clement thought one looked like a much slimmer Olive and guessed the other might be Sidney's grandmother, her sister. There was not a single photo that showed any man who may have been a husband. The house reminded Clement of that of his widowed aunt Patricia. Her husband had died when Clement was so young he could not even remember meeting him. Unlike Aunty Patricia, who unfathomably did not keep a pet despite what must have been a lonely existence, Olive clearly had some four-legged company. A pet bowl sat on the floor. Beside it, stacked high, were seven or eight large bags of unopened pet biscuits. Along a wall was a small sewing table on which resided an old Singer machine. A pattern had been left open and a little purple thread flecked its base as if there hadn't yet been time to sweep it away.

'Would you mind if Detective Earle checked over Sidney's bedroom?'

'I don't mind. You won't find anything.'

She indicated a room towards the back of the small house. Earle put on gloves and aimed for it. Clement came as far as the threshold and looked in. Sidney Turner's bedroom was surprisingly neat. Well, perhaps not that surprising when you considered the rest of the house. The single bed was made perfectly. It smelled fresh too.

'You sew?' he offered, by way of making conversation. Olive Pickering stayed at his shoulder where she could make sure Earle wasn't planting anything.

'Worked for nearly thirty years for Mr Jeffrey.'

The tailor. Clement saw him now, as he had when he was ten or eleven, outside looking in through a plate glass window – stooped over his counter, lean, balding, impeccably dressed even in this climate.

'Always wore a bow tie.' He was remembering aloud as he pictured him.

Olive looked at him curiously. 'You from around here? I don't remember you.'

'My family had the caravan park.'

'Ah,' she said and nodded sagely as if she had already made some unspoken judgement on him. Her eye flicked back to check on Earle.

'What became of him?' Clement wasn't just making conversation now. He was curious. The man had been background to his everyday life as a kid for three or four years but then one day he was gone. He hadn't spared him a thought for a generation.

'He retired, died.'

Clement was appalled by the impermanence of life, not so much life itself – with the job he worked, that was a given – but our place in other people's perceptions of it. The hunched elderly gentleman in the bow tie, a man of a different era, odd, comical to the young Clement listening to Prince on a Sony Walkman, had yet still been part of the fabric of his life. The tailor probably had a wife, children, dreams, secrets, but now perhaps only Olive Pickering was there to vouch that he was no figment of a schoolboy's imagination.

'I was fifteen when I started sewing for him,' she said. 'The nuns taught me.'

She offered no more insight into whether he had been fair, tyrannical, finicky – though one almost naturally assumed a tailor would be. Clement tried to picture the location of the old shop.

'What's there now?' he asked.

'Hairdresser,' Olive Pickering said.

Clement thought there was some insight into modern humanity in that: men no longer cared about their appearance but women still took trouble with their hair.

Olive Pickering proved to be right about finding nothing in the bedroom. Clement guessed that whatever way Sidney was ingesting ice, he was doing it off premises. Earle was as careful as he could be in returning the room to its previous state but Olive still made a show of neatening it all up. They found nothing in the lounge room. Clement did not wish to insult Mrs Pickering by asking to check her bedroom.

...

As it was, there was plenty of evidence against Sidney in the satchel. Clement stared at it now on the long desk in the squad room, spread out in plastic evidence bags: seven phones minus sim cards, four cameras, a watch, several pieces of jewellery, fifty-six ecstasy tablets, a big pouch of pot. Turner had been carrying five hundred and sixty dollars in cash. Given he'd had no job since returning to Broome, it was a fair guess that this money had come from wallets which had then been tossed away. The woman driver had been charged and di Rivi had driven her home. Turner had been interviewed but was now claiming he'd found the bag. His attempted escape, he claimed, was just a reaction to being freaked out by the big guy – Josh Shepherd – yelling at him. Clement had tried to get Turner to implicate Mongoose but Turner was sticking to his guns.

'Nearly five dozen eccies. We can charge you with dealing. Are you working for Mongoose? He gives you crystal in return?'

'I told you, I found the bag. I don't do drugs.' His body language said otherwise. Lack of the drug was already starting to bite.

'This might be the best thing for you, Sidney, a chance to get off it.'

The boy looked at him, guilty, knowing it. 'I found the bag. I'm not saying any more.'

They'd locked him up. There would be a bail hearing in the morning. Clement had determined Shepherd should handle it all himself, give him some responsibility. He'd sent him off to brief the police prosecutor.

'He's a flight risk so we have to oppose bail but there's no indication he's violent. Make sure he's checked regularly through the night.'

...

It was now close to 5.00 pm. Earle was busy writing up the report on the arrest when Scott Risely walked through the door with an older man who seemed familiar.

'Good stuff on getting the B&E guy. This is Richard Lane. He's working privately for the Feisters. I assured him he would have full cooperation. I'll leave you guys to chat, bring each other up to date. And see you tonight.'

Clement extended his hand to Snowy Lane, that's the name he remembered him by now. No wonder he seemed familiar. Snowy Lane had cracked the Mr Gruesome case. The guy's handshake was like Iron Man's.

'Afternoon, Inspector.'

Lane obviously didn't recognise him. Clement considered mentioning an earlier crossing of paths but quickly expunged that thought. It would probably be embarrassing to bring it up. Snowy Lane had been a legend at one time long ago and he didn't want to highlight a failure.

'You like a tea or coffee?'

Lane waved that off. 'I'll have a beer when I get back to the hotel.'

Clement pulled up one of the plastic chairs for him and they sat facing one another with the long squad table on one side. Clement cleared a space among the exhibits for Lane to place the folder he was carrying.

'We had a successful afternoon,' he explained.

Lane studied the haul but didn't say anything. Clement felt obliged to make some light conversation before business.

'Where are you staying?'

'The Mimosa.'

Of course that's where he'd be staying if Feister was footing the bill.

'When did you get in?'

'Couple of hours ago. Drove up from Hedland.'

That did for niceties.

'I'm sure the Super filled you in: we've put the word around to all our people and Fisheries, Parks et cetera. We've had two flights a day checking a radius from Sandfire, which we've gradually expanded, and I've sent a memo to all the mining companies who fly over the area to be vigilant.'

Lane nodded with each of these steps as if offering approval. Clement didn't care if he approved or not. He felt no ill will towards the man who had helped solve one of the biggest cases in Perth criminal history. In fact he respected him. However, that was many moons past. Good luck to Lane for landing Feister as a client but he didn't need the guy reviewing him. Lane seemed to study the tabletop again, then shook that off and turned back to him.

'You were the one who collected the Sandfire footage?'

'Yeah. You've seen it?'

Lane had. 'The family are concerned about the boyfriend. I don't know about you but I didn't see anything that suggested there was any problem between them.'

'Same.'

Lane sighed, scratched his eyebrow. 'It may be nothing. The girl has done this before but ...'

Clement completed the thought: '... she was carrying a large sum of money and it's odd we haven't found any sign of her.'

'Yes.'

They sat in silence for a few seconds. Lane broke it. 'I've been told there's been no recent abductions, murders, carjackings up this way.'

'It's not North Queensland.'

'I don't know. I heard you had a few bodies here a year or so ago.' He winked.

Clement didn't want to like the fellow, he just wanted a neutral professional relationship, but there was some force of life about him that was oddly compelling. Still, he resisted the overture for camaraderie.

'We've got an Aboriginal aid, Jared Taylor, works with us. He knows every crevice, every creek and probably the nickname of every bloody goanna from here to Kununurra. I've been waiting to send him up the Gibb River Road but he's had a family death up Beagle Bay. He's due back tomorrow.'

Graeme Earle sidled up with his jacket slung over his shoulder. 'Finished. See you tomorrow.'

Earle acknowledged Snowy Lane and took his leave. Mal Gross had already handed over to the evening shift and left.

Clement said, 'You got any thoughts on how you might proceed?'

'I'm going to ask in shops, show the photos ...'

'There was no sign of the car on any CCTV.'

'The car might have carked it. They cadge a lift ...' Not for the first time Lane left his thought dangling for Clement to nibble on. Clement had to concede the possibility and was annoyed he had not seen it himself.

Lane was continuing. 'It's not much to go on but they had mentioned heading to Broome. Now, whether they just meant the general direction or the town, who knows? Perhaps they had a specific reason to travel here, meet somebody, say. I'd like to rule that out. Besides, I might meet somebody else fresh into town who just had a barbie with them at Fitzroy Crossing or wherever. I'll do the pubs tonight. Coffee shops, supermarket, chemist tomorrow. Doubt I'll need to check real-estate agents or hairdressers.'

Lane's thoroughness told Clement he'd not been taking the whole thing seriously enough. The thief, the wedding, Louise, had all been blurring focus.

'I've got dinner with the boss tonight, otherwise I'd be glad to come with you.'

Lane waved the offer away. 'Appreciated, but sometimes it's better not to be a cop or even around one.'

Lane stood to leave. Clement reminded him he was welcome to call him if anything turned up and handed him a card.

...

By the time Snowy Lane walked out the building it was close to 6.00. There was still time for a quick call to Louise. But that's what it would be, quick and cursory. Clement needed to get home and shower. And he couldn't get Marilyn out of his mind; like a shape that had appeared on the perimeter while he'd drawn sentry duty, he wanted to get closer, get a better look. Was she waiting for him to challenge her assertion they didn't have a future together?

He found himself in the car heading away from the station without remembering the steps in between. Idly he studied faces as he cruised by, Snowy Lane's hypothesis playing in the background. Could Feister and Coldwell have driven to meet somebody specific and then met foul play? If that were the case, the best chance would lie in finding that vehicle. He drove to the wharf and parked in front of the chandler. Would a text be enough? Show he hadn't completely forgotten Louise? Or was that the coward's way out? He sat in the hot car and hit the phone keys. **Sorry missed you. Flat out. Dinner with boss. Call tomorrow.** He stopped. A whole new problem had loomed out of the ocean Moby Dick–like. You can't put 'love', he told himself, but you put nothing and it seems curt doesn't it? He found a solution by scrubbing out **Call tomorrow** and replacing it with **Looking forward to catching up tomorrow**.

He got out of the car feeling sticky and climbed the stairs.

...

Sometimes when you spend several hours on a boat you get off and the earth feels like it is swaying. That's how I felt after I left the police station. Not literally. I mean I hadn't been on a boat for a start but things didn't seem quite as they should. The reason was mental not physical. One of the worst things you find as you get older is that, whereas a few years earlier you would have an answer at your fingertips with the merest hint of a question, now you knew you knew the answer but couldn't find it. It was shoved down the back of your memory, crumpled and hidden. There was something I'd heard or seen when Clement had been talking to me that should have grabbed me like a high-kick long-legged chorus line but it might as well have been the featureless Great Northern Highway I'd stared at for the last day or so. Was it something about the Feister girl? Not exactly. Something else. It was pointless to waste time on it, it would bob up eventually. Meantime I had questions to ask. The burger I'd eaten at the roadhouse was still sitting heavy in my gut so while I should have been dying for some fine food, I wasn't. The cops had already done the rounds at the Mimosa Resort and other pubs, asking if they had seen Ingrid or the boyfriend, but I figured there was no harm trying again. Like I'd told Clement, sometimes people won't talk to a cop, especially if they've been with those you were asking about, smoking weed, or shooting up or whatever. Starting at the Mimosa, fuelled by a welcome mid-strength beer, I worked my way around Broome showing pictures of Ingrid, Coldwell and their car without uncovering any definite leads. A couple from Queensland thought the car looked familiar from two days earlier on the Gibb River Road. A pretty girl from France believed Ingrid might have been at the airport. I made notes. At the Cleopatra Tavern, I got the same negative response but on the flipside there was a poster advertising sExcitation for the following Monday. I'd meant to try and track them down but had put that on hold after I couldn't locate any website of that name. The poster indicated a Facebook page. Despite Tash's continuous urging, I wasn't on Facebook myself – hey, I'd stubbornly resisted flares too when they were the rage and believe me there was no regret – but it was proving to be a useful investigative tool.

By 11.30 that night I was back in my unit at the Mimosa. It was a perfect night, with a cool breeze blowing from the ocean but not strong enough to clear the scent of the surrounding gardens. I ran through Facebook and located the page for sExcitation. According to their schedule, they were in Tom Price tonight and, as the poster had suggested, Derby Saturday, then Broome the following Monday. I didn't expect to get anything from them but, having come this far, I was going to tie up every possible lead. After messaging sExcitation, pretending I was interested in hiring them, I sat back with time on my hands. For once my timing meshed with Barcelona. It would be late afternoon. I pushed my IT skills to the limit, logged on to the Mimosa internet and checked Skype. It said Tash was online so I gave it a go. I sat listening to my modem or whatever it was calling across vast oceans and was given to thinking that each ring was a modern day pebble thrown against Juliet's window. I was old enough to remember television before satellite, cricket on a radio wave, the FA Cup, something for the morning paper's late news on a back page in pink ink; and while I'd been mightily impressed when it became reality that we could sit in our lounge chairs and watch live the first ball of a Lord's Test as it hit the infamous ridge, or a Gunner netting at Wembley, nothing was quite so impressive as this: staring into the eyes of the object of my affection who was on the other side of the world. That the mundanity of our conversation – the reference to weather, the furnishings of the rooms we found ourselves in, the checklist of tourist highlights – fell so far short of the beauty of the technology and the perseverance of the human spirit that had allowed it was a shame but not a disaster. After all, people had wandered past Van Gogh's paintings without blinking and no doubt propped themselves against David for a quick slash after too much vino and some ducal hijinks. Most of us are unable to elevate ourselves to the plane on which reside the greatest achievements of our peers. That's what makes us human. But all of us yobbos, no matter how emotionally inarticulate, are grateful for anything that helps us see, hear, draw closer to, our distant loved ones.

Unfortunately Grace was off having coffee with a friend. Nothing Tash or I said to one another impacted any aspect of the world in the slightest, and yet the simple joy of talking to her coursed through me. One day maybe we'll be able to skype the dead and I'm sure we'll have the same inane conversations. I doubt we'll be sitting around waiting for wisdom on how to make the world a better place, how to save the planet from greed or plague. I reckon we'll just gaze into the eyes of our departed loved ones and chat about the weather and ask if plants are blooming and what we've been eating.

After fifteen minutes, we'd said all we could. Tash kissed the screen and I was a young man again.

I pottered for another twenty minutes writing up a report and emailing it to Dee Vee. Just after midnight I switched off the computer and the lights and went to bed where I tossed and turned for another fifteen minutes. Then I got up and peed because that's what men do post fifty-five. I slipped outside for a minute and gazed up at a million timeless stars that looked like they'd been hurled from a bucket and stuck. With the smell of fresh salt air in my nostrils I slipped back under the sheets and gave myself to sleep.

...

I ate breakfast like a Viking. Well, there was space in there. I'd fasted since yesterday's lunch but there's something about eating under a clear blue sky off a big white plate, with cutlery heavy enough to anchor a tinny in a cyclone, that increases appetite. The bacon and perfectly cooked eggs lasted less time than an Italian parliament. I never swim straight off after eating; however, the breakfast hadn't even registered in my stomach and with unusual foresight I'd packed my bathers, though to be honest I assumed I'd be swimming in chlorine. But here I felt an irresistible pull.

I'll just go for a look, I told myself.

Within a few minutes I was on Cable Beach standing on a cape of white sand that stretched endlessly to my left and right. Ahead was a sheet of Indian Ocean, flat as a spirit level. The waves were too polite to lap, they softly hushed. A couple of people in the water about two hundred metres north were having a dip, otherwise it was deserted. If I hadn't checked and rechecked it was safe from box jellyfish this time of the year, I would have thought that was the cause. Reason told me there'd be no great whites up here, didn't mean there weren't other sharks, crocs even. If I was ever to swim in the ocean again though, this had to be it. I had my budgies on under my shorts. I dropped them and my cotton shirt, a birthday present from the girls, and walked towards sea. I was not scared, on the contrary, as I eased myself into the water I felt an amazing privilege, and a sense of awe. Maybe this was how monarchs feel when they are anointed. This was my cathedral and I was the chosen one, inducted into a line of the specially blessed in a place that suggested a Power infinitely greater than me. I crouched down so the chill water reached over my shoulders to my chin. I could hear the frenzied shouts from the day Craig Drummond had perished, as clear in my head as if a soundtrack was playing. I had no vision of Craig like you might see in a movie, no flashback but – and I know this sounds like a cliché – I sensed him with me. I began to swim and any fear or residual tension left me. My body was out of practice, the muscles not too bad but my breathing slightly shallow. For maybe twenty minutes I swam parallel to the shore, and with each stroke I became more comfortable. I floated a few minutes on my bed and thanked Craig, and then I swam back to the shore and walked back along wet sand to where my shirt declared itself on an otherwise snow-white backdrop. I'd not brought a towel but by the time I walked back to the car I'd pretty well dried. I put on my shirt and brushed the sand from my feet, whole again.

After I'd showered, I redressed and began hunting through the town, again proffering the photos of Ingrid Feister and Max Coldwell. After ninety minutes I had nothing to show. Maybe it was the earlier reminiscence of Craig Drummond that did the trick, I don't know, but as I passed by the little watchmaker jeweller on the way to the chemist, something slapped my consciousness. I stood staring through the window at the rings, necklaces and watches, and I knew what it was that I'd seen without seeing at the police station last night. In one of the evidence bags on the long table had been a bluebird pendant. I should have recognised it straight away. I'd stared at that damn thing day after day, night after night, for months. It didn't look like a bluebird really, more like a flying swallow, and that was why I knew it was the one-off piece designed and sold by a small London jeweller in 1989 to a visiting Australian businessman looking for a gift to his daughter. That daughter was Jessica Scanlan and she had been wearing it nearly twenty years ago when she'd gone missing.

CHAPTER 16

'Is Jared back yet?'

Clement's bark was like a handful of chips thrown to a bunch of seagulls, not meant for any one in particular, but everybody automatically looked to Mal Gross, the only person who had any idea of rosters, car pool, the comings and goings of personnel.

'I can check.' Something in the sergeant's manner transmitted to Clement he needed to dial back the aggro.

'Wasn't he due back today?' Clement made a concerted effort to rein in his irritability. He should never have indulged in that last bottle of red with Risely.

Gross said, 'Due back in town but he's not rostered on till tomorrow.'

'Oh. Can you check anyway?' Clement wanted to get Jared Taylor started on the Feister disappearance as soon as possible. He beat a retreat to his office, safer there. It wasn't their fault his ex-wife had placed him in this situation. He'd answered honestly, albeit spitefully, that she shouldn't marry Brian. His encounter with her had tainted everything. He would surely have called Louise by now except for Marilyn ambushing him like that. It had thrown him completely. The obvious conclusion was she was having second thoughts, realised she would never have with Brian what they'd had together. Yet the reality was she had divorced him and then reiterated they had no future. So now he was what – some best-friend sounding board? He checked the time: 11.45. He'd wait half an hour then call Louise as promised. He rang Bill Seratono to soak up a few minutes.

'Any luck on that car and couple?'

'Nothing yet. I got the word out. I'll let you know if anything comes back. You want to meet up tonight after work?'

'I'm in the middle of stuff. I'll buzz you if I'm free.'

'What about the girl? How's that going?'

'Slowly. Call me if you hear anything.'

He hung up. There was a knock on his already open door. He expected Mal Gross but it was Meg the civilian receptionist.

'There's a Richard Lane says he needs to see you urgently.'

He must have turned something up on Ingrid Feister, thought Clement, and told Meg to bring him through. He was not really hungover, not with a headache anyway, but too much wine and not enough water made him feel like there was a smudge across his medulla. Risely had been good company, his wife Chantelle pleasant. They had talked little or no work apart from some old-case glory days but the bottom line was he had overindulged.

Meg pointed Snowy Lane into the office and withdrew. Clement had caught sight of some TAB tickets in her handbag on more than one occasion, so he suspected a closet gambler but Meg did not mingle with the rest of them.

'That bluebird pendant ... you still have it?'

The words punched out of Lane like desperate men bursting from their prison transport. Clement was completely lost. Lane gave him no chance to seek clarification.

'It was on the long table yesterday, part of the bust you did.'

Clement might have been oriented towards the finish line but the blindfold was still firmly in place.

'The evidence bags you mean? I don't remember any bluebird.'

'It doesn't look like a bluebird. Have you got the evidence bags? I'll explain.'

Clement reluctantly got up and poked his head out. Josh Shepherd was on a computer on the far side of the room.

'Josh, where did you put the evidence from the Turner case?'

'Current Court Cases.'

Clement moved to the rear of the building, leaving carpet for concrete. He felt Lane at his shoulder. A narrow corridor led to a locked evidence room protected by a key-code pad.

'You need to wait here.' Clement punched in the code.

Lane said, 'It's a sleek piece of silver, looks almost like a plane, sapphire for the eye.'

Clement switched on the light in the hangar-like room of steel shelves.

At the back of the room was a larger area for bulky pieces of evidence. There were three small safes and a firearms cabinet. The drugs would have been tagged and locked in one of the safes but he surmised Shepherd would have left the other pieces together in a simple box. He located it correctly marked, and sorted through the plastic bags till he found the pendant. Only now did he notice the chain seemed to be broken. He signed the book, recording the time. Lane was waiting for him on the threshold, in hyper-drive, his eyes wide and alive, his body craning in though his feet remained where they should.

Clement held the plastic bag up to Lane who studied it a long moment then almost whispered, 'That's it.'

'That's what?'

'That's the pendant Jessica Scanlan was wearing when she disappeared in Claremont, August, two thousand. It was not found on her body.'

Lane did not need to explain who Jessica Scanlan was. Every cop in WA had the names of the three girls who had disappeared near Autostrada nightclub burned into his or her brain. But now Clement was angry he'd indulged Lane. The guy had been tangentially involved in the investigation and had clearly become obsessed, probably trying to find a way to skate back under the limelight. Well, Clement wasn't going to be used for Lane's agenda.

'You don't remember this, but I shared a lift with you back when George Tacich was running the case. You came in with some big theories and wasted the task force's time. George Tacich got rolled. Ian Bontillo did it.'

Lane absorbed the hit without flinching. 'The case is still officially open.'

Clement knew that was a sop to public sentiment. Tregilgas who had replaced Tacich had won his way to commissioner on the back of that case; it was never going to be overturned.

'Bontillo killed himself. There've been no repeats.'

'That you know of.'

Clement sidestepped the barb, swapped insult for logic. 'There could be a hundred of these.' He shook the evidence bag a little for emphasis.

'There's only one.'

Lane pulled out a sheet of A4 on which was printed an old press report with a photo blown up, showing the pendant. The piece was identical.

'One?' Clement had no recollection of that detail.

'One-off designer piece sold by Emerson's of Piccadilly to Jessica's dad. Listen, even if it was Bontillo, you don't know if he had an accomplice. We trace this, we can tie the case up officially. We might even be able to find those girls' bodies. You imagine what it's like for their parents?'

Clement could. Phoebe was his life. He had no time to feel embarrassed that he'd slighted Lane, his cop's brain was busy running the implications.

'Sidney Turner's too young to have been involved in any way. But he is a thief.'

Snowy Lane was already there, waiting with the next question. 'So who did he steal it from?'

...

The old Broome Regional Prison was supposed to be closed down, but reality had set in and it was now used for remand for prisoners pending court cases. As prisons went, it didn't look the worst from the outside: single level, well-tended garden, open design. Clement drove to the prison faster than he should have. Lane had infected him with the same fever: putting a full stop to the Autostrada case was the Holy Grail of criminal investigation in this state. More importantly it would give the parents closure. Unless somebody had copied the design of the pendant for some unfathomable reason, this was a huge breakthrough. At the gate, Clement explained who he was and was told to drive to reception. He threw a look at Lane whose eyes were far away. The drive was short. He parked and they climbed out of the car. Somewhere a bird warbled. It had the stillness and quiet of a hospital. Clement addressed another intercom that was on a short pole in front of a porch area. A female voice told them to advance to the door where they would be met. A female prison officer, with a pleasant face and curly blonde hair, was waiting on the other side of the glass door. Clement had met her before but for the life of him could not remember her name: Barbara? The door slid back and they stepped into a cool area that offered a water fountain and a coffee table with some very old magazines, in front of a well-used but still firm sofa.

'Afternoon, Inspector.' The woman prison employee turned her smile from Clement to Snowy Lane to show he was included. A male officer remained behind a desk. Clement thought he had the look of a man who led a greyhound to its starting box: smoker, drinker, slightly undernourished because he gambled money that should have gone to food.

'How can we help, Inspector?' asked the woman. Clement was becoming more convinced her name was Barbara.

'A remand prisoner we brought in yesterday, Sidney Turner. I'd like to see him.'

The woman looked unsure and glanced across to the male officer for support.

'He's gone,' said the male officer. 'He got bail.'

...

It had been like having a dog barking outside your door for fifteen years. Now, finally, a chance for peace. And these bozos cock it up. I got the gist as we hurtled out of there towards Turner's house. Clement called his constable and had him phone the prosecutor, a cop. The prosecutor said the aunt had hired a defence lawyer who had asked for bail. The prosecutor had said the boy was a flight risk, the aunt had said via her lawyer that she believed he would not flee and was prepared to bet her house on it. The magistrate was a member of the boy's former hockey club and remembered him as a good young man. He also noted the boy had been injured by a DUI driver the day before and thought prison might not be the best place for him. He set bail at a hundred grand. The aunt stumped it up. The prosecutor hadn't had time to communicate this to Clement and his team because he was overloaded and onto the next case. A perfect storm. I wasn't panicking yet. Maybe the boy wouldn't run anyway, maybe the aunt was right. It was less than two hours ago, so chances were he wouldn't get far. I had no doubt this kid had stolen the pendant. All we needed off him was to find out where. The sense I'd had while in the ocean of Craig Drummond's presence hit me afresh. I'm not sure if I fit the mould of a spiritual guy; I go to church Christmas, and the crowds seem pretty strong. I'd rather believe in God than not, but the older I got the more certain I was that there was something bigger than me, bigger than what you could see or hold in your hand, something formless and inexplicable that connected all of us from the caveman down, something that every now and again we could detect, as if a beam set off something deep in our DNA. And that's what I felt now, like I had some part to play still, like I'd been given a second chance. I dare not waste it.

CHAPTER 17

He couldn't believe he was back at Aunty's house. He thought that was it, he was going inside, and it scared him bad. He had been stupid to think being fast was enough. Sooner or later they were going to get you. He was so lucky to have Aunty. It was only bail though. He'd have to go court and they'd find him guilty and he would go to prison. That wasn't so bad was it? They'd get him off the crystal. He could come back here, live with Aunty, play hockey again. They had been the happiest times of his life. To know you're good at something, that was cool. His mates, they all played footy. Not that he was bad at footy but he was light and he couldn't kick so well when he was at full speed, but then he found hockey, that was his game. The coaches said he could play state.

He should never have gone to the city.

Darren had mocked him: 'Hockey? That's a girls' game, dude.'

That first time he didn't even know what was happening. Darren just came out the shop, shoved a bag at him and told him to run. The store security guards had no chance. They couldn't bust Darren because when they searched him he had nothing on him. Darren was too smart to let the camera catch him. Then Darren stole that car and it all turned to shit. Trying to impress that skinny girl, Jasmine. She was cute though. He was pretty sure she'd been flirting with him but what could he do? Darren would have beaten the crap out of him like he did that time he had to ditch the bag and jump the fence to get away. Like it was his fault. So, he would go to jail and do his time. He had no choice. They'd caught him cold. It was prison, for sure.

Unless he ran.

But no, he wouldn't do that. He promised Aunty. Trouble was, he recognised one of Mongoose's men in the court. He didn't know his name but he was one of the close ones he'd seen at the house sometimes. Maybe he was there to pay a fine or something? Or maybe not. Maybe Mongoose had sent him to check him out.

He couldn't relax. He'd sit for a second on the bed and then jump straight up again. He wished Aunty hadn't gone off but she said she had to do things with the lawyer. She was a good sort, the lawyer. Once they got him inside though, she wouldn't be able to help him. No one could. He hadn't talked. He'd kept Mongoose out of it. But what was to stop Mongoose wanting to make sure he stayed silent?

He couldn't think clear. If only he could have a hit, just a little one, clear his head. No one was going to stake him but. Not now. Shit, shit, shit. He didn't even have those pingers. The house felt so small. He was pacing from one side to the other and back. Like that cocky in a cage they used to have at the club: the 'hockey cocky'. Could it still be alive? Damn thing gave his finger a real good ...

The rumble of a car outside pulled him up. Mongoose had a Subaru sounded just like that. He couldn't see anything from in here. The windows were at the side of the house. Even if he opened the front door, he might not see anything because Aunty's little driveway had trees and bushes hiding it so you couldn't see out to the street. If the car drove straight in, then you could see it. The car was still rumbling. What to do? He edged to the front door and opened it a crack, peering out. Nothing in the driveway.

The rumble stopped. His heart kicked in. He could imagine Mongoose climbing out with a cricket bat. Please come back, Aunty. He shut the door. His eyes travelled to the phone. The police? No, because then he'd have to say why he called them and once he mentioned Mongoose they wouldn't let up. Maybe it wasn't Mongoose, maybe it was some other car. Plenty of cars rumbled, not just Mongoose's. What he could do was sneak out the back, go over the back fence through the property behind, walk down Axton Street, turn down Morris Street, back down the other side and look at the car from the corner. If it wasn't Mongoose, he could come back inside and relax. If it was he could hide till Aunty came back. That's what he'd do.

He grabbed five bucks from Aunty's drawer, just enough to buy himself a milkshake or something. He put on thongs and cracked open the back door. He looked left and right. Clear. He ran quickly and lightly up the backyard, his thongs flipping against his heels. He vaulted the picket fence easily into the property behind, crossed through sand and bush that did for a backyard and ran up the path that ran along the side of the house. Inside a dog barked but that was okay, he was on Axton Street in a flash, jogging to the corner and then turning down Morris Street. There were a couple of cars parked on the street but he couldn't see anybody. He slowed as he got to the corner of Aunty's street. Fortunately a big old wattle tree provided good cover. He edged under it and looked to the left.

Shit, shit, shit. He could see the back of the car parked about fifty metres down blocking Aunty's driveway: Subaru. Shit. Nothing for it but to get lost for a few hours. Maybe he could find the lawyer's office? She might even buy him a hot chocolate. He turned to head back. The shape of something so close it was a blur leapt out at his head. Whack, the blow stunned him, he felt himself drop. Words hung just out of reach. He felt a hand on his shoulder, but it was weird ... it was a rubber hand ... and then something pricked his neck.

'What the fuck?' He thought he said it aloud. 'Mongoose, please ...'

He tried to locate him but there was wattle in his eyes and nose and when he looked up the sun was so bright it was like a stick in your eye. 'Man,' he gasped, trying to stand but his legs were rubber. He felt weird, clammy, everything turned to film negative ...

CHAPTER 18

As we swung into the street, a Subaru passed us coming the other way. At the time I didn't think much of it. We parked on the opposite side of the road, got out and walked across to a driveway that was narrowed by thick old trees on both sides. Don't ask me what kind of trees they were, botany was of as much interest to me as a bus timetable. The narrow dirt driveway looked rarely used. Certainly there was no car in it now as we approached what some people would call a quaint weatherboard. A tabby cat watched us from the porch near the front door but scrammed when we got close.

'Does she have a car?' I asked. It was the first thing either of us had said for minutes.

'I don't think so. There wasn't one here last time.'

I followed Clement up three low steps to the porch and Clement pushed the bell. Nothing sounded inside, so he knocked. When a repeat knocking brought no response, Clement offered the obvious.

'They must be out.' He pulled out a card and wrote a note on it to contact him. 'I've got everybody out looking for them. His aunt's not going to let him skip.'

I had the impression he was attempting to reassure himself as much as me.

...

Never take anything for granted. That's been a maxim of mine my whole detective life. If I needed reminding of it, which I didn't, I learned it again in spades. We were back at the police station.

More than an hour had passed and there was no sign of the aunt or Sidney Turner. Broome is not that big a place you can be out on a street for an hour without the police spying you. If they were here, they were indoors somewhere. The supermarkets had already been checked. I sat on an office chair, my fear growing as inexorably as the nation's debt. Clement was across the room talking to an attractive young woman in civilian garb, a navy cotton dress, sandals. I saw him hand her the evidence bag with the pendant. She went off with it down the corridor. He walked back to me.

'Lisa Keeble, our head tech. She's good. Chances of fingerprints aren't great but you never know.'

I'd had time to ruminate on Turner and his great-aunt. 'It's possible they're talking to his lawyer,' I said. Clement made a call to find out who the lawyer was. Whatever he heard turned his face flat and white as an envelope.

'What is it?' I asked but he ignored me, dialled and walked off by himself on the phone. I sat there for five minutes. It felt like fifty. Clement returned. His colour had improved to pastel.

'The aunt is with the lawyer. She's just leaving. She says she left Turner home by himself. We're collecting her.'

The lawyer's offices were five minutes away. They were waiting out the front, the elderly Aboriginal woman and the lawyer who reminded me of Natasha ten years ago, poised, the looks of a newsreader. The body language between her and Clement was easy to translate. If they hadn't shared a bed they'd thought about it plenty. It was going to gall him, I thought. He'll be trying not to let it get to him, that she got the kid bail and he's a flight risk. Maybe he wouldn't have cared that much before, but he was involved now, like me, I smelled it on him. Nearly twenty years of desert on Autostrada and then you come across a well, sweet water, enough perhaps to get you all the way home. The kid could have slipped out for a minute. He might have been scared to open the door thinking he was going to be arrested again. It really didn't matter so long as he was at home.

...

He wasn't.

The back door was open and nearly fifty dollars was still in a drawer. The aunt said that was almost everything that had been there, maybe a little loose change, under ten bucks. She still believed in the kid. She said he wouldn't run off and I could see she was genuinely worried. So was I.

On the off-chance, we cruised the surrounding streets but there was no sign of him. So we drove back to the house and were met by two other detectives: the solid guy with the beer gut, Earle, and the young guy who looked like he worked out while standing in front of a full-length mirror. There were two uniforms as well. Clement set them about doorknocking nearby houses while he got a list of names from the aunty – the kid's friends, people he hung around with. When he finished with the aunt, I sidled up to him.

'Funny he went out the back door,' I said. Clement, who looked like a golfer watching his drive curve towards the trees, didn't offer an opinion. I dressed up the implication. 'I mean, if he's just doing a runner why not head out the front? Unless he thought you had eyes on him.'

Clement gave me coal eyes. 'You're saying he slipped out the back because he was worried somebody was out the front.'

That accurately represented my position.

'When you picked him up he had a big bag of eccies on him and grass. I'm guessing he was dealing those to pay for his meth. He have any cash?'

'Five hundred and sixty dollars.'

'So, could be somebody is out of pocket. And maybe not happy about that.'

Clement thought it through for all of five seconds. Then he hauled the detective constable from his doorknock to join us and called out to his sergeant.

'Graeme, I'm heading to Mongoose's with Shepherd. You run this.'

The older guy nodded. I liked him, a kindred spirit. Somewhere in his past he'd taken back soft-drink bottles for the refund and foraged a golf course for balls to resell to happy hackers, using the cash for bubblegum footy cards. Clement was harder to get a bead on: intense, driven, maybe moody. I could imagine him furiously chopping wood by a Swedish lakehouse populated by sparse furniture, Lutheran in the original sense. I'd liked his thoroughness with the CCTV stuff but I guess I was still miffed I'd needed to convince him I wasn't an aged obsessive, raking over his last case. I didn't blame him, mind, it was a natural conclusion, but that doesn't mean I liked it.

'Shepherd, Snowy Lane.'

I was surprised he'd used that moniker to introduce me. It meant nothing to the young dude.

He was forced to add, 'He's a private D.'

We both made for the front passenger door. Shepherd reached it first but his swagger deflated when his boss told him to climb in the back. And that's how easy it was for me to start liking Clement again.

···

I don't know the geography of Broome well enough to describe where we were heading but it seemed to be away from the water. The street we turned into was wide with fewer trees than Turner's aunt's place. The front yards were mostly bare, the earth red-brown, though there were a few acacia trees dotted here and there, they're about the only brand I recognise. There was one house bigger than the others. It sported a long but narrow concrete veranda on which sat a few old chairs. Cars, mainly iridescent utes, dotted the driveway and front yard but it was stark, bare of trees or shrubs, with the absence of any feminine touch; a gang place if ever I'd seen one.

'His car's not here,' commented Shepherd from behind in a thin, cheap voice that could have been manufactured in Guangdong.

'What does he drive – Merc?' asked Clement as he parked in the driveway and killed the engine.

'Na, hotted-up Subaru.'

CHAPTER 19

Sidney Turner woke with the smell of dry dirt in his nostrils. Forcing open his eyes, he saw rotting wood and mudflat close up. He was on his right side. He went to push himself up off the ground but realised his hands were tied behind his back, and feet bound. Tilting his head as far as he could manage, his left eye detected a darkening blue sky. Late arvo? Somewhere in the near distance birds were screeching and chattering. His head felt like it had been kicked by a kangaroo. He split the smell of dirt and bush apart, zeroed in on a cloying odour of sap and wild honey mixed with something else ... still water. His muscles had melted. He had no strength. Where was he? Sleep still held him in a headlock but it was not normal sleep, this one made you dizzy and weak. The recent past came to him, not in a fluid stream but like one of those old black and white movies he'd seen on some show on Aunty's TV, movies that had no sound, and where the images came in jumps and jerks. He remembered looking through wattle, then turning and wham! Somebody had hit him from behind. Mongoose, must have been, must have suckered him. Got out of his car and been waiting, knowing he would come out of the back door.

Panic gripped him. In his balls was where he felt it most.

'Listen, man, I didn't tell the cops nothin'.'

His words were sucked into a maw of dead silence. What was happening? If it was around 5.00 now, he must have been out for hours. He was so thirsty. As his brain thawed, thoughts broke free in chunks and fear rose like so much mist, slowly forming into a solid shape, a knowledge: they were going to kill him and bury his body where it would never be found.

The adrenaline jolt helped him roll on his back. Insects buzzed around him.

'Mongoose?' Even though his throat was raw he called as loud as he could. He had to explain he hadn't talked. Beg for a chance to let Aunty pay off his debts.

Yet again his voice choked on itself. Maybe they'd gone somewhere thinking he was still out to it. Or it could be this was just a warning. A warning he didn't need. They'd dumped him in the bush. He'd have to find his way home. Now his brain was functioning better, he seemed to grow in physical strength too. He summoned his energy and tried a sit-up but couldn't hold it. As he dropped back down, this time to the left side, his eyes tracked a grey shape, log-like, spitting distance. He felt his bowels shift. His heart jumped to his throat. He couldn't breathe. Was it ...?

Using hip and shoulder but with the greatest care he was able to fractionally lift himself to confirm ...

Oh fuck.

Less than three metres from him, a big croc lay on the creek bank just the other side of a narrow strand of low bush. Sidney's bladder wanted to release but he did not dare. He barely dared draw breath. Had it not heard him, smelt him? Perhaps it had been preoccupied with the birds dotting trees like toilet paper chucked around by some naughty kid. He had to be so careful now. If he made a sound, the croc would come for him but he couldn't just lie there. The volume of birds' cries seemed to come in waves, he noticed. Scattered individual cries would start to congregate and then swell for a second or two in one big mass before breaking apart again. With great care Sidney drew his legs behind him. He waited until the cries reached peak volume, then using his arms in concert with his legs he pushed backwards, once, twice ... and then rested as the sound fell away. He fought to raise himself again but this time as he lifted, the croc, as if sensing him, swung its head around. He dropped into the earth, his heart thumping out of his chest. Please, please ... his muscles tensed, his ears primed for the sound of the croc's advance. He did not want to go that way, dragged into a creek by a crocodile, death-rolled till he drowned, stashed underwater and eaten in stages. The birds' cries were swelling again. They reached a crescendo. Did he dare? Closing his eyes, Sidney Turner pushed again, once, twice. He expected at any moment to be seized by jaws of iron. The painful throb in his head did not even register, for every other internal organ seemed to be fizzing, whizzing, clattering, clanging, thumping, pumping. The next time the birds' cries massed, he pushed again, once, twice, three times now, a worm slithering away through spiky grass. He followed his routine twice more before he started to feel some optimism.

For the first time he had driven himself back towards some proper trees, paperbark. He rolled onto his back and, wedging his flank and hip into the trunk, managed to sit up. He'd dragged himself maybe ten metres from his original position but the sun must have dropped, for the air was charcoal now and he couldn't be sure where the croc was. While the rope on his hands was tied tight, the rope around his ankles was much less so, and had been loosened during his wriggling escape. He tried rolling onto his back and rubbing his ankles against the trunk of the tree but all he did was scrape his legs with crumbling bark. However, by alternately stretching his legs, pulling ankles apart as far as he could, and trying to crisscross them, he began slowly lessening the tension, working a wider circle in the rope each time. Finally he was able to angle his right foot down and then slide it up through the hole. Once that was out he was able to stand, albeit shakily. He felt an incredible burst of joy in his body and, heedless of the sticks and thistle that poked into his bare feet, walked, or more accurately stumbled, from the creek to a distance he thought was safe. The rope around his left foot snagged and dragged so he stopped and used his right toe to further free up the rope until he was eventually able to drag it off his leg. By now dark had dropped. Once more the ache in his head and the dryness of his throat surfaced.

What to do? What to do? What to do?

Had Mongoose left him there by the creek hoping he would be taken? Or was that just a coincidence? If Mongoose knew there was a croc in the creek, why not toss him in? Shit. He wished he could think straight. If it was just a warning then maybe it was safe to try and get back home. But where was he? Before he could think anything through, he saw headlights appearing through the bush. It might be Mongoose coming to check on him, see if he was dead, and finish the job if not. Sidney began running fast, blindly through bush, the headlights bouncing with the car over uneven ground and threatening to expose him. He hit a bare patch of ground that allowed him to hit top speed. In a few seconds he would be safe in the thicket ahead. Just as he reached the very apex of his acceleration, something, a twisting tree root most likely, but something absolutely solid, dark, unseen, low down like a devil's fist, grabbed his ankle. He heard the snap and felt the rest of his body continue at an unnatural plane, so he spun in the air and flipped like a TV wrestler. With his hands behind his back he could not break his fall in any way. Instead of canvas, his head landed on hard rocky earth with a terrible thump.

...

Richie Laidlaw, everybody called him Richie Rich, stopped his truck and climbed out. He thought he'd seen a shape, running in the distance, probably a roo but he couldn't be sure. The police had asked all the Parks and Wildlife people to keep a special eye out for a white girl and her boyfriend driving a Landcruiser, and when he'd asked old Warry, who was camped a few k east cooking up a parrot for dinner, whether he'd seen anything unusual, he'd said earlier today he'd seen a car heading through the bush towards the waterhole. Bloody stupid he reckoned, everybody knew there was a croc down there, you could hear the birds going crazy. Warry hadn't seen the car coming out but admitted he might have been sleeping. He'd had a good nap. He wasn't sure how long ago it was he'd seen the car as he didn't eat lunch today and that usually helped with time. Maybe three or four hours he thought.

Richie Laidlaw stood totally still, listening to the rhythm of the breathing bush the way a mother listens to a sleeping child. It seemed as it should, undisturbed, normal. And yet, the ranger sensed something, some alien presence.

'Hello? Is there anybody there?' he called out loud and clear. He thought there was the faintest sound, a low one, like a gum groaning. He grabbed a flashlight and walked forward twenty metres calling out again, sweeping the torch left and right. He held his breath but this time he heard nothing. He waited in the same spot for nearly five minutes. A fluttering above made him shine the torch: black-shouldered kite.

He walked slowly back to the car and waited another ten minutes, listening in vain. He drove as close to the creek as he dared and shone his spotties. The water was dark as blood. He thought he could see a flattened area a metre or two from the bank that looked as if a croc might have lain there, probably after a lazy bird at sunset. The croc and whatever birds may have been there had since gone. Reluctantly he climbed back into the car making a note in his head to check in with Warry every couple of days. That old fella was almost as good as having twenty-four-hour CCTV. He slowed one final time where he thought he'd seen the roo and wound the windows down but again heard only the same sounds this bush had yielded up for a thousand years. He was hungry now. He had pasta back at the house. He bet a thousand years ago his ancestors would have killed for a microwave.

CHAPTER 20

'So where were you between when you left Sidney Turner's house and three-thirty-five pm when you returned?' Clement had not made up his mind whether he thought Mongoose Cole was lying in his claim that he had called in to see Sidney Turner but that nobody had answered the door. It was possible Turner had already fled, or fled when he heard or saw the distinctive car. Cole's suggestion that he had heard about Turner being in court and had gone over to offer him 'the support of a bro', he did not believe for a second.

'I just been drivin' round. Bought a chicken burger.'

That burger part was likely true. The car had smelled of it. Cole had allowed them a cursory check. No obvious blood, boot vacant but that didn't mean he hadn't used another vehicle.

'You didn't visit anybody?'

'Nope. Just drivin', listenin' to the iPod, chillin'.'

'We can check.'

'Course, you're the man.'

Graeme Earle shot a look over at Clement that suggested he would have given him a quick backhand for the insolence.

'Okay, Cole, you can go. Don't leave town.'

'If I hear anything, I'll let you know ... Officer.'

Clement asked Earle to show him out. When they had shuffled out of the interview room, Clement stopped the tape and sat there carving one big word out of the thick atmosphere: If. If he had spied the bluebird pendant like Lane had, they would be well on the way to knowing where it came from. If bloody Marilyn had let him be, he would not have ignored Louise, they'd have been in contact, she would have mentioned she was representing Turner, he could have anticipated he might get off, be a flight risk. Now he was stuck with the ugly possibility that Turner had been silenced. He'd left it to Mal Gross to chase up the list of associates the aunt had given him but none of them claimed to have seen Sidney. The doorknock had turned up no clues at all. Graeme Earle walked back in.

'What do you think?' Clement valued Earle's input. Earle had been a cop up here a lot longer than Clement, and you had to allow for regional differences in the way people acted, criminals, cops, everybody. What a crim might do in Perth might be very different.

'From what I've learned,' Earle said, 'Cole's a brutal bugger. Beat up one of his women dealers so bad she had to be hospitalised. If Turner had something big on him, he might have got rid of him.'

'Why not just beat him up? Turner hadn't told us anything.'

'You can't expect any kind of normal behaviour from these mutts. Each one is worse than the one before. Each one goes that bit further. It's like ice has pushed everything to the edge.'

This was true. Only two weeks ago a paramedic had been bashed by a meth addict wielding a metal bar. Two weeks before that there was the incident at the hospital.

'Could Cole be involved?'

This time Earle was deferring to his boss's expertise.

'With Autostrada? No.'

Cole was thirty-four. Technically he could have been old enough but Claremont was a world away from here, not just geographically. An Indigenous teenager would have stood out in white-bread Claremont. Cole's file said he'd grown up in Derby.

'Turner is a thief. Odds-on he nicked that pendant.'

'His last job was the motel.'

Clement was thinking the same thing. He made a decision. 'I want you and Shepherd to concentrate on locating Turner. For a start, go through every CCTV camera you can find and see if we can pick up Cole's car between eleven am and three-twenty-five. And get Cole's phones checked, and the aunt's. We need to know if Turner arranged with anybody to pick him up.'

'Turner might have had a mobile.'

'Everybody says he never had one.'

'Could have used a stolen one.'

That was a good point. He might have kept one or two phones back from any one of his thefts. They would be handy for covert meetings. It was no certainty that victims of his burglaries had cut off their phones, so many tourists, empty houses, they might not have even realised yet, thefts might be unreported.

'Go back over his known robberies, make sure all phones reported stolen have been found, double-check victims gave us details of all their stolen phones. And tell Mal we want to be informed of any report of any stolen phones in the last forty-eight hours, particularly today.'

'You?'

'I'm going to brief Lane. He can go through the motel people with me. I owe him.' He wondered if Earle would object, complain that he was stuck with hack work while a civilian was doing his job, but the big man just accepted it. 'Do what you can till, say, nine. If nothing breaks, go home and start first thing tomorrow.'

'What about Perth?'

A question already on Clement's mind: should he contact the hierarchy in Perth? Officially the Autostrada case was still open but the Commissioner considered he'd personally closed it. If he contacted Perth he ran the risk of interference, worse, media. It would be a nightmare; any chance to lay a trap would be blown. Ultimately it was Risely's call.

'I'll have a talk to the boss.'

'Josh?'

So far the only people in on the loop about the pendant find were Lane, Earle and Mal Gross. Keeble he'd asked to check for prints but without explanation. It reminded him he needed to follow up. He had discretely shown the pendant to the aunt who said she had never seen it before. But what to do about Josh Shepherd? Josh could be a loose cannon.

'Not yet. Let him think this is all about the drugs. You okay with this?'

'Sweet as a nut.' Earle saluted and left.

En route to Risely's office, Clement called Lisa Keeble at the lab.

She said she was just about to call him. 'It was hard but in the end I got enough of a thumb print off the pendant: Sidney Turner. Nothing else I could lift.'

Which was as he had expected. He told her he needed to speak with her about something and they arranged to meet in his office in thirty minutes. He rang off and tapped on Risely's door.

'Come in.'

One word occupied his brain as he entered: If.

...

Following on from the breakfast, I ate the counter-tea fish burger at the Cleopatra. The two best meals I'd had since the girls had been away, in the one day, in Broome. Tash watches those cooking shows – she has to because of the magazine and, let's face it, the locations are always amazing and the chefs make everything sound delectable – but you just can't go past bacon and eggs for breakfast, and fresh barra on a lightly toasted bun with crunchy iceberg for dinner, especially when you haven't eaten in between. Once I'd recognised that pendant, the day swirled around me like I was standing in the middle of the Indianapolis 500 track watching the cars. Food didn't penetrate my consciousness. All I wanted was to hear they'd found the kid. It was lucky I'd spotted the drug dealer's Subaru outside Turner's. Clement had missed it. I wished I'd have been allowed in on the interview but I understood them keeping me out. For three or four hours there I pretty much forgot I was a civilian. I was back! Prior to the Mongoose Cole interview, Clement had called and advised me to check out the Cleo fish burger. He'd debrief me in person if and when he could. I was grateful. Plenty of cops would have frozen me out. It was only when I was attacking my burger that I remembered Ingrid Feister, and then only because a text arrived from Dee Vee asking if there was any news. I ignored it for now. Not long after Dee Vee's text I got another, this one from Clement asking if I was still at the Cleo. When I confirmed, he texted he was on his way. It was around 6.15.

He joined me ten minutes later and accepted my offer of a cold beer, which we drank while he ate. Through mouthfuls of burger he told me what they'd got from Cole: a big fat nothing. I'd held onto this case for seventeen years, like one of those bog men they pull out of some hill in Wales still clutching a bag of coins that he is supposed to enjoy in the next life. Well, this was my next life, and I was not enjoying it. I was frustrated, maybe not in hell, but purgatory for sure. Sidney Turner was the key but he'd been lost down the stormwater drain. I blamed Clement and his crew, naturally, and he knew it. But I had to stay cool. It was a long time since I had any close friends in the department.

When Clement was finished he wiped his hands. 'I know you're frustrated. So am I. But if you want, we can work this thing.'

I noted the pronoun with interest and budding hope.

'I talked to my boss. He's happy for us to keep it among ourselves for now. I've briefed Lisa Keeble and asked her to confirm, if she can, the pendant is Jessica's, not some copy. Graeme Earle and Mal Gross know too. As far as everybody else is concerned, we're looking into the disappearance of Sidney Turner and we're concerned he could come to harm. That's all true and all we need to say.'

'What about the aunt, you ask her if she recognised the pendant?'

'Said she'd never seen it before. She's straight as they come.'

He had brought some zipped-up folder case with him. He held it aloft.

'This is the file on the burglaries. Chances are whoever Sidney stole that pendant from is in here. Wanna go back to your place and take a look?'

He didn't have to ask twice.

...

Clement pulled up a chair. I sat on the bed, file spread open in front of me. It wasn't that hot, so I had the fan on low.

Even though my clients were paying and there was a full bar fridge, a vestige of Depression-era penny-pinching had carried down the paternal line of the Lanes and I stocked up on beer at the Cleo. Given the Mimosa was a classy establishment, ceiling fan *plus* air con, I'd felt obliged to get Peroni to match the atmosphere. I handed Clement one.

'Turner's a meth-user so I think it's safe to assume that he cashed his spoils straight away.'

I couldn't disagree with Clement's reasoning and stated the obvious. 'So we look at his last known burglary first.'

'Yes. Pearl Motel. I was there.'

'On the job?' I wasn't being clever. I actually meant 'as in working', thinking he might have anticipated the target.

'On the job is a pretty accurate description.'

'Oh.'

He saw me glance at his finger. Even though I'd already done that and noted there was no band, habit had shoved me that way.

'Divorced,' he offered. 'My place is not exactly conducive.'

Contrary to what women might think and perhaps unlike themselves – this I'm basing on my female clients and that I admit might be a skewed sample – Aussie men don't generally go into detail about a night of sex. It might be that most of us don't think we're very good at it; it might be we're too drunk to remember it. Clement offered no further embellishment of who, when, how. He explained he'd been sleeping when the guy in the unit next door started shouting. He gave a brief account of the chase and wash-up: six rooms burgled, five wallets stolen, three purses, two cameras, seven phones and some jewellery and watches.

'Let me guess, nobody mentioned the bluebird pendant?'

'Between picking Turner up yesterday, getting him to hospital, Shepherd having himself checked out, we hadn't had enough time to reconcile the complete list. We never found any wallets on him so we were mainly worried about reconciling cash and the phones.'

The pieces of jewellery and watches, other than the pendant, had been taken from three different rooms. One of these was occupied by the Bernards, a South African couple who were not even in Australia seventeen years ago.

'Of course they might have innocently picked the pendant up there or here but then surely they would have mentioned it on their list of stolen items.'

I agreed.

The other room where jewellery had been taken was that of two young women from Adelaide. They would have been about four years old when Jessica Scanlan went missing. Their families weren't on the radar for anything criminal. Their taste in accessories was different too, cheaper, mass-produced mall variety. We didn't fancy them as being involved. So who did not report stolen jewellery?

'Bruce Henderson, fifty-six, works on a rig off Onslow, watch and wallet. He maintains a flat in Perth, divorced, no criminal record apart from a drunk and disorderly in the early eighties.'

He would have been late thirties at the time of Autostrada, almost too old for the profile I'd imagined but not quite. The lack of criminal record counted for nothing. I didn't think the killer would have much of a record or the police would have found him. We agreed we couldn't rule out Henderson. Of the three other victims of that night only one seemed promising: David Grunder, forty-three, married, living in Sydney, on holiday with his wife and daughter Keira, eight. Clement had checked. Grunder had been born in Perth and held a West Australian driver's licence up to 2001.

'He works for ANZ, some corporate finance job.'

I was surprised Clement knew so much about him and asked if he'd questioned the motel staff.

He smiled. 'Facebook.'

David Grunder interested me a great deal. He was a perfect fit for the age group. He had lived in Perth but moved away ... and the abductions had stopped. Moreover he was in the kind of job that screamed university degree. Claremont would surely have been his stomping ground. I said all this to Clement as I processed it. We were both excited and that fuelled our drinking. He took it upon himself to hit the bar fridge to replenish the beers.

'I'd love to know if he was interviewed by the task force,' said Clement. 'But then I'd have to tell Perth.'

'Maybe not,' I said, took a gulp and winked. I explained I had a list of all the people the task force had interviewed, although not the actual interviews.

'Tacich?'

I told him I couldn't reveal my sources.

'And you still have the files?'

'I still have the boots I wore in my first league game. Unfortunately I only ever needed one pair. I kept my old computer. It's basically my filing cabinet.' I didn't confide in him that so far as I was concerned, the case was never closed. I didn't want to come across as one of those obsessed old investigators, but in truth I was, it was just vanity protection. The first thing I had done before heading to the Cleo and its vaunted fish burger was to call my young pal, Dylan, who lived in the same strip as my office, in a flat above a hairdresser. Dylan was studying philosophy at uni and came cheap when I needed shit work done like getting the car cleaned, or cataloguing. My call found him in Bunbury, well south of Perth, visiting his family. He said he would be back to Perth sometime the next day. While Dylan was talking I was running through alternatives. I could call my mother-in-law Sue Holland but she was a bit old to be up on the technical side of things. There was nobody else I really trusted.

'I can have the files sent sometime tomorrow afternoon.' I explained the situation to Clement.

'You can put stuff on the cloud now, pull it down when you need,' said Clement.

'You even know what that means?' I was suspicious of a guy like Clement talking technical jargon.

'Nah, I have a tech guy,' he admitted.

My method of a previous computer (there's no point backing up because you have to check the USB anyway to see what's on there, and by the time you have a dozen that's as big a time waste as gardening) plus calling on Dylan might have been outmoded but it was reliable and simultaneously allowed me to feel as if I was a patron to higher education. Clement wasn't fazed by the delay.

'I'll find out where Grunder and Henderson are. I can interview them as follow up to the robbery without blowing it. Meanwhile we'll keep looking for Sidney Turner.'

'Grunder and Henderson could still be at the motel,' I hinted.

Clement began to search for the number on his phone but cut that short. 'Bugger it. Just as quick to drive.'

'You need to use the loo?'

He shook his head. Two beers at my age was equivalent to a case at his. I had my slash, locked up and found him at his car on the phone. I gathered it was his DS on the other end. The temperature had cooled considerably. Above me unseen branches were shaking tambourines.

'Great stuff. Call it a night, see if you can pick up where he went after.' He ended the call and turned to me. 'That was Earle. They picked up CCTV of Cole's Subaru heading to the airport around one-forty this arvo. Tomorrow they'll go through all the CCTV they can find out there.'

The interior of Clement's car was sparser than mine: no old sneakers or beach towels. CDs were scattered in the door pockets. A song came on midstream as he fired up the car and swung out of the Mimosa carpark. I couldn't believe it.

'*Babylon*?'

Clement looked at me, curious. He picked up a CD cover, Dr John.

'You know him?' he asked.

'I had my best sex ever to Dr John.' And before you point out that I said not so long ago that men don't talk sex, let me be clear there was no elucidation. 'It's more surprising that you know him. I thought REM would have been more your speed.' I hadn't meant it as a putdown but realised when it was out of my mouth it might have seemed that way. Clement was impervious.

'I like REM too.'

'Yeah, they're okay but .... how come Dr John?'

'I was on a case. I listened to the victim's record collection while I sat in his house trying to suss it out.'

My first judgement on Clement was sounding accurate: a driven guy, internal, a thinker. Him being a Dr John fan was a big positive.

'You think Grunder would keep that pendant with his wife and daughter around?' he asked.

'The sick fucks that abduct women and murder them, anything's possible. If it was him, he might have even given it to one of them as a gift.' I wasn't the only one who couldn't explain the twisted individuals who got excited at their so-called trophies being displayed. We'd already reached the motel. Clement parked right out the front in a set-down area.

Green lights shone on shrubs in a small corner garden of bark chips and native plants. The doors slid open easily. It must have been near 9.30 but the desk was actually manned, if that's the right word, by a young woman who was so plain that 'generic' is the only adjective that comes to mind. She was watching something on her computer. She looked up with an effort at perkiness.

'I'm sorry, we're full up tonight.'

Clement explained who he was and showed her ID. 'I'm wondering if the Grunders are staying here? Also a Mr Bruce Henderson.'

The young woman checked the desk computer. Without taking her eyes from it she said, 'No.'

I could see Clement was about to ask if she meant both but she jumped in. 'But the Grunders are booked back in tomorrow. I think they went up to Beagle Bay.'

Clement left his card with a message for them to call him when they returned. In case I hadn't thought of it, which I hadn't, he explained to me that he wasn't sure if they'd have their phones back on yet.

'The phones all had their sim cards removed,' he elaborated. 'Presumably by Turner to stop us tracking him.'

Then he turned back to the girl and asked for a printout of all the guests who had been staying there on the night of the robbery. It was like the pilot had collapsed at the control and she'd been asked to land the Dreamliner. She made a phone call to somebody who knew the finer points of the reservation system, ended the call and asked if it would be okay for her boss to send the names through tomorrow.

'I don't know how to work this computer. I'm just the night clerk.'

Her addendum was redundant. Clement told her that would be fine. We stepped back out into the cool night air and Clement asked if I fancied a drink.

...

There is something about the thrill of the hunt that works up a man's thirst. He drove to the Roebuck Bay Hotel and we found ourselves in the Thursday night throng, guys and girls hoping to ride each other's bones. There were more accents than an AC/DC song, a lot of blond hair, a new-wave Viking invasion. We took our beers outside where marijuana and cigarette smoke hung like faded bunting.

'It wasn't like this when I grew up.' Clement gestured with his beer and gave me a run-down on the Broome of his youth. I mentioned my previous experiences up here. We lasted a good twelve minutes before drifting back to the case. Both of us were hyped on Grunder, not altogether forgetting Henderson.

'I shouldn't have let Sidney Turner walk out like that. I should have known about the bail.'

I found myself turning one-eighty. 'You didn't know the significance at the time,' I said. 'It might not have made any difference. Cole could have just waited till the coast was clear anyway.'

'That's very fucking insincere, Snowy,' he said and we shared a bitter laugh. Thing is, investigative work is probably no different to running a stock portfolio or a fruit shop. You make calls all the time on what your focus will be, what's going to pay off, what it's going to cost you. Sometimes you make the wrong call. He told me he had a good mind to go to Mongoose Cole's now and roust him till he spilled his guts on Turner but we both knew it was just a wish, like winning lotto. Back in my day though, Dave Holland, Tash's old man, might have done just that.

'You want another?' he asked dangling his empty. But we'd both had enough and the grouse were safe for another day. Tomorrow was shaping as big.

As we were leaving Clement said, 'I suppose it's occurred to you that we might have a serial killer up here, and Ingrid Feister has disappeared?'

I am ashamed to say that it had not. I simply hadn't put the two together. By the time I was back at the Mimosa the thought had seeped into me like a creeping infection heading to the lungs and I found myself sharing my bed with the cold corpse of past failure. Under the regular thunk of the ceiling-fan blades, excitement gave way to fear.

CHAPTER 21

Clement scrutinised David Grunder's face for any tell as, along with his wife and daughter, he peered at the pendant inside the plastic evidence bag. With her usual efficiency Lisa Keeble had been through the Autostrada files and confirmed that identification markings listed by the Piccadilly jeweller on Jessica Scanlan's original piece were indeed present. It was not a copy. Grunder, fried egg perched on his fork, looked towards his wife, Yvonne, as if for guidance. She was shaking her head.

'No. It's very stylish but not mine and too old for Keira. And it was stolen too?'

'Yes, but we can't be sure it was from the motel.'

Despite what Clement told himself about being impartial, he was deflated. While Grunder, if he was indeed Jess Scanlan's killer, would have had plenty of time to prepare for this confrontation, his reaction seemed entirely natural: a husband who wasn't sure exactly what jewellery his wife and daughter might possess. Clement had received the call from them just before 10.00 am and had arranged to see them while they had breakfast. He wanted Yvonne Grunder and the girl there when he produced the pendant so that if they had ever seen it they might drop Grunder in it. Grunder seemed the kind of gormless, well-fed, soft type who littered the offices of multinational financial giants, did the winter sleep-out at the behest of his boss, occasionally made it to the corporate box when the home side was playing a less popular team, Melbourne or the Bulldogs say, travelled business class, and had a salary twice that of Clement's. Not that this ruled him out of being a killer. Clement agreed with what Lane had said, if the killer – and of course this assumed Bontillo was innocent or not alone – was an obvious type, he probably would have been found already. Of fair complexion, Grunder's skin was pink from unaccustomed sun, and his hair, still quite blond, receding but relatively thick. Clement had ordered himself a coffee to give him an excuse to linger. He pretended he was interested in their Beagle Bay trip, and in truth when he looked at Keira, the Grunder daughter, he recalled fond days with Phoebe at that age. But any emotion piggybacked on his pragmatic intention. A small child at a nearby table was emptying salt all over it. The parents ignored it while they checked different phones. What was happening to the world?

'So is this your first time to Western Australia?' he asked. Yvonne Grunder explained that her husband was from here. She had grown up in Newcastle and Keira had been born in Sydney.

Clement smile pleasantly at David Grunder. 'You didn't grow up here, did you?'

'Perth.'

'Whereabouts?'

'Willagee.'

A southern suburb that had been housing commission in the old days and was now quite gentrified.

'So you went to uni?'

He had done a commerce course at UWA. Fortunately he was almost the same age as Clement, who was able to draw on shared experiences of bands.

'Every Friday I'd be at The Sheaf in Claremont,' he lied.

Grunder acknowledged he'd gone there more than a few times. If he was the man who had killed Scanlan he must surely get the hint that he was suspected. However he showed no anxiety, no change in manner.

'And when did you go to Sydney?'

'Just before Nine Eleven,' he said. 'Awful, but it's something you don't forget.'

...

Later Clement sat in his office trying to lay out the threads of the pendant discovery, making sure he had the possibilities covered. The pendant was that which had belonged to Jessica Scanlan. It was ninety-nine point five percent certain it had been stolen by Sidney Turner. It was eighty percent certain it had come from the motel where the two main persons of interest were Bruce Henderson and David Grunder. Both had been in Perth in 2000 at the time of Jessica's disappearance. Neither had suspicious criminal records. Mal Gross had located Henderson working at the desert goldmine Telfer. Clement had interviewed Grunder and could not establish anything astray. He was waiting on Lane's files to see if either was interviewed back at the time of the original investigation. He bore in on Turner. He may simply have run, not caring about his aunt. Ice quickly weeded out any decency in its addicts. Alternatively, he could have been silenced, either by Mongoose Cole, or by Scanlan's killer who, having realised what had been taken, found it imperative to silence Turner. How would that person have known, though, that Turner was the thief? His arrest had come pretty quickly from the time they learned his identity. Nonetheless Clement had to concede, people talked – and here he immediately thought of Josh Shepherd shooting off his mouth – although it could have easily been word spreading from the hockey club. It could even be somebody present in the court. Shit, thought Clement, I still haven't followed up on Louise. It had all been so promising with her in what seemed an age ago.

He struggled to get back to the case. His life was a mess, so be it, but it must not interfere, not with this, the only thing he'd ever been really good at. Suspects ... When Turner disappeared, Henderson was already back at Telfer and Grunder was in Beagle Bay. Clement still favoured Cole as the solution to Turner's disappearance. Cole admitted having been at the house. He could have had a second vehicle standing by. It would be worth going back over the CCTV, see if any cameras picked up Cole's Subaru before he arrived at Olive Pickering's house, see if he was accompanied by such a vehicle. He made a note for follow-up then checked his email and saw that while he had been breakfasting, the Pearl Motel had sent over the names of all guests on the night of the robbery. He printed two copies. At a glance there were seven rooms and ten names. Damon Kelly and Shane Shields were in the right age group. He would need to look over all the other burglary victims before the motel job too. He couldn't assume the pendant came from the latest robbery. Turner may have been delayed in selling it for some reason. His phone rang. It was Snowy Lane. He now had the original task force files.

'Come into the station,' Clement said without elaboration, and then called Mal Gross into his office and handed him one of the printed lists. 'I need background checks on these people. I also need checks on the other victims of Turner's burglaries.'

'Got it.'

Scott Risely squeezed in as Gross exited. Before he could speak Clement updated him.

'A couple of promising leads from the motel but they haven't paid off yet.' He elaborated on Grunder.

'If there's any suggestion this is too big for us, I'll have to inform Perth.'

'At the moment there's nothing they could have done that we haven't. We've established the veracity of the jewellery, we've got people looking for Turner, Graeme is checking Cole, and I will shortly have a copy of the original task force files ... You don't want to know,' he warned before his boss could ask him how he obtained them. Risely was no fool, he'd guess Lane was the conduit.

'Don't let it come back to bite us; glory is one thing ...'

'It's not glory. Can you imagine if the media got hold of this? And if it goes to Perth it will. Someone will talk. Believe me, I know, I worked there twenty years. Once it's out of the bag, our killer is going to be very careful.'

'You've got my support,' Risely said. 'Do you need any more bods on the ground?'

'Stay on Parks and Wildlife re Turner. He's still the key.'

'Done.'

Risely left. Clement needed a coffee but it would be cutting it fine to make a café before Lane arrived so he headed to the kitchenette. Jo di Rivi and Nat Restoff, recently promoted to senior constable, were chatting. All of a sudden Clement remembered the pooch.

'How was she? Did you get the biopsy back?' He carefully measured the instant powder.

'The vet rang this morning. It's cancerous. He says it will kill her eventually.'

Clement felt confused, duped. It wasn't supposed to be like that. It was supposed to be one of those things where the vet goes, 'It's benign.' He felt hollow, like the world had let him down. 'I'm so sorry.'

Di Rivi was handling it calmly. 'We think she's about nine. She's probably got another three years.'

'Can he operate?'

'It's expensive.'

'We could all chip in,' offered Restoff.

Di Rivi seemed to have made up her mind. 'She's going to be thoroughly spoilt for the rest of her life. I'd rather we put the money to finding homes for some of those other abandoned dogs out there, give them a few years of quality life.'

Clement admired that matter-of-factness. He was too sentimental: an observation that threw back to Marilyn. He was due to have Phoebe Saturday. The pick-up might present a chance to talk to Marilyn? But maybe that would be a mistake. He'd enjoyed his time with Louise. If he left it too long ...

He pulled himself out of the deep ditch of his navel back to the present. The kitchenette now had the vibe of a de facto morning-tea break. Manners, the IT guy, had wandered out of his area holding his giant-sized mug. To Clement the size of the mug was inverse to the personality of its owner. Manners was somebody you didn't dislike but had to force yourself to be interested in. His mug read MAY THE FORCE BE WITH YOU and was decorated in the motif of check crime tape: a pun no less. Clement suspected Manners was one of those who dressed up in *Star Wars* or *Doctor Who* costumes and went to conventions to mingle with mirror images of themselves. He remembered his mental note to himself.

'I want you to try and find Cole's vehicle on CCTV preceding Turner's disappearance, see if it was travelling in company with any other vehicle.'

'Any one in particular?' Manners slurped more than sipped.

'No.' Another thought jumped into Clement's head. 'Those phones that were stolen from the Pearl. There were no sim cards were there?'

'No. He stripped them all out.'

'There are a couple I want you to run the records for me. Grunder and Henderson.'

'Sure,' Manners helped himself to a soggy biscuit and kept looking at Clement, expecting to be briefed on why. Clement, who had no intention of informing him, saw Lane being shown through into the squad room by Meg and went to meet him. He was about to offer him a coffee but saw Lane had supplied his own.

'Wise man,' he said and beckoned Lane follow him, wishing now he had taken the time to head outside for a shop espresso. For years he'd been more than happy with instant but lately the unthinkable had happened and he'd decided he preferred the other. Maybe it wasn't too late? Maybe he could change big things in his life as well? Images of Marilyn and Louise flashed up side by side as if it were some TV reality show. He banished them. Lane placed his laptop on the desk. They waited while it fired up.

'Slower than a bishop's apology,' Lane cautioned.

'How did you sleep?' Clement asked out of politeness, his whole focus now on the computer.

'Not well. Your parting shot worried the shit out of me.'

Clement struggled to recall exactly what his parting shot had been, caught it, wriggling away. 'Oh, about Ingrid Feister.'

Lane sipped his coffee. 'On the positive side, I realised this morning that Grunder wasn't in WA when she went missing, right?' The computer had loaded up. 'Needs your internet password,' Lane reminded him.

Clement pulled it towards him and punched in the password, probably against regulations but he was too fired up to care about bureaucracy.

'That's right. Henderson too, I'm pretty sure. Think he was at Telfer. I can check.' He swivelled the computer back to Lane.

'Haven't looked at these for a while,' Lane admitted. Clement walked around to the other side of the desk and stared over Lane's shoulder as he scanned the list of those interviewed in the original investigation. Neither Dave Grunder nor Bruce Henderson appeared. There was a Thomas Henderson, and Clement made a note just in case he might be some sort of relative. He slid the list of the other motel guests over to Lane. Clement had highlighted the names Kelly and Shields.

'No bells,' Lane said, 'but it's been a while.' But when they punched the names into the Autostrada files they also returned a blank.

'I've got Mal Gross looking for any criminal history.'

A tap on the door swung them around. Scott Risely stood there. He looked grim. 'A body has been found in the desert.'

...

The body may as well have been on the moon, thought Clement. It was a fluke it had been found at all. A geology team had been heading west from no-man's land in the desert after a week's surveying and sampling and had almost driven over it. There were no roads here, just a few tracks of compacted red earth if you were lucky. Outback four-wheel drives were the only vehicles that you would trust, and even then you'd want to have a couple, each with a big water supply. The heat desiccated you, gave your clothes the crispness of dry gum leaves. Mind you, Clement counted himself lucky, this was one of the cooler months; he put it at about thirty-seven degrees Celsius. He chug-a-lugged a canteen and threw a sideways glance at Lisa Keeble and her assistant, a bald guy named Mason – Clement had never been sure if that was his first or last name – who were working the corpse and the surrounds. He'd already interviewed the three men who had found the body – a geologist, a surveyor and dogsbody – and let them be on their way. He felt sorry for them stuck out here for the nearly four hours it had taken him to get here, and that with a chopper. It could have been much worse. The location of the body, a little over three hundred k south of Broome on the edge of the Great Sandy Desert was just within the helicopter's range. Clement had thought hard about driving instead. The chopper would be conserving fuel, taking it easy, while the highway south would be as fast or faster, but then you had to cut inland for another hundred and fifty k of scrubby, red nothing.

He concluded these hours might be critical and that he and the two techs should fly in the chopper with two vehicles following. He called in Graeme Earle and Josh Shepherd from their Mongoose Cole inquiries and told them to take Snowy Lane. Shepherd looked none too impressed and Clement guessed this time Lane would have to sit in the back. Jo di Rivi and Nat Restoff were also coming, bringing a van into which the body could be loaded, although there was an option to chopper it.

En route, plenty of thoughts ran through Clement's mind but the one sticking its chest out for the tape was that the corpse was either the Feister girl, her boyfriend, or Turner. The geology party, who had got through on a sat phone, were finally raised again just as he and Keeble were getting to the helicopter. From what he could tell, they were saying the corpse looked like it had been there a while. He'd told them to wait and leave the remains intact. When the chopper eventually got there, flying low over endless rust-coloured dirt, not a living creature in sight, he directed the pilot to land a good distance from the site so as not to disturb the ground with its rotor. They then trudged through the furnace. Some days it got upwards of forty-five degrees C here so this was practically air-conditioned.

One glance told him this wasn't Sidney Turner. The heat and wind of the dry desert had mummified the remains, which looked not unlike some of those images from Howard Carter's tomb-raiding expeditions: leathery skin stretched over bone, teeth and nails intact. And hair. There was plenty of it. Clement reminded himself that Max Coldwell had long hair. The body was not totally intact, chunks were missing. Snap judgements could come back to bite you so Clement held off on any interpretation as to the cause. For the same reason he did not rule out the corpse being that of an Indigenous person. There were no reports of other missing persons, however, so he knew what odds a bookmaker might give. The loudest gong of doom playing in his head was the body appeared to have been nude. Maybe animals had carried off the clothing but he'd just completed a hundred metre radius sweep without finding a scrap of fabric. He'd already had the pilot take the chopper up for a quick sweep of the area in case there was any sign of another person or body. Unfortunately the fuel limitations meant that the search had to be circumscribed.

He checked his watch: 4.40 pm. He thought the others might still be an hour off. The pilot was stretched out under his chopper in the little shade there was. Keeble, in her tech suit despite the heat, strode towards him.

'Looks like wedge-tailed eagles and lizards got to her.'

'Her?'

'Definitely female.'

'How tall?'

'One seventy.'

He wished he could remember Ingrid Feister's size. Lane would, surely.

'No clothes?'

'Not a stitch. These will be helpful.' She produced a small jar of beetles. 'I'm thinking two weeks. Rhino will want a look.'

Rhino will love those, he thought. Keeble had learned most of what she knew from Rhino. She might have outstripped him on ballistics and other technical areas but he was the insect specialist.

'You think all that damage is animal activity?'

'Three years ago I had a case near Shay Gap. Rider came off his bike, nobody missed him for a week. I saw that body, I thought it was Jack the Ripper's work but it was just our desert creatures doing what they do. The smell those first few days, it would have been like an invite to a smorgasbord.'

Clement could have done without the simile but every tech he ever knew who worked bodies adopted the same black humour. He was a detective, he had the luxury of thinking of the dead as their living selves, the techs had to treat the body as an inert site from which to scientifically extract evidence.

'Having said that ...' she had pricked his interest, '... lots of bones seem to be broken.'

'Like what? She was beaten?'

'More likely run over.' She obviously wasn't prepared to hazard any further opinion. 'You're thinking it's the Feister girl.'

Now it was his turn to be coy. 'Not until you get me her DNA.'

She made a short snort. 'Good luck with that.'

'You don't think we'll get anything?'

She pointed at the sun, sulkily heading down but with a way to go yet.

'Better than bleach. It's going to be a real long shot.'

He'd half expected as much.

'Might be a chance with fingerprints.'

That was something.

'You got casts of the geologists' tyres?' He'd asked her to do this for elimination in case they found tyre tracks.

'Mason did. But I haven't seen any other marks at all. They probably blew away.'

Or somebody dumped the body and then wiped them.

...

I was in a far-off mental state, part of a surreal landscape of burnt orange, bumping over ground, alternately sandy and scrubby rock. I could have been one those emperors of olden times being carried on the shoulders of odd-sized servants. In front, Shepherd and Earle were exchanging a few words but not so loud as I could hear clearly, even had I wanted to. My mind was still back at the station when my fingers had played over the computer keys, the years peeling away to a time when Grace was in a highchair and Perth gripped by mistrust and fear. It might have been baseless but I felt I'd let myself down, my colleagues down, my city down, my clients down, and most of all those girls. This was supposed to be my second chance. Out of the ether, there it was, the missing pendant, in front of me, somebody who would recognise it, maybe not instantly but soon enough to follow the trail. It was as if the whole case centred around me, like I'd been specially chosen; I was the young King Arthur. But then in an instant that stupid egotism of mine was used against me, like a judo flip. I was twisted in mid-air so what was up was now down and vice-versa. Then I was dumped on my arse. I was supposed to be looking for Ingrid Feister but I'd sidelined her, belittled her importance. Now I was being punished for my neglect. Only at the last minute did I save myself from praying the body was not hers. In my rush for self-preservation, that would have been a new low. Whoever had died out here, accident or murder, deserved my prayers, not me. Maybe I was too old, maybe I was already past it seventeen years ago. If that was the case, I should just get out of the way.

...

By the time we reached the site, the sun was nearly done. Clement warned me the remains were far from pristine. I didn't try to get too close, didn't need to. He sent the others to drive around in their vehicles in case there was a survivor or, more likely, another body. At some point I heard the drone of the light aircraft he'd called in to look further out than he'd managed with the chopper.

'Keeble says female. How tall are Ingrid and Coldwell?'

I'd brought my folder just in case but didn't need it.

'Five eight and five ten and a half.'

Clement did the calculations. 'That's definitely not him. We've got the victim as five seven.'

Bones were broken, scavengers had attacked the corpse and I couldn't be certain how accurate the given height was anyway; everybody makes themselves taller if they can and the data could simply have been copied from a form Ingrid herself had filled in sometime. In the absence of any other missing persons I had to assume it was her.

'I suppose the DNA will tell us for sure.'

He explained we might not be that lucky. Now I felt ignorant as well, a virgin in Victoria's Secret.

'If there's a way, the Feisters will pay, I'm sure of that.' I asked if he had to tell Perth.

'I suppose I could wait, see if we can get a cause of death but we've got two missing persons and a body. It's up to Risely. I'm guessing he'll call Feister, see if they want to go public.'

When the cars returned without having spotted anything, Clement went off to talk privately with Graeme Earle. I waited around kicking dirt. There was a lot to kick, which was just as well. It was a while before Clement came back.

'We'll load the remains in the van with the uniforms. They'll drive to Derby and leave them at the hospital. By the time they get there it will be too late to fly them out today. You, me and Keeble will fly back in the chopper. Lisa will go to Derby first thing and accompany the remains to Perth. Earle and Shepherd will head back now. They've got some stuff happening with Mongoose Cole. The other techs will stay here and do another search first thing tomorrow.'

...

No matter how much life wants to grind you down, you can find something that reaffirms your place on the earth as blest. For me it was savouring a slice of pepperoni pizza sitting on Cable Beach under the stars. For now the horror of the desert had been parked, along with contemplation of our own mortality. I had flown back in the chopper mired in dark thoughts, postponing calling Dee Vee until the morning. A late-night call was only going to have people worrying. By the time we'd got back to the station it had been near 10.00, and Clement and I were starving. Clement suggested pizza. So here we were eating slices out of the box, the waves breaking softly in darkness. Keeble had politely declined an invitation to join us as she was looking at a 5.00 am start to get to Derby and ride shotgun with the body. Which was probably a more entertaining prospect than joining two losers feeling sorry for themselves. It had been too noisy to talk on the chopper so apart from our short parley at the site we'd not really checked the scoresheet since before we'd left for the desert. Now there wasn't much else to do except swallow.

'Earle hasn't made much progress on Cole.' Clement licked a piece of cheese off his bottom lip. 'They didn't find any footage of his Subaru with any other vehicle before Turner went missing. All we have is that CCTV of his car heading out to the airport around one-thirty.'

'Was he alone?'

'That's what it looks like. He didn't go to the main terminal but to the light aircraft area. There we got more vision of him meeting with the pilot of a plane that flew in from Wyndham. We're thinking drugs. The Feds have found evidence of a drug trail from Malaysia to Timor. It leaves Timor by boat, mid-sea swap, then maybe it goes to Wyndham and Cole collects this end.'

'How long was he at the airport?'

'All up, around half an hour. We're trying to find some eyewitness who might have seen him park, load, or leave. Then we lose him and pick him up in the chicken place buying a burger at two-fifty.'

'Maybe he hid Turner in the back, organised Turner a flight out?'

'I just don't see Cole being that worried by a little meth-head. It's possible he dropped Turner off somewhere, then collected him after the airport and did God knows what after that. Earle is solid. He'll keep looking for those missing hours.'

'So we still have Sidney Turner unaccounted for,' I said. 'The body is not his. Coldwell and Feister are also missing and have not been seen now for three weeks. Their car has also vanished. The possibilities with Feister and Coldwell haven't changed much. The best case scenario: they've dropped out and tuned out. Alternatively, one or both have come to harm.'

He said, 'The likelihood of an accident, I think, is receding. Even if that body is not hers, we've had planes, choppers and eyes on the ground searching for them. They could have met with foul play and the vehicle has been deliberately hidden for some reason. Agree?'

'Yes. Foul play possibilities if we assume the body is Ingrid's: Coldwell has killed Ingrid, deliberately or accidentally. Question then, where is he? Interstate? Or somebody has killed both of them.'

'You don't think he's been abducted?'

'I can see why you kill the guy to keep the girl but not vice versa.'

His turn to agree. I spun it out. 'Now, if they are dead, we have some evidence – the pendant – of a serial abductor-slash-killer having been in the area. Is that a coincidence? Do we have a Bradley Murdoch opportunistic road-killer type out there *and* a serial killer who so far as we know is still dormant? Or is it the same guy?'

'She fits the profile of the Autostrada victims: young, affluent.'

'Except she was with a guy.'

Clement pulled a face. 'Maybe he couldn't help himself this time. Maybe he didn't realise there was a guy?'

I could concede those points. 'If it's the same killer, it is not Grunder or Henderson, right?' I like to go over a scenario again and again.

Clement dusted his hands. He was done for pizza. 'Correct. But then, maybe we are jumping the gun and it isn't the same killer. Feister withdrew six grand in cash. For a lot of people, that's a million bucks.'

He stood. I think he was as annoyed as me we were chasing our tails.

'Time to go and check on those previous Turner burglaries. I haven't had a chance yet.'

We started to trudge back to the car when he stopped and said, 'Shit.'

I would have been less surprised at Margot Fonteyn twerking.

'What's up?'

'I'm supposed to have my daughter. Now with all this stuff ...'

He checked his watch, pulled out his phone. He was going to cancel.

'Don't. The body won't be in Perth till midday or something. You'll be wasting a day you could spend with your kid.'

'There's Turner to follow up, the other burglary victims.' He wanted to hear me but his professional duty was like a pair of headphones clamped on his ears. I spied an out for him.

'Why don't we hit the pubs now, ask around about Turner? I'm guessing Friday night just about everybody in town is out and about.'

...

The next two hours we canvassed every venue in Broome showing photos of Turner, Feister and Coldwell. A couple of people recognised Turner but hadn't seen him recently. Clement asked them who Turner normally hung out with, just in case the police had missed them in their earlier inquiries. I had some young South Americans who reckoned they might have spied Coldwell at one of the gorges the previous week. They thought it was Manning Gorge but couldn't be certain. He seemed to be fishing, they said. Other than a cursory 'hello', he hadn't spoken to them and had left fairly quickly. That in itself was suspicious. Up this way human interaction is usually cherished. They had not seen his vehicle. I took their details and passed them onto Clement when we were back in his office. It was close to 1.00 am now. A few of the night crew were coming and going. Even though neither of us had consumed alcohol, we were both struggling. The day seemed to have lasted longer than a Geoff Boycott fifty. He pulled out the list of other burglaries Turner had committed, mainly businesses. None of the victims seemed a likely demographic match to the Autostrada killer but we checked the old police files anyway, to no avail. There is an old Mental As Anything song, 'Spirit Got Lost'. That was how I felt, split into two, half of me floating away.

'Stumps?' I suggested and he agreed. Later I would have to call Dee Verleuwin and give her the bad news. Somehow I felt I would not be enjoying a swim and a bacon breakfast.

...

After Lane had gone, Clement walked to the car at the rear of the building, opened it and sat for what seemed a long time. He could not remember ever feeling so alone. This, he imagined, must be what it is like for a shipwrecked sailor drifting in an unfathomable vastness. It was not his work that precipitated this. If he applied himself methodically, he knew over time this miasma would be defined into discrete, potentially understandable elements. The core of his problem was Marilyn, yet he could not blame her entirely.

What was her crime: to seek him out and ask his opinion? Of course it was insensitive, she knew how he felt, but that did not make it wrong. Meanwhile, he'd had ample opportunity to call Louise back. Indeed, he should really have interviewed her about Sidney Turner, seen if Turner had let anything drop in the course of their deliberations that might give a clue as to where he was now. Instead he had avoided her, like he was some monk whose sole duty was to worship Marilyn. He thought back to the night at the Pearl Motel. He drew his mind across the naked curve of Louise's body; the easy conversation echoed even now.

Just a few minutes later he was out the front of Louise's house, still in his car, without any real memory of how it got there. He thought of criminals he had interviewed, murderers, rapists: 'I don't remember when I got there. I was just there.' How many times had he heard that? Now he was forced to trawl back in his brain to actually bring back the physical sensation of turning the car key and driving out of the station. Tiredness? Perhaps. Her mother would have returned home by now. 'Two days longer and I get my house back,' she'd said over dinner.

There was no light on but that didn't matter. In fact it added some bravado and a whiff of romance. He could call her now, apologise for disturbing her, tell her he'd had one hell of day and he was out the front. The worst that could happen would be she would scream at him and say she never wanted to see him again. Or perhaps the worst was that she was with somebody else. But then he'd be off the hook and not torn north and south. And if she didn't reject him, if she sleepily said, sure come in, would that not be the sail on the horizon, the rescue? He would curl into her and not be alone.

For one night at least.

But then, perhaps the next night and the one after, he might find himself in the same situation, dependent, and that was something he would not live with. Clearly there was something lacking within himself, some flaw that kept him forever balancing on a dividing line, an emotional twilight. Fear? Insecurity? Distrust? This was not a result of Marilyn, it had been part of him in that relationship too. And yes, you could blame his ambition and his addiction to his work, her restlessness and sense of entitlement, but it did not alter the fact that until he changed something fundamental within himself all he would be doing was creating another need. He should be with Louise, or any other partner for that matter, because of what he could offer them, not what they might offer him.

While he had been thinking all this, his phone had been warm in his palm like the beating heart of a dove. He placed it down in the console of the car. Then he started up and drove home.

CHAPTER 22

He had panicked. He saw that now. Even if the police found it on the Indigenous boy they probably would not even recognise it. And most likely he had sold it already for drugs or whatever so it had already distanced itself from him. He should never have kept it but he could not bring himself to throw it away. It was all still so vivid, like yesterday. Sometimes he could still feel her lips on his. Even so, it had been a stupid, unnecessary risk. He put on his iPod. Pet Shop Boys came up first. He restrained a smile at the irony. He liked them. The music took him back in time to the time he first saw Jess. I must do everything in my power to know you better, he had told himself. He could feel her delicate arm in his grasp, smell her perfume. No, he must not pursue the thought. This was a new start. It had not been easy but he had managed to build a life where the past was dead and buried. Like Jess. Such a beauty and such a waste but you could almost say she brought it on herself.

He was lying on his bed naked but for a pair of silk boxer shorts. Picking up the catalogue he studied the lingerie models. He much preferred these girls in short teddies, homely, slightly amateurish, to those brazen, nude types spreading their legs. He wasn't a prude by any means but they weren't for him. These were the best age he thought: seventeen, maybe nineteen, before the world had corrupted them. His hand reached down his silk shorts and lingered ...

No. It was no good, not while the boy was out there. How long since he'd had a proper sleep? He had to get over that. The police just weren't that competent. He finished where he began; annoyed with himself for panicking.

...

What was I going to do? Hang around all day twiddling my thumbs? In spite of what I'd told myself the previous night, I rose at 6.00. Just four hours sleep but it had been as deep as a Chinese proverb. I drove to Cable Beach, slid into the ocean, swam. My breathing was getting better, my stroke a little more powerful. I sealed my brain to images of the desiccated corpse but allowed myself to wonder if this might be my last day on the job. If so, I was undecided whether to head straight back to Perth. I doubted I would. The Autostrada killer might be up here right now and we had unfinished business.

Back at the Mimosa, I grabbed all the free maps and travel guides I could find in reception and studied them while I ate a fruit breakfast in my room. The South Americans had claimed to have seen a man who resembled Max Coldwell, they thought, at Manning Gorge. That was probably an eight-hour drive from here. The first two to three from Broome to beyond Derby was on a sealed road. After that it was going to be hard yakka bouncing over hard, rocky ground. Still, if I left now I could be there mid to late afternoon. I checked my notebook. The girlie revue sExcitation was playing Derby tonight. There was a slim chance I could get to the gorge, take a look around, and if I struck out still make it to the revue. That's if I still had a job. What the heck, I may as well take a look at the gorges. Right after I'd called my employers.

...

'Yes.'

Dee Verleuwin's voice was sleep-stained. I imagined her turning a blurry eye to a digital time display and cursing me.

'There's a body. It could be Ingrid.' That woke her up quick. I gave her all the details I had, including the bad news on the DNA.

'So what can we do?'

I imagined her searching for a cigarette. I told her I was off to follow the Coldwell lead but nothing about Autostrada.

'I don't know what reception is like out there, so don't expect to hear from me until tomorrow,' I warned. She said she would contact Feister and asked me to try and get back in touch with her as soon as possible.

It still surprises me that you can drive hours anywhere in this world and not see another soul but that's what it's like up here. Quite a few vehicles passed me en route to Derby but once I swung up to the Gibb River Road, traffic became a trickle, and then dwindled to nothing at all. Two and a half hours later, having passed a total of three vehicles, I stopped at the Imintji Roadhouse and enjoyed a tea and a pie. And I do mean enjoyed. I felt I'd earned it, like I was the latest in a long line of Leichhardts and Forrests. The tea wasn't billy, and my arse wasn't sore from riding camels or mules for days on end, and I'd had the luxury of a fast vehicle and air conditioning and Weddings Parties Anything on the CD player but, I tell you, I had felt keenly the isolation and the slim thread of my humanity in this crucible where, like a recumbent giant, prehistoric dead-earth and rock dwarfed me. The woman who served me at the roadhouse, her name was Jenny, was pleasant and chatty. I guessed even for her and her husband, who was absent at that time, a little human interaction was welcome. I told her who I was and showed photos of Ingrid Feister and Max Coldwell. Like a lot of people she thought the idea of being questioned by a private detective was exotic. The police and rangers had already asked her and her husband to keep an eye out but so far nothing. I mentioned I was heading to Manning Gorge and spoke about the South Americans, and was pleased she remembered them passing through. It gave them credibility and at least encouraged me that the cramps in my feet and the unrelenting vigilance weren't futile. When I asked if it was possible the vehicle could be around without being detected, she replied that if it stayed away from the roadhouses and carparks there was a load of land and very few people.

'But eventually somebody will spot you.'

...

I bought water, went to the toilet and, refreshed, slipped back into explorer mode. It was heading towards four by the time I reached Mount Barnett Roadhouse. It was hacienda style, red earth and gums. A young couple ran the place and they too were duly impressed by my occupation. They also remembered the South Americans, and had been primed by the police, but had nothing to report on Ingrid Feister, Max Coldwell or the vehicle. I paid the fee to gain access to the camping ground and gorge.

'Is it possible to get to the gorge without coming through here?'

'By foot, yeah,' said the young guy, 'but you'd need to be desperate.'

The sun had been beating its fist angrily on the car body for hours but my air con was holding out with a Rats of Tobruk spirit. It could have been worse. I guessed the temperature at a few degrees under forty. The flies were a problem though. They sought me out, crammed into my face. I drove a few k up the road to the campground, parked in what shade

I could find and started on the path leading to the gorge. There was not a vehicle in sight. I was wearing shorts, runners and a long-sleeved army-style shirt. It was a weird experience, like I was the only person left in the world. My mind drifted to whether Coldwell had indeed had a falling out with Feister, killed her, maybe accidentally, and now was hiding out, unable to face the consequences. I walked the path for a while and then saw I had to cross the river to get to the gorge. Thoughtfully, polystyrene boxes were provided to swim your gear across. I only bothered with my shoes and socks. The water was cool and refreshing, the sky azure. I wished I had Tash and Grace with me, they would have loved this.

Once across the river I put my shoes back on and continued to follow the path, my clothes drying quickly. The sun isn't part of life up here, it is life. It defines everything. The atmosphere was snap dry, the moisture in my clothes leaving me the way a former lover leaves their last kiss, quick and shallow, so it's a memory before it has even ended.

Out of red earth studded by the odd big gum, there suddenly appeared an eruption of plant life. It wasn't exactly lush but it was almost thick, with a variety of shrubs, some sporting little orange flowers. Cutting across this surprisingly green border I was confronted with an ancient landscape: rock pools, flat sheets of water trimmed here and there by a sprinkle of rivulets, and across the way low hills of rock, almost pink in the sun, made from chunky Lego-like pieces scattered by an infant god. I edged forward and stared down the gorge. A few hundred metres ahead the bush thickened. Trees edged down cliffs like a herd seeking water, or clumped in little headlands, poking right out into the surrounding pool. Some seemed to sprout from the rock itself. There were no cascades, maybe it was the wrong time of the season for that, but it was much bigger than I could have imagined, with many pools to swim in. The futility of me trying to locate any person up here hit me right then. You might have a chance from a chopper, maybe a plane even, but otherwise forget it. I spent the best part of an hour exploring, not from any belief I might find a clue but simply taking advantage of the opportunity to sightsee.

I was totally alone in one of those prehistoric dimples even nature itself seemed to have forgotten. If the long neck of a dinosaur had suddenly appeared over a ridge it would not have surprised me. I would have stayed but it was too long a trip back. I retraced my steps to the campground, swimming the gorge again. I couldn't quite dry out on the way back to the car and had to wipe myself over with a spare shirt when I got there.

I stopped at the roadhouse and let them know I was heading back to Derby. It's funny, when you're in the outback you instantly feel part of the community. I guess it's the magnitude of space and the paucity of humans. I pulled up next to a dirt-covered diesel four-wheel drive and headed inside.

Sometimes it's dumb luck that drives your investigation on. Inside the roadhouse were two young guys, modern Leyland brothers but with beards and tanned skin. They were slugging Cokes.

'You should speak to these guys,' said the young woman owner when I stepped in. 'They might have seen the Landcruiser.'

Their names were Ben and Liam. They told me they were just leaving Adcock Gorge, about forty k back towards Derby, and had driven inland for a look around. In a slightly more wooded area they had seen a white Landcruiser. It was odd because it was away from the gorge. They saw nobody around and wondered if it was somebody illegally camping there.

'Tom's already called the police,' said the young woman whose name, I belatedly discovered, was Emily. I thanked them all, got the boys to draw me a map and left, driving fast. It wasn't just that it was a white Landcruiser – heaven knows there would be a few of them up this way – it was more that the car had been parked in such an odd place. Pushing as hard as I dared, it took me a good forty minutes to find the turn-off. The map they had drawn was surprisingly accurate and seven or eight minutes from the turn-off was the car, unmoved. You would have missed it if you hadn't driven this way and reason told me not many people, after taking the turn-off, drove in the opposite direction to the gorge. I parked and climbed out, my excitement mounting.

It was Ingrid Feister's car alright. Stained with red dirt and dead insects, but it was the car. Nobody was around. There was no sign of damage to its outside and the interior looked innocent enough, a couple of shirts and a blanket tossed on a seat. I mulled my next move. The sensible thing would be to wait but then a flock of birds took to the air in a sudden rush, over in the direction of the gorge. On impulse I climbed back into my car and drove through bush onto the main road to the gorge, keeping an eye on the position where I'd seen the birds scatter. I crossed a small creek, parked near the otherwise empty carpark and got out to find the temperature for the first time that day heading south. I beat a path through the bush, which was thick and spiky here, then angled back towards the gorge.

It was a pretty, box-like gorge with deep rock walls and white gums.

A small sound, like somebody slapping water, pulled my head to the right and I glimpsed for the merest fraction of time, a figure. Male or female I couldn't tell, but part of a limb, leg or arm, I wasn't even sure. Curbing my instinct to yell out I circled around and down through sloping trees and rock ledges and edged around to where I had seen the figure. Up above me now, another plume of birds scattered to the blue sky. I made my way up the rock face as quickly as I could but I was not so young now and had to be careful not to slip. I reached the top in time to see something running away through the bush about fifty metres ahead. I gave chase and this time I did shout.

'Max? Is that you?'

The pursuit was short – maybe ten seconds – and then I was back into much clearer territory of occasional spinifex. There was no sign of any figure ahead as I scanned left or right. That seemed impossible. Unless ...

I heard the sound too late and turned to see a branch driving towards my head.

...

Clement sat on the floor cross-legged watching Phoebe roll dice and meticulously count out squares. It was her favourite Harry Potter board game, which he kept here in the Derby house for their times together. How much longer, he thought, would it remain so? How much longer would he know what her favourite anything was? She already had Facebook although that was heavily monitored by her mother. Snowy Lane had told him his wife and daughter were in Barcelona. One day that would be Phoebe with Marilyn ... and Brian, no doubt. Would she even keep his name? For the first time it occurred to him that he may have another family of his own in the future. A young woman like Louise – and he wasn't in any sense planning a future with her – but any young woman would likely want her own children. Complication upon complication, he thought as he rolled the dice. He'd hoped Marilyn might have been there when he called to pick up Phoebe but there was no sign of her, and Phoebe was waiting outside ready with her backpack. Perhaps when he dropped her back? When I was Phoebe's age, he thought, life was so simple, wasn't it? You read comics. You were the Human Torch or the Hulk. You rode your bike, you were driving a Formula 1. You remembered how many runs you had made when the backyard game restarted the next day. Of course there were bullies, kids at school who had it in for you. There was anxiety, no denying that, it wasn't nirvana. Nevertheless, before puberty it was a lot less complicated. Nothing in life is harder than finding the right partner – except keeping her – that's what he thought. He imagined Marilyn in the room with them, playing too, or just sitting on the sofa reading, and the intensity of his loss was so keen he could have cried.

CHAPTER 23

'You okay?'

Clement's voice down the line seemed thin, as if strained through mesh inside my head. It was near midnight and I was existing in a chair in casualty at Derby Hospital. The closest I could describe how I felt was the afternoon of New Year's Day when the hangover is subsiding but hasn't yet disappeared. A giant moth dive-bombed. It was a toss-up which was bigger: it or the lump on my temple. The doctors wanted me to stay the night, I begged discharge. They insisted on keeping me for a couple of hours to have another examination before I was allowed to sign out, absolving them of all responsibility.

'I should have stayed with the car.'

It was pre-emptive. I knew Clement would be thinking the same thing. A short silence confirmed as much but the guy was polite. Somewhere down the hall somebody started jabbering incoherently, DTs or Ice.

'Jared tells me you didn't get a good look at your assailant.'

Jared Taylor, the police aide, was the one who found me, sitting in the shade under a tree. I figured it was about twenty minutes to half an hour after I got hit. I'd pulled myself over and waited to feel well enough to drive. I was bleeding from the temple but my guess was it was superficial.

'No. I saw a branch coming towards me, then, stars. There was somebody at the waterhole but I couldn't say if it was man or woman. They haven't located the car yet?'

It had been gone by the time Taylor arrived.

'It's a matter of time. There are only so many roads up here. Are you alright to drive back?'

Taylor had organised his mate to drive my car back to Derby while I rode with him to the hospital but now I was on my own.

'In two hours I'll be cherry ripe. Thank Jared for me. I hope I haven't ruined your time with your kid.'

'No, your timing was perfect. I'd just dropped her home when I got the call. Listen, I've got a place just outside of Derby. You could stay there.'

'I'll be fine, truly. I've had a lot worse.'

'You tell Feister about the body?'

I explained I had communicated the situation. Dee Vee had left three messages to call her when I had a chance. I should be ringing her now but why make my headache worse?

'I'll see you tomorrow morning,' I said. 'Thanks for checking in.'

He told me to take it easy and reaffirmed they would find the car soon. I wished I could curl up in Tash's arms but she was on the other side of the world and all I had for companionship was a silent television and torn, out-of-date magazines.

...

Clement hung up, thinking it was stupid of Lane to have gone in alone. But perhaps he was stupid too, allowing a civilian this kind of access. On the other hand, there was no guarantee Jared would have made it in time to clock the Feister car. At least this way they had confirmation on the vehicle and surely it couldn't get too far now. Taylor had radioed ahead for people on the Tanami Track to keep an eye out. All the other major towns had been informed. He'd informed Risely who said tomorrow they would get aerial support. As to why Lane had been attacked, he could only surmise it was somebody who had committed a criminal act already, either Coldwell on Ingrid Feister, or a third party who at the very least had stolen the car. Clement was standing on the dock outside the chandler's place. The breeze was pleasantly cool. His hope of seeing Marilyn when he returned Phoebe home had been dashed. There had been no sign of her and he had been forced to deal with his mother-in-law, Geraldine, to whom he ascribed a lot of responsibility for the marriage break-up. In spite of this setback, he was on the verge of digging in his heels and waiting for Marilyn but then got Taylor's call informing him he was on his way to Derby with a bleeding Snowy Lane. Clement had then driven back through town and stopped in on Turner's aunt, Olive Pickering, just in case she'd heard anything. She was very upset. She'd heard nothing from her nephew and was sure something bad had happened.

'He wouldn't do that to me,' she kept saying.

She was worried now about losing her house. Clement tried to reassure her but in truth he had little idea how these things worked. Sidney Turner was a foolish young man but not, Clement believed, an evil one. And yet in his wake he had left physical and emotional destruction. Clement rechecked with her there were no friends of Sidney's she had not already mentioned. There weren't. He promised Olive Pickering they would keep looking.

'He was a good boy,' she said, 'until he went to Perth.'

The sound of a small outboard reached out to Clement from the black. He remembered nights like this when he was young, anonymous out the back of the campground his parents ran, music from a cassette radio hanging thick as fruit in the warm air. On impulse he dialled Louise. The phone rang and rang. He was about to hang up, chiding himself she was probably already in bed, when she answered.

'Hi, it's me.'

'Hello stranger.'

He could detect no reproach, she seemed relaxed. He stared out at the dark water. There was hardly any moon.

'I know. Things have been crazy.' He did not tell her he had sat out in front of her house last night, and then wondered why not. His own motivations were as hidden from him as the water out there.

'Have you found Sidney Turner?' she asked.

'No. We've checked his friends. We're chasing down a couple of things. I dropped in on his aunt. She's very worried about her house. Could she lose it?'

'It's possible.'

'Could you talk to her? I think she needs some guidance.'

'Of course. Do you want to come over?'

Yes he did. 'I had better not. There's a lot going on at the moment and I have to be up really early.' He wondered if he had blown it. 'I'd like to, I really would.'

'That's okay.'

For the first time there was a hint of wound in her voice.

'Did Turner say anything to you?' He had to be careful here. This would have been so much simpler if he'd seen her in the interim.

'I can't go into our conversations, you know that though.'

'Of course. But did you get a sense of his mood?'

'He was scared of somebody, a dealer I think, but I can't say any more than that.'

Clement wondered how far he could go in touching on the Autostrada case.

'There was a critical piece of evidence pertaining to another case, something Turner stole ...'

'Is *accused of stealing*, I think you mean.'

He didn't blame her for coming on all lawyer-like but it irked him. 'Yes, found in his possession. We desperately need to know where it came from. Did he give you ...'

'He never went into any detail. There wasn't time for that. I was looking at his good record and an argument to get him bail.'

Which has been the cause of this whole problem, thought Clement. But he had the will to hold his tongue. They dithered for a minute longer but the body had slipped from the conversation and left them only with garments intended for decency. Clement ended the call promising to catch up soon. He'd made a hash of it.

...

Hubris comes at a price. It wasn't bad enough I'd tried to act like I was still twenty-five and copped a whack on my head for my trouble. I also rejected out of hand Clement's offer of the use of his house. Not satisfied with those errors, I resisted the doctors' suggestions I take a room at the hospital, insisting I could ride it out in casualty until they cleared me. They didn't. They told me I was grounded until 8.00 am. I tried to sleep across seats. A nurse took pity on me and offered me a pillow. Finally they allowed me to go. The drive back to Broome was interminable and I felt nauseous, from the hit or lack of sleep or both. Twice I had to pull over thinking I was going to throw up. It must have been around 11.00 in the morning when I stumbled into my room at the Mimosa. After talking with Clement I'd turned my phone off and did not turn it back on. I fell on the bed and slept. A knock on my door finally woke me a little after 3.00 pm.

Clement stood there.

'Hi there, champ,' he said. 'You weren't answering your phone. I thought you might be dead.'

'Dead to the world.' I stepped back to let him in. 'Please tell me we have something.'

'I wish. The word is out. Jared Taylor is checking every one of the gorges with the Parks and Wildlife people. We have a plane up but it's Sunday, so it's tricky. Also means no autopsy but I spoke to Rhino. He's checked the beetles from the body. He puts date of death close to August nineteenth.'

The day after Ingrid and her boyfriend Coldwell were last seen at Sandfire.

'You want a coffee?'

'That,' I said, 'is an excellent suggestion.'

...

We availed ourselves of the café at the Mimosa. It was expensive but worth it. Not just because the coffee was good but because my legs still were rubbery and my hip sore where I must have hit the dirt hard. It took me back to my famous game when South Fremantle's Timmy Wittenoom cleaned me up. As if by some mutual truce we didn't talk the case, or cases as they may have been.

'So, you had a good day with your daughter?'

'It was great. Sometimes it's the only thing I can keep hold of. You know what I mean?'

I did and told him so.

'How many times have you been married?' he asked.

'Once.'

He scraped away the fern pattern on his cappuccino froth. 'You're lucky, then. It makes you feel like a failure you couldn't get it done, see it through.'

'I know plenty about that: Autostrada being one example.' I thought back to the Gruesome case. I got it right in the end but I missed what was under my nose too. In the spirit of bonhomie I took a stab in the dusk.

'The night at the Pearl. That wasn't with your ex?'

He shook his head. 'She's got a fella. Getting married in a few weeks.'

'The lawyer?'

He looked up sharply. 'Somebody talk, or you figure that out yourself?'

'I picked up the vibe when we called around. She's beautiful, you don't mind me saying so.'

He shrugged, no objection.

'Love of my life looked like that, back when I was a young man and video players were the newest thing on the block. Guess that's ancient history for you?'

He smirked. 'We didn't have a video player. I had to rely on friends. And up here there was never anything new to watch.'

'Supposedly we're the envy of the world. We've had twenty years or something like that without a recession but I don't see any improvement. People have to work harder now than ever to pay off a home: that's two people working instead of one. You can't get into a hospital or, if you do, you'll get a worse infection than you started with. We used to leave bottles of beer for the garbos at Christmas. They'd know your street, know the women who were pregnant and if one wasn't around when they called they'd ask: has she had it yet? Now it's one guy you never see in a truck. Next it'll be robot trucks.'

Clement was in step with me. 'They've already got those up here for mining. What I miss most, everybody was pretty equal. Like holidays. When our caravan park first started you'd get businessmen, doctors and their families, right next door to a tradie with his kids. By the time my folks closed, it had all changed. I can't see it's for the better.'

'We don't make anything anymore,' I said, like the curmudgeon I was. 'Not even biscuits.' Mind you, this didn't stop me eating the tiny packaged Italian biscotti that came with my coffee.

'Exactly.'

'And yet,' I said, unable to keep from saying it, 'he's still out there.'

I didn't have to explain. Clement knew.

'Not for much longer, right?'

He held out his cup and we clinked. I prayed that wasn't more hubris.

CHAPTER 24

Because of the volume of things to do, Clement made sure he was at the station 5.30 Monday morning. He had slept well, which was surprising with so much running through his head. Sidney Turner was still missing but Earle and Shepherd were to follow that up, at least from the Mongoose Cole end. Lisa Keeble had said the autopsy would be first thing today. He guessed that might mean around 8.00 am. They'd got nothing on Jane Doe's fingerprints. Jared Taylor and his posse of sorts were still searching for the Feister vehicle around the gorges. Getting more planes up would be Risely's concern. Clement guessed they'd get started soon. Until proved otherwise, he was going to treat the Autostrada investigation as separate to the body-in-the-desert. The next stage would be to interview all those motel guests – particularly the four men of the right demographic – about their whereabouts back during 1999, 2000. Whether it was him who got to do that was moot, although ...

His eyes fixed on the map: the dot that was Telfer out in the desert. He certainly could speak to Henderson. Graeme Earle arrived at 6.00. Clement filled him in about Snowy Lane. They talked about Mongoose Cole. Risely and the AFP were pursuing the drug-running end. Clement knew the AFP would not take kindly to him or his people muddying those waters. They'd want Cole to think he was in the clear while they monitored him. Josh Shepherd arrived in time to be the beneficiary of Clement's distilled thoughts.

'If Cole won't crack, maybe somebody close to him will. Try and get one of his men busted in the act. Then we can offer a deal. He tells us what Cole did to Turner, we go easy on the charge.'

Both men had plenty of informants they could tap. No sooner had they left, than Risely arrived. Two planes were up covering the Gibb River Road to Wyndham.

'It's an enormous stretch. If he keeps the car covered, it will still be hard to spot.'

Right now Clement didn't need Risely's lack of faith, even if it was justified. On the other hand, his boss was optimistic about the Mongoose Cole situation and busting a major drug supply ring. The Feds, he said, were 'very interested in our intel'.

Mal Gross arrived, clocked his superiors in discussion and went to his desk. Clement waited till Risely had left, then approached his sergeant. Gross was prepared. He had pulled records on all the known victims of Turner's burglaries. The ancient and minor transgressions of Bruce Henderson were the only things he'd found in the way of a record. It was possible however that something might crop up from one of the other state police. He had asked them to check the backgrounds of people listed.

It was nearly 8.00 by the time Clement finished with Gross. A sense of unease seemed to have taken possession of him, his personal relationships, these cases, all seemed out of his control. After leaving Lane, he had driven to Louise's but their last disastrous conversation pressed on him like an unwelcome hitchhiker and once again he had not found the courage to stop. Instead he'd gone home and intricately checked his bearings on every aspect of the two cases he was running in tandem. Despite his sound sleep none of his sense of powerlessness had dissipated. He made his way to the kitchenette, not so much needing a coffee as hoping it might provide a timeout, some breathing space. Manners was already there, his monster chalice in his mitt. He beat Clement to the punch.

'I ran those phones for you.'

It was one of those little loose ends Clement had reminded himself of last evening: he had asked Manners to run the numbers called and received on all the phones Turner had stolen. He didn't know what he was looking for really. If the Autostrada killer ran a double life maybe there might be some discrepancy: calls to bondage sites, a link to somebody from the original case. TV cops would so often look behind the book that didn't sit quite right on the shelf and, lo and behold, discover an important clue hidden. Okay, nobody seemed to read these days, but it was not a bad metaphor, he thought.

'Anything interesting?'

The idea that he may have been expected to analyse anything himself seemed to shock Manners. He muttered he'd just collated the data and dashed off to get it. It was just the interruption Clement didn't need. His doubts came gushing back. How dumb was he? He should have stopped in at Louise's last night, banished Marilyn with great sex. Now he'd not spoken to her since Saturday night and that absence of contact had amplified vague unease into something almost tangible. Would she even want to hear from him?

Manners returned with a bunch of pages. 'I listed all the calls in and out: Who To, Who From.'

At least that was something.

'What should I do with this?' Manners held out a mobile phone still in its evidence bag.

'What do you mean?'

'It was one of Turner's stolen phones but nobody claimed it.'

Clement fought to keep his anger under control. 'That's been sitting there?'

'I guess.'

'Why didn't you tell somebody?'

It would have been so easy to take that silly mug out of his hand and dash it on the floor. The severity of the rebuke forced Manners to blink.

'I told Josh.'

Still roiling, Clement dialled Shepherd. Soon as he answered, he went in hard, all the frustrations finding a focus.

'Manners says he told you there was a spare phone in Turner's haul.'

Shepherd sounded offended rather than chastened. 'That's right. Hey, if they're not going to ask for it back, I'm not chasing it up. We've been flat out, and my shoulder's still knackered.'

The hazard of keeping Shepherd out of the loop now loomed big and clear. Shepherd had no idea of the significance. He thought it was just a piece of loot that had been retrieved from a burglar.

'You should have told me.' Clement stabbed the phone off with bitterness.

Manners had the look of a man fearing he was next for execution.

'Do you know whose phone this is?'

Manners, edgy about giving a suitable reply, hesitated mid-sip. 'I wrote it down.'

'Could you go get it please?'

Manners put down his coffee cup and once again moved off in haste. Meg appeared, sensing something had gone down but not letting that affect her. Nothing much affected Meg.

'The detective bloke's here.'

'Send him through.'

Lane arrived before Manners had returned. Clement's gaze was drawn instantly to the right temple.

'Some wag at the servo asked me if I was a Dockers supporter who'd forgotten to remove the facepaint.'

Clement couldn't suppress a smile. Truth was it was almost as purple.

'They're not big on empathy up this way,' Clement said and was surprised to see Lane offering him a takeaway coffee.

'I saw the way you looked at me last time. Thought you might bushwhack me for this. I played the odds: flat white. I drank mine on the way.'

Clement thanked him and sipped as he gave a cursory run-down of what was in train to find the vehicle and hopefully the assailant.

Manners appeared with a list printed on A4.

'Phone's owner is Chelsea Lipton, Perth address, no landline.'

Clement scanned his memory. 'There was no Lipton on the motel list was there?'

He directed the question at Snowy Lane rather than Manners, but they both answered 'no' in unison.

'What about the earlier burglaries? Could it be from there?'

Clement could not recall a Chelsea Lipton being a victim.

Lane said, 'He could have stolen it from a beach bag, or coffee shop.'

Manners jumped in. 'It's an old android. I could check for photos.'

'Good thinking. Be careful about fingerprints, just in case.'

It was a long shot. Most likely Sidney Turner's would be the only prints found, but you never knew. While Manners was engaged he asked Mal Gross to see what he could find on a Chelsea Lipton.

'Perth address.'

He beckoned Lane follow him to Manners' room, which was full of electronic gear he had no idea about. I should be up on all this, he told himself. This is the future and I'm just a more recent version of Snowy ... a poor man's version, without the instinct.

Manners looked up from his computer. 'There are a few pics.'

Clement leaned in for a look. He felt Lane behind him. The photos started with two typical highway shots from a driver point of view inside a car. They appeared to be somewhere around this region. Then came a shot of a very long train, wagon after wagon, winding their way into the distance. Clement guessed Port Hedland. The next five shots were all of young women on stage in skimpy, see-through clothes. One close-up showed a brunette singing into a microphone.

Lane's big knuckles flicked his shoulder. 'That's the pub at Port Hedland. This must be sExcitation.'

But it was the next shot that really yanked Clement's attention. It was a much wider snap of a fairly large room and a party of sorts seemed to be in progress. There were open pizza boxes, long necks, other spirit bottles scattered around. In the background, sitting by himself with what looked like a sizeable spliff in his fingers, was Max Coldwell. Front and centre, laughing with a couple of the revue girls, was Ingrid Feister. Lane spoke a shared conclusion.

'This has to be the party, the night before Ingrid disappeared.'

A charge roared through Clement's body. Sidney Turner had stolen a phone that nobody had claimed. The phone and the pendant could have been stolen from the same person. If they found the phone owner, they likely had the Autostrada suspect. There were another seven photos but they were all tourist type snaps of Broome, nothing incriminating. Clement came back to the photo of the party. There was only one question on his mind.

Who had taken that photo?

CHAPTER 25

The thin column of smoke was about a kilometre to the north. Richie Rich gritted his teeth and flattened the accelerator. A fire in these conditions was always a concern. It didn't seem to be growing larger so he had to assume that for now it was just a campfire. Tourists were stupid with campfires, Aussies no better than the international people, in fact probably worse because the others tended to read up on what was acceptable practice. Rather than wait for the track, which was nearly two kilometres ahead, and then cut back around, the ranger figured he was better off cutting through the bush direct. The ground here was sparse enough for him to pick his way through with his big four-wheel drive, dodging the odd larger tree. With his windows down he could now smell the smoke quite clearly and soon found himself driving across open ground to its source. Surprisingly it was old Warry who stood there, turning his way. Though this was Warry's neck of the woods, he invariably cooked early morning and evening so Laidlaw had not even considered him as the fire's author. The old fellow was gesticulating and running off a stream of words in the old language before Laidlaw had even managed to stop. As Laidlaw decamped from his car, he was able to see that Warry had not been cooking. The fire had been a signal. Warry had been carefully tending it to supply smoke with a minimum of flame. This realisation came as he was deciphering Warry's turbulent speech, which was a jumble of words, only some of which Laidlaw knew: there was a young fella and he thought he was dead. Warry pointed out the direction, then doused the fire as Laidlaw grabbed a first-aid kit from the car and ran, foremost in his mind the missing couple from Perth. Warry had made his fire where it was safest, for this part of the bush suddenly thickened, with hostile tendrils trying to trip Laidlaw, bully him to a different route. A yell from Warry behind and a hand gesture sent him further to the right, and that's when he saw the body sprawled in the dirt, the right leg lying at an unnatural angle so he could tell at once it was broken. It was a young Indigenous fellow, not somebody he recognised right off. He was very still and his first thought was that he was dead but, checking his neck, he found the faintest pulse.

...

I don't know if I had ever been so excited yet so frustrated. Winding the clock back, I suppose with my first girlfriend, Sharon, when our ardour pushed us down the slippery slope towards the promise of ecstatic sex, only to find the road blocked by common sense ... hers, her hand lowering like a boom gate and stopping mine. We had the phone of somebody who likely had been involved in the Autostrada abductions and the known death of Jess Scanlan but we were stymied for now on their identity. Clement had been on to Perth asking for a couple of uniforms to go and interview Chelsea Lipton at the Como address given on her driver's licence details. The question could be a simple one: your phone has been found, had she given it to anybody? He had yet to hear back. So far he had not notified HQ. I thought his precautions were sensible. Clement didn't strike me as the kind of guy who big-notes himself. Hey, I'm sure, like me, he wanted to be the one who solved the biggest mystery in WA history but his motivation was genuine. Once the press got hold of this, the killer – if he did not already know we knew – would be alerted and could once again slip through our fingers. The guy had to be smart to have remained so long unknown and I feared the likelihood was he was already far from where he'd lost his 'trophy'. But the next question rose as inexorably as a pimple after Easter: Was there another more recent trophy to take its place? Had he abducted Ingrid Feister? Maybe stolen her car. Was Ingrid Feister dead?

Whichever way I looked, the odds seemed bad, the omens bleak. He'd been at Port Hedland when she and Coldwell were there. They had left the next morning and not been seen again. More dark speculation sprouted. Could the body in the desert be Lipton? Even if it was, that didn't mean Ingrid wasn't also a victim. Something might have kicked the killer off again, another spree the result. I wondered if these ideas had occurred to Clement. Generally he was a beat ahead of me but at the moment he was in his boss's office on a phone call to Keeble at the Perth autopsy of the desert corpse. I kept my head down in the squad room, flicking through the phone photos that Clement had since transferred to his computer. The sExcitation people were due to play Broome tonight. Thanks to being cracked on the scone, I'd missed the Derby show. I wondered what time they'd get in and where they were staying. Maybe I could front them before then. Clement re-entered the main room.

'No positive ID on the corpse yet. Chances of DNA are skinny. Rhino confirms Keeble's likely time of death.'

His phone rang. He answered and spoke in bursts short as Phar Lap's starting price. I waited rather than piece dots. It didn't take long.

'The uniforms I asked to check on Chelsea Lipton. No sign of her but a neighbour says she's in New Zealand.' I floated the idea about her being the victim. The way his face clouded I could tell that this time I'd been ahead of him.

'I hope you're wrong.' He announced he was going to try her next of kin and disappeared into his office. I heard the low rumble of his voice and studied a cobweb on a light fitting, trying not to think. He stepped back in on a cordless, speaking aloud for my benefit.

'You spoke to Chelsea last night and she's fine.' He gave me a thumbs up, mouthed "her mother". That was something. He slid back into his office. I could hear him getting Chelsea's New Zealand contact numbers. I was left sitting there, redundant. I'd been a cop. Last thing you wanted was some civilian taking up space in your squad room. I eased out to get Clement and me another coffee. My temple had been sore to sleep on but the fog had gone from my brain and my senses were as clear as the Broome air. I could smell desert, ocean and scented flowers right up to the threshold of the café where bacon and coffee took over. Out of nowhere I felt an almost physical pang: the absence of my women, Tash and Grace. I think it was probably in the background the whole time and the instant there was a gap in all the crap surrounding me, it just dove in. I went through the motions of ordering two coffees to take away but all I could think was how I missed them. It was early hours in the morning in Barcelona now. I'd thought of Skyping them last night but I was bushed and I didn't want to worry Tash about me getting sconed. Grace is a teenager, the world revolves around her – actually it does – hence her mother being in Spain. I'd have to be on life-support before it kicked in that her old man was flesh and blood and might be worth worrying over. She was spoilt, of course she was, she was all we had. Not a brat though, a nice kid, kind to her friends.

Sometimes I wondered if she'd had a brother or sister would she be any less self-obsessed but I doubted it. We would have liked at least one other kid but even before Grace, we agreed that if Tash didn't get pregnant or couldn't hold a baby to term, we weren't going to investigate our fertility and travel down the road of IVF. We might have adopted if we were able. As it turned out we were lucky, Tash got pregnant pretty quick, nothing much went wrong. But it was a one-off. For whatever reason she didn't fall pregnant again. My brain made connections, skipped back to Gerry and Michelle O'Grady. I desperately wanted to give them closure over Caitlin. I realised I was staring at a sExcitation poster for the Cleo tonight. That prompted me to stop indulging myself with personal shit and get to work. The hotel phone number was in the bottom corner. It was near 10.00 as I took my coffees; it would be open. I called. Some guy answered.

'Hi, this is Mitch from the *Post*.' A copy of the local paper was right in front of me so I improvised. 'Could you tell me when sExcitation get into town and where they're staying?' I figured they'd tell a journo, thinking, free publicity. Otherwise I could be any perve. The guy I was speaking to had no idea what time they got into town but they were staying at the Boab Apartments. I thanked him and started back with my coffees.

...

The squad room was all action. Something had gone down. Clement appeared, moving fast from the direction of the gents.

'A ranger near King Sound found a young guy matching Sidney Turner's description close to death in the bush. He's on his way to Derby Hospital with him. It was quicker to drive.' He saw the coffee, deduced. 'Me? Thanks. That's two I owe you.' He grabbed one of the cups.

'Is he conscious?'

'Not from what we can gather. Shit.' Something had occurred to him. He was back on his phone. 'Keeble, me. Need you back here. We found Turner, alive, just ... soon as.' He ended the call, yelled for Mal Gross to get uniforms to secure the area where Turner was found, and turned back to me as he scooped keys. 'You coming?'

'I'm going to follow up on the dancers.' The last thing I wanted right now was more hours on the road and another visit to that hospital.

Clement was moving towards the back door where Graeme Earle waited with it open.

'Stay in touch,' called the vanishing Clement.

Car doors slammed and they were out of there. Everybody except the IT guy had vanished as quickly as they'd appeared. He was standing at the kitchenette holding a massive mug.

'You know where the Boab Apartments are?' I said.

...

Workwise the day had been undemanding but he'd been unable to concentrate. He couldn't stop thinking about the kid. Pure panic, and dumb, the whole thing. The dose was wrong but he'd extrapolated as best he could. He could have waited, tried to get more information, but he was worried somebody might turn up, catch him in the act. The problem was he acted too hastily. What were the chances of the cops even identifying the pendant? Say they had, there were plenty of innocent explanations as to why it might be in his possession. Okay, they'd dig but could they actually prove anything? No, but his life would be wrecked.

He'd shut himself up. It was dark back here. It reminded him of that night ... Jessica. Why did she have to struggle? It was her fault really. She'd come to him, hadn't she? Placed herself in jeopardy. There were plenty of warnings about the girls who had disappeared. She could have stayed away. She should have stayed away. You couldn't put it all on him. It was fate.

For the umpteenth time he went through the list he'd made before: hypodermic, disposed of in bush, no prints. The hunk of wood tossed in a different location. There were no traffic cameras near the kid's house, he'd made sure of that. He started to calm. He was safe, he was safe, he was safe.

But still he felt ... edgy. Music would help. Music while he worked. Where was his iPod? He checked the desk where he thought he'd left it. No. Then perhaps ...

He slid open the drawer but it was not there either. He looked all over. No. No. His sense of unease grew. When was the last time he'd had it? Yesterday? No ...

He remembered now. He had it when he was preparing the syringe. He could recall the song he was listening to, Huey Lewis. Surely he hadn't taken it with him? Or had he? Before the kid, he'd had things to do. He'd been rushed. Fingerprints wouldn't be a disaster but there'd be other ways to crack an identity, an account number, notes ... He had to act quickly, there was no time to dither. Maybe he had taken it with him after all. The car! It had to be in the car. He'd done that before. He dashed outside, fast, obsessed.

But even before he reached the car he slowed, a sense of dread enclosing him like a net. It couldn't be in the car. He'd washed and vacuumed it thoroughly, every centimetre. Even the undercarriage. He'd replaced the tyres, just in case there might be trace. Fevered, he searched regardless: glove box, under seats, through pockets. His shirt was soaked with sweat. The iPod was not in the car. It was not here. It could have fallen out. It could have fallen out when he got the boy in or out of the car. The kid had been hard to wrangle. It might be out there now, in the bush, a beacon pointing the police towards him.

CHAPTER 26

'When I found him he still had his hands tied behind his back.'

Laidlaw exuded common sense. Clement had warmed to him immediately. The nickname Richie Rich didn't fit at all.

Clement examined the severed rope in his gloved hand. Good quality but common garden rope.

'You cut it?'

'I had to hurry.'

'I understand. You did the right thing.'

Laidlaw was smart enough to have brought it back with him. They were sitting in a corridor at Derby Hospital on office chairs that had somehow escaped from their usual location. Turner had gone straight into emergency. The female doctor treating him had told Clement it was touch and go whether he would survive. He was severely dehydrated and appeared to have suffered head trauma. She saw no chance of him being conscious in the immediate future. Two hours of hard driving it had taken to get that news and Clement did not want it to be all for nothing. Graeme Earle had gone to find them a light beer. They were over coffee, tea or water, and the one Pepsi already consumed was enough for a week.

'You didn't see another piece of rope?'

'Nope. I was in a rush.'

Earlier, Clement had managed to talk his way into the treatment room on condition he observe from a distance. He asked the doctor to tell him if Turner's ankles showed any sign of having been restrained. She couldn't say for sure but the signs were not 'inconsistent'. She wouldn't hazard a guess as to what had caused the trauma to the back of his head, not at this stage.

What conclusion could he draw? Turner had been abducted? No, that was a bridge too far. Turner may have gone willingly with another party. What seemed indisputable was at some point his hands and feet had been bound. Had he been beaten first then tied up? Or was the trauma the result of his fall when he tripped? One likely scenario: he'd managed to get his feet free and made a break for it but this still left the question as to the scenario preceding that. Had he been beaten, tied up, left for dead? If somebody wanted to stop him revealing where he'd found the pendant, why hadn't they finished the job? Had Turner escaped before they could? On the other hand, if this had nothing to do with the pendant, if it were Mongoose Cole or somebody in his employ, perhaps they'd dumped him as a warning to keep his mouth shut?

Laidlaw had said something.

'Sorry, what was that?'

'I was out there the other night. I thought … I don't know what I thought … maybe I heard … I looked around, you know. I must have missed him, the kid.'

'Which night?'

He watched Laidlaw count backwards, his lips moving oh so minimally. 'Thursday night.' It was Monday now. 'I had pasta. I was worried. There's a big croc out there, didn't want some tourist getting taken.'

'Is it common knowledge, the croc?'

'With the locals, sure. Old fella who camps out there, seen her a few times, tells anybody he comes across.'

Could somebody have tied up Turner and left him for the croc? Jesus, that would be the pits. It reeked of something Cole might do. If Turner survived, he would have got the message, and if he didn't … problem solved. A helluva lot of variables but there was still a chance whoever had lost that pendant didn't know it wound up with Turner. Graeme Earle arrived, his bag clinking in time with his step. The beer was a lifesaver.

'Any news?' he asked.

Clement looked back down the corridor to the room where Turner was being treated. There had been little movement. Was that a good sign? 'Nothing so far as we know.'

Earle offered Laidlaw a beer but he waved it off. Clement surreptitiously pulled out a stubbie and twisted off the top. He was just about to get the amber to his lips when his phone rang. Why is it always the way? he thought, putting relief on hold.

'Clement.'

'It's Chelsea Lipton. I got a message to call you.'

'Yes, Chelsea, thank you. I'm a police detective in Broome investigating a series of burglaries. Your mobile phone has turned up.'

'Broome? Really?'

Clement was well attuned to falsity. He detected only genuine confusion.

'You never gave it to anyone?'

'No. I left it in the drawer in my bedroom. I didn't think there was any point bringing it on my holiday. Roaming charges, all that.'

'How long ago did you leave?'

'Two weeks. I'm skiing. Here for four more days.'

'You have a boyfriend or relative who might have taken it?'

'My boyfriend is with me.' There was the slightest pause. 'There's my flatmate.'

'What's his name?'

'Her. Sonia Rochdale. She's a flight attendant.'

Clement elicited a phone number. Chelsea Lipton was still bamboozled.

'I'm sure she wouldn't take it ... she would have told me.'

'When did you speak to her last?'

'I skyped her about a week ago. We've been texting. I use my boyfriend's phone. She never mentioned a robbery or anything like that.'

'She married? Boyfriend.'

'No. She's a bit of a party girl.'

Clement read casual sex, recreational drugs.

'Do I need to cancel my phone?'

'No, we have it here, but it's evidence. We might need to hold onto it for the time being. Why don't you enjoy the rest of your holiday and we'll work something out when you get back? We can probably send you back the sim card. Do you know a Dave Grunder or Bruce Henderson?'

She did not. Nor Shane Shields or Damon Kelly.

'One last thing. You don't possess a pendant do you?' He described it.

'No. Nothing like that.'

He finished the call and explained the gist to Earle.

'Somebody took it. The uniforms didn't mention a break in?'

'No, but they might have missed it.' Or, Clement was thinking, some 'friend' of the flatmate could have helped himself. He dialled the number for Sonia Rochdale he'd been given and hit voicemail. He left a message for Sonia to call him as soon as possible. They finished their beers. Laidlaw had been sitting there, quiet, patient. Clement's phone rang again. It was Mal Gross. Justin Coulthard, one of the detectives on the night shift who specialised in drugs, had popped one 'Jungle Jim' Thornley the night before, carrying eccies. Coulthard told Jungle Jim his grief would be lessened if he spilled on Cole and Turner. Thornley said as far as he knew it was nothing to do with Cole. He denied Turner was dealing for Cole, said he was too 'squirrelly'.

'What did Coulthard think?'

'He was inclined to believe him. The tablets we found on Turner aren't anything like the batch Thornley was carrying. That rang a bell. I went back and checked an email from the Pilbara boys a month ago warning of some eccies that were cheap and nasty. They look identical to Turner's. I'm sorry, boss, I should have picked it earlier.'

'Don't worry, you do a great job.'

He relayed the info to Earle who chewed it over. 'Turner could have travelled to the Pilbara for his little earner.'

It was true, a bigger can of worms, one that would have to wait.

'Of course, if he was dealing in competition to Mongoose ...' Earle didn't have to complete the thought. Clement understood. Cole might have been out to eliminate that competition. He spoke to Laidlaw. 'This old fellow you mentioned who camps out where you found Turner?'

'Warry.'

'Can you take us to him?'

'Sure.'

'How far from here?'

'Forty minutes.'

He was calculating. The uniforms would have cordoned off the area by now, Keeble's crew would be arriving any minute, Keeble herself was still probably an hour off landing, plus the drive. There was no sense hanging around.

'We'll follow you.'

They got up. Clement felt a twinge in his knee. The first sign of age. He told the others he would meet them outside. He needed to notify Olive Pickering but did not have her phone number on him. He called Mal Gross and got it.

She answered on the second ring. He imagined her waiting right by the phone, the slow tick of a clock the only sound.

'Mrs Pickering, it's Detective Clement.' He heard the intake of breath.

He imagined her praying the next words out of his mouth would not be 'he's dead'.

'We've found him.'

Little gasps, a sob. He did not want to build her hopes.

'But he's in a very bad way. He's unconscious with a broken leg and head injuries. He's in Derby Hospital.' He ran through the bare bones of it. 'There is no guarantee he will survive.' She was babbling, part thanks, part fear of the worst outcome. 'I will arrange a police car to bring you here.' He was already thinking Jo di Rivi. 'Would you like that?' Eventually he got a yes. He called Gross back and told him to give di Rivi a car and for her to bring Olive Pickering to Derby to see the boy. 'Ask her to call me first.'

He finished the call, walked down to Turner's room and cracked the door open. The doctor was still there. She was young, thirties he guessed, Indian, Sri Lankan maybe.

'No change?'

'We're just trying to stabilise him.'

'I'm organising a policeman or woman to be on call. If he regains consciousness please notify them. It is extremely important.'

'You could be waiting a long time. He may never regain consciousness.'

He hoped to God she was wrong.

...

They used to call it a motel but I guess apartments sounds better. No, I'm being disingenuous there. Motels always have concrete as a motif, a second-level balcony with iron railing or a long narrow porch. The Boab Apartments were single level and eschewed a long concrete porch for small wooden ones. The apartments were built in four blocks of four, each block two apartments side by side with matching ones behind. The porches were higher than the old-style single concrete step; two wooden steps plus the apron. They also featured an overhang roof that gave shade, plus wood-chip gardens, but I was guessing there was still a slip to order breakfast the night before and a kettle for you to make your own complimentary weak tea from bags as skimpy as the costumes the girls wore. No doubt too, a few of those long-life milk pods that proved impossible to open without squirting something nearby. The other thing that hadn't changed was the kidney-shaped pool surrounded by a few chunky wood lounges behind a steel fence erected to prevent the drowning of unsupervised toddlers while their parents slept to the rumbling of a temperamental air conditioner. I'd stayed in a heap of these places down through the ages. My clients rarely ran to more than three stars and their cheapskate husbands, or their wives who were having affairs with somebody else's cheapskate husband, seldom performed their sins in luxury love-shacks. I'm not saying it doesn't happen, just not in the circles from which my clientele is drawn. Which I suppose reflects on me. That said, I'd rarely had the experience of standing at the edge of one of these pools looking at four hot young women sunbathing. These were clearly the sExcitation dancers. Now, when I say 'hot' I'm not talking supermodel or super-athlete hot. All the girls had about them an aura that suggested a prior history of stacking shelves, hairdressing and early-teen body-piercing; however, compared to the fare normally on offer around the communal blue kidney bean, female or male, they were noteworthy.

I walked to the gate. 'Hi girls.'

The girls looked up and waved. It's a funny thing, endearing, girls who had worked low-pay, sore-feet jobs were nearly always open and friendly, even to an old guy like me. I think they felt the world was smiling on them. They were happy, and happy to give it back.

'You're the dancers,' I said. They were split fifty-fifty between brunette and blonde.

'Yes, we're on tonight.'

'At the Cleo.' I wanted them to know I was a fan. 'You guys did Hedland a couple of weeks ago, is that right?'

One of the blondes seemed to be a little more the spokesperson. She confirmed what I already knew.

'My name is Richard Lane and I'm a private detective.' I could see the scepticism on their faces.

'I bet you say that to all the girls,' laughed the blonde and the others tittered.

'No, seriously, I am. I used to be a cop but I've been doing this thirty years.'

'That how you got this?' One of the blondes cheekily pointed at my scarred forehead.

'In the line of duty, yes.' I wanted to shift it on from my less than glorious effort. 'There was a young couple at your Hedland gig, they partied with you guys afterwards. They left next day and have not been seen since the roadhouse at Sandfire.'

Now I really had their attention. Only then did I open the childproof lock on the gate to join them. I got their names: the talkative blonde was Sierra, the other blonde, Dana, the brunettes Briony and Teagan. I hoisted up my folder.

'I'm sure you'll remember them.'

I opened it and produced photos of Ingrid Feister and Max Coldwell. Two of the girls were hazy but Sierra and Teagan reacted.

'Oh yeah,' they said in a kind of lopsided unison.

'This is a photo of the party, see?'

I produced the photo that showed them eating pizza after the show.

'You think something's happened to them?' one of them asked while I was busy sorting photos.

'That's what he's trying to find out,' Sierra said on my behalf.

'What I'd really like to know is, who took this photo? Anybody remember?'

In turns they all squinted, shook their heads.

'There were a few people hanging around,' offered Sierra.

I pulled out one of the other photos that showed Dana strutting her stuff on stage.

'Here's some other shots the person took. You remember somebody taking phone shots of you?'

They laughed. 'We get so many guys doing that,' Briony said.

I was growing twitchy. I felt so close. 'What about this girl?'

I pointed to the fifth dancer. She wasn't present here.

Teagan said. 'Kelly quit.'

I felt like Scott of the Antarctic must have when he was down to his last dog. 'Did you guys take any snaps of the party on your phones?'

Blank looks. Sierra said, 'You should ask Alex. She's our boss. She videos all our shows.'

A jolt went through me: smoke on the horizon, a supply ship to rescue me. 'Where do I find Alex?'

Sierra pointed towards one of the blocks of apartments. 'Number three.'

'Thank you, ladies.'

They waved me adieu and told me they'd see me tonight. I was trying to keep a lid on it. Maybe this could pay off after all. It was hotting up, honky nuts were scattered over the bitumen where they would store up the heat. A memory echoed, Tash telling me to sunblock. But they were no more than dust motes. My brain was ninety-nine point nine percent full of one idea: a video of the Hedland show.

...

As I approached the apartment I heard music from inside. The same track was being stopped after a few bars and restarted repetitively. I didn't recognise the song but I could guarantee the clip featured the young female singer surrounded by a dozen male dancers who looked like nobody I've ever seen at my barber's. I reached the open door and called out but the music must have been too loud, nobody answered. I knocked, and poked my head inside.

A slim young woman with long red hair was working on a dance routine in a bikini. A pocket-sized woman, muscular like she did aerobics, and wearing a singlet and three-quarter leotard, watched her carefully. The redhead saw me first. The other woman turned too, killing the music. She was probably forty or just shy, with a hardness I've seen in women who worked mining camps or were ex-army: too much sun, drinking and a divorce, but a sense of fun too.

'Sorry to interrupt. Alex? My name is Richard Lane. I'm a private detective. I'm hoping you can help me.'

The older woman appraised me, spoke to the dancer.

'Take five. Work on the left turn. It's sloppy.' The dancer skipped outside. We were in an all-in-one living room and kitchen area. The furnishings comprised bamboo-style couch and armchairs, a small glass dining table with two tubular chairs. The couch and armchairs had been shifted to create a space. Alex moved to the fridge.

'Water?'

'Thanks.'

'Got a show tonight and a new dancer. Trouble with this business, they don't stick around. They get money in their hot sweaty palm, or some bloke whispers sweet nothings, and they're out of here.' She poured water, offered me a glass. 'So?'

I pulled out the photos of Ingrid Feister and Max Coldwell.

'These people disappeared the day after your Port Hedland show. The family hired me to find them.'

She studied the photos, shook her head. 'Sorry.'

'They came to a party the girls had after the show ...'

'I can't help you. After the show I'm packing up and counting money. Then off to bed for my beauty sleep.'

That ruled out her identifying the cameraman from the party.

'I believe you take a video of the performances.'

'Yeah, check the girls are doing the routines right. Put it up on our Facebook page. It's the way these days.'

'Would you still have footage from the Port Hedland show?' My heart was pumping against the roof of my mouth.

'I dump it all on the hard drive.' She jerked a thumb at a laptop sitting on the table.

'Would it be possible to take a look? These people haven't turned up. We can't rule out foul play. I want to see if there's anybody suspicious.'

She looked me up and down. 'Don't see why not. Richard?' Like she was checking she had my name right.

'Lane. People call me Snowy.'

I got the sense she was sifting memory to see if she'd heard of me. Evidently not.

'You can check it here if you don't mind us rehearsing.'

'Of course not.'

She moved to the computer and found the file. 'I shoot the routines. I file them under the name of each dancer if it's a solo, or "group". Most of the time you'll only get backs of heads because I'm near the lighting desk. You might be better off checking this file.' She pointed at a folder marked CUTAWAYS. 'I do grabs of the audience.'

I clicked on the folder. There were a dozen files in it. I opened one. It seemed simple enough to work.

'So it could be some nutter?' I heard her hunting for a packet of cigarettes. 'Plenty of those up this way.'

She crossed to the door and called out, 'Gabby!'

I smelled the smoke as Alex lit up, the last thing I wanted, but I wasn't in a position to complain. I heard the girl from before come back in and they started back up, dousing the audio of the pub gig I was watching. The visual quality wasn't great. It was too dark in a lot of places to make out faces, but I saw what the girls were talking about: half the guys in the audience held phone-cameras. Alex must have been standing side of stage right as she videoed. Every now and again you caught a glimpse of the dancer as she moved to the front. I was especially keen to see Dana because I knew our camera guy was filming right then. The people near the front were fairly clearly visible but I knew from where the Dana camera shot came that whoever took it was about middle of the room, pretty close to centre stage, maybe slightly to stage right. I went through three files: bupkis.

I was on the fourth file, vaguely aware that in present time Gabby must have been getting better because she was being stopped less often, when on the video, I saw Ingrid Feister with Angus Duncan and the Chinese guy, Shaun. They were over near the wall stage left. It was only fleeting and I couldn't make out whether anybody was paying undue attention. Of Coldwell there was no sign but Shaun had a smile on his dial bright as Shanghai by night. I made a note of the file number but when I struck out on the next three I was back to being Scott of the Antarctic as he roasted his last dog.

The Chinese believe number eight is lucky. And it was on the eighth file that everything happened: the fragmented, fractured puzzle suddenly cohered. Alex was shooting but slower, lingering a little more than the quick sweep of the other audience grabs. Dana ever so briefly sliced through frame, two perfect butt cheeks in a spangled thong shaking, I later discovered, to an INXS song. I zeroed in on the section of the audience where our unknown photographer had been hanging and hit the motherlode. There was one guy with a phone-camera, half-lit, good enough for ID but his camera arm was blocking his face. And then the number must have stopped because people were applauding and he dropped his arm. Bingo. There he was. I made him as late thirties to forty, average height, average everything. I found rewind and went back to recheck. I got the shot again and hit pause.

What the ...?

My pulse wound so fast the watch-face shattered, the springs fell out. I was sure I recognised the guy. Or he looked awfully like somebody I knew. My brain was treacle. I picked out film actors: no, no, no ... think. I forced myself back to 2000. Out of nowhere I saw Cathy Freeman in her special spacesuit. Post-race photos. The race I never saw because I was camped out in Mosman Park, watching this guy smoke dope by the ocean, then breaking into his car. I had him now.

Shane Crossland.

CHAPTER 27

The old fellow had not seen a car. But he had heard one, Thursday around lunchtime. He wasn't sure where exactly, his hearing wasn't so good these days, but he knew it was somewhere down the mangroves where he'd seen the crocodile. 'Those fellas are in for a surprise,' he thought to himself. Here he showed a gummy smile. One tooth stubbornly clung to his upper mouth and three to his lower. They were sitting on the ground at Warry's campsite. Warry himself had the luxury of a small fold-out stool, his bony knees rising up in front of him. Behind him was a modern, tautly assembled tent. His swag consisted of a bedroll, a small aluminium pot, some cutlery, a fishing handline and, incongruously, a pair of small, modern binoculars.

Clement was grateful he had Laidlaw to help out on translation. Old Warry spoke his own version of pidgin and it would not have been easy to follow. He had not heard the vehicle leave; by that time he was off, heading further east looking for dinner.

'So you never heard a vehicle between Thursday and today when you found him?'

Warry had not. 'Only when he come.' He pointed at Laidlaw. That had been Thursday evening. Today Warry had been heading west tracking a goanna. Well, he found a bloody big goanna, didn't he! Here he laughed himself silly, flashed all four teeth again. He pointed at his heart, scared him to death! His laughter wound down. Soon as he found the fella, he ran back to his camp and started a fire. He knew that would bring the ranger.

Clement asked if Warry recognised the kind of vehicle he'd heard. Warry shook his head. There had to be a good chance of tracks, there'd been no rain. He checked his watch. Keeble would be arriving at the airport soon. Her assistant techs including Mason were already here. Graeme Earle was supervising them in the restricted area that started fifty metres or so west of this spot. Clement's phone rang. His first thought was it was the hospital. He'd arranged for a uniform from the Derby station to be standing by. His second thought was Jared Taylor had located the Feister vehicle. But the ID showed Snowy Lane.

'Yes, Snowy.'

'Got him.' The fever in Lane's voice was audible even through the tiny speaker.

'Who?' Clement told himself to be patient.

'The camera guy from Hedland who used Chelsea Lipton's phone. Our guy.'

Everything incidental fell away. Clement was aware only of Snowy's voice.

'I went and saw the dance troupe. They had a video of the Hedland audience. I matched the video to the angle of the shot. I recognised a face.'

Now Clement was being lifted off the ground, weightless. 'Who?'

'Shane Shields. The sExcitation girls remembered him at the Hedland afterparty but didn't know his name. I took a copy of the video shot to the Pearl. The receptionist recognised him. Only he wasn't called Shane Shields when I made him as a suspect in the original investigation.'

Clement's throat constricted. He could barely make a sound. 'He was a suspect?'

'My suspect. Back then he went by the name of Shane Crossland. I was sure there was blood in his car. The techs told me it was smoke. He was a dope-head but he knew at least one of the girls.'

Clement said, 'I'll meet you at the station.'

···

They were powering back in record time. He had Earle drive so he could think more clearly: Crossland was at Port Hedland the night before the Feister girl and her boyfriend had vanished. He'd been at the Pearl Motel when Turner had burgled it but never reported the phone missing: because it was stolen, because it would lead the police to him when they found the pendant. It had to be him. What were the chances of anybody else with the pendant being in the same motel on the same night as a suspect in the original Autostrada investigation? Turner could nail it for sure, but there was no news from Derby Hospital. Jo di Rivi had called to say she was there with Olive Pickering. It had taken three calls, replete with dropouts, to get the gist. That had been half an hour ago. There had been no change in Turner's condition. He suggested she use the radio for updates and had to deduce from its silence that nothing was changing. One thing that didn't jive if Crossland aka Shields had done away with Coldwell and Feister and stolen their vehicle: why hadn't it been seen in Broome when he stayed at the Pearl? It seemed complicated to hide it on the Gibb River Road where Lane had come across it. How would Crossland have got back to Broome? He ran the question past Earle. He was good for this stuff, logical. Earle digested at a hundred and forty k per hour.

'Only thing I can think of is he had an accomplice.'

That made sense but it complicated everything. Another possibility occurred: the car had been dumped but then stolen by somebody else and they were the ones keeping it out of sight. Snowy Lane could have been clouted by a simple car thief. Clement tried to call Lane. He imagined him guzzling coffee, checking his watch five times a minute. Unfortunately the signal still wasn't strong enough to get through. He wondered if Lane had asked the Pearl if Crossland registered a vehicle when he stayed there and made a mental note to follow up. Before leaving Derby he'd called Mal Gross and asked him to get everything he could on Shane Shields aka Shane Crossland. Clement found himself watching low grass speed by. It must be what it's like to be a cheetah, he thought. His brain skipped to Louise. He should call her, let her know about Turner. He tried her number. No reception. A minute later the radio buzzed. It was Mal Gross.

'Yes, Mal.'

He expected it would be about Crossland. It wasn't.

'Jared just radioed in. He's got a ranger who has spotted the Feister vehicle on the Mitchell Plateau – Kulumburu track about halfway between the Gibb turn-off and Drysdale. He's on his way now.'

This was a whole other thing now. If it were Crossland in that vehicle it could not be left to a ranger and a police aide.

'Tell Jared not to approach. Same for the ranger. Just keep an eye on it. We'll fly in.'

They were thirty minutes out of Broome, maybe less. The track was back in the direction from which they'd just come and then some, back along the Gibb River Road where Lane had been attacked and further to the north. Sometimes you just couldn't win. This region was so enormous. He relayed the latest to Earle and added, 'I better inform the boss.'

'You should have reception now.' Earle had travelled these roads for decades, fished in remote areas. He knew its anatomy. Clement did what he suggested. He'd not spoken to Risely since immediately after he'd left the hospital to give him an update on Turner. Earle was right of course. Clement waited as it rang. Risely answered.

'Has he regained consciousness?'

'No, and that could be a long way off. I need a plane. Graeme and I are about twenty minutes out. Things have been moving fast. Taylor has eyes on the vehicle on the Mitchell Plateau track and there's a shitload more Snowy Lane can tell you about. He's in there now.'

'I saw him hanging about. What's the plan?'

'Fly to Drysdale River Station, get them to loan us a vehicle. Bring in the closest chopper for support. Move whatever ground units we have up the track.'

'I'll have a plane ready for you by the time you get to the airport. You have vests?'

'No.'

'I'll make sure they are in the plane with some food, radios, the rest of the fruit. You want Shepherd?'

'Yes, good idea.'

Risely said he would get a plane sent from Derby too with three more bodies for backup.

Clement was appreciative. He ended the call and told Earle to head for the airport. Then he called Lane.

'Sorry, mate. This has to be police only.' He felt for Lane. He'd been the one making the big breakthroughs. Lane said he got it. 'I've told the boss you'll update him.'

'He's heading my way now.'

'I'll let you know as soon as.'

'Please do.'

Lane wished him luck. Clement was happy to accept.

...

Shepherd was waiting at the Cessna with the young pilot, Stephanie. She'd flown Clement a few times. He felt sorry for her. He had no doubt

Shepherd would have been hitting on her. Earle excused himself for a quick slash, after which they piled in. It was 3.30. Clement had done ten hours straight, driven around five hundred k already and was about to fly as many again before at least another hour's drive.

'I reckon I'll get you there just after six.' Stephanie's voice was nasal. She had blonde curly hair and the kind of smile Clement could use right now. Six was not optimum, it would be sunset or just after. They'd have to drive in the dark. Shepherd was garrulous and eager to speculate on who might have the Feister vehicle – he still had no idea about Crossland or any Autostrada lead. His voice was like a drill in Clement's head, so much so that Clement was actually grateful for the real mechanical sound of the engine that made conversation too difficult to bother with. The sandwiches were tomato and cheese, melted and squished. Neither Earle nor Clement cared. They'd consumed nothing but a stubby of beer. They tore into them.

How quickly we lose our gentility when we are starving, reflected Clement. He rolled the wax and brown paper into a little ball and slipped it inside their kit. He could easily have eaten another two. Flying had never affected Clement much one way or the other. Like most people he sensed in himself some innate fear of crashing but otherwise he approached it like a bus ride, an uncomfortable necessity. Lately, however, he had come to enjoy being aloft over vast tracts of land, skinny rivers, railway-model shrubs, lonely twisting roads. Up here the concerns of the world could be contained; an enemy uselessly waving arms beyond a castle's moat. This could be my life, he thought. The river down there was Marilyn and me, winding through arid, barren nothing. It never really occurred to him it would dry up. I have to let you go, he thought. I have to, I have to ...

Then woke with a jolt, realising he'd been dozing, and was embarrassed he might have spoken aloud. But a glance told him Graeme Earle was out to it in his seat and Shepherd was hanging over the co-pilot seat probably boring Stephanie senseless. Even if he had talked, the engine was too loud. But he'd been asleep longer than he might have guessed. The light through the windows now was yellow-orange, the colour of decay, of times passed, of opportunity lost. Clement watched the yellow fade to light, then dark grey.

As far as Kimberley landings went, Drysdale River Station was a Heathrow. There was actually a long gravel strip. Clement had several times had to put down on nothing but a grassless paddock or dirt road.

Stephanie was true to her word. It was 6.07 as they started in for the landing. The Derby aircraft had already arrived. Clement could see it, through the gloom, parked off the strip. Earle's eyes flicked awake as they bumped and skidded down the strip, little rocks flew. They pulled to a halt and Clement clambered out. His legs felt stiff. The smell of earth was strong with the arrival of dusk. He was pleased to see the Derby contingent included Sergeant Dave Drummond and the leviathan Luke Byrd, promoted to a senior constable. The third man he hadn't met before.

'Con Katzios,' said Drummond and they shook hands.

Clement said, 'Gentlemen we don't know what we have here. A couple have been incommunicado but we can't be certain that's not by choice. However, we do have an unidentified female, deceased, time of death a good fit with when the couple was last seen. We also have an assault on a PI who was hired by the family to find the couple. The ID of the assailant is unknown. We also have a suggestion of a historic criminal potentially having a presence in the Kimberley.' He noted Josh Shepherd's shock. 'However, we have no evidence he is the assailant. So, let's tread carefully. Let's try and solve this simply by a stealthy approach. Best we take him or them by surprise.'

They had two four-wheel drives at their disposal, both filled with diesel. While the others loaded up, Clement made radio contact with Jared Taylor. His position was fifty k south-west. He was about a kilometre from the Feister car, which was lying about four k east of the road in reasonably dense bush. His own car was a further three k back with the ranger's vehicle. Taylor had hiked through bush leaving the ranger back at the cars. Clement asked Taylor how long he thought it would take them to get there.

'Cross-country, dark, you're looking at an hour at least.'

Clement told him to stay in radio contact and repeated he was not to act even if the vehicle made a move. Then he went and joined the detective vehicle with Shepherd at the wheel and they pulled out. The Derby guys dropped in behind. The moon was out but there wasn't much more than an eyelid showing.

As expected, Shepherd started right in. 'Who's the historic criminal? Mongoose?'

'No. And we don't even know if the guy is a crim but he might have links to an abduction investigation. That's all I can tell you right now.'

Earle met his eye, he understood: that's all Clement wanted to tell him.

It was a moonscape out there. The first twenty-five k was fairly simple. There was a well-worn cattle track they could follow and they made good time. Clement navigated and picked the point where they had to go totally bush. In the wet season it might have been unnavigable but apart from hard bumps in the rutted ground it wasn't too bad. They had almost reached the coordinates of the ranger and police vehicle when the radio crackled into life.

'Somebody has left the car and is wandering around. I'm not sure what they're doing. It's dark.'

'We must be close to your vehicles. See you soon.'

It was less than five minutes on when they saw something iridescent and red to their right about three hundred metres away. Shepherd changed direction. The headlights of the second vehicle followed. Shepherd's headlights picked out the red again.

The ranger was waving a red glowstick. They cruised in quietly. Clement got out. The ranger was a young guy, not more than twenty-five. Clement introduced himself and learned the ranger's name was Donald.

'Jared's down that-a-way.'

He pointed at eight o'clock. Earle had got out now too. 'What do you think? Take the cars or not?'

Clement had been wrestling with that the whole way. He didn't want to risk the quarry driving off. On the other hand, if the guy was armed ...

'We'll go in on foot. Have the others standing by.' He relayed information to the Derby car. Byrd was driving. 'I want you guys to circle around to the track in case they make a break back that way.'

Drummond rogered that and they moved off. Clement, Earle and Shepherd checked their weapons. Clement didn't want a vest on yet. It was too far. He bagged them and made Shepherd haul them. He radioed Jared Taylor again.

'We've left the cars, we must be about a k off.'

'I'll shine the torch your way.'

They saw the distant light and adjusted accordingly. Clement killed the radio. The three of them spread out as they approached Taylor's position. Without the torch he would have been undetectable. He was crouched behind a ring of taller trees. Clement shook his hand.

'Any more action?'

'The figure headed into the bush. I thought he was carrying something, maybe a rifle. Then I heard movement on the far side about a hundred metres from me. I think they are still there. Might be having a crap.'

'What about the car?'

'Nothing.'

He signalled for the vests. Shepherd broke them out and they fitted them on. They re-checked their pistols.

'Jared, you wait here. Graeme, you take the car. Josh with me.'

With a jerk of the head he signalled they move forward carefully. The ground was sparse but they weren't skilled enough to avoid twigs and branches in the dark and their stealth left a little to be desired. Fortunately there was a wind blowing now behind them and leaves were rustling above. Then Clement heard it, a murmur like somebody praying. He cautioned Shepherd to go even more quietly. The adrenaline in his body was more than counteracting the fatigue. His palms were sweating up. The voice was closer now, a man's voice ... melodic and ... that was music.

That was the point that Shepherd stood hard on what must have been a much a larger branch. It snapped like a gunshot. The figure let out an oath and swung towards them.

Shepherd raised his weapon and yelled, 'Gun!'

Clement threw his hand up to block the shot.

'It's not a gun, it's a guitar.'

Clement swung back now, pointing his torch. Max Coldwell stood blinking in the beam.

CHAPTER 28

Coldwell was thinner than Clement had expected and his beard had grown, Ned Kelly–style. He was jumpy, his head swivelling every time one of the others passed by where they were sitting on fold-out chairs. Shepherd and Earle were gloved up, examining the car thoroughly using ultra-bright, brick-shaped torches. Of Ingrid Feister there was no sign.

'I told you. She hitched a ride.'

'With a South Australian couple. This morning.'

'That's right.'

The detail of the couple being from South Australia rang true if Coldwell was the simple, hippie-nik he projected. It was also the kind of thing calculating killers made up to sell their story. Clement was sure the kid was hiding something. But then, that was exactly what you wouldn't expect from a calculating killer. It made Coldwell a conundrum.

'You get a licence? Names?'

'Um, Jenny and Keith.'

'I mean surnames.'

Coldwell shook his head. His eyes bobbled. Jared Taylor and the young ranger were in quiet conversation with Drummond and the Derby cops who had driven around to link up. It looked like they were heating soup on a primus.

'I don't know what the problem is. Ingrid didn't feel well. I wanted to stay out here, see the falls.'

Clement ignored the plea for an explanation. 'Her people were worried about her. Neither of you has been seen since Port Hedland.' He wouldn't mention the body yet.

'That was the point. You don't come to the outback to meet people.

There's no phone reception out here.' He pulled out his phone and threatened to throw it away. 'We wanted it that way.'

'You didn't even stop for food.'

'We had stuff with us.'

All Earle had found in the car were a couple of muesli bars.

'Maybe you did at first. There're not many supplies now.'

'We've been living off the land.'

'You fished?' Clement put together the earlier reports.

'That's right.'

He could tell Coldwell suddenly felt on safer ground.

'So, this South Australian couple were ...'

'Heading to Derby. I told you.'

Clement made a show of checking his watch. 'They should be there soon.'

'You think I did something to Ingrid? That's crazy.'

Time to peel a layer.

'Ingrid's family hired a private detective. He found the car near Adcock Gorge. Somebody hit him on the head with a branch. Was that you?'

'No!'

The denial was a bit too shrill.

'You didn't hit this man?'

'No, I didn't.'

'You didn't see him there?'

Coldwell's Adam's apple bobbed. 'No.'

Clement did not for an instant believe him. 'He was knocked out not far from your car.'

Coldwell continued to shake his head. 'I never saw anyone, I never hit anyone.'

'You heard nothing? He said he was calling your name.'

Coldwell shrugged: search me. Jared Taylor arrived with a cup of hot soup for him.

'Jared here found the guy, knocked out, didn't you, Jared?'

'That's right.'

The whites of Coldwell's eyes were expanding. Clement offered him the cup.

'You hungry? Would you like some soup?'

'I'm fine.'

'No, you look like you're going to keel over.'

This time Coldwell took the cup. It was too hot to sip immediately. Clement wanted it for himself. He was still famished. While the soup cooled he changed subject.

'You're a singer.'

Coldwell said he was, took a tentative sip.

'I wish I had that talent. You know Doctor John?'

Coldwell did not. Clement was hardly surprised. He did not make this observation public, however. Now was empathy time.

'It's amazing out here, isn't it?'

'Yeah.' Coldwell sipped more hungrily, more relaxed now.

'I'm sorry if it seems like we're coming on a bit strong but bad things happen out here sometimes. We found the body of a young woman in the desert.'

Coldwell looked down into the soup, sipped more quickly.

You know something, Max, Clement thought.

'We're pretty sure she died around the time you guys left Hedland, so, no offence, but you see why we're curious when Ingrid isn't here.'

Coldwell looked him in the eye, more resilient again. 'She's on her way to Derby. She might be there now.'

...

I hadn't felt tension like this since the last quarters of the 2005 and 2006 grand finals between the Eagles and Swans. Grace and I watched them together. She was six or seven. It was yesterday. I cooked. Okay, I heated up: party pies and sausage rolls. Her whole life she'd been indoctrinated that the only team that mattered was East Fremantle but that train had been hijacked by Victorians and a few carpetbaggers who purported to have WA footy's best interests at heart. I and a handful of other chumps were left on the platform holding our valises, laden with personal history, while full carriages rolled by crammed with those who believed in the Promised Land of AFL and national domination by the super team the West would inevitably assemble. It was my fatherly duty to set Grace free of her heritage and I duly obliged but she never really felt any real affiliation to Eagles, Dockers or anybody else. The sausage rolls had given way to tapas. I bet if those bars in Barcelona put up a party pie or two they'd be a sensation. I could have done with a few of them right now. This wasn't my station house, not my squad room, and my only real ally, Clement, was hours away. I felt isolated, incidental, and didn't like it. I paced,

I stretched, I thought of Skype and Tash and dismissed it, thought of calling Dee Vee and dismissed that too, because sure as I did, something would break here. The other cops mostly ignored me. Scott Risely checked on me early on and then cloistered himself in his office. Mal Gross updated me as Clement's convoy drew near the Feister vehicle. I tried to assemble my thoughts coherently, it was impossible. I kept telling myself I'd know soon enough, why waste energy on 'if' and 'but'. Gross entered, chewing something.

'Five minutes away,' he said. I'd peed not twenty minutes before but went for another slash. What did that waste, two minutes? I couldn't take it, my blood pressure was too high and I felt light-headed. I needed air. I slipped back towards the front desk manned by the night roster, a young uniform male with curly black hair and a nose that suggested the Colosseum and togas. He was bent over a book studying something. My phone went. Dee Verleuwin. I was half a mind not to answer. The other half won. I figured my clients had a right to know we'd found the vehicle.

'Hi, Dee we're about to ...'

'She's fine. Safe and sound in Derby. She rang her father twenty minutes ago.'

'Ingrid did?'

'Yes.'

It's appalling to admit, but in that instant I felt deflated. I should have been euphoric. It was like I'd been hoping Coldwell and Ingrid Feister were murdered so it would fit my half-arsed theory. Dee Vee was talking on, and the back of mind caught the gist the way the mesh catches rubbish on a pipe outlet. A jumble, a few shiny objects: Ingrid and Max had split up earlier, she didn't feel well, he wanted to stay, she didn't want to wreck his trip. She'd hitched a ride to Derby.

I got back on even keel. 'You want me to check her out?'

'No, she assures her father she's fine.'

'It's definitely her?'

'I think her father recognises his daughter's voice.'

It was a good old-fashioned chide at my expense. She ran through details. My service was terminated but I would be paid till the end of the week. Mr Feister thanked me for my assiduous work. She told me to file the last leg of my expenses when convenient. As for the physical trauma she understood I had endured, while the client accepted no responsibility, Mr Feister was pleased to offer a five hundred dollar bonus. Her language was distancing me already. I wondered if she was annoyed I'd kept her so much out of the loop or if one of her employers was listening in but it wasn't our usual cosy repartee. The phone was inert in my hand when Mal Gross entered to say they had located Max Coldwell at the vehicle but not the girl.

'She's in Derby,' I said.

...

The carpark was full but I jagged a space close to the front door. A bunch of young men stood nearby smoking. No doubt about it, sExcitation could pull a crowd. Where else was I going to go to celebrate and drown my sorrows in equal measure? The answer appeared to be 'Not here' because there was a hastily handwritten FULL HOUSE on the door. I thought my senior years might cut me some slack.

'No way, José,' said the doorman putting three fingers on my chest. I couldn't fault his originality, he possessed none. His arms were fire hoses when the water's pumping. I was about to turn away.

'He's with us.'

The voice came from my right. The diminutive Alex finished the stump of a cigarette and ground it under her high heel. She still favoured the mini.

'I thought you weren't going to show, Snow.'

I didn't recall giving her my name. She saved me brain effort.

'Your name was familiar. I looked you up online. You solved the Mr Gruesome case.'

'It seems a long time ago.'

She moved towards the door and the big man stepped back to allow us both through.

'It *was* a long time ago,' she quipped. 'I was three.'

The place was jammed, broad backs in singlets and body-shirts obscured the stage.

'Not bad for a Monday night,' I observed.

'That's why I love these tours. They want entertainment and they are prepared to pay.' She somehow found her way through to a clear space. I could see the stage now. 'Last break,' she confided. 'Like a drink?'

I offered to get her one.

'Don't bother. We're on the house.'

I said a beer would be fine. She caught the eye of the distant bartender besieged by thirsty patrons. There were few women present. She yelled for a beer and bourbon and Coke. The backing tapes were half volume. She ran her scanner over me.

'You look depressed.'

Nailed me in one.

'I finished my job tonight.' Cryptic as a losing footy coach in the post-match.

'So you're at a loose end,' she winked.

'I'm married and too old for you.'

'Now you're flattering me. There's still more buff than puff about you, Snow.' The barman reached through the crowd. Good-natured blokes passed our drinks across. 'But I respect the marriage rights. Lord knows somebody has to. My ex left a lot of ground for somebody to make up. We can still talk, right?'

'Of course.'

But I was already thinking of Shane Crossland and where he might be this very second. Mal Gross had made inroads on his background but he wasn't sharing until Clement was back, likely around 1.00 am. With hindsight it was flimsy stuff that had led me to suspect Crossland had done Feister and Coldwell. Clement's instinct about the vehicle had been right. I sipped my beer: cold, heaven in a glass.

The music suddenly powered in, the lights went starburst. Sierra took the stage, high kicks, a cartwheel without hands, a superb bum in tiny shorts. The audience loved it, especially when the shorts ripped away to reveal a thong. The girls did solos first, worked duo and trio routines before coming together for a full flush. No stripping, that wasn't allowed these days, but the wowsers hadn't yet found a way to ban suggestive dancing and acrobatics. As it was, it paled in comparison to some of the video clips Grace watches. Alex groaned at the new girl, rolled her eyes at me. I thought she was harsh. The girl wasn't as slick as her teammates but she'd get there and her red hair found favour with the crowd. I found myself looking around for Crossland. Okay, I'll be honest, that's the main reason I came here. If he was in the area maybe he couldn't resist. After all he'd taken snaps at the Hedland show. I divided my time between the girls and the audience. Like they'd said, lots of cameras.

I asked Alex to tip me on the final number, told her I wanted to beat the crowd out but would wait for her. She did, and I was able to set up in prime position. They started coming out five minutes later in a knot, followed by a short rush and then a steady trickle. Car engines caught and rumbled, spirits seemed high, no fights. It was twenty minutes before the staff ushered out the barnacles. I had not seen Crossland. Alex appeared at the door.

'You got wheels? Follow us to the motel. I'll be about ten.'

It was more like fifteen. Fifty percent more time to brood. Risely would have to notify the task force now. He couldn't keep Crossland off their radar. Maybe we had twenty-four hours but that was probably stretching. I checked my forehead in the rear-vision mirror. Still a little untidy. A perky horn sounded. Alex was at the wheel of a Tarago, the girls sequestered behind. I pumped my lights and followed through dozing Broome. Monday night and everybody who was up must have been at the Cleo. The town was a crypt.

We were greeted by four other vehicles snoozing in the Boab carpark. Our doors echoed. I complimented the girls on their show. Some of them were going to swim. Their eyes laughed at Alex and me as we walked to her apartment. They assumed we were going to get it on. Alex made her trademark drink of bourbon and Coke. I accepted a tumbler. She'd left the door open and the breeze hummed around us. I took a lounge chair, she went the sofa, slipped off her shoes.

'Long day,' she said and rubbed her feet.

I toasted her. The bourbon proved to be a fist in a velvet glove. She examined me over the rim of hers.

'Walk into a door?'

I realised she hadn't been there when I'd told the girls about my war wound.

'My client's boyfriend; hit me with a branch.'

'The ones you were looking for?'

'Yeah. I wasn't sure until now it was them.'

'With clients like that ...'

'Exactly.'

I asked her how she wound up in the business. She'd qualified as a bookkeeper she informed me.

'But the only place I could get a job was Woop Woop mining camps, books and paymaster. The money was good but there was nothing for the guys there to do. First chance they got they'd head to the races, or the brothels, or catch a plane to Perth and burn money.'

She had sensed a business opportunity but everybody said girly shows in pubs couldn't work now that stripping was banned. 'I always thought it was more about what guys wanted to see, than what they got to see.' She put the show together, refined it, and it had been running five years. 'The trouble is keeping the girls. It's high turnover. Sometimes they don't even tell you they're going. A few of them are on drugs: E and coke mainly. I warn them. They don't listen. Eventually they get slack. Or they meet some fellow, he splashes around a wad of cash. Three weeks later they're begging for the job back. But once bitten ...'

She let it trail off. After a little time she said, 'Tell me about the Gruesome case.'

She knew of it, sketchy bits. I ran her through a censored version over the course of the bourbon.

'Another?'

'Thank you but I'm completely bushed, though I am grateful for the hospitality.'

There had been a few shrill calls from outside as the girls had initially hit the water but even these had faded. She walked me to the door. It was like one of those school-day dates, pleasant. She stood on her toes and pecked me on the lips.

'You have a card?' she asked.

I fumbled around, came up empty. She handed me hers instead.

'If you're ever at a loose end in an outback town, have a look around, we're probably there.'

...

The pool was deserted by the time I climbed into my car. I wondered where Crossland was this minute. I was angry. This could have been avoided if the right moves had been made twenty years ago. I pulled out and drove the dark road. There were no streetlights and the moon was mean with what it offered. My phone rang. Clement.

'Hi.'

'Thought you might still be up. Just lobbed in Derby.' It was 12.51 by my phone.

I told him I was heading back to the Mimosa.

'Or you could turn around and crash at my place in Derby.'

'It'll be near three before I get there.'

'More like two-thirty. And I'll make you breakfast in the morning. We have a lot to talk about.'

He was right about that. I dropped anchor.

'You got a GPS?' he asked and yawned.

'Yeah.'

He told me the address. 'I won't be up but I'll leave the door open. You can stay in my daughter's room. The bed should be long enough. I've got a toothbrush and razor if you don't want to have to drive back to the Mimosa.'

Twenty minutes extra sleep sold me. I was already on my way to Derby.

CHAPTER 29

Something shook me awake. I had no idea where I was. Taylor Swift was looking down on me.

'Wake up, Snow.'

I tried to focus through gloom, detected Clement. He was real, Taylor was glossy and paper thin. Things began to make sense. I had driven to Derby, found the house, one of those holiday-type places on stilts. I was in his daughter's room. I couldn't have been asleep five hours ... could I?

'What time is it?'

'Five-fifteen.'

I'd hit the sack about three. By 3.01, I was stone.

Clement was talking, in socks and pants, buttoning a shirt.

'Richie Laidlaw the ranger called me. He saw headlights in the bush a couple of k from the Turner scene. The techs finished up last night. He thought he should let me know.'

I was sitting up by now in my jocks. My clothes I'd folded neatly on the floor. I pulled them on. I had to aim to get my feet through the leg hole; even then I miscued twice.

'You okay?' Clement asked.

'Do I look okay? Where's the bathroom?'

He gave me directions, told me to help myself to a new toothbrush. I splashed water on my face. The bathroom reminded me of my own since I'd been batching, neat and passing a man's threshold for clean but would only have got a 'participation' from Tash; mirror smeary, sprayed but not wiped over twice, shaving cream pooled on the washstand. Plenty of new toothbrushes and paste and I noted the pink mug with the kid's toothbrush and the collection of mini perfumes. Yeah, I remembered those days. Now

Grace had the expensive real stuff. I gave the pegs a polish and was ready. I'd been such a brief time in bed I had no need even to pee. I found a mug of tea in my hand.

'Let's go. You can drink it in the car.'

It was still dark. My stiff legs descended the external staircase, my brain floating somewhere behind. There was a sense of a boat under the house but I couldn't swear on it. I oriented towards the cabin light of the car, which glowed bright yellow.

'How far?' I managed to ask as I slumped in the seat.

'Half an hour.'

We were already gliding into the gloom, a submarine leaving port.

'It might be nothing,' he said. It was pleasantly cool now. I sipped my tea and the world became three-dimensional again.

'So last night was a waste of time.' At the moment I was a glass-half-empty man.

Clement ignored the doom in my voice. 'Not entirely. We established Coldwell and Feister are okay.'

'Which means you have an unidentified corpse.'

'There's that,' he conceded. He picked up his radio and put a call through to the Derby station. He told them he needed some support and gave them a grid reference he'd written on his wrist. They only had one car available. He told them to send that. I was still mulling Coldwell.

'What did you make of it all? You buy Ingrid was sick?'

There was not a car on the road. We turned off down some minor road, thin bitumen, chipped on the borders so every now and again the tyres dipped and thumped dirt.

'Hard to tell without seeing her. I think they had an argument. You know how much cash he had on him? Eighty bucks, maybe not even enough to get back to Derby. He denies hitting you.'

I made the kind of sound you make when you've just heard a politician tell you he'll make you better off.

'I warned him we would be in touch but I want to see what she has to say first.'

It was all a secondary concern.

'And Crossland?'

'Shane Shields is an alias. He's never changed his name. He has a Queensland driver's licence and address these days. Gold Coast police checked on the address last night. It's defunct. He moved out three months ago. Manners is running the Chelsea Lipton phone and Crossland's phone and checking on recently called numbers. We'll have those by nine. Risely will be in touch with the task force this morning.'

And I would be sidelined again.

'Chelsea Lipton's flatmate called me. She brought a guy named Shane home one night. She identified Crossland off his photo. Odds-on that's when he stole the phone.'

She was lucky to be alive and didn't even know it.

'Do we have his vehicle?'

'He hired a white Toyota Corolla in Perth on August tenth, unlimited k's. Mal has circulated the number plate statewide. He can't hide for long.'

'Any locator device on the hire car?'

'Unfortunately not.'

I don't know how long we'd been driving. The tea was lukewarm. I sat there uselessly holding the cup until we saw the ranger's vehicle up ahead through murk, pulled off to the side of the road. We got out. Laidlaw advanced towards us. He was around six foot, big powerful shoulders, a gut that suggested he liked his tucker. Laidlaw didn't give time for introductions.

'I saw headlights in there. Nobody has come out that I've seen.'

We'd clearly beaten the Derby guys. Clement asked Laidlaw to wait for them while he and I went in. I don't know what I was thinking. I wasn't optimistic, that's for sure, not after my latest theories had been blown sky-high.

'The techs left at one am, apparently.' Clement had already started in.

'You think somebody was waiting for them to go?'

'It's possible.'

I've had longer conversations from a phone company's automated voice menu. That was fine with me, I shut up and followed. He seemed to have some idea where he was heading. There were a number of big trees, gums I supposed. I think we both saw the light at the same time. I was pretty sure it was a torch. It was about eighty metres away.

'By the mangroves,' he whispered. We edged closer. He added, 'Look out for crocs.'

I don't know how good he thought my eyesight was but it was still dark grey all around us. We closed another twenty-five metres. I could hear something now, somebody moving, like in a small area, fretfully. There was the light again. We began to edge forward more rapidly.

Radio static suddenly cut the air, off Clement's hip.

'Alpha One, this is Bravo. We can't seem to find you guys.'

The Derby cops at the worst possible time. The light up ahead doused. We were talking twenty metres. I heard somebody breaking away.

Clement yelled, 'Stop, police!'

We both charged, Clement faster than me. Up ahead came a splash as somebody entered water. Clement burst through shrubs to a muddy, mangrove flat. Just visible in the middle of the creek was the churn of water, somebody swimming.

'Fucking idiot,' said Clement and yelled 'Stop!' again to no effect.

I don't know why, maybe it was the shame I was still carrying from Craig Drummond's death and my hesitation then. Maybe it was thought of twenty years of mental pain and its potential relief being so close, or maybe I was still not quite conscious through lack of sleep. I knew there were crocs around, I just didn't care. I ran to the creek and started wading. I heard Clement shrill behind me but I couldn't tell you what he screamed. The creek was narrow, twenty-five metres perhaps. I began swimming, fast. Where my quarry was I had no idea. I didn't look up till I was within five metres of the opposite bank. I heard somebody up ahead, running, probably just topping the shallow bank as I reached shore. All of a sudden the light was pale grey. Sunrise somewhere. Too late for me to catch a glimpse, the rim of the bank truncated my line of sight. Then came my mistake. When I reached the edge of the creek I tried to run straight up the bank ahead of me but it was pure mud and I slipped straight back down to the water's edge. I lost valuable time picking myself up and tackling the bank at a slower pace where strips of wild grass provided a foothold. When I topped the rise I heard an engine catching and a vehicle pulling out. The sound of rubber and metal and broken bush taunted me. I ran blindly yelling, 'No, No!' as if my frustration was powerful enough to hook an anchor on the car's bumper.

It wasn't.

...

His heart was beating through his shirt like a foot pedal on the skin of a drummer's bass drum: boom, boom, boom. Where the fuck had they come from? He drove haphazardly through bush, hit a connecting track, he thought it was the thin one he had used while surveilling the tech team. They had pulled up stumps last night. They had taken down the tape but he waited to make sure they weren't coming back. He had meant to go in sooner, around 3.00 am, but had fallen asleep and not started till about 5.00. Was it a trap? Had they found the iPod and lain in wait for him? Were they already aware of his identity? Though terrified, he'd jumped into the creek; what choice did he have? All he could think of was the crocodile. He'd expected to feel the vibration of his own bones being crushed as monster jaws closed around him and dragged him under. The death roll. He could imagine his lungs bursting. But it was a risk he had been prepared to take.

No vehicle seemed to be following yet. It was still too dark for aerial surveillance. His pulse was slowing, finally. You've been through this, he told himself, what's done is done. You have to move on. You moved on once before, you left it behind you, you started again.

The first rays of light were just starting to creep through the trees but it was still dull.

Create space. Cameras, think cameras, they'll be looking for vehicles on the roads around this time.

No cameras on this strip. He'd taken the precaution of removing the number plates, and it was dark. He didn't think the police had seen him, that bark of the radio gave him just enough warning. Now was a crucial time. Avoid Derby at all costs, drive across country, loop around south, cross the Fitzroy River if needs be or head to Willare. You've brought a tent, fishing and camping gear. Even if they have the iPod what does that prove? The kid was a thief. He could have stolen it without you knowing.

You fucking idiot. He banged his head on the steering wheel. You risked everything and you could simply have denied it. 'Yes the iPod is mine but I never saw that pendant.' Maybe there would be prints, but maybe not. The kid's prints would be all over it. Or whoever he might have sold it to. The police probably don't have it. The kid was in hospital, unconscious, may never regain consciousness. He'd overheard that last night while lying there in the deep grass just out of range of their electric lights. He'd given serious consideration to just leaving. They weren't even searching in the right place. But then he thought, if they do have the pendant, then the iPod would betray him. Again he'd panicked because, as he had now just figured out, the kid was a thief. There were alternative explanations. Even if the kid came to and said where he got it, who was to say somebody else hadn't left it there? Yes, he'd been interviewed about the killings but so had thousands of others. A good defence lawyer would make short work of that. He wound down the window. No pursuit yet. The advantage of having parked on the opposite side *of the creek, just in case. He checked his car clock. Twenty minutes now, still not light. Put the plates back on, suspicious otherwise.*

He stopped, got out the car and screwed the plates in. He listened carefully for car engines but heard none. All he needed was for that luck to continue.

...

It was an hour or so after my dip in the creek. Clement and I sat in a coffee shop in Derby, an old-fashioned type where you got a toasted sandwich on laminex and the coffee was scalding but never tasted quite right. I'd just demolished a ham and cheese toastie, Clement was only halfway through his. I supposed I had forfeited my free breakfast from Clement and would be paying myself. He went to take another bite of his sandwich, put it down.

'What the fuck were you thinking?'

The question had no doubt been festering but Clement had been too polite, or busy, to chew me out publicly. He'd had to wait for me to circumnavigate the creek, then hike back towards Laidlaw who he'd radioed to drive in. We didn't know where our quarry had gone and by the time I joined the others, he had a fifteen to twenty minute start. The Derby police were only just arriving as we were leaving, so there was nobody on the northern side of the creek where the vehicle had disappeared. It took another forty minutes to get a chopper up. Nobody had seen the vehicle, nobody had seen whoever it was I had pursued. I could not even be sure it was a man. In my heart I expected it was Crossland, though why he'd be out there was a mystery. As big a mystery as why I'd jumped into that creek.

Clement was still waiting for an answer. I had a stab.

'What was I thinking? A hundred things, nothing. I didn't want him to get away again. I didn't want to be a coward. I didn't want to toss and turn at night telling myself I suck.' I told him then about Craig Drummond. 'I still wonder if I'd have been quicker ...'

I wasn't trying for empathy. Clement gave it anyway.

'You were in shock. I've seen it a thousand times. Doesn't matter how much you train, part of you is telling yourself 'this isn't real', and it's only when somebody moves, you get that validation. It's not cowardice, it's sheer bloody disbelief.'

The fact that he made the effort to justify my behaviour did make me feel better. But only better like when the horse you back runs second:

you're still a loser, just not as hopeless as the other losers. I felt obliged to state the obvious.

'It may not have even been Crossland.'

'I don't think you believe that. Otherwise you wouldn't have jumped in.'

'You should be a detective. What would he be doing out there?'

Clement threw up his hands. An idea needled me.

'Perhaps he lost something when he dumped Turner.'

'The techs didn't find anything special but they're running fingerprint checks on cans and other crap.'

'But they weren't looking there, right? They could have missed something.'

'They're on their way back out anyway, see if they can find tyre marks or paint, anything we could use at a trial.'

We sipped our hot, weak coffee.

'So, the task force has been informed?'

'Yep.' He wasn't any happier about it than me but we both knew it was for the best. He rethought his answer. 'Well, there isn't a task force any more, just a cold-case team of two detectives. But they'll increase that now. They were on their way to Crossland's parents and brother last I heard.'

'What about his own phone? Can you track it?'

'Not at the moment, which means he could still be in this neck of the woods. Last call was to Brisbane. The task force will follow that up.'

I asked him how long he thought before it all became public.

'Forty-eight hours if they are ultra-careful.'

'What about Turner?'

'It's not looking good. He's not improving.'

Shit all round.

A young woman entered the coffee shop. Even in her sunglasses I recognised Ingrid Feister. Her hair was wet, probably freshly washed, worn out. She sported shorts topped with a plain t-shirt, light blue, some kind of sandal. She was slimmer than a racist's logic but there was no sign of her being off-colour. I nudged Clement as she studied one of those menus where little white letters and numbers are pushed onto a black background and invariably go missing. Right now I guessed she was looking at 'COFF E $2.50'.

'Miss Feister.' Clement stood. His chair scraped. 'Detective Inspector Daniel Clement, Kimberley Police.'

She looked his way, removed her sunglasses, checked him up and down, and in that moment I caught something of the rapier that was also present in her father's gaze. Her voice was surprisingly sturdy.

'I'm so sorry if we caused a problem. We didn't understand people were looking for us.'

'But you weren't in touch with anyone since Hedland.'

'That was the whole idea. Well, Max's idea. You know, no phones, no iPads, no Facebook. It was okay for a while. And then I found there was no reception anyway.'

Very neutral, Clement said, 'You didn't even visit any roadhouses.'

She rolled her eyes. 'Max. He wanted to be Bear Grylls, you know, catch our own food. He thinks he's Indigenous.' Her eyes strayed back to the menu.

'I'm sorry. I didn't mean to keep you from ordering.'

A pimply girl slouched behind the counter like she could care less anybody ordered anything.

'No, that's fine. Is there anything else?'

'There is, actually. Your family hired a private detective to find you. He was assaulted at Adcock Gorge. You know anything about that?'

Her hands went to her face. It was a narrow face, more pretty than plain, but she wasn't going to be the Yoghurt girl on a bus billboard anytime soon.

'Is he alright?'

Clement pointed at me. 'That's him there.'

She gushed at me. 'I'm so sorry.'

'I'm fine, Ingrid. Nice to meet you, finally. Your family was very concerned. Me too.'

'My brother and sister will probably be disappointed.' That acid tone again. 'Are you sure you're okay?'

I told her I was sure.

'It was an accident ... well, not an accident exactly, but we were scared.'

Clement said, 'Max denied it.'

'He's not going to be in any trouble is he?' Her eyes pleaded with me. 'Poor Max, he gets frightened of authority figures and panics. Just being with my dad turns him into a blubbering mess.'

That I could understand.

'He was just trying to do the right thing, to protect me. All my life I've had it drummed in to me to be on the alert for kidnapping. It's second nature to me. And I had quite a bit of cash. Max came back to me in a panic. He said there was a man snooping around the car and he'd hit him with a stick. It's as much my fault. I just wanted to get out of there. We knew there was no way to call for help.'

Clement pushed out his bottom lip. 'You could have gone to the next roadhouse.'

'We were scared. We only heard about you last night when I rang home. I am so, so sorry. Please, I'm sure Dad will ...'

'That's taken care of.'

She turned back to Clement. 'Are we in trouble?'

'Mr Lane says he's okay, so, as for the assault, I think we can let that slide. But I would advise you to tell Max not to lie to police in future. We could charge him with obstructing an investigation.'

'Of course. Max is on his way here. I'll let him know.'

I said goodbye. She shook my hand, thanked me again and once more apologised.

...

Outside the sun was flexing in preparation for a big day.

'You don't think he was beating her up, do you?' I asked. He'd met Coldwell, I hadn't. Going on his photo, he was as dangerous as a sheep. But he'd given me a solid whack and there was something about her manner, like milk left a smidgeon too long out of the fridge. I didn't buy her being sick. She looked thin, tired, but not worse than the people on *Survivor*.

'No physical sign. You?'

I agreed in the negative.

Clement said, 'I think they had a blue, maybe about hitting you or maybe general lover stuff. She said 'fuck you' and took the money. He got to keep the car.'

I wondered if that reflected something of Clement's personal experience.

'Anyway,' he said, 'she's no longer my problem, but Jane Doe is.'

...

We were heading back to Clement's house so I could get my car.

'Are you going back to Perth?' he asked.

'What do you think?'

'Chance in hell?'

'Less. What happens with Crossland? Are you off the case?'

'No. If he turns up here, we'll be involved. But first priority is going to be the corpse in the desert.'

I said I couldn't believe there had been no missing persons reported.

'It's a different world here, Snow. None of that parking every day in the same underground car-space. Very few things defined. People are wandering thousands of k's on their own, or in small groups. Some of these remote communities, the kids just take off and there's nobody to look for them.'

'Your Jane Doe is not Indigenous, though, is she?'

'Indigenous or not, it's a transient world. People fly in from Sydney or Brisbane, work, fly out two weeks later. You've got holiday-makers and adventurers and wanderers, people who don't fit in. She might not have been missed yet.'

'But employers ...'

'A lot of them take it for granted they'll lose staff. People just up and go. Say it was a girl about to fly back to Melbourne. She never makes her flight. The airline calls her mobile. It could be anywhere out there, good luck finding it. Or she could be somebody touring through, hitching.'

Something he'd said pinged on my sonar. We were pulling onto the wild grass that did for his front lawn. What was it? Something about employers taking it for granted. And then I saw the above-ground pool he'd done for his daughter, and pieces got sucked together, images and words: Pool, Employer, Young Woman. I was back at the Boab Apartments, music was stopping and starting over and over. Alex was teaching the redhead replacement: the other girl, Kelly, had left without notice.

Clement had turned off the engine. He was looking at me now. 'What's up?'

'The desert girl died around the time sExcitation played Port Hedland. We know that because we thought it might have been Ingrid and that was when she'd been last seen. One of the girls in the show quit suddenly. I'm pretty sure Hedland was her last gig. I wish I could remember what Alex, the owner, said: something about drugs or rich guys, the girls think they have it made and quit at the drop of a hat.'

Clement was already on my wavelength. 'And Shane Crossland was at the Hedland show.'

CHAPTER 30

What had depressed Clement about having to call Perth in on the pendant case was not sharing any subsequent glory but that he had not already brought the case to heel. Police, he thought, were no different to any other profession – they liked to call their own tune. And he'd had that privilege but squandered it, right from when he'd chosen to keep Shepherd in the dark about the pendant and thereby missed getting earlier to Chelsea Lipton's phone. From this point on he would be an appendage acting on whatever Perth determined. However, Snowy Lane's revelation had re-energised him. The body in the desert was still his case and he could pursue that as he thought fit. That it may be related to Crossland was a bonus. They were back in his lounge room now. Lane had called the mobile of the dance troupe proprietor, Alex Mendleson, but received no answer. While Lane tried the Boab, Clement searched his desktop for the sExcitation Facebook page. It wasn't that easy to find. His search engine query threw up ten pages of suggestions. It occurred to him the world seemed to be able to wean itself off cigarettes and oil but sex was a different matter. He assumed it must still be lucrative.

Lane ended his call. 'The girl at the Boab says they left about an hour ago. She wasn't sure where they might be headed.'

'I can't find it here yet,' Clement was forced to admit.

Snowy Lane referred to the card. They switched to Facebook direct and typed in the address. As if by magic the girls appeared on screen. Upcoming Dates was easy to find.

'Dampier, tomorrow night.' Lane tapped the screen. Clement had seen it already. Dampier was on the coast south-west of Port Hedland.

'They'll be hours yet.' Maybe if he got lucky, he'd get a call through to

Alex Mendleson near Port Hedland. His eyes flicked over the five young women on the screen.

'Which one is she?'

'I think she's already been removed. That's the new girl.' Lane pointed at a slim redhead in a bunch of posed shots. There were some historic photos in the gallery but the girls were distant in them, their features indistinct. Fortunately Clement had brought his laptop computer with him from work and it contained the downloaded photos from Chelsea Lipton's phone, photos they assumed Crossland had taken. He refilled tea while the laptop loaded. He wondered if Louise would be in court at this very second and chastised himself for letting things drift. He found the file with the Port Hedland photos and opened it.

'That's gotta be Kelly,' said Lane as they scrolled through them. 'I recognise all the others.'

There were at least two good shots that showed Kelly on stage, full length.

A pretty girl, thought Clement, more striking than the others, higher cheekbones.

'What's that?' He had spied a mark on her lower leg. He zoomed in. 'Tattoo? Birthmark?'

'Tattoo for sure,' said Lane, peering in real close.

'Can you make it out?'

Lane shook his head. 'Too blurry, but it's a tatt.'

Clement was certain there had been no mention of a tattoo on the corpse from the desert, otherwise it would have cleared Ingrid Feister as the victim as she had no known tattoo. He dialled Lisa Keeble. She was in her lab sifting through stuff they'd found at the Turner location. She'd sent her team back to look for anything from this morning's activity.

'Don't get your hopes up on this lot. We were there till at least one this morning. I'm running prints on what we have. You might get more from today. Sounds like you disturbed him.'

'We did that alright.' He asked if she recalled there being any tattoos on the desert corpse.

'No, no marks, but the body was not intact. There was damage to the lower legs.'

That was right, animals or insects had got to work.

'But there was some flesh, right, mummified?'

'Yes, quite a bit.'

Clement asked her to call the coroner asap and get him to check. He thanked her for her efforts. It can't have been fun labouring through things: negative, negative, negative.

'Maybe it was wishful thinking about it being Kelly,' said Lane who had picked up a lot of what had gone down.

Most cases, you found yourself a balloon, you inflated, you deflated, over and over.

'It's a good thought. Let's see what happens. You know what it's like. They miss things sometimes.' Clement couldn't indulge himself any longer. He had to get back to the station. He asked Lane his plans.

'He might still be up here. I want to see it through. I'll keep my room at the Mimosa. For now I'm going to head back there and sleep.'

The man was prepared to risk being taken by a crocodile, Clement couldn't deny him that.

'I'll let you know what I can but it might get tougher with Perth involved.'

'It will get tougher,' said Lane. 'But I still want to be around.'

...

'They're excited.' Risely was in his office, pacing as if he too had the fever. It always seemed so uncluttered in here to Clement.

'I'll bet they are. Have they said who will be running the case?'

'I get the impression the Commissioner himself.'

Risely didn't have to editorialise, they both got it. The cold-case detectives would find themselves out in the cold so to speak. The Commissioner had his reputation at stake, he'd want to protect his legacy, or at least create a new one if the old one wilted under new evidence. So long as he didn't bury it.

'How did Perth go with Crossland's parents?' Clement asked.

'They last saw him a little over three weeks ago. His mother was ill after an operation and he came to see her. He told his brother he was living on the Gold Coast and working in construction. He said he was flying back there. His phone has been inactive for eighteen hours. The last calls he made were to old pals back in Perth. They claim he was just saying hi after catching up with them three weeks ago. He told them he was 'up north' but was not specific. The full list of calls is on your desk. They want us to follow up any Kimberley numbers. By the way, Feister called the Commissioner to thank him for our help.'

'Did he offer to pay for our planes and personnel?'

'Now, now, Inspector, somebody might think you resent us being an organ that helps the people.'

'Which people is the question. We seem to be pretty selective.'

'Don't get too cynical, Dan. We've expended a fair bit on the Turner boy too.'

Which reminded him, he needed to check in on him.

He took his leave and returned to the squad room. Graeme Earle looked up from his desk.

'Still no answer.' Among other things, like double and triple checking missing persons to see if anybody fitted the desert corpse profile, he'd been tasked with calling Alex Mendleson every ten minutes. 'I had a thought.'

'Fire away.' Clement liked it when Earle had thoughts. Usually that element was on standby because of fish or beer.

'We could see if there are any road patrols on the highway. Get them to pull over the bus.'

'Go for it. And contact Sandfire, tell them to keep an eye out and get Alex Mendleson to call me.'

'Done. I've put a list of all known Turner burglaries on your desk. Josh did a good job.'

Meaning, give him a pat on the back. It was something Clement often forgot. Mind you, where Shepherd was concerned, there were scant opportunities to praise his work.

'Where is he now?'

'In with Manners looking for CCTV of Crossland's vehicle on major roads.'

Clement made a mental note to check with the Sandfire Roadhouse for any footage of him. Something about Sandfire and the Feister case echoed but he couldn't haul it in. Too much on his plate right now. He shut himself in his office and imagined dissecting the space staring back at him. First he sliced it in two. One side was Shane Crossland, the other the desert victim. Step one: track Kelly the dancer and any other missing persons. That was in hand. Next: press release circulated nationwide. Then he switched to the other side of the dissected void: Sidney Turner can link Crossland to the pendant.

Clement transferred that thought into black marker pen reality on his whiteboard and wrote CALL DI RIVI. He did and found her at Olive Pickering's.

'I drove her back this morning. She needed a break.'

There was no change in Turner's condition. The doctors were pessimistic he was ever coming back to consciousness. He hung up and thought again about the pooch. The dog was dying and didn't know it. How much of our lives are dying every second without us realising? Not just our cells, but our love, our hopes, ambition. We're perpetually shrouded in ignorance. Maybe that was a good thing?

He fought it off, went back to the whiteboard. Was it Crossland at the creek this morning? He wrote KEEBLE, ANALYSIS. He wasn't hopeful of getting much from the tech but whoever was there this morning panicked; they might have left something. From his desk he picked up the list of calls assumed to have been made by Crossland on Chelsea Lipton's phone. It was not a long list, maybe a dozen to fifteen numbers. The people who owned the phones had been listed. At a glance Clement could see the early landline numbers were in Perth. The mobile numbers he couldn't tell but someone – he was pretty sure it was Mal Gross – had circled a mobile number belonging to a Dwayne Laughlin and written DOPE-HEAD. The same was noted against Jeff Hunter. So presumably they were local. The other account, Crossland's personal phone, showed no numbers of any individual who had been identified as a Broome resident but there was a number for the tour people who organised camel rides on the beach, and one for a diving tour company. On the face of it, typical things a tourist would do. They were for a week ago, Tuesday morning. That night the Pearl Motel was burgled by Turner. There were also two numbers for individuals in Pilbara towns, both women. As Risely had said, most were identified as Perth numbers. There was also Brisbane, Gold Coast and Sydney represented. But curiously neither Dwayne Laughlin or Jeff Hunter's numbers reappeared on the personal phone. He called in Mal Gross.

'Did you make these annotations?'

'Yep. Both big pot-heads. Laughlin's probably into eccies, speed as well.'

'So they live here?'

'Yep. Small-time, users, deal a bit.'

Snowy Lane had said Crossland was a dope-head. That made sense. But what was interesting was that when in Hedland he had called them on the phone he stole but not from his own phone since he got here. That reeked of him being cautious.

'Let's go speak to them,' he said to Gross. His phone rang. He recognised the number. 'Hi Marilyn.'

'Is now a bad time?'

Out the corner of his eye he noted Mal Gross peeling off to grab the car key. Mal always liked to drive.

'I wish I could say it wasn't. I've been trying to reach you.'

'There's a lot ... I'll call you later. Or you call me.'

And just like that she was gone again.

...

Hunter had a job packing meat at the abattoir on the town outskirts. Clement remembered a visit to an abattoir in his school days. A few of his classmates wound up working there. Those were the days when you could leave school at fifteen and make your way in the world for better or worse. Now everybody had to be 'educated' and then unemployed because there were no industries any more, well, apart from tourism. He was certain that these days a school visit here would not be encouraged. The principal would be put in stocks for traumatising his charges. Grief counsellors would be employed. Today kids were taken to the theatre and encouraged to take up a profession that would lead to them waiting tables. He wondered how long this place would be allowed to operate. Surely it was only a matter of time before eating meat was banned. Clement actually wasn't a big meat eater and he had nothing against vegetarians but certain attitudes increasingly annoyed him. The kind of attitudes Marilyn's friends had. They'd definitely be against abattoir visits. They'd all gone to university and they all felt the same way about everything, just like their lecturers. Slaughtermen would be equated with paedophiles. If he said – and this is what he would like to say – the visit is what you make of it, it's good for kids to understand the reality of death, blood and slaughter; life isn't all about tannin in wine and sundried tomatoes ... well, you can imagine the response.

He caught himself then: he was pissed off and annoyed, not because of the nation's inexorable drift to becoming one big café for former humanities students, but because he yearned to speak to Marilyn, to share with her, like in the old days, his excitement and fear of failure, and she had picked almost the worst possible time to call. He was even more annoyed he hadn't said bugger it, and kept talking anyway. Mal Gross was a vault. But he hadn't been courageous enough to follow his desire, had he? He didn't want his vulnerabilities on display for a colleague to witness.

As soon as they'd got out the car, flies had swarmed. It didn't matter how clean you were, flies loved slaughter. Mal Gross had gone to fetch

Hunter. Clement studied ubiquitous hygiene signs while he waited not far from the building entrance on a concrete apron under the high tin roof. Men's and women's voices rose and bounced. The constant sound of a high-pressure hose being turned on and off gave time its borders, bone saws on high rev its stitching, and though the smell of blood enveloped him it was perfume compared to the smell of human death. There must have been fifteen to twenty people working the floor, the saws in the far distance; closer, at benches, men and women in health scrubs chopping and cutting meat. He felt a vibration in his pocket, pulled out his phone, the noise too high for its ring. Lisa Keeble's name was on display.

'Yes, Lisa.'

'The Coroner's Office just called, mucho apologetic. There was definitely ink on the body's left ankle.'

He felt his heart kick. 'Thanks, Lisa.'

Kelly the dancer was looking so much more likely now. And that meant Crossland was right in the crosshairs.

Mal Gross returned, accompanied by a young man, Hunter presumably. He was small, wiry and wore a blood-smeared apron and a hairnet. When he got close Clement noted his interesting face, Japanese somewhere back in the past he was sure. A lot of Japanese divers had come to Broome working pearl boats way back when and had settled. Ironically the Japanese had also bombed Broome during the Second World War.

'Jeff Hunter, Detective Inspector Clement.' Gross made the introductions and stood at ease.

Hunter looked cautious. Clement got to the point.

'You have been in contact with a person of interest in a major homicide case.' He saw Hunter blink: that was news. 'Shane Crossland, aka Shane Shields. Do you know where he is? I advise you most strongly to tell the truth or face a charge of impeding an investigation.'

Hunter moved his jaw but no words came out. He took another breath. 'I hardly know the guy. We worked on a building site once.'

Clement had no patience, not today. 'You can save us a lot of time and yourself a lot of grief if you tell me the truth. I know he called you three weeks ago from Port Hedland.' Hunter was about to go for some glib response. He could see it in his eyes. 'Think very carefully. This is not an ordinary investigation.' He watched Hunter swallow like he understood the gravity involved. Good.

'I really don't know where he is.'

A couple of workers walked by trying not to look but the way they stopped talking as they passed gave them away.

'I am not a drug cop on this case, I'm a homicide investigator. I'm not going to trick you but you must tell the truth. Did you see him in Broome?'

Hunter's eyes darted. Clement could feel him weighing which way to play it.

'Yes. But only for like ten minutes.'

'When was this?'

Hunter was jumpy. 'I don't know, a week ago.'

'Did he say where he was staying?'

'Some motel. The Pearl maybe?'

An encouraging start. 'Was he buying drugs off you?'

'No! I don't do that shit.'

The first denial rang true, the second clanked.

'Last chance. Don't lie to us. You won't be charged on any drug business.'

'He rang me from Hedland. Said he was coming to Broome for a holiday and he had some gear for me at a good price. But he never delivered. He turned up here after my shift, said he got robbed. All his weed and eccies. You can't bust me, right? I never bought anything.'

'I told you, we're not going to bust you. Tell me everything.'

'He asked me for some drugs. I had a little bit of weed. I gave it to him. By the time he saw me he'd already scored some eccies. I don't know who gave him those but he said they were top quality, better than what he'd been carrying. He was going to try and score some wholesale. I told him there were some heavy dudes had the territory here. He said he was going to the source. That's the truth. I never saw him after.'

Clement established it was a Wednesday this took place. Six days ago. That was the night after the Pearl robbery. Crossland was supposed to deliver drugs but never did. It was falling into place now: Mal Gross said the tablets found on Turner were not Mongoose Cole's. The reason was they were Crossland's, stolen at the Pearl along with Lipton's stolen phone. Crossland had, to use a pun, not let the grass grow under his feet. He'd immediately tried to source more supply.

'So Crossland is a dealer.'

'Not like, big-time or anything. He just buys up some gear and travels around the country selling it.'

'Working holiday.'

Hunter allowed himself a grin. 'I guess.'

'He say where he scored the eccies from?'

Hunter licked his lips, anxious. 'No.'

'Your guess would be?'

'My guess would be he went to the nearest pub, asked around.'

'Thank you, Jeff. You've been most helpful. If he gets in touch, or you hear where he might be, give Sergeant Gross a call.'

Mal Gross handed him a card.

'That it?' said Gross as they strode away.

'He told us all he knew. Call the station, tell Josh and Graeme to be ready for a takedown, vests and guns.' He called Risely. 'I've got an idea on where Crossland is heading. I need a plane.'

'Of course. Where?'

Crossland had scored Mongoose Cole eccies. They were the pills he'd shown Hunter. Somebody, maybe Laughlin, had told him where they were sourced. Crossland wanted to buy those drugs to fulfil his orders but he wasn't going out to Broome airport right under Cole's nose. He wasn't that stupid. Or, if he had been, he was lucky enough to have avoided every CCTV camera in Broome.

'I think he's going to the source of the drugs, Wyndham. One problem. We might be muddying the AFP case.'

'Fuck the AFP. That's not my response, that's what the Commissioner is going to say because that's what the Minister is going to say to him. That's who pays our salary. I'll warn Perth. How sure are you?'

'Fifty-fifty.'

'A hundred percent, good, that's what I'll tell the Commissioner.'

...

He was back wrapped in the familiar blanket of plane drone. The three of them plus the Wyndham lot should be plenty to nail Crossland. He'd not called Snowy Lane and felt bad about it. Lane was manic enough to swim through a crocodile-inhabited creek. Clement couldn't risk him hiring a plane or chopper too and turning up in Wyndham as the bust was going down but he had texted him about the coroner's discovery. Immediately after Clement called from the abattoir, Risely had alerted Wyndham to be on high alert for Crossland's vehicle. A half hour into their flight Mal Gross had radioed to let him know the highway patrol had stopped the sExcitation bus near Sandfire. Clement had told Gross to get all details on the former dancer Kelly, check whether anybody from the troupe had heard from her since she'd left.

'Let them go on to Dampier. Tell them I'll be in touch.'

They were flying just inland from the coast, mangrove and crocs to the left, desert to the right. For a brief moment Clement was able to marvel at the fact he was the sheriff for this huge incredible area of land, a place the size of Ohio with waterfalls, desert dunes and mudflats. He drifted for a while, not asleep but in contemplation. He thought of Marilyn. He lusted for Louise. He lusted for Marilyn. He thought of Louise. He imagined wartime aircrew on bombing missions flying low over occupied territories, their own death just a puff of smoke away, the death of others at their fingertips. He felt himself in their bomber jackets, reeking of nervous cigarette puffs in the bracing chill before boarding, considered their desire for a girl they'd met at a dance and fondled in an underground shelter while London burned, imagined their indecision, the girl back home in Iowa, the English girl won easily with a box of assorted chocolates. He wanted to equate his mission with their wartime reality, knew it was self-serving, dissembling, but he forgave himself this much: he had never strayed from Marilyn, never would have; his moral question was whether he had any right to censure his ex-wife while he pined for Louise or, on the flipside, courted Louise while he pined for Marilyn, even though it was hopeless, even though ...

'Clem.'

It was Graeme Earle nosing towards the pilot, who held the radio out for him. It was Mal Gross again. He could not hide the excitement in his voice. Crossland's vehicle had been spotted just outside of Wyndham's main drag at a camping site. Clement told him to tell the locals to keep their distance. The last thing he wanted was Crossland running and some siege or shootout developing. He passed the message on. The tension exuded by Earle and Shepherd ratcheted up a notch. He checked his watch: 2.30 pm. A thorn pricked him. It was too early. He hadn't expected Crossland till maybe 4.00 or 5.00. Could Crossland possibly have got from a creek near Derby at 6.00 am to here in that time? It was a nine hundred k drive along the Gibb River Road. He had to start in scrub. Over a hundred k an hour might be viable on a major highway but here? It jarred. So did the fact the vehicle hadn't been spotted on the Gibb River Road. Surely that was the only way he could have got here in anything like that time. They had eyes everywhere along the road. Yes, he might have diverted off-road through bush but he couldn't have maintained that speed. Perhaps the vehicle at the creek had nothing to do with Crossland? He parked the thought, went neutral for now, contemplating the catch. It had to go smoothly.

'Vests on,' he commanded. Shepherd and Earle complied and checked their weapons.

They landed and taxied to where a local cop, a uniform sergeant in his mid-forties, waited for them by his car. Graeme Earle knew him of course. He knew every cop in the Kimberley. The sergeant's name was Stevenson. They piled in. Stevenson talked as he drove.

'DS Warren and DC Penny are waiting up by the road leading to the caravan park in an unmarked, as per your instruction, sir.'

Clement asked if there were any other roads to or from the park.

'Nope, she's the only one. The campground is on the river so that's the only way out to the north. I've got a couple of my boys in civvies pretending to be fishing.'

Earle laughed at the 'pretending'. 'That's all these blokes do up here. Stevo here caught the biggest bloody grouper I've ever seen.'

To the east and west of the campground was bush. That would be the only way out but all the roads were covered. Crossland was ultimately going nowhere.

...

It took them about ten minutes to reach the campground road. They passed two vehicles. It was a beautiful day, gums stretched tall for the sun, which was lowering itself but still heating the town to around thirty degrees Celsius. Shepherd, who was drumming his palms on his knees as the expectation built, asked how the weather had been.

'Beautiful cool nights, low twenties. Perfect,' said Stevenson.

Clement spied the unmarked police vehicle up ahead, off the road under a shady tree. Stevenson pulled alongside. Clement and the local D's wound down windows. Clement had met them a couple of times before, so no introductions were necessary.

'The car hasn't moved.' Warren was the driver and the closer to Clement. 'He's in a small unit, front door, back door.'

'How many people in the complex?'

'Seven units hired and about six tents pitched. Looks like around half are out. I make it ten civilians, including the owners and staff.'

'Follow us in. We'll go to the front door. You guys take the back. You might want to get your vests on now.'

They climbed out of their car and did so. Clement heard birds twittering. It seemed out of context with flak vests and handguns. When the Wyndham cops were ready and back in the car, Clement gave the signal. Stevenson rolled forward slowly with the locals behind. The ground was low-lying right by the riverbank. There were caravans and a number of discrete small units built in a log cabin style. Each unit was about fifteen metres from the next. The car was outside number five. They pulled in quietly either side.

...

He was almost resigned now. Everything would be determined by Fate. He'd done his best, waiting through the night for his opportunity. He should not have fallen asleep but he couldn't change that. Whatever cordon they might have established had been too late to get him. He'd circled around in a big loop making better time than he had thought. And now here he was again, alone. He was hungry. He remembered he'd grabbed a packet of cracker biscuits the other day to eat while he waited for the thief. Where had he put them? His brain was all over the shop. His backpack. That's right. He walked over to the backpack, unzipped it and pulled out the crackers. In the end he'd only eaten a couple, he'd been too nervous. When he put the backpack down he noticed a weight in the front flap. Frenziedly he unzipped it and reached in. He shook his head in a mixture of disbelief and joy. There was his iPod. He ran his fingers through his hair, stupid, stupid, him. All that for nothing. It was going to be okay after all.

...

Clement positioned himself in front of the door. Shepherd and Earle flanked him, hands on their weapons. There was a shuffling, then the door opened. Before him, a confused expression on his face, stood a shirtless, shoeless Crossland in a pair of dirty shorts. His hair was matted and his eyes red around the rims. He reeked of dope. Clement could see into the small room. There were no other occupants. Some clothes and a backpack were strewn on the floor. Was this the face those girls saw in their last moments alive? Up until now Clement had been able to imagine nothing but a shadow, a monster carefully and artfully rendered more terrifying by the suggestion of his presence rather than his physical form, a human Jaws. But all Clement saw here was yet another selfish loser. Crossland seemed to eventually take in the vests and weapon readiness.

'What's the problem?'

'Shane Crossland?'

'Yeah? What's going on?'

'I'm Detective Inspector Clement of the Kimberley Police. I'm arresting you for theft.'

'What?'

'The phone of Chelsea Lipton.'

Crossland pointed at Shepherd and Earle. Spittle flew out of his mouth. 'This is bullshit. Over a fucking phone I borrowed?'

Clement had heard them all, a thousand times over. 'There's also intent to supply drugs. Come on, Shane, let's not make this harder than it needs to be.'

Crossland's eyes were full of resentment and veiled threat. That was a look Clement had seen a million times before: the instant when they realise you have them. He'd either lash out now or put down his head like a lamb.

Meekness won. Crossland's head bowed. He allowed himself to be shuffled towards the vehicle by Shepherd and Earle. He was muttering something about the hire car. Clement didn't hear. He was listening to the bird chirping again in preparation for the soft fall of dusk.

CHAPTER 31

I woke, then heard the hotel phone ringing beside me and realised it must have been the catalyst. The red display on the clock said 4.20 pm. I'd been out like a Von Steiger brother after Mark Lewin had applied the sleeper hold. It had to be Clement, they'd found Crossland. I grabbed for the receiver, missed and knocked it off its cradle. It clattered on the dressing table and I had to haul it in like a fish.

'Me.' I said it short and quick as teen sex. I was expecting Clement's voice. I guessed he'd called me on the mobile and I slept through it.

'Snowy, it's Alex Mendleson.'

I'm ashamed to say it meant nothing at first. Then I oriented. 'Yes, Alex.'

The words swarmed around me. I got the gist: police had stopped them on the highway, she'd called Clement. He was too busy to take the call but the Sergeant had asked about Kelly. Had she been in contact, what was her full name, where did she live? And so on. All he would tell them was they were trying to eliminate her from an inquiry. After the policeman rang off they'd tried calling Kelly's phone but there was no response at all. She'd had a terrible sense of doom then. She'd remembered an article in the local paper about a woman's body found in the desert. She couldn't think straight. She questioned the other girls: none of them had heard from Kelly since she left. The last time Sierra spoke to her, Kelly had said her ship had come in and she'd be heading overseas. There was talk of ten thousand dollars.

I had the impression Alex was driving. While she talked, I checked my mobile. There was a long text from Clement: the desert corpse had traces of tattoo ink on the lower left leg. Alex was still talking.

'I remembered you said you were at the Mimosa. I want to hire you,

Snowy, find her or find out what happened to her. I'm tough, but this ... she's not a bad kid. I rang her mum, she's in Perth. She hasn't heard from her in nearly a month. Normally she'd call her mum every couple of weeks. She thought she was with me.'

I asked her to try and calm. 'Look, Alex, I'm not totally in the loop but I can tell you what I know. The body of a young woman was found in the desert. She probably died around the time of the Hedland show.' I heard her gasp. 'She was approximately Kelly's height and there were traces of tattoo ink on what was left of her left leg.'

'Oh my God, Kelly had a dolphin tattoo. It's her, isn't it?'

'I think we're looking at pretty solid odds.'

'Is it the guy who took the photos? I'll kill the bastard. The girls told me he offered them drugs. They only just came clean. Teagan and Briony took pingers. They didn't say anything before, they didn't want to get into trouble.'

My brain was two-timing. Clement knew how important it was to speak to Alex. If he was too busy it could only mean he'd located Crossland or had a hard lead.

'Did they say if they saw him with Kelly?'

'Wait a second. Teagan.' Her voice rang shrill in my ear.

Teagan's voice came on the line, shallow. 'Hello.'

'Teagan, you got drugs off the guy I pointed out in the photo?'

'Me and Briony.' Dropping her mate in right away.

'And Kelly, did he give her drugs?'

'I don't know. She was hanging with the girl you showed me. He might have.'

'Did you see her with any drugs?'

'No. We kind of went back to our room.'

'With the guy or on your own?'

'He tried.'

'So he didn't come back?'

'No.'

It was like trying to feed a cat a pill. 'Did you see Kelly speaking to that guy?'

'I don't remember. We went back to our room. He might have gone back to the party.'

I asked to speak to Briony. She made Teagan sound like Geoffrey Robertson. But her answers were the same.

'Where did he give you the drugs? At the party?'

No. He'd been waiting at the back door of the stage.

In turn I spoke to all the girls. Sierra and Dana both confirmed what they'd told me before: they didn't specifically remember Crossland speaking to any of them – they'd only just found out about the drugs he'd supplied the others. All they remembered was that he'd been lurking.

'With Kelly? Think.'

As usual, Sierra was the most productive.

'Kelly was hanging with the girl whose picture you showed me, and the Asian dude in the suit, for quite a while. Then I'm not sure. I lost track of her. Then I saw her in the loo. She said, "Don't tell A" – that's what we call Alex – "I'm quitting." I told her she was crazy. She said, "I'm getting big bucks. I was going to quit anyway when we got back to Perth and it's what I'd make in a month." We get two grand a week so it had to be real big bucks.'

If only I had the legs.

'What kind of girl was Kelly. I mean, how did she see herself? Ferrari, Hollywood...'

'No, that's more Teagan or Briony. Kelly was, I don't want to say up herself, that's not fair, but she would buy *Vogue* and talk about investment properties. You know, I think that kind of rich New York thing, a lot of class and style, oodles of money, a husband, children, horses to ride.'

'Did you see her leave?'

'No. Dana and I had enough, we went to bed. Some of the bar staff were there, you could ask them.'

Dana's memory was no better. I was thinking of the Autostrada case. The girls were there, then gone. Crossland could easily have crossed paths with Caitlin O'Grady. Emily and Jessica were known to him. What had he told Kelly? We can travel Australia, go to Bali for a break. He probably showed her the cash he had from dealing drugs. He was likely flush. Don't tell anyone. I could hear him now.

Dana was still on the line.

'Was Kelly into drugs at all? Buying, selling?'

'Not in a big way. She'd snort a line of coke if it was offered.'

I asked for Alex back.

'You're not going to like it,' I said.

'She's dead.' She was trying to prepare herself.

'The man in the photo is a person of interest in a homicide.' I wasn't going to blow Autostrada. I imagined her smoking, trying to hold it together at the wheel of a rattling mini-bus. 'This one is out of my hands but Dan Clement is as good a cop as I've seen. I'm sure he'll call when he gets the opportunity.'

We talked on for a few minutes, saying the same things over. We rang off eventually, unsatisfied with reality, unable to change it now. The girls couldn't place Crossland and Kelly leaving together. They'd mentioned pub staff being at the afterparty. Maybe one of them could? But the cops would speak to them soon enough.

Although ... if they'd been taking drugs would they spill to a cop? All that was needed was somebody to admit to seeing Crossland and Kelly together after the party broke up. Of course, I had no business with this, except I had. I'd fingered Crossland seventeen years ago and been treated like a Carlton supporter in the Collingwood cheer squad. Clement was good but his role would be diminished from here on. The Commissioner was the same cop who'd cocked up the first time. I didn't trust task force cops I'd never met. I thought back to how they'd missed the video of the van parked at the cemetery when I'd thought it was that SAS guy. I was going to see Caitlin O'Grady got justice. Might Ingrid Feister have seen anything? She'd been at the afterparty. I tried her phone, got a voicemail and left a message asking if she could call me. Then I did the same with Max Coldwell for the same result. I wondered if they were talking to each other now, if the romance had been rekindled. I had a brainwave. I checked my file and dialled Giant Resources in Port Hedland.

'Angus Duncan, please.'

'He was up at Tenacity Hill. I'll see if he's back.'

The guy who answered didn't even ask who was calling. After a minute, Duncan came on the line. I told him it was me.

'Hey, Snowy, good to see Ingrid return safe and sound. How can I help?'

'I'm not sure you can but I thought I'd try. That night of the sExcitation show, there was a fellow there ... I've got a photo ... I'll send it through in a minute. Anyway, one of the dancers has gone missing. They thought she'd up and left but it's possible there was foul play. I'm trying to establish if they left together.'

'Are you working on this?'

I understood his confusion.

'Not really. Doing a favour for a friend.'

'I'm sorry, I don't see how I could help.'

'I'm talking about the party after.'

'Oh, right. Not really a party, just pizza and a beer. We didn't stay that long from what I remember. Left about one.'

'Maybe if you see the photos. Would you mind?'

He said no but didn't sound hopeful. I told him I'd ring him back in five after I'd sent them from my phone. He gave me his mobile number. It took quite a few minutes to send the photo I had of Kelly and the still I'd taken off Alex's video. That one in particular was pretty poor quality. I watched the clock tick by and called. I was already figuring other possibilities if this hit a wall.

'I remember the girl,' he said. 'The best looker, I thought. She chatted to Ingrid for a while. The guy seems familiar but I couldn't swear.'

I apologised for the photo quality.

'Like I said, Snow, we didn't stay that long. I'm too old for pubs, even if the sheilas are cute young things and Shaun, my client, was tired after a long day.'

'I thought I might try Ingrid.'

'Don't think she could help. She and Max left with us. They had an early start.'

It was all less than I hoped for. I thanked him and rang off. Should I call Clement? No, out of necessity he'd delisted me from what was now a big official police investigation. If I told him what I was doing he'd order my arse out of there, officially at least. I chucked my stuff together. I could make the Sandfire Roadhouse for dinner.

...

As he'd been led to the plane, Crossland had asked constantly what it was all about. Clement had said nothing other than it concerned the theft of a phone and conspiracy to distribute drugs. On the plane ride Crossland had fallen into a sullen funk. Mal Gross radioed through with an update on Kelly, now identified with her full name Kelly Davies. There was no signal on her phone and it had not been used since August 17, the night of the Port Hedland gig. Prior to that gig she'd been surfing Instagram and Facebook but there was no activity since. Her mother had not heard from her, nor had the sExcitation girls. They were awaiting his call in Dampier. Clement had no doubt now that Kelly Davies was the dead girl in the desert. Gross also told him that, as per his instructions,

Lisa Keeble and her tech team were already on the road to Wyndham. They had been standing by at Derby and left as soon as Crossland was in custody. If Kelly Davies had been in any part of Crossland's vehicle, he was certain Keeble would locate traces.

...

By the time they entered the station it was close to 11.00 pm. The day had begun in the gloom of the mangrove flats near Derby. It seemed interminable. Risely was waiting for them.

'Perth says you can start questioning.'

Mal Gross led Crossland into the interview room. Nat Restoff was tasked with watching over him. Shepherd stretched out on the sofa and announced he was starving. Clement told him he could go home.

'No, I'll stick around.'

Everybody wanted in on the glory. Gross had bought a burger for Graeme Earle. It was cold now but Earle stuck it in the microwave. Clement had declined the offer. He'd make do with toast if he got hungry.

'You okay?' he asked Earle.

The microwave pinged.

'Will be after this.'

It was weird, thought Clement. They all knew they were on the verge of solving the state's greatest crime mystery but it was as if they were embarrassed to admit that.

Clement grabbed a coffee. It was probably a dumb idea. His head was thumping. It seemed he'd been flying and driving for as long as he could remember. In his office, he popped two Panadol from a blister pack and swallowed them dry. He picked up the report on Kelly Davies assembled by Mal Gross, scanned it to make sure Gross had given him all the relevant facts and then sent a text to Snowy Lane. **Got Him.**

While Earle ate, Clement went to the bathroom and splashed water on his face. He'd been running since 5.00 am but he felt charged. He made a quick call to Alex Mendleson. She sounded worn down. She told him she'd spoken to Snowy Lane and he had warned her to expect the worst.

It was 11.30 pm by the time he and Earle were sitting opposite Crossland. Clement passed a white coffee and two biscuits over to Crossland then switched on the camera, gave the time and date and introduced the parties. He asked Crossland for his full name.

'Shane Jason Crossland.'

The answer was given begrudgingly. He showed Crossland the Lipton phone, which was sealed in a plastic bag.

'Recognise the phone, Shane?'

He shrugged. Clement asked him for an answer on the record.

'I might. Can't say. Plenty of phones look like that.'

Clement watched Crossland sip his coffee. He's off balance, thought Clement. He wonders how much we know. Clement began by asking for an account of his movements that day. Crossland lolled his head, bored and annoyed.

'From when I got up?'

'Yes, Shane.'

A sigh. 'I woke up about eight, eight-thirty, I pissed in the bush.'

'Where were you?'

'I don't know. In the fucking bush near Kununurra.'

Clement tried to show no surprise. 'You sure it was Kununurra?'

'Yeah. Everybody said go see Kununurra, so I did.'

According to Crossland, he'd been at the pub at Kununurra till 10.30 the previous evening. He'd then driven towards Wyndham but got tired and pulled off the road, 'doing the right thing, like they tell you', about 11.00 pm. He'd then woken up and pissed and driven to Wyndham where some time late morning he'd had a breakfast. He didn't know the name of 'the joint' but described where it was and the waitress. 'She should remember me, I gave her a five buck tip.'

Clement didn't detect false bravado. He'd already been sceptical that Crossland could have made Wyndham from Derby. He was ninety-eight percent certain now that whoever had been at the creek wasn't Crossland. He took Crossland through a chronology of when he had hired the car and driven north from Perth. Crossland claimed he was doing a 'north-west holiday'.

Clement checked his watch. It was after midnight now. 'So,' he said, 'tell me all about your trip.'

...

It was close on 8.30 when I wheeled into the Sandfire Roadhouse parking lot, rush hour. Three big rigs, a couple of campervans and a handful of cars were scattered like mahjong tiles beneath a breathtaking cape studded with the most brilliant stars. I stepped out into fresh, cool desert air tainted by tobacco smoke. A couple of blokes stood by the tavern door, fags in their mouths, beers in their fists. It felt sacrilegious. Inside, the community of travellers tucked into steaks and hamburgers. I took my spot, ordered a burger with the lot and a beer. By now Crossland might have been shot dead trying to escape whatever Clement had going down, or he might be in custody and have already confessed.

Or they could still be looking for him.

I tried Clement's phone again just in case and got a voicemail. I left a message to call me when he had a chance. The burger, in Australian tradition, contained beetroot and while it wasn't the Taj Mahal of burgers, it did the job. There was no need to rush, I sipped my beer while I traced my steps back seventeen years to when Grace was a baby and I'd first begun on the case. Could I really be at the end of that long journey? Resisting the urge for a second beer, I paid up, filled my tank, had a pee and stood under the stars. For an instant I was once more a tiny figure in a huge volume of space. I guessed an astronaut must feel like this when they float outside their ship. It was wonderful and uplifting, and I laughed at the absurdity of forcing myself back into the tiny cramped confines of my little metal ball and hurtling south towards Hedland. But that's exactly what I did.

...

Driving a lot faster than I should have, I reached Port Hedland in well under three hours, still too late for the pub to be open but I headed there anyway. I swung into the area out front. It looked dark inside. I checked my phone. One text, Clement: **Got Him**.

I didn't feel elation, just relief. I might have given up then, gone and pressed the night bell at the motel and asked for a room, but I saw a side door of the pub open and a young woman exit, smoking. I walked to where she'd emerged from, a saloon bar, low light inside, a few young men and women having a drink and eating potato chips: staffies, an Aussie tradition. You stayed sober till you'd got everybody else pissed, then had a go yourself. I was still kind of floating, I don't know how else to describe it. Nearly twenty years of your life you've had this thing, pricking you, one minute light as a feather, another, deep in your soul. Part of me still didn't believe it could all be finished. I had to make sure it was. The door had snapped shut so I tapped on the glass. A young guy I recognised from my time here before got up and wandered over to open it for me. He didn't recognise me.

'Sorry mate, we're closed.'

His name leapt out of the ether.

'Dougal. Richard Lane, Private Detective, remember?'

He did with that prompt. I asked if I could have a few minutes of their time. He let me in, locked the door and kindly offered me a beer. I was more interested in the potato chips, I was starving. There were three young women and three guys. I introduced myself.

'I don't know if any of you guys remember the night of the sExcitation show here. There was a bit of a drinks and pizza party upstairs afterwards. Did any of you go to that party?'

Two of the guys and one blonde with an English accent, sunburned cheeks and curly hair had.

'Do you remember this guy at all? He might have been with one of the dancers.'

I produced my phone and showed the best photo of Shane Crossland I had.

The blonde girl giggled. 'Yes, I remember him: Shane. He wasn't with a dancer though.'

One of the other girls smiled and slapped her playfully. 'You didn't?'

I'm old and slow. It took me a beat to catch on. 'Are you saying you were with him?'

'Yes.'

'How long?'

She made a distance sign with her hands. The others burst out laughing. I wasn't in the mood for jokes.

'Sorry,' she said, 'couldn't resist. Basically the whole night. I had to kick him out at a quarter to ten next morning, my shift was starting.'

CHAPTER 32

'I don't remember her name but she's a Pom, blonde and curly hair, and she was deadset up for it, so she's lying if she says she wasn't.'

Crossland was more at ease now, toying with his second cup of coffee, enjoying the cream biscuit Clement had offered. He was a lot more relaxed than Clement, the headache was back, pounding harder this time. Maybe it was because he wasn't getting the smell of fear he'd expected from Crossland, or because the doubts about the time line were growing. They'd blazed past 2.00 am. Clement nodded to Earle, his turn to recap.

'So, according to you, you left Perth, drove up through Geraldton, Carnarvon, Exmouth, lapping up the sunshine...'

'I told you, I don't like the cold.'

'... you went to the sExcitation show in Port Hedland. You took some photos with the stolen phone ...'

'It wasn't stolen.'

'... you went to the after-show drinks for a while ...'

'Not that long. Fifteen minutes. Then I scored the Pommy chick.'

'And you went back to her room in the staff quarters at the hotel and had sex all night, waking at about nine-thirty next day.'

'That's right. She woke me up, she had to go to work.'

Clement chopped in. 'When you left the drinks, who was still there?'

Crossland shrugged. 'Couple of the staff, couple of the dancers, some dude smoking a big spliff. Couple of others. I wasn't paying much attention.'

'What did you do next?'

'Took a drive to Newman, then back up to Karratha, Dampier back through Hedland.'

'Looking for work?'

'No, just kicking back. I find the desert very relaxing.'

'You've got people who can confirm this?'

'Course. The motels I stayed at.'

After some to and fro, they established Crossland's account of his time. He'd spent August 18 at Mulga Downs, then August 19 to 21 at Newman in the desert. He'd driven all the way back to Karratha on the coast and spent the next three days there. He cruised on to Dampier for three days, then back through Hedland for another three days. The 'Pommy chick' wasn't there so they had not hooked up again.

What were you doing, thought Clement, looking for victims, selling drugs, both?

According to Crossland, he'd driven to Broome on September 1st.

'I stayed at a place called the Divers Retreat, something like that.'

The Divers Rest. Clement knew it.

'How long were you there?'

'Just a couple of days. I thought it was a bit expensive so next time I tried the Pearl.'

'And after Broome, where did you go?'

'I drove up to Beagle Bay.'

He said he'd spent a couple of days relaxing there before returning to Broome and booking at the Pearl.

Earle said, 'Under the name Shane Shields.'

'That was just a bit of fun.'

'Did you use that name at the other motels?' Earle playing the hard man.

He grinned. 'It was an adventure.'

Earle threw to Clement, knowing he would want the meat. Clement sensed he was getting to the climax and his one shot before Perth took over, probably first thing tomorrow.

'The Pearl Motel was burgled that night and Chelsea Lipton's phone stolen. You didn't report it. If you hadn't stolen it, why was that?'

Crossland had his back to the wall and knew it. 'Alright. I took the phone, okay? Mine was on the blink and I was about to go away. Come on, I'll buy her a new one. You guys must have something better to do.'

'No, Shane, this is what we live for.' He wanted to get his timing just right. He pulled the drugs taken from Turner and tossed them in front of Crossland in their plastic evidence bag. 'These were stolen off you too.'

'What? No way. I knew you'd try and fit me up.'

Confronted with the hard evidence, Crossland was not such a good actor.

'Shane, we know you were selling these, we know they were stolen from your hotel room. Along with this.' It had all been building to this moment. He'd seen Crossland lie twice now. He could read him. He felt the weight of nearly twenty years of police investigation on his shoulders. He pulled out the pendant and dangled it.

Crossland sat back and folded his arms.

'I've never seen that before. Or the gear. This is bullshit.'

No false note on the pendant but the denial on the drugs had a hollow heart. One more time on the pendant.

'You've never seen this before?'

'Stolen is it?'

'Just answer the question.'

'No, I've never seen it before.'

There it was, the brick wall. Perhaps Crossland was such a consummate actor he could seem transparent on the drugs but convincing on the pendant. Clement would have liked to take the questioning along the Autostrada line but that would be wrong. Even if he got something, Crossland could claim he was fatigued, didn't know what he was saying.

'Can you account for your actions on Thursday the seventh of September?'

'Give us a break.'

Clement walked him through the days.

'I think I was on some diving tour. I'm not sure.'

'What diving tour?'

'I don't know. I walked into their shop in the main drag.'

'Kimberley Diving?'

'That's sounds right. There were about ten of us on the boat.'

'Do you know this man?"

Clement produced a photo of Sidney Turner.

'Nope.' Nothing that showed recognition.

It was almost 3.00 am.

'Alright, Shane, that's it for now. You'll be charged with stealing the phone and attempting to distribute drugs. You'll spend the night in the lockup.'

...

An eager Risely was waiting for them when he and Earle emerged. Clement had made a list of notes he wanted double-checked, foremost Crossland's Hedland alibi with the barmaid, and his claim about being on a diving tour the day Turner went missing. Before he spoke, Clement made sure Crossland had been escorted out the back to his lockup transport.

'He copped to the phone, lied about the drugs, claims he has an alibi for the night Kelly Davies disappeared, denied he'd ever seen the pendant. I have to say, on that he was convincing.'

'Well, he would be.' Risely though looked deflated.

'Even if his alibi with the barmaid checks out,' said Earle, 'it's not really an alibi. He could have killed Kelly Davies, stashed the body in his boot, gone back, rooted like a rabbit, then driven into the desert the next day and dumped the body.'

Clement was worried that Crossland's car wouldn't make it into the desert.

Risely said, 'He might have borrowed or hired another one.'

All that was true. And yet there was something, that internal alarm, that Crossland just had not set off. Risely asked Earle what he thought.

'I don't have your experience. I thought he was bullshitting about the drugs. I reckon he came up with a bootful of drugs and worked his way around the Pilbara selling. The pendant, I couldn't say.'

Risely clapped Clement on the shoulder. 'You've done exactly the right thing. Detectives Collins and Stroghetti will be arriving first thing tomorrow to take him back to Perth for questioning. We are to continue to pursue the Kelly Davies case and let them know of any convergence.'

Clement fought the frustration of having to hand over Crossland. There was no sign of Shepherd, not surprising.

'The footy star head home to bed?'

'No,' said Risely, 'he offered to help Manners on confirming the time lines Crossland gave us for arriving in Broome. They are checking CCTV.'

Clement felt bad for thinking the worst of his constable. He was proud of the whole team, Risely included. They were out on their feet but grinding on till the last. Mal Gross was hovering.

'Yes, Mal.'

'I sent photos of the ecstasy tablets through to the strippers in Dampier.'

Clement didn't bother to correct him on the job description, it was far too late and he was too tired.

'The girls confirmed them as the same tablets Crossland offered them.

I've spoken to Hedland and they are chasing up the Hedland phone numbers on the Lipton phone. They recognised at least one as a drug user.'

'Check out the others. If he's telling the truth, he did Newman, Karratha, Dampier. My guess is he used Lipton's phone when he was dealing. Any news from Keeble?'

'She's still going but her initial examination of the hut revealed no belongings relating to Kelly Davies and no blood in the car. There was also a message from Snowy Lane.'

...

We're just puppets in a big shadow play somebody has written, thought Clement as he sat on his bed in the small flat above the chandler's. We think we're the star but then we're sent off stage while the next scene plays out with new characters. Sidney Turner thought he was the main man but he's no more than inert sticks and string now. And what was Clement if not a bit-part player?

He lacked even the energy to make himself supine and for now just sat. When they had been alone, Graeme Earle had asked his opinion of Stroghetti and Collins. Average, that's what he thought, Commissioner's choice to filter everything through him. Collins was a misanthrope who had finally made inspector by sucking up to Tregilgas. Stroghetti was hewn from the same lump of wood.

Lane's message, which he picked up after he'd spoken to Risely, had been another kick in the guts: he'd interviewed a barmaid from the Hedland pub who had told him Crossland had spent all night with her, Thursday August 17 through to the morning of Friday August 18. This confirmed Crossland's alibi. She said she'd had to wake him close to 10.00 am and there was no chance he'd slipped out anywhere during the night. Lane felt she was credible and totally unprompted.

Trust Snowy to be a step ahead. It was theoretically possible that Crossland could have gone outside while the woman slept, encountered Kelly Davies, killed her, stuffed her in his boot and dumped the body the next day. But the vehicle worried him. It was no four-wheel drive. It couldn't have made it into the desert where the corpse was found. So what did that leave? Either Crossland didn't kill Kelly Davies or he killed her, and gave her body to somebody else to dispose of. Back to an accomplice.

Clement finally found the energy to stretch out on his bed but not to remove his jocks and singlet. He'd untied his shoes and slipped out of his suit earlier. Once he relaxed he remembered Marilyn had called him. That fact had almost been lost in the crush. He'd had to brush her off. His brain flickered. Sidney Turner might be the only ...

He was out before he could even finish the sentence.

CHAPTER 33

I was back in the same unit at the Kookaburra Hotel I'd been in around a week before. I was too wired to sleep, especially after my late snooze. What did I know for sure? Well, Mal Gross had said they'd got Crossland in Wyndham. I clicked on my computer and checked distances between Derby and Wyndham. No way he was swimming croc creek at 6.00 am and getting all the way there. Plus there were cops along the Gibb River Road almost immediately after that, on the lookout. He was not the guy. But who was, and why would you take that risk to get away? If you were poaching crocs you'd just stick your hands up. Maybe they had something to do with Turner. Maybe Crossland had hired a third party to get rid of him and they'd stuffed up. I liked that theory. Crossland would know criminal types for sure. I made a note to run it by Clement: check Crossland's phone calls. Probably he was already on it. My brain jumped to the body in the desert: the girl we now knew was Kelly Davies, tracked back to here, the night Kelly disappeared. The bar girl was a hundred percent credible. She'd played hide the sausage all night with Crossland. She hadn't thought he was weird in any way. He was a normal sort of guy, no mental genius but well built. I could see the penny dropping when I kept asking about him but I deflected her questions. I wasn't going to say she had a close shave with a serial killer. It was possible that at some point when she slept – even though she denied that, people do drop off without realising – Crossland had slipped out, killed Kelly Davies, stuffed her in the back of his car, returned to bed and coolly driven off the next morning to dump the body in the desert. Okay, his car wasn't perfect for the job but if he was careful maybe he borrowed a car. There was something about the body I should have been homing in on but I had too many ideas pushing and shoving. I forced myself to play devil's advocate.

Could Crossland be innocent of Kelly's death? Could it be a coincidence? Who was the last known person to see Kelly alive? According to the accounts I had, Sierra. She said she had seen her in the ladies. Could the girls be lying to me? Jealousies on tour, where would they lead? I only had their word Kelly had said she was going to quit anyway. But like Crossland's car, their van would never have made it into the desert to dump the body. They'd need help and, unlike him, they weren't criminals.

I suppose I could check their time lines but I just couldn't sell it to myself. I was starting to get antsy. I wondered if Crossland had confessed already. Doubtful, Clement had promised me he would let me know right away and I believed him.

It was just after 2.00 am I reckoned that was around 8.00 pm in Barcelona. My computer was running. I signed up for the pub internet and launched Skype. Presto. A little icon told me Tash was online. And then I was looking at her beautiful face and wanting to hold her and realising all over again how deeply I missed her. We chatted for ten minutes about their adventures. Gaudi had become their hero.

'It's as if he takes our stupid modern lives and turns them into a beautiful mystical tale.'

We talked about her work. She found Barcelona inspirational. She asked about my case. I trimmed: successful outcome, big payday. She read me even via an internet cable.

'So what's the problem?'

I spilled on it all: the body in the desert, Crossland – leaving out his name – I trusted her but was paranoid of speaking into anything electronic. I told her I'd recognised the pendant. I told her it was so clear and obvious and a vindication of my work way back when ... except it wasn't. Things didn't add up. She listened for a good twenty minutes. We didn't lose the connection. It was like I had my personal therapist. When I started going over everything the second time, she interrupted me.

'You told me, Dad told you once, a poor detective doesn't reach, but a good detective can be guilty of the same error in reverse and reach too much. You remember that?'

I have to be honest, I didn't remember telling her that, but I did recall her father Dave Holland, the best detective I'd ever known, giving me that piece of advice when I first started. My memory was fading, I guess. She was still talking.

'You mustn't fit the case to your theory, no matter how beautifully it seems to work.'

And now it was like she was inside my head, decoding the intuition I'd felt over the last fifteen or so hours.

'If the facts say it's not your suspect, maybe it isn't.'

'But ...' I started. It was as far as I got.

'Yesterday Grace and I were walking down Las Ramblas and we'd been talking about her getting her licence. I told her about how the first time I drove as a licensed driver, I broke down in Barrack Street. There I was, middle of the city. I was petrified. I didn't know what to do. And there's a knock on my window and there was John Norton, her grandfather's friend, and he helped me.'

I knew there had to be some point to the story. I held my tongue.

'We had lunch and walked around and started back to the pensione and who do we see? Oliver. I'm not joking. Oliver Norton, John's grandson. He's on a break from uni. Coincidences happen, Snow. Maybe the girl decided to quit the troupe, was hitching and got picked up by the wrong guy.'

...

Later I lay in bed with those thoughts still zipping through my head. What Tash said could be true. The coroner had said Kelly's body had been crushed. A big rig would do that. She could have hitched ... coincidences happen ...

Stop it, I told myself. You're grasping at straws and you know it. I hadn't told Tash about my swim through croc creek. Maybe one day I would. I conjured her beside me, became drowsy. I saw Grace's life in flashes: in a highchair, face covered in yoghurt, wobbling on a bike, the first time she won a school prize. I drifted. I was in dappled light, on the edge of a mangrove swamp. There was a big croc right in front of me, I had to get out of there but I was frozen. Clement, no Dave Holland, was there too but couldn't see me or hear me or was paying no attention. Someone else was in the shadows on the other side of the swamp. If I wanted to see who it was I would have to get past the croc. There were magical shapes, buildings. Tash was taking photos. It was a city, it was Gaudi, but somehow it was right next to where I was in this mangrove swamp. Dave Holland was saying something, mumbling numbers, distances, repeating that it was impossible, it didn't add up. The shadowy figure was getting away from me. They were more lit now but only their back. I wanted to advance. The croc was getting ready to spring at me. I realised there was a branch above me. Perhaps I could jump for it ...

...

I woke with my legs jolting from the imagined leap. Light streamed through a gap in a blind. Outside a cleaning trolley jolted. Reality smothered me. I checked the time on my watch on the bedside table: 7.50. First thought, check my phone. Yes, a text from Clement. I was lucky, I didn't need glasses yet. Well, maybe I did, my eyes got a bit blurry when I got tired. I'm sure I held my breath.

No dice. Only admits to phone theft. Perth have him tom.

Shit. I suppose I more than half expected it but I'd always thought there might be a chance he'd cop to Autostrada. I lay there enfeebled by the dream and the text.

A proper breakfast was calling.

The weather was glorious, the sky the colour blue I remembered from old Westerns. It was warm but with a freshness you no longer got in Perth where every summer was more humid than the one preceding. I wandered the streets. Cars, front and back, had been feasting on red dust. The gentrification of Port Hedland was well underway. I knew this as soon as I spotted a Dôme café. Dôme was born in Perth, a sophisticated version of Starbucks. The originators hit the zeitgeist full on: baby boomers – who had travelled OS where they'd bought leather jackets in Manhattan, boots in Milan, and gallery prints in the Tate – had slowed down, generated families and traded Jim Beam for espresso. Dômes carried the spirit of Singapore's Raffles, ceiling fans, rattan-themed furniture, open space where cutlery clatter ascended to the cupola, the underside of the eponymous dome. Those who played bongos in parks, sucked fire and still rolled their own shied away, too middle-class. Everybody else thronged. This Dôme sported an impressive, long, latticework veranda replete with hibiscus. Inside, the place was thriving with morning trade, white collar and hi-vis vests evenly split. I ordered tea and the big breakfast, out of sentimentality selected my old guernsey number fifteen for my table number, and found an unoccupied two-seater. A previous incumbent had left half an *Australian* and the local rag. I skimmed the *Aus* – terror and taxes – and turned my attention to the local as the tea arrived. The Hornets had flogged Karratha in netball. Front page told the town it would be shortly be welcoming the Premier and Federal Minister for Industry for the inking of the big deal between China and my former employer Giant Ore. I thought there was supposed to be a glut of the red stuff but I suppose I was wrong. Nelson Feister was clearly still able to make a buck. The big breakfast arrived: bacon, eggs, sausage, tomato. Barcelona could keep its tapas. Unfortunately it still had what I truly treasured, my girls.

I sat back as the food hit and contemplated my next move. I could drive back to Perth, that's where Crossland would be heading. On the other hand, there was unfinished business here. What had happened to Kelly Davies? Who had led me through croc creek, and why? The phone rang. Clement. I wondered if he'd caught any sleep or been working through. I answered through bacon and tomato.

'So he didn't put his hand up.'

'No. He admitted to the phone, denied the drugs. I showed him the pendant. He hardly noticed.'

Crossland was practised. He'd been there before.

'Where are you now?' I asked.

'Sitting on my bed getting dressed. Sounds like you're out and about.'

'Big breakfast, Dôme. You got some sleep?'

'Three or four hours. Tell me about the bar girl.'

I told him everything she'd told me. 'She's not lying. She's genuine. Okay, it's possible he snuck out in the middle of the night ...'

Clement cut in. 'I know. But it's a stretch. And the car bothers me. I wondered if he could possibly have had an accomplice.'

I told him the same thought had crossed my mind. I remembered what Tash had counselled about reaching too far and then promptly ignored it. 'Maybe he had a trail bike or something in the car,' I said.

'Or one of those James Bond jet packs he strapped to his back.'

Okay, I was asking for it.

Clement said, 'Perhaps Crossland being at the Pearl really is a coincidence.'

I was poked by the absurd thought that Tash and Clement were in cahoots.

'I don't like coincidence.'

'Me either, but probability is a weird thing. If you have twenty-three people in a room, what do you reckon the probability is of two having their birthday on the same day?'

'Really, Dan?'

'Indulge me.'

'Three hundred and sixty-five days to a year, twenty-three people ... what's that about one in fifteen? Seven percent.'

'Fifty percent. See, you have to work out the probability of having that many people who don't have a birthday on the same day. There were a lot of people interviewed over Autostrada. Perth isn't that big a place. Maybe one of them was bound to be in Broome when we found the pendant.' He sounded liked he was trying to convince himself.

'You don't have twenty-two other people, just Crossland.'

I think it worked. He sighed. 'Keeble's going over his clothes and car but there's nothing obvious. Are you heading back?'

'I haven't decided. I want to help with Kelly Davies. I've got money in the bank from the Feister job. I'm not in a rush.'

He had to go. I told him I'd let him know if I was staying. We ended the call and I finished up my breakfast and ordered a coffee. I was waiting for it to arrive and replaying in my head my conversation with Clement when wham.

Sometimes you say something as a joke and have no idea of its significance. Out of the mouths of babes and all that. I called Clement back.

'I'm driving,' he said.

'Can you get me into Hedland police, or better still the AFP?'

He heard it in my voice. 'You've got something.'

'Maybe.'

'Should I drive down?'

'Let me have a look first.'

'At what specifically?'

'CCTV of the airport road.'

I could almost hear his brain clicking. 'I'm coming.'

'You'll be hours.'

'I'll fly.'

...

Apparently we were lucky. The Crossland arrest could have buggered up an AFP drugs operation but Crossland hadn't actually made contact with the drug supplier before his arrest, so Clement was still in good odour with the Feds. Now we sat in front of a computer screen watching road traffic to the Hedland airfield at midnight August 17. Clement had flown in from Broome by himself. The rest of his team had been working non-stop so he'd given them the morning off. I'd been waiting at the airfield and we'd discussed my reasoning on the way to the Federal Police building.

'When I asked who Kelly spent time with that night, the dancers all said Ingrid Feister. Angus Duncan told me she and Max Coldwell had an early start and had left early with him and his Chinese client. But I rang the girls again and Sierra, who is the most reliable, was sure that when she and the other girls left, all four of them and Kelly were still there.'

'So, what, some threesome that got out of hand?'

I didn't see Coldwell as that kind of guy or Feister as that kind of girl.

'You know what it's like: go to the character of the victim. The girls said Kelly wanted the life of the rich: big house, international travel, kids, horses. She was attracted to bankers not would-be pop stars.'

'And what made you want to look at the airport road?'

'Her injuries.'

So here we were perched in front of the computer looking at the screen showing night, no traffic. Clement was dubious.

'The airfield is closed this time of night. You can't fly.'

'You mean you're not supposed to. This is still the Wild West. It was you talking about having a jet pack that got me thinking.' Minutes ground by, all the same: dark, nothing.

'There.'

Clement sat up and pointed at the screen. A car had pulled up at the gate, the logo on the door clear even with this low-res: Giant Ore. A driver got out. Angus Duncan. He punched a keypad and climbed back into the vehicle. It slid forward through the gate, Ingrid in the front passenger seat, Max Coldwell behind her closest to the camera, two other people in the back blocked by Coldwell. The gate glided back, the car faded into black.

...

It was literally the middle of nowhere, thought Clement, as if the tableau of his internal life had been externalised in these physical surrounds, this moonscape. Tenacity Hill was an arid hump in a bunch of arid humps. It was mild today, around mid-thirties. The sun would get higher yet and beat down on these tents. There were three of them. Two were smaller three-man tents; the other larger, rectangular, serving as some kind of mess tent. Two four-wheel drive vehicles sunned themselves adjacent to two Cessnas parked nose-to-tail on a long, thin roughly graded strip.

Stephanie, the pilot, was drinking water in the largest of the tents.

'We choppered in a little grader.' Duncan made it sound like a mum dropping a school book off to a kid at lunchtime but Clement could imagine the cost involved. He watched Lane poke around the tents. Duncan had already said there was a three-man geology team off beyond Tenacity Hill.

'What's it like here at night?' asked Clement.

'Pleasant.'

Clement guessed Duncan knew they hadn't flown here for a chat but all Clement had said so far was they wanted to ask a few questions. Out the corner of his eye Clement caught Snowy Lane showing a great deal of interest in a cut-down forty-four gallon drum which served as a makeshift incinerator.

'What was it like the night of August seventeenth, or early hours of August eighteenth?'

Duncan made a helpless gesture.

'I don't remember what day that was.'

'The night you flew out here after the sExcitation show. You, Ingrid Feister, Max Coldwell, Kelly Davies and your client, Mr Li. Shaun. We've got video footage.'

Duncan looked away to nowhere. His neck was red even though he wore his work shirt collar raised.

'Alright. We came here to have a bit of a party. The pub was closing, Ingrid suggested it. She said she wanted to see her family's business. There's always lots of grog here.'

Clement jerked his chin at the strip. 'Bit dangerous, though, night-time landing here. Not to mention illegal.'

'I could do it with my eyes shut and one hand tied behind my back.'

Clement could picture it all now. The excitement of the night, the still beauty.

'So. You got here and what happened?'

Duncan took his time, weighing how much to say. 'It was a beautiful night and Shaun wanted a private dance and was prepared to pay.'

'We understand he talked about it with the girl before?'

'I wasn't privy to that. Ingrid wanted to come out here. She's the daughter of my boss. My client wanted to bring a girl. End of story.'

'Except it wasn't, was it?' Snowy Lane had sauntered over. 'Something happened, something bad.'

Clement noted Duncan showed the first sign of stress. He put two hands to his face and brushed his hair back.

'Yeah. The dancer, she'd scored some drugs back at the pub. Ecstasy, I guess. We hung here for a little while. I broke out some grog. Coldwell was already stoned. He and Ingrid went off to that tent; the dancer, Kelly, and Li that one. We were all going to sleep the night here and I would fly them around next morning then drop them back in Hedland. I was in the mess tent on an air mattress.'

According to Duncan, about two hours later Li came running into his tent and woke him up, babbling in Chinese. He knew something was wrong.

'I got to the tent and she was stone cold with some sick around her face.' He threw his hands up. 'I didn't know what to do.'

Yes, you did, thought Clement. You knew exactly what to do for your employer.

'You could have called us.'

'You have any idea how much this deal is worth to this country? We're talking billions. If Shaun got involved in that, the whole thing could be shut down.'

Nothing shocked Clement any more. His dismal assessment of humanity was simply reinforced.

Lane said, 'Shaun was involved.'

Duncan blustered. 'She OD'd on her own drugs.'

Lane said evenly, 'Was she wearing clothes?'

'She was naked. What arrangement Li and she came to was none of my business.'

Clement had figured out the next bit, albeit with Lane's assistance. 'So rather than call us, you took off with the body and dumped it out of the plane where you thought it would never be found. Dumped the girl like a piece of meat.'

'It was too dangerous to land. I wasn't thinking straight.'

'Straight enough to burn her clothes and her bag first.' Lane jerked his head towards the makeshift incinerator. 'There're buckles in there, and I'll bet techs can match them to her bag.'

Duncan stared straight at Clement. 'You put yourselves in my shoes.'

Clement was thinking the steps through. The body and evidence had been disposed of. 'When did Li fly back to China?'

Duncan shuffled. 'He flew to Singapore that day.'

'What about Ingrid Feister and Max Coldwell?'

'They slept through it.'

'A plane taking off and landing?'

'They were out to it, completely.'

Lane said, 'They didn't find it surprising Kelly Davies wasn't there the next morning?'

'I told them I'd dropped her back in Hedland, then come back for them.'

Clement was thinking of the vision of Feister and Coldwell at Sandfire. He recognised that body language now: they'd been part of something traumatic. He didn't buy Duncan's story.

'And you flew Ingrid Feister and Max Coldwell and Li back to Port Hedland.'

Now Coldwell and Feister running off into the outback made a lot more sense.

'That's right.'

'You wouldn't be trying to protect your employer's daughter?'

'No, I would not. They didn't know anything about it.'

'And then you lied to me when I asked where Ingrid was,' said Lane.

Duncan protested. 'I tried to convince you there was nothing to worry about. That she was fine.'

Clement drew an arc in the sand with the toe of his shoe.

'You're facing a heap of charges including illegal disposal of a body, hindering police investigations, withholding evidence.'

'Wrong place, wrong time,' was all Duncan offered in his defence.

'Alright, you'll fly back with us to Hedland and be charged.'

'What about my plane?'

Clement said, 'It contains potential evidence. Our techs will check it over.'

...

They were back in Lane's room after returning to Port Hedland where Duncan had been charged with the offences threatened. Lane had made them an instant coffee with the powdered milk supplied. Up until now they had curtailed any discussion of the case in front of Duncan or other police.

Clement sipped. As a rule he didn't mind instant but this brew was pretty awful.

'You saw that CCTV footage at Sandfire,' Snowy said.

'Yeah. Coldwell and Feister knew what had happened. They were traumatised.'

'The question is, was that all he lied about?'

Clement spelled it out as much for his own sake. 'The client gets rough. She resists ...'

'You'll have to interview Ingrid Feister and Max Coldwell. They might give you the real story.'

Or they might not. At the very least they'd concealed evidence. Clement wondered if, now that the background was known, the pathologist would be able to tell anything about how Kelly Davies died.

Lane said, 'Will you take it on or leave it to Perth?'

'No, my case, my burden.' He couldn't drink any more of the coffee. 'But we can rule out Crossland.'

'Ironically, if he supplied the drugs and Duncan isn't lying about how she died, Crossland could be up for that, some manslaughter charge.'

Once again Lane was ahead of him.

'You should sign up again. We need some good detectives.'

Lane seemed amused. He was obviously still pondering the facts. 'If Crossland didn't abduct Turner, we're talking another coincidence.'

'Crossland probably never knew who took the pendant. How would Crossland know Turner had been arrested for the break-ins unless he was hanging around the court? I'm thinking it was Mongoose Cole abducted him. Maybe he didn't do it himself. He's got plenty who would. But we'll probably never know. Turner is as good as brain dead.'

Clement stood. 'I have to be getting back. I'll be flying to Perth no doubt.'

Lane got up too. 'You might make it before me. I'll take my time down the coast. Please let me know about Kelly Davies. I'd like to inform Alex Mendleson and the girls.'

'Of course.'

They shook hands.

'We did good, Inspector.'

Clement's shake was not convincing and Lane read it.

'You're still not sold on Crossland for Autostrada?'

'I suppose it has to be.' Lane knew Clement was skirting the question. 'But?'

'When he saw the pendant I might as well have been waving a biro.'

'He's had years to practise.'

Clement supposed so. Lane suggested they catch up in Perth if Clement ever had the time.

Clement told him he'd look forward to it ... if he ever had time. Right now he had to fly back out to Tenacity Hill.

...

There were four techs going through the tents and the incinerator drum. Lisa and Mason had Duncan's plane to themselves. The geology party had returned and been told they would have to stay with their vehicle until the company could fly them out; apparently a plane was standing by but with three planes already on the makeshift strip there was no room. Clement finished off his bottle of water and walked over to Duncan's plane. Lisa Keeble saw him and climbed down. Things hadn't stopped for her and her team.

'There's no sign of any blood, I can say that much.'

'Any way to tell if Duncan's lying about the overdose?'

'I don't reckon you'll get anything like a tox screen from the body.'

'Strangulation?'

'So many bones were broken it might be difficult. And there's no way to tell really if they happened post-mortem. Grabbing, dumping a body ...'

He understood the difficulties. It would be up to Ingrid Feister and Max Coldwell to paint a true picture of what happened.

'Did you see the reports on Sidney Turner? I put them on your desk.'

Clement explained he'd had no time.

'Turner had a large volume of horse tranquilliser in his system. I also retrieved a partial tyre tread from behind the creek on the second visit. There was nothing of significance from our first examination and nothing else of interest in location two near the creek except for one thing.'

She was reeling him in.

'Which was?'

'A very small trace of wattle, which might not be unusual except there was none in the immediate area and it was an exact match of the wattle from the tree on the corner of Olive Pickering's street.'

Clement made the jump immediately.

'So, the person near croc creek the second time could have been the same one with Turner the first time?'

'Or at least have been around his street at some time recently. There was hardly any sample at all. My guess is it might have come from the first visit, probably off the sole of a shoe and onto the mangrove root where I found it. There was probably more originally. We would have missed it if someone hadn't gone back.'

Clement was thinking it through. 'Ketamine in his system. Plenty of users go for that, right?'

'Not in these quantities. There was a needle mark but Turner is not an intravenous user. I'd say he was dosed into a stupor.'

'Mongoose Cole would likely have access to a large quantity of ketamine. Did you find the wattle in his car?'

'No.'

Which didn't mean he couldn't have cleaned his car or had somebody else snatch Turner. Why had they gone back? Lost something? Taken somebody else out there? Shit. They'd have to search the creek and that meant trapping the croc.

...

She had lost none of that haughty beauty that was her trademark. Even from where he sat in the Mimosa garden bar looking into the sun, he recognised her from the way she carried herself. She saw him and walked over. The frock was white, naturally elegant. She wore a wide-brimmed hat, the kind you might see at the races but without the fruit. She could get away with that and she was very sun conscious which was why he had chosen a table in the shade. He had already ordered her a chardonnay. When he'd called her upon his arrival back in Broome, he'd said he could come over to the house right away but she had said Brian was home today and she didn't want him present.

'Thanks for seeing me. You must have been flat out.'

She seated herself, smoothing her dress beneath her bottom, and raised her glass in a 'cheers'. He was on soft drink. After this he had to fly to Perth to confront Ingrid Feister and he wanted all his wits about him.

'Yes, it's been unbelievably busy. I'm sorry about last time we sat down,' he said, not truly meaning it.

'I doubt that, but it's okay. I probably wasn't being fair.'

They talked about Phoebe, easy stuff to settle them both. She was doing well at school but could do better. She was becoming too interested in social media but then she was hardly alone in that regard. They both monitored her and there was no area of conflict here. Small talk had spent itself quickly. The breeze lifted slightly. Marilyn pulled his eyes to hers.

'You think the wedding is a mistake because you're a romantic at heart. You also think no man can know me like you, which is probably true and why I asked for your advice, but that doesn't mean you're better or more desirable, necessarily. It does mean you are special.'

Clement tempered his response. 'That's a relief.'

She let it slide by. 'Brian asked me to marry him over a year ago. I said no. Don't ask me to tell you why, I probably couldn't tell you, except that it hurt when we broke up. It really hurt that we failed ... I failed.'

'I can take my share of the responsibility.'

There was a far-off look in her eyes and she was staring down at her glass as if trying to remember, for all time, the exact shade of yellow of the wine.

'Brian has cancer. I feel I owe it to him.'

Clement was rocked. It was the last thing he'd expected. 'What sort of ...'

'Prostate.'

Prostate, that was barely a cancer most of the time, more an inconvenience. He did not want to appear dismissive though, even if part of him was.

'There could be a lot worse. They get it early?'

'We think so. It appears to be contained.'

'And you want to know if I think it's a good enough reason to marry somebody you don't love?'

'I do love Brian. I can't tell any more if I wanted to marry or not but I think it's the right thing. Just, before you say anything, put yourself in his shoes.'

Clement did not want to put himself in anybody else's shoes, Brian's especially.

'You should do what makes you feel good,' he said. 'If that's marrying Brian, for whatever reason, marry him. If marrying Brian is going to make you miserable, then don't. You're right, romance isn't a valid reason for marriage. If it was, we'd still be together.'

And that's how you give up, he thought. With the breeze wafting in slowly, opposite a beautiful woman in a white dress, you renounce ownership of what might be and settle for what is. He wanted to feel sorry for Brian but he couldn't. Cancer or not, Brian had Marilyn. He'd won.

CHAPTER 34

Squally rain lashed the window of Clement's hotel. Winter's last gasp, he thought, as he gazed out on the Swan River. A couple of sails were visible through the grey. The water was flecked with whitecaps. It had been a little while since he'd been back to Perth in the cooler seasons and he felt disoriented, as if it were a different country. The sensation rekindled thoughts of when he'd first come here from Broome as a teenager. How strange everything was, how rushed. Prostate cancer. What could you say without seeming inhuman? He didn't want Brian to have cancer. He didn't want him to have a cold. He didn't want him to have Marilyn, that's who he didn't want him to have but it was moot, even cancer had conspired against him. He checked himself in the mirror. His shirt was brand new, his suit drycleaned. In his days down here on Homicide, he'd found that you got better results if you dressed like them. Budget restrictions had meant he'd not been able to bring Graeme Earle but he chuckled now as he thought of what Earle might have looked like, probably wearing his shorts. Risely had been very cautious about the whole idea. His boss really would have preferred Perth detectives to do the interview. Nobody wanted Nelson Feister as an enemy because that meant the Minister and Commissioner would be your enemies too. In the end, the boss had supported him, agreed it was their case and only appropriate he do the interview, but Risley's concern bubbled close beneath his skin. It was Clement's job to try and get Ingrid Feister and Max Coldwell to admit they knew what exactly had happened to Kelly Davies. That might incriminate them and the client, Li. Of course Clement would offer them a deal for their cooperation. Otherwise he'd get nothing. Risely had got a call suggesting a meeting at 9.00 am sharp at Feister's lawyer's office on the Terrace. That meant heavy monitoring and little chance to appeal to the better nature of the two hippies.

Clement strode to the elevator and mingled with the businessmen and women out to joust for the day in the corporate tournament. He wondered if he could ever have made a go at that life. At school he'd done well at math and there was an attraction in the impersonality of numbers. They couldn't hurt you like people. The elevator travelled smoothly. Its surfaces were clean and shiny and brought to Clement's mind the pristine water in the Kimberley gorges. Leaving the hotel he joined the foot traffic and passed a parking inspector booking a courier van in a no-standing zone. I don't miss that, he thought. Nor the rain which, though weak as the shower in a cheap motel, was surprisingly cold and dreary. A few pedestrians chanced their luck with umbrellas far too flimsy for the wind. Most preferred to jostle each other for the lee of the buildings and Clement quickly got into the swing. He had the size to take the best line and, apart from the top of his right shoulder, remained dry.

Two blocks along dulled by rain slick he found the discrete brass plaque that said ARMSTRONG – Feister's legal firm. He entered a building that had been constructed sometime in the 1890s, all dark wood and brass and the echo of leather on ancient stone. Yellow lamps fought the gloom and revealed a young woman with a severe bun, wearing a charcoal suit too expensive for a receptionist. She stood waiting for him, bone dry. The detective in him deduced an underground car-space and direct elevator.

'Inspector Clement? Abigail Lisle.'

He shook the proffered hand. He'd anticipated a waiting room of some sort, a coffee table, copies of the *Financial Review* but it was an empty space. Before he could break the ice with a mention of the miserable weather, Lisle indicated a large door, one of those that reaches all the way up and you expect to lead into an old-fashioned courthouse.

'They're in here.'

He followed. Halfway to the door, he got it. They didn't need a waiting room or receptionist, Feister was their one and only client. Despite their size, the doors opened with a whisper at Lisle's touch and revealed a large meeting room. A beautiful oval table was in the centre. At one end Max Coldwell sat in a chair, picking his nails. He wore an expensive suit and tie clearly alien to him. A silver-haired man around sixty sat directly opposite facing the door and stood as Clement entered. This was no doubt the lawyer, Gleeson. Clement wasn't sure if his boss was Armstrong or that was simply the firm name from a bygone era. At the opposite end of the table to Coldwell sat an older woman in a well-worn twin-set, pads, pencils, a recorder and computer splayed on the highly polished surface in front of her; some sort of stenographer, Clement guessed. The room was comfortably warm but there was no sign of anything so plebeian as a radiator. Lisle asked if he would like tea or coffee. Silver pots were ready on a sideboard. He declined. She shut the doors and pulled up a chair.

'Please,' Gleeson indicated the seat directly opposite him and began to lower himself. 'Miss Feister will be ... ah.' He stood again as a recessed door opened in the wall behind Clement. Ingrid Feister entered. She looked hardly anything like the woman he had encountered in Derby. Her hair was freshly washed with a wave and sheen that would have done Marilyn proud and she wore a navy blazer and long pants with Marilyn's style. If the other Ingrid was Woodstock, this one was Martha's Vineyard.

'Hello again, Inspector.' She smiled and took her seat.

Gleeson spoke. 'We are all now aware of the unfortunate incident that took place at Tenacity Hill and of the lack of judgement of a senior and trusted employee of Giant Ore, Angus Duncan. Miss Feister and Mr Coldwell are very keen to help however they can in your inquiry. I will be speaking up if I feel your questions or their answers may be inappropriate. Ms Lisle here may do the same.'

Clement found the stenographer's scratching on the pad off-putting. He did not like being lectured to by lawyers.

'This is a serious matter, and I will ask the questions I deem necessary to establish the truth. I thank Miss Feister and Mr Coldwell for their presence.' He looked directly at them. Coldwell couldn't meet his eye and fidgeted. 'I want to assure you that we will be extremely grateful for your help and candid answers. You will not be charged for some minor offence.'

'You won't bust us for smoking pot?' Ingrid Feister had a playful look on her face.

'No. I won't. On the night of August seventeenth you attended an afterparty at the Kookaburra Hotel, with the dance group.'

'Yes,' Ingrid Feister answered clearly. Coldwell slid in his chair.

'Angus Duncan and a Chinese man, Mr Li, also attended.'

'Yes.' Feister was answering for both of them.

'You met Kelly Davies there.'

They had. Things had begun to break up after midnight but the five of them weren't ready to stop. Li didn't speak English but it was pretty clear he was up for some fun.

'I knew Angus flew and I wanted to see the desert at night. I suggested he fly us to Tenacity Hill so we could wake up to a desert sunrise. Right?' At her prompting Coldwell looked up nervously and nodded. You really don't want to be here, thought Clement.

'What happened when you arrived?'

'We drank, danced. Or actually Kelly and I danced. There was an old CD player there, I remember. Max smoked pot. Kelly did a kind of lap dance for Shaun. She had a handful of pills. Eccies. She offered them. We didn't take any. Shaun might have.'

'Do you know where she got the pills?'

'No. It was clear Shaun appreciated her dancing. They started kissing. She was drinking Vodka neat, from the bottle.'

'Did either of you see her take any pills?'

Feister said she saw her hand go to her mouth but wasn't keeping tally.

'What about you?' Clement homed in on Coldwell.

'I saw her swigging vodka.'

'Max was pretty well out to it. He was tired. I said we were going to head off to bed. I didn't want to miss sunrise. Kelly took Shaun's hand and led him over to the other tent. I went out like a light. Max too. We woke up a bit late, just after the sun was up. Kelly was gone. Angus said he'd dropped her back to Hedland for her bus. There was a bit of a weird vibe, but I didn't think anything of it.'

Clement looked to Coldwell. 'You?'

'Same.'

'Neither of you heard the plane take off or land again?'

Feister said, 'I might have, in the back of my brain, but I didn't wake up.'

She was straightforward. Clement found it hard to judge the veracity of what she said.

'The CCTV footage we found of you at Sandfire made it seem like you were both upset about something.'

With the drollness that probably scored him good points at his law club, Gleeson said, 'They were holding titles like the silent movies?'

Clement held his gaze on Feister and Coldwell.

Feister said, 'We'd probably been arguing. I don't like Max smoking too much pot.'

For the first time Clement detected a false note. He did not linger however.

'You see, you disappeared, off the face of the earth so to speak. Which is consistent with you two having knowledge of something unpleasant.'

Gleeson said, 'It's also consistent with the purpose of the holiday.'

Ingrid Feister played with a nail. 'The phones don't work up there anyway. You know that.'

'Hitting the private detective who had been hired to find you, with a lump of wood, that's pretty extreme.'

'As I told you in Derby, I've always been warned about abduction. Max made an honest mistake.'

Clement leaned towards Coldwell. 'Is that right, Max? It wasn't because you knew Kelly Davies had been killed and dumped in the desert and thought people might come after you?'

Coldwell huffed and puffed. 'No! Like Ingrid said, we thought he was going to hurt us.'

*

When Clement rang me I was in a sports bar in a Geraldton pub. I'd wound my way down the coast the way a royal grows bald, steadily and without the stress of pending work. By the time I made Dampier, sExcitation had already left so I'd had no chance to talk direct to Alex but over the phone I had passed on what I knew.

'They're not budging,' Clement said.

It wasn't a surprise. Angus Duncan was prepared to take the fall and one could only speculate for how much. I asked Clement for his take.

'Turns out Ingrid is a chip off the old man. Coldwell's a flake. They're sticking to the drug story which means more trouble for your pal Crossland.'

I was looking at a baseball game on the wide-screen when Breaking News came on: a historic video of George Tacich leading a search in bushland, other shots of Bay View Terrace and Autostrada circa 2000.

'It just broke,' I said.

'What did they last? Three days? That's a bit longer than I thought.'

POLICE INTERVIEW PERSON OF INTEREST IN AUTOSTRADA CASE crawled across the screen. Clement told me about the horse tranquilliser found in Sidney Turner. It was looking more like an unrelated abduction to do with his involvement in the drug scene.

'If only we could have interviewed him.' I heard the bitterness in his voice.

'Don't beat yourself up. We've got the guy.'

There was a prolonged silence. I envisaged him sitting there, stewing on what might have been.

'I better go,' he said finally, told me to drive carefully and rang off.

I contemplated whether I should call Michelle O'Grady but judged it was better I did not, at least not yet. I'd wait a few days and let the police narrative take hold. It didn't help that I'd been right all those years ago. It didn't help that they had Crossland. Nothing would bring back the girls or Ian Bontillo for that matter. I wondered if Crossland had been able to stay clean all that time. Surely he had killed again, we just didn't know where.

I hoped Crossland had the decency to talk and let the parents claim their daughters' remains but I wasn't optimistic when it came to psychos like that. I ordered a beer and savoured it as befits a near twenty-year wait. I thought of George Tacich, the clandestine meeting at the zoo. George had retired now. Nikki Sutton, the young policewoman on that case, was now the Super in charge of Major Crime. Craig Drummond had lost his life in a shark attack.

Yet, here I was, the last man standing ... or, to be more accurate, sitting on a bar stool.

I finished the beer and watched the froth slide all the way to the bottom. I didn't order another. I felt maybe a sense of vindication but no triumph. It was a long, awful chapter in my life but at least I could close it. But that didn't leave me satisfied. There's a principle we have banged into us from the days when our folks gave us lunch-money: the one about how we're all equal under the Southern Cross, how it doesn't matter if you're rich or poor ... but I am a believer in this principle born from the days of convict settlers building stone houses with their bare hands and, later, diggers on the goldfields, skin burned raw by unrelenting sun: everyone deserves a fair go. Kelly Davies deserved a fair go. I hadn't given up on her yet.

PART THREE

CHAPTER 35

The others had long left for the Anglers or venues of choice. It was the first of the AFL elimination finals and the entire station house was empty. Even the night shift was nowhere to be seen. Probably holed up at one of the pubs watching the big screen too, thought Clement without any malice. Years past he would have gladly joined them but he was overcome by a kind of stubborn inertia, resisting cleaning his whiteboard of the vestige of the Turner–Crossland case even though he'd accepted, albeit reluctantly, they had the right guy this time. It was still cat-and-mouse with Crossland. So far he had not been officially charged with any murder and was maintaining his innocence. Clement had suggested they try to match Crossland's DNA with the Karrakatta rape as per Snowy Lane's original thesis. Reluctantly they agreed but it was no match and apparently the Commissioner ridiculed Clement's faith in Lane. The fact that he himself had hounded an innocent man to his death didn't seem to impact him. The press was frustrated. They wanted to release the suspect's name and had stories lined up ready to go. Once they found out he'd been arrested in the Kimberley, they'd badgered Clement for details. He'd palmed them off to Risely. Snowy Lane had called: somebody had indicated he'd played a key role and the media were hounding him too. Lane of course gave them nothing. He hadn't given up on Kelly Davies. Good for him. Clement's hands were tied. He'd wished he could have offered Lane some closure on who he'd chased through the crocodile creek. Two days ago he had finally been able to interview Mongoose Cole in his remand cell. The AFP investigation had climaxed with the arrest of Cole and his Wyndham supplier. The reality had yet to sink in for Cole. He was still acting the big man. Clement had given him every opportunity to admit to Turner's abduction. He'd said he could put in special requests for privileges for his cooperation. Cole was in denial: he was going to walk. He was almost swaggering.

'Why would I need to abduct that little dickhead? He was never going to say anything because he had nothing to say.'

Clement thought it was a case of Cole rewriting history. Why else had he been around at Turner's? He'd fished, suggested there may have been no intent by Cole. They'd taken Turner and left him in the bush as a warning. What had happened was a genuine accident.

'What part of no don't you get, bro?' Cole had answered.

'Bro'? Even in Broome, crims were thinking of themselves as LA gangstas. What hope was there for any of us?

They'd found no ketamine when they raided Cole's place but he'd had plenty of chance to get rid of it, and there were a number of his customers who had admitted sourcing it from him in the past. But Cole wouldn't cop, and Clement couldn't convince himself to draw a line through the Turner case. Risely was beside himself with pride. They'd had major impact on a Feds drug case but the jewel in the crown had been cracking Autostrada. The AC had called Clement to congratulate him. Nikky Sutton, the Super, had called him too. He knew her quite well from his days at Perth Homicide. He'd deflected her praise, explaining Snowy Lane was the man who made the breakthrough.

'Snowy Lane of Mr Gruesome fame?' She was clearly excited. 'I met him back at the start of Autostrada. He was too clever for them. Apart from George Tacich, they hated him.'

He'd asked if they were close to charging Crossland.

'Very. He has no alibi for any of the times when the girls went missing. To be honest, they thought they would have cracked him by now.'

Clement had slowly come to accept that if it looked like a duck and quacked like a duck, it was a duck. He'd been thorough, no offence to Snowy Lane, but Lane was far from objective on Autostrada. Clement had needed to be convinced that there was no viable alternative suspect. He had personally gone back over the work Shepherd and Earle had done while he'd been in Perth. They had recanvassed all Turner's earlier break-ins and found no connection with anybody who had been in Perth over the Autostrada period. Earle had even flown to Telfer to interview Henderson, the miner from the Pearl, who'd lived in Perth back in the late '90s. Earle found nothing suspicious. Clement personally called David

Grunder and interviewed him specifically about the Autostrada case. He had an alibi for Caitlin O'Grady. He was in Bali, checked and confirmed.

One constructive thing Clement had done was to call Louise. He had bought a bottle of wine and they had shared takeaway Chinese on the beach under the stars. Then they'd gone to her place and pleasured one another. He had not stayed though. He wasn't ready for that. Maybe after the wedding. It was set for Grand Final Day. Only Marilyn and Brian – whose interest in sport was Sunday golf and, of course, basketball – could have been so ignorant as to opt for a Grand Final Day wedding. When he'd pointed this out to Marilyn in the only communication they'd had since, she started in on him.

'It was the only date available by the time we got back to the minister.'

The implication being it was his fault for not urging her sooner to get married. Unfortunately Louise was not here this weekend. She'd flown to Perth to be with her mum. Clement picked up the wiper and cleared the board. Done, whether you like it or not, he told himself. His phone rang. It was Jo di Rivi.

'Yes, Jo.'

'The hospital called me. Sidney Turner just passed away.'

...

People are always telling me how great Kurt Cobain is. I don't get it myself. Iggy Pop, yes, hell, even Ignatius Jones from Jimmy and the Boys, but they are adamant Kurt was a genius and I'm prepared to concede that if somebody ignites that much passion they probably are, although maybe not in the selection of their women. Imitators of Kurt Cobain however, I'm sorry, I can't make an argument on their behalf. See, this is another reason why it's so wrong to get rid of factories because it means people like Max Coldwell, who might have made an excellent fitter and turner, or forklift driver, had nothing to do in his life except practise his guitar and try and write songs like Kurt Cobain and then inflict the result on the handful of us who sat in this Fremantle basement bierkeller place drinking overpriced grog. I think there were seven of us, eight counting Max, who didn't recognise me back in the shadows. Ingrid Feister was not among the Magnificent Seven. Mercifully, the set came to an end. When Max started packing up, I walked outside and around the back lane where he would load out. It was cool, breezy but not wet, the smell of the port drifting on the wind. A few minutes after I was in position, Max emerged at the back door carrying his guitar and amp. No autograph hunters had delayed him. When he opened his boot I stepped out of the shadows.

'Hi Max.'

He looked up with that bovine smile. Clearly he didn't recognise me even out of the shadows.

'I'm the guy you whacked with a piece of wood.'

He shat himself. He wanted to run but he was still holding his guitar and amp and couldn't bring himself to drop either.

'It's okay, I'm not going to take it out on you.'

He was still wary. I noted this was not Ingrid's car but an old Hyundai. I held up the boot lid while he slid in the amp and guitar.

'What do you want?' he asked not looking at me.

'I want the truth. I want to know what happened back there at Tenacity Hill and I think deep down you want to tell me.'

'I told the police,' he said and made for the driver door. I grabbed his arm. I could have snapped it like a candy cane.

'No, from what I heard, Ingrid told the police, you were just along for the ride. I'm not the police, Max. I just want the truth, and you owe me that. Different car, I see?'

'Ingrid and I busted up.'

'Yep, those rich heiresses do tend to gravitate towards the billions.'

His bottom lip was jutting, trying to be defiant. 'Let me go, please.'

'Or what, you'll scream?'

He didn't know what to say.

'I saw the CCTV of Sandfire. I watched it over and over. It told me you were upset. Ingrid too, but you were the one who was really hurting. Because you knew what had happened. Am I right?'

He didn't dispute it. I was halfway there.

'And then I remembered something else. When they found you, you had eighty bucks. That was all. Yet Ingrid withdrew six grand before you started. She must have still had five grand left. Why would she take all the money ...'

'I had the car.'

'Yeah, but she didn't give you the car, did she? Or you'd be driving it now. I think it went down like this. I think you saw what happened to Kelly Davies and you wanted to tell. Ingrid said you couldn't. It would kill a huge deal. She probably said her old man would look after you. And then you said "shove your money" or something like that. You actually grew some balls. Because you knew it was wrong, that Kelly's family deserved better.'

He was near tears. He started talking then.

'It was all like Ingrid told the police, up until we went to the tents anyway.'

'Kelly had drugs?'

'Yeah, a few eccies. I didn't take one. Ingrid did. Maybe the Chinese guy. We were asleep. We heard a scream, real loud. It woke both of us up, I guess. We were kind of groggy. We lay there then heard a more muffled something, a groan, I don't know, but it didn't sound good. We got out and ran to the other tent. It was dark, just moonlight, but he had his hand around her throat and he was shaking her, the way a dog shakes a toy, you know? Ingrid yelled, get away or leave her or something, and he dropped her and she just ... dropped, like a rag doll. They were both nude. I think Ingrid tried to revive her but ... nothing, and the Chinese dude was just sort of staring and then Duncan came in and checked her and told us she was dead and we all had to shut up and think it through. And I said, we have to get the police or some help, and Ingrid said we can't help her now, and Duncan said he'd deal with it, we had to forget it ever happened. He told us to go back to our tent. We just sat there. I couldn't think of anything. We didn't talk. I smelled something burning. Her clothes I guess, out in the drum. We heard the plane take off. That sort of snapped me to. I told Ingrid we had to report it but she said no, we couldn't do that, there was too much at stake. Then Duncan flew back and the three of us got on the plane and flew back to Port Hedland. Duncan said we weren't to tell anybody anything. He dropped us back at the hotel and then he and Shaun drove off.'

Coldwell started sobbing then. He fell into my shoulder and cried like a little boy. I felt sorry for him, but not as sorry as I felt for Kelly Davies and her family. Coldwell got himself under control. He looked up at me. His eyes were red, more tears than dope this time.

'I want to tell the police,' he said.

CHAPTER 36

Watching the old lady carefully pour the tea in a long steady stream affected Clement in a powerful and, initially, inexplicable way. Or maybe he could explain it this way: she belonged to a bygone era when women kept home accounts in little notebooks with small sharpened pencils, when sewing and mending were valued skills, when people actually served you face to face, filled the petrol tank, cleaned the car windows, an era when you inherited furniture built for several lifetimes. Of course, he supposed, it might be different for Olive Pickering. She might well remember it as a time when her people had no voice, when their babies could be taken away 'for their own good'. Whatever, the fastidious manner of his hostess elevated her dignity. She offered him a neatly cut slice of fruitcake that he was pleased to accept.

It was good. So was the tea. She had warmed the pot, waited for it to brew. The silence had been excruciating. She did not pour herself a cup but sat quietly watching him while he indulged.

'You're not going to have one?'

'I'm alright.'

A big part-Persian cat sat watching him from on top of a stack of bags of expensive-looking cat biscuits.

'You have a few?' Clement indicated the cat.

'No, only Tiger. Sidney bought all of those for her. He loved Tiger.'

Clement found himself thinking 'bought it with stolen money' before he could bury the thought.

'I'm so sorry we haven't been able to find the person or persons who took Sidney.'

'Constable di Rivi told me you were trying. She said "My boss won't stop looking".'

'Anything you might learn, please, call me.'

'Of course.' She sighed. 'He should never have gone to Perth. He was such a good boy. But the young ones they all want to go to the big smoke.'

'You always live here?'

'Every day of my life. What's out there we don't have here? You stay with your family. But I'm all that's left here now. Me and Tiger.'

...

For weeks now he'd been watching the reports unfold. The first time he heard it he couldn't believe his ears: the police were questioning a man in relation to the Autostrada case. The man, who had been investigated by the original task force, had been arrested in the north-west of the state in relation to a minor crime and had aroused the interest of police. There was an unconfirmed allegation the man had been in possession of an item belonging to one of the missing girls. The man was now being detained on drug charges. The news report mentioned that the police had never closed the case although Ian Bontillo, a teacher who suicided, had widely been regarded as the prime suspect up until now. For the first few days he'd thought it was a trap. Thought they knew. Thought they were setting him up and would come bursting through the door. Then he thought maybe they didn't know, only suspected, and they wanted him to run. A man who would run out on his wife and children had to be guilty. But these last two days he had come to the conclusion that they genuinely believed they had the man. There must have been some kind of fateful chain from Turner to this suspect. Turner was not going to regain consciousness, he had found that out from a contact at the hospital. It was easy to put that kind of thing into everyday chitchat. All his worry had been for nought. He was in the clear despite all his mistakes, keeping the pendant, taking it out of the safe and forgetting to put it back. I will be a good man, he promised himself, I have made mistakes but I have learned my lesson. I will never go down that false path again.

...

'They won't prosecute.' Risely delivered the news over a chicken wrap at the Honky Nut.

Clement felt his jaw clench. 'I spoke to Coldwell after Lane called me. He's prepared to change his statement.'

Risely sat back, edged his plate away from him. Clement thought he detected a sigh.

'I went as high up as I could go with the Crown Prosecutor. I got "no".'

'Because of a billion-dollar deal with China going down the toilet if they did.'

'You're a cynical man, Inspector.'

'That's the reason. We both know it.'

'Even if it is *a* reason, they have others: Duncan won't change his story ...'

'He's obviously being paid a huge quid.'

'... Ingrid Feister won't change hers. And they're not going to have the taxpayer footing a bill for a trial that's lost before it's started.'

'You should speak to Coldwell.'

'Normally I support you to the hilt, Dan, but you're wrong on this one. By his own admission, Coldwell is a dope-smoking, unemployed liar who, by the way, also bashed Snowy Lane.'

'What's in it for Coldwell? Why would he make up that story?'

'Spite: the jilted boyfriend. That's how they would paint it. Look, we do what we can, we present the evidence. You've done a great job on that. We can't impose our ideas. DPP might agree with us but they can't win. If Coldwell goes up against Ingrid Feister he's taking on Nelson Feister, not to mention a few government ministries. By the time Feister's people are through with him, Max Coldwell will be lucky to have a shred of credibility left. His family will be brought into it. He'll find himself charged for offences he didn't know existed and wind up in prison.'

It was true, all of it. None of the forensic evidence was conclusive. In the end it was Duncan and Ingrid Feister versus Coldwell, and even if they sidelined Duncan, nobody was going to believe Max Coldwell over Ingrid Feister.

'That is not justice.' Whatever appetite he might have had was gone.

Risely said, 'It's a far from perfect world, Dan. We just police it the best we can.'

Maybe our best isn't good enough then, Clement thought.

...

Back at the station, he was still brooding. Josh Shepherd was talking incessantly about why the Eagles would win the premiership, though they had to win the preliminary to even make the Grand Final. That shoved the wedding back into Clement's path.

'Haven't you got something better to do?' he snapped. Josh moped off. Earle shot him a look that said he should go easy. He walked to the water fountain to give himself a timeout and was pleased to see Jo di Rivi with the pooch. Lisa Keeble was making a big fuss. He had not had a chance to thank di Rivi for her efforts with Olive Pickering, and did so now. The policewoman brushed it off.

'She's a lovely old lady. I'd want somebody to do the same for me.'

Keeble was rubbing the dog. 'How's she doing?'

'Good. The vet said she's no worse than she was a month ago.'

You're marked for death, old girl, but then we all are, aren't we? Clement filled a cup with water and went back to his office. He sat and drank his water looking at the clear whiteboard dead ahead. Something was whispering to him, trying to get through the closed door of his brain. What? He knew something without knowing it. The pooch. Why was the dog important? And why when he saw the dog did he see Olive Pickering's cat Tiger, sitting regally on a stack of ... he was getting it now ... cat biscuits. Expensive ones. 'Sidney bought them.' Really? Sidney used his stolen money to buy cat biscuits? No, Sidney used his money for drugs. Maybe one bag he might buy. And now he saw something else. He saw the parking lot behind the vet's and a glazier van. Ketamine.

He sat there for a long moment in his office tingling with the kind of chill that heralds the onset of a bad dose of flu, simultaneously fevered and icy. He went straight to the Sidney Turner file, the day he was abducted, Thursday, September 7th. He ran out of his office to where Lisa Keeble was making herself a coffee.

'Where's di Rivi?'

'Taking the pooch home.'

He jogged down the corridor to the back area and out the door. Di Rivi had the car door open for the dog to jump in.

'What day did you pick up the dog from the vet after the biopsy?'

She must have understood it was important.

'I'll check my calendar, hang on.' She studied her phone. Clement had no idea how that worked.

He thought he could see it all now, the glazier, he and di Rivi talking about Turner, the pet food.

'Wednesday, September six.'

...

I was gardening when Clement called. Okay, I was actually sweeping leaves but that counts, right? We have a big gum that clogs up the gutters and drops leaves all over the brick patio. Usually it's Tash who does it, she claims she finds it relaxing. I was only doing it because it made think of her, and at the same time stopped me from thinking about everything else. Clement's number was blinking at me. I knew he'd taken Coldwell's statement and put together a submission.

'How did we go?'

'No dice.'

I whacked the rake down on the bricks. It was one of those widespread, light ones especially for leaves and I don't know how it didn't snap.

'I know, mate,' Clement was saying, 'but it's a no go from DPP.'

And that meant it was the end of it. There was no way anybody like Kelly's family could take a civil action. You'd be going up against Nelson Feister.

'That's not strictly why I'm ringing.'

The same way you can tell a guy is going to miss a shot for goal just by the angle he stands, you can tell from somebody's voice when their spade has hit the rim of a treasure chest.

'You got something.'

Autostrada, neither of us had to spell it out.

'You remember there was a vet at the bottom of Bay View Terrace.'

'Yeah, middle-aged woman. I interviewed her myself.'

'There was also a master's student working out of there.'

I vaguely recalled that. 'I don't remember his name,' I said.

'Robert Plaistowe.'

'I definitely don't remember that but as far as I recall he was cleared.'

'He was. I'm checking your notes, the ones a certain unnamed source gave you. Thing is, Robert Plaistowe is a vet, right here in Broome.'

My heart kicked like Graham Melrose. Boom. Vet and Ket rhymed. I got it.

'Don't tell me. Turner broke into his place.'

'No report. But the day before Turner went missing, which was right after the Pearl Motel, not before, I saw a glazier at the back window. And then I went inside and told di Rivi, who was in there with her dog, that we had a lead on our break-in artist. He would have overheard Turner's address.'

...

I had to pay for my own airfare but I didn't care. I would have sold my entire collection of *Phantom* comics. Clement was not going AWOL on this one. He played it smart. He rang Superintendent Nikki Sutton who apparently was some sort of fan of mine. He told her he had a major breakthrough but, as it pertained to the Turner case, she didn't have to call it to the attention of the Autostrada boys just yet. She was happy to read between the lines. The Commissioner had been attempting to grab the glory for himself with Crossland; this time she thought Clement and his team deserved a shot. The team included me, although I could not take part in official questioning.

Clement and Earle picked me up from the airport. He had news.

'Lisa Keeble checked the tyre. It matched.'

We cruised through the streets. It was just after lunch, fine and clear. I tried to put every second into my memory. I asked him how he was going to play it. He still wasn't sure. We parked out the front.

He said, 'I took a look at the new window. I'd say it's the toilet. It is right on the parking lot, bars, but wide enough for a skinny bean like Turner to slide through.'

Clement and Earle led the way in classic detective suits. I was in a sports jacket. Earle said, 'He might recognise you anyway. You have to figure he's been following the case.'

There was a young woman with dark red hair wearing a beach sarong at the counter blocking my line of vision. She had some sort of prescription and I could hear that reassuring drone that chemists and vets have down pat when it comes to what tablets when. It was only as she swung away and left that she noticed the three of us and I saw her eyes register a fact that didn't quite fit. Now I could see Plaistowe. Ordinary nailed him in one. Not that tall, say five ten in imperial, he was pasty of complexion, some achievement for a place like Broome. Once he would have had a shock of flaxen hair bobbing over his forehead but, like all those of Viking origin, his hair had thinned. No glasses, but I suspected contacts. He wore a striped short-sleeved shirt, the kind that ten years on would be on racks in St Vincent de Paul in their hundreds. He was at ease with Clement.

'You after Jo?'

'Not today, Robert. We actually wanted to speak to you.'

There it was, just for that scintilla of a second. That sense of surprise that was not surprise but of a surprise half-expected.

'How can I help?'

I noticed his hands were entwining like a marriage celebrant. His voice was steady.

'You know a man named Sidney Turner?'

He frowned as if he was about to say no but then cocked his head to one side.

'I think ... was that the guy you arrested?'

'Yes. That was him. You never had any dealings with him did you?'

'No. Wouldn't know him from a bar of soap.'

Earle spoke for the first time. 'He broke into a number of businesses. We thought maybe here too? We're trying to put some stolen property back with the owners.'

'Oh,' his mouth formed a nice round circle. A man appeared at the door. Plaistowe raised a finger and said, 'Sorry, I'm a bit busy. Would you mind coming back in fifteen?' The man, a young guy in casual gear looked at him oddly and left without a word. Plaistowe didn't miss a beat. 'No. Not here, fortunately.'

Clement said, 'Although you did have a glazier here to fix the toilet window. Right around the time Turner was most active.'

'Somebody in a truck backed into it. Obviously they had some load.'

'Sidney Turner was abducted. The abductor subdued him with ketamine.'

Plaistowe lifted his chin to indicate he understood now why they would be here. 'Well, I keep good records. I will have a list of people I supplied. However, it is very common with drug users, people of that ilk. As I'm sure you know.'

Clement gave the impression he was actually taking that in. 'But see, there was a tyre mark matching your vehicle out at the creek where Turner was left.'

That hit him hard. He tried to regain his balance. 'There must be lots of vehicles ...'

Like the good cop he was, Clement went straight back at him.

'Where were you on Thursday, September the seventh?'

'Probably here.'

Earle said, 'No, we've checked with the other businesses. You didn't open till after lunch that day.'

'Right. Let me check my diary.' He made a show of looking in his diary. 'Yes, that morning I had a client over Derby way.'

I could tell Clement had had enough. 'Robert,' he said it in the way my uncle used to talk to me when he'd found I'd been reading his *Penthouse* magazines. 'We have the bags of cat food Turner stole. And that other thing, the pendant.'

Plaistowe's eyes went dull. He offered some guttural moan and crumpled on the floor like a dropped sweater.

...

It was the first time Clement had seen it happen to a suspect. Regrettably there were at least three times he recalled that people had collapsed when he'd had to tell them a loved one had been killed: twice way back when he was a uniform, and once as a detective when remains of a missing person had been found. The worst time was the second. An eight-year-old girl was one of two who had perished. A class had been playing at a beach on a school excursion when a sand wall collapsed. There had been no way the mother could prepare for that news. She had cut sandwiches, applied sunscreen ... tragic. Plaistowe, on the other hand, had had years to prepare, certainly weeks since the break-in.

As it turned out, the vet was only out to it for a few seconds. Thank God, thought Clement. For an instant he'd been assailed by the idea he may have taken some suicide pill. Earle found a small kitchen out the back and brought a glass of water in. Once Plaistowe had that in him, he revived. All the same, they couldn't just proceed. They called ahead to a clinic.

'Do you have any heart complaint or other existing illness?' Clement heard himself asking.

Plaistowe shook his head. 'My blood pressure's a bit high but I've been resisting going on tablets. They say there are a lot of side-effects.'

A serial killer worrying about his hypertension medication. Clement wondered if he was in some surreal story.

'We'll get you checked out.'

The vet got shakily to his feet.

Clement unclipped his radio and told Mal Gross to send in the techs. He was pleased to see Lane hadn't moved.

'Snow, you better wait outside.'

Lane saluted him and shuffled out. Clement shared a knowing look with Earle, then they escorted Plaistowe gently out front. The clinic was only a block away.

Lisa Keeble and her team arrived in two separate vans.

'You can have our space,' said Clement. 'We're just having Mr Plaistowe checked out.'

They parked at the rear of the clinic. Clement entered first and spoke to the receptionist who indicated a room had been set aside. Clement then brought in Earle and Plaistowe. In the waiting room a surfer dude with a bandage on his toe sat staring at his phone. A young mother with two children looked annoyed she'd been bumped.

The doctor, a man about forty-five who probably knew Plaistowe, emerged from a different consulting room and pointed.

'This way.'

'I'll leave you to it.' Clement whispered to Earle. 'Anything important, give me a call.'

A warrant had already been secured for Plaistowe's house and car as well as the shop. A second tech team should be arriving at the house now. Clement left the car for Earle and walked back to the vet's. Could this really be the culmination to nearly twenty years of police work, he wondered? All those thousands of man-hours, rolling up under a blue Broome sky while the main suspect has his blood pressure checked.

Snowy Lane was standing quietly out front.

'Your forensic is out the back in the carpark. You think anything's wrong with Plaistowe?'

'Not physically.'

Clement found Keeble suited up and examining the van, rigged up with a rear cage for animals in transport. This is where he shoved Turner, thought Clement, like some large dog he was moving. Risely himself and Josh Shepherd would be accompanying the techs to the house about now. If he kept one trophy, chances were he kept more. Snowy Lane emerged after him and leaned against a car, watching on, knowing to keep clear.

Mason came out of a rear door. 'There's a small safe in here.'

...

Plaistowe sat opposite him and Graeme Earle now in the interview room. He'd been given orange juice and a glass of water, and been well mannered. The doctor had declared that Plaistowe had probably hyperventilated and would be fine if he took it easy. Goodness knows what he made of it all, the local vet and a detective in his room. They had brought him to the station and charged him with the abduction of Sidney Turner. The camera was running. They had been through the preliminaries, establishing name, date, location. An audio feed led directly to the adjoining interview room where Snowy Lane sat by himself listening in. Risely and Shepherd were still at the house dealing with a shell-shocked Mrs Plaistowe.

'I didn't kill Jess,' said Plaistowe, his lips wet and seeming fleshy with the liquid he'd been drinking. 'I had nothing to do with any of those girls.'

Clement wanted to steer him away from that for the time being. Lisa Keeble had already told him that the van had been thoroughly vacuumed. She'd found no trace of wattle in it. She was hoping for a result on Plaistowe's clothes.

'I'd like to talk to you about the matter you've been charged with, the abduction of Sidney Turn –'

'Yes.' Plaistowe added for good measure, 'Yes, I admit it.'

Clement was always worried when things went this easily.

'You admit you abducted Sidney Turner?'

'It was stupid. I panicked. I wouldn't have done anything. I wouldn't have known who it was who had broken into my shop except for Jo and you talking. I panicked.'

'Why did you panic?'

'You know why: Jess's pendant. I thought this would happen. If anybody found out where he got it from, they'd think I hurt Jess, but I didn't.'

Clement was not going to allow him to drag them down that path. Not yet.

'Could you describe how you abducted Sidney Turner?'

'I waited in my van, thinking he might show. He didn't have a car that I could see. I was parked in the side street. I'd filled a syringe with horse tranquilliser. I still wasn't sure how to do it, or if I would do it, when I saw him. I jumped out and snuck up behind him and injected him. I dragged him to the van, tied him up, just his hands really.'

'Didn't you hit him first?'

'Um, yes, I might have. I had a block of wood the size of a brick.'

'So you hit him and then injected him?'

'That's correct.'

'And then you loaded him into your van and drove him to an isolated creek south of Derby and what? He escaped?'

For the first time Plaistowe looked at Clement with some hostility. 'No. I'd had time to think by then. I just left him there.'

Earle spoke with doubt in his voice. 'You just left him, tied up, sedated, on the banks of a creek where a crocodile was known to be active. You wanted it to do your dirty work.'

'No. I didn't know there was a crocodile there.'

Earle played the sceptic. 'It was in the papers.'

Plaistowe was agitated. 'It was just bush. I didn't know what I was doing.'

Clement found himself circling. 'You just took Turner to the bush to what ... question him about what had happened to the pendant that belonged to Jessica?'

'That's right.'

'But, help me here, Robert, you already knew we had it or it had been sold on, right?'

He's looking trapped thought Clement. He's starting to see his error. Plaistowe said nothing. 'And here's the problem for me. If he didn't know the significance of the pendant before, Turner was going to know once you questioned him. He'd be able to give us a description. And if you thought we had the pendant but hadn't worked out its significance, then by removing Turner you removed any link back to you.'

It was not the first time Clement had made somebody confront their darkest self. That part of us we can sweep under the bed, pretend doesn't exist.

'You took him there to kill him. And either Turner escaped, or you changed your mind.'

'I don't why I took him there but he didn't escape. I left him there. His legs weren't tied that tight. I had no reason to kill him.'

The last sentence was strident. We are there now, thought Clement, we can talk about Jessica Scanlon.

...

It was a weird sensation, alone in this room, listening to the voices from next door. Like a play going on in my head. I admired Clement's skill as an interrogator. He'd got the admission from the vet he had abducted Sidney Turner and he'd all but got Plaistowe to admit that at the very least his initial intent was to kill Turner. Now we were where we were always destined to be.

'I didn't kill anybody. The police at the time questioned me. I was at Lake Grace the day Caitlin O'Grady disappeared.'

There was a rustling of paper, Clement making out like he was checking notes but of course he and I had already been through this.

'You claim you were in Lake Grace the entire weekend after that Australia Day.'

'That's right. I have a cousin there.'

'Three hundred and forty-five k, that's the distance.' It was Earle this time. 'But you could drive that in, say, four hours. Leave Lake Grace at nine, be in Claremont around one am. Drive back again.'

'No,' high-pitched. 'You're trying to frame me. I never left the farm.'

Clement came in again, reasonable. 'Okay, let's say you're telling the truth. You're telling us you didn't know Caitlin O'Grady or Emily Virtue?'

'No. Only Jessica. She was friends with my brother.'

According to Clement, the safe in the shop had contained nothing but drugs Plaistowe used in his work. Last I'd heard, nothing had turned up at the house but it was early days.

'So how did you wind up with her broken pendant?'

There was a long pause. I held my breath. Was he going to demand legal representation? No. He began speaking. Thank God.

'I was working at the vet clinic that night, Friday, after uni. I was doing a study on the symptoms presented by animals and the likely choices of treatment by vets. That was my master's. Just as I was arriving, Jessica got off a bus from town. She was meeting friends for dinner up the street. I always liked Jess, and I got the impression she liked me. She was flirty, you know, she'd always touch you and laugh ... and I said I was here at the vet and if she wanted to after she'd had dinner, I could give her a lift home because it was dangerous out there. Everyone was freaking out.'

Because of you, I thought.

'And, you know, the whole time I was thinking about Jess coming back to see me. I had a bottle of gin I used to mix up with lemonade while I worked. Which was mainly going through the computer and the notes, you know? And anyway, there was a knock at the back door at, whenever it was, and there was Jess. She said she was going to get a taxi but there was none at the rank and was it still okay to get a lift? I asked her if she'd like a drink while I was finishing up and she said sure. And I was at the computer and she was leaning over my shoulder and I could smell her perfume and feel her, you know her breast against my neck, and I just thought, "she likes me". And I turned around and kind of stood up and kissed her. And she freaked.

'She pushed me away and said, "No, what the fuck are you doing?" or something like that. And I felt so ashamed, and maybe angry because she'd kind of led me on, you know, and I reached for her to tell her to calm down and say "I'm sorry, okay", but me grabbing her freaked her out even more and she shoved me again and I grabbed for her and got her necklet and it snapped. And I was standing there with it in my hand and she just ran out. Out the back door, it wasn't locked. And there were some dogs there and they were going crazy and I just stood there with this thing in my hand for like, five seconds. And I thought, no, I have to give this back, I have to put things right. And I ran out and there was no sign of Jess. But there was a car's brakelights heading out the carpark towards Leura Avenue. I knew she had to be in that car.'

Clement said, 'You're saying there was no sign of Jess and it was five seconds?'

'Maybe twenty, maximum. It seemed longer but I've thought this over thousands of times since. It had to be less than half a minute. I know I was thinking I would see her when I ran out.'

'And what did the car look like?'

No hesitation. 'It was a station wagon, dark red I think.'

I was rocked. That was something I was not prepared for.

...

You've kept your secrets for eighteen years, Clement was thinking as he tried to read the man opposite. This could be just another lie.

Earle asked, had he got the registration? No, he'd wished every day for the rest of his life, to this very second, that he had.

'I was standing there in shock. I tried to tell myself that it might be someone Jess knew, or that it was a Good Samaritan who had seen her upset. She'll be fine, I was trying to tell myself. The car swished to the left and accelerated up towards the railway.'

Was he too convincing? There was about Plaistowe something haunted, something of the loss he'd felt, something that echoed with Clement's own fears over losing touch with Phoebe. But maybe Plaistowe could still feel that, even if he was a killer.

'So you're standing there with the pendant in your hands, what did you do then?'

'I didn't know what to do. I went back to the vet's and locked up. I was still telling myself, she's okay. I didn't have her phone number. There was a phone box in the Bay View Terrace across the road. I went there, called triple zero and reported a dark red station wagon in Bay View Terrace that had been cruising suspiciously. I didn't give the exact location because it would come back to me.'

It seemed he was hurting, but how could you be sure?

'And later when Jessica was reported missing, you didn't get in touch.'

'I'd be a suspect. I'd argued with her. The police had already interviewed me. I was in Lake Grace when Caitlin O'Grady went missing but I know how you think. I'd reported the car. I didn't know anything else. I had no more information.'

'You could have told us Jessica was there one second, gone the next.'

He was looking down at the table now. Clement waited for more, nothing came.

'So why did you keep the pendant?'

He continued to look down. 'I just felt I should. I couldn't throw it away. It seemed wrong.' He looked up into Clement's face. There were tears now, for himself or Jessica or both, Clement couldn't say. 'I only tried to kiss her. I didn't want to believe that something ... that I ...' He regained composure. 'Whatever you think about me, that's the truth. I did not harm Jessica and I never had anything to do with the other girls. I kept that pendant in my safe at work. And then one day I had to fit some boxes in there and I moved it and forgot to put it back. And that was the night that Sidney Turner broke in. I think it was Jessica, Detective, I think she guided it all so you could catch the real killer.'

CHAPTER 37

Twice I'd tried to pin the Autostrada abductions on Shane Crossland, twice I'd been wrong. Crossland was nothing but a small-time drug dealer who'd been in the wrong place at the right time and now I had to face that mistake. I'd been angry at Tregilgas for his dumb stubbornness but was forced to recognise the same flaw in myself. Crossland had never had Jess Scanlan's pendant, that had all been Plaistowe, so the question had to be: was the vet lying? Had he abducted and killed Jess Scanlan, and likely therefore Emily and Caitlin? I wasn't going to let the myopia I'd shown with Crossland repeat. Plaistowe could have abducted Emily Virtue. According to Clement, the records of the original interview did not give him an airtight alibi. He had been in a Nedlands share house at the time but could nominate nobody who was with him that Saturday night, early Sunday morning. Caitlin was a different story. He was confirmed as being at Lake Grace, an awful long way from Perth, till around 9.10 pm. It was just possible he could have done it, got back to Claremont and abducted Caitlin but we were talking a ten to fifteen minute window, so he would have had to drive non-stop and practically grab the first girl he saw. Of course the Geiger counter clicked loud when it came to Jess. He admitted he was with Scanlan the night she was abducted, seconds before she was abducted in fact. He had even maintained possession of her broken pendant. That spoke of a violent struggle and that made him a prime suspect, with the task force and Tregilgas licking their respective lips.

Clement told me he didn't hear a false note in the confession. I didn't have the advantage of seeing Plaistowe's face but that can be a distraction too; sometimes the consummate actors work their visual emotions better than their voice, and I had to say, his voice sounded as true as a David Warner pull over mid-wicket. But, of course, if Plaistowe was the culprit, you'd expect him to be a consummate liar.

One thing I've learned is that if a man kills once, he won't have much compunction about killing again. If Plaistowe killed Jess Scanlan, he would have killed Turner after abducting him. Unless Turner escaped. Was that likely? Here's a guy who can snatch women from under the noses of police in a crowded nightclub district, wouldn't that guy be able to deal with Turner way out in the lonesome bush? Okay, maybe he'd reformed, maybe he'd lost his knack as well as his yearn to kill, maybe he couldn't be bothered with a male victim, it just didn't do it for him, and so he grew slack and Turner got away. I'm sure that is what my old pal Collins at the task force and his boss, the Commissioner, would be suggesting.

On the other hand, if Plaistowe did not kill Scanlan, his account dovetailed with other facts I'd uncovered. He claimed he'd seen a dark red station wagon leaving the carpark moments after Jess Scanlan ran out. The roadie, Party Pig, saw a dark-coloured station wagon parked beside his truck the night Emily Virtue disappeared. The night Carmel Younger was raped it seemed the vision caught SAS soldier Mathew Carter on camera. At the time Carter owned a maroon wagon. Carter had been my original suspect but his DNA did not match the swab from the rape kit.

'But the sample I got was from a hair from a hairbrush in his room. You see what I'm saying. Maybe somebody left their brush there, or used his brush. Maybe that wasn't Carter's DNA.'

Clement took a bite of his fish burger and chewed slowly, thinking. We were back at the Cleo post the interview.

'But you said the night Scanlan disappeared his squad was in Northam.'

'He could have got back. Maybe they were on some all-night exercise and he had time. Come on, Northam's a lot closer than Lake Grace.'

Clement wiped his mouth carefully with a napkin. 'We'd need an ally to approach the army.' He put the napkin down, still thinking.

'Nikki Sutton helped me once before. You said she likes me.'

'She's a superintendent now.' He said it like somebody tells you the nag you just put a fifty on has a bad limp in the mounting enclosure. For good measure he added, 'You're poison as far as the Commissioner is concerned.'

'Maybe she cares about truth more than the Commissioner's approval.'

Clement mulled. 'Alright. I'll ask her. Any idea where Carter is now?'

'No. He had two friends, well not exactly friends, but guys in the squad.

I don't remember their names but I have my notes. There are also the other two guys he shared the house with. Filbert and Hinton or Holton, some name like that. I've got all the files still.'

We agreed I'd run my old contacts while he followed police records on Carter.

'What's going to happen to Plaistowe?'

'The task force guys are picking him up tonight.'

We finished up our burgers and Clement dropped me at the airport. I kissed goodbye to Broome in the hours of dusk, its scent lingering in frail air. We'd had a short yet tumultuous affair: crocodiles, lingerie dancers, beers on the beach. I hoped we'd see one other again sometime when the guns were silenced and justice had been served.

...

Everything was in a frenzy as the footy season climaxed. After that Australia would hit a lull until the Melbourne Cup. It was a time when the bees start to buzz again and all the corporate bigwigs take holidays so they don't have to stand in line at airports with the December plebs. It's a great time to be outside but today I had to forgo the pleasure. I was in my poky office. It took me hours to find my old computer files on backup disk. The files I needed were on floppy disks of the era before I'd instituted the better strategy of simply keeping an old computer forever. This reminded me why. It took me hours to locate possible backups and half of them didn't work on the new computer. I had a vague memory of printing a hard copy and eventually I found what I was after in the second of my lever-arch folders marked simply CAITLIN. I'd never stopped thinking of Caitlin and the O'Grady family but I'd kept them in the background, not wanting to give false hope. I was glad I had. I would have blown it with Crossland. For now they could find out whatever the cops wanted to tell them.

By the time my plane arrived in Perth the night before, there was a text from Clement to say Sutton was on board. I'd driven home, slept till 6.00 am and come straight to the office, so it was around midday before I found the names I was after. The two men who had hung with Carter in Timor were Luke Whitmore and James Feruggi. Whitmore I'd met. I remembered him now, fair hair, slim face. I guessed he wouldn't look anything like that seventeen years on. I tried the old number I had on him and got a woman with an Indian accent who had never heard of him. Clement would be the surest way of locating him but I was going to have a stab at Facebook first. I got lucky. There was a photo of the guy I remembered, not that different, still sinewy, hair slightly thinner but wavy. I was going to apply to be his Facebook friend but I thought there might be a quicker way. His profile photo had him wearing a Cottesloe Rugby Club jersey and there were other guys behind him in the same shot. I had an old pal, Manto, who was associated with the club. Manto was no gazelle, and as far as I knew had never excelled on any sporting field, but he was an excellent sportsman when it came to off-field activities like carrying an esky or organising smart, attractive women for the trivia night. I called him and we swapped long losts.

'I haven't played for years,' Manto said, 'but if he's a member somebody will know him. Call you back in ten.'

He was true to his word. The Whitmore number was a mobile. I rang and got voicemail. I said he might not remember me but we'd met once before years ago and I wanted to speak to him about Mathew Carter and would he mind calling me. I was about to pack it up but figured I may as well try Feruggi. There weren't too many James Feruggis in Australia. One looked about eighteen. The other was the right age and lived in Darwin. I sent a friend request. My phone rang: Clement.

'Mathew Carter was bashed to death in a lane in Richmond, Victoria, in two thousand and three. He'd left the army and had joined the Hells Angels.'

I'd never caught wind of it and that surprised me. Mind you, it was over in Victoria and I remembered that in 2003 Tash and Grace and I had gone on a holiday to Vietnam, so maybe that coincided.

'Suspected biker related but never established,' embellished Clement.

I'll admit, the first thing I thought was good riddance to bad rubbish. The next was, we're never going to find what happened to those girls. Not for the first time on the Autostrada case, I felt I'd been punched in the guts. But this wasn't about me.

'I'd still like to close out the case,' I said. 'The families need it.'

Clement agreed. 'They'll have some sample of his DNA on file in relation to his death. Sutton has put in a request to the army for files relating to Northam exercises.'

I brought him up to speed on my efforts and suggested if I could get onto Whitfield I might be able to get some idea of what they did at that camp.

'It's a long time ago,' he said with naked scepticism.

That was true but who knew how long before the army would respond. If they were like most government departments, it would drag on like a school presentation night.

We agreed to keep each other informed and rang off. Our conversation had left me in an emotional no-man's land. If Carter had been dead since '03 it might go some way to explaining why there'd been no repeat. No more abductions and murder was a good thing but part of me still felt cheated in the way a man who has prepared himself to defend his house against a bushfire suddenly finds the fire has swung in a different direction and the day is saved anyway. I wished Tash was there for me to bounce off. I went back home, cooked an omelette and hoped the phone might ring, the way I would in my youth after a nervous first date. To milk the mood I put on an Esther Phillips CD and got deep blue stewing on what had happened to Kelly Davies. I drank a Heineken, something I couldn't have done in my youth because we were a one-beer town, Swan. Supposedly we had become sophisticated but allowing imported beer wasn't a pass mark. You don't get sophistication by copying glossy photos of piazzas. Like everything else in life you have to earn it the hard way, and sometimes that means change from within, a lot harder process. Wherever I looked, I still saw one big pit. Whether it was gold or nickel or iron ore didn't matter, in this state power still came from who held what land where. We weren't an ideas city, or a tourist mecca, we could let Sydney or Melbourne hoodwink themselves into that lie. Sure, every now and again there'd be some campaign featuring the Bungle Bungles or red wine and surfing in Yallingup but that was like the donation a rich man gives to the beggar outside the opera. It helped us hide who we really were from ourselves. When it was founded the city had a governor, a polite word for a state-appointed dictator. Nelson Feister was no dictator but he wielded just as much power. I didn't mind him being rich. I didn't care if he shot skeet with plates of pearl but I didn't go much for letting his business associates get away with homicide. The ringing phone pulled me out of my funk. It was Luke Whitmore. He said he remembered who I was, though he was pretty vague on our last meeting, it was a long time ago. I asked if he might be able to meet with me and talk about his time in the army with Mathew Carter.

'You wanted to speak about him last time. Why?'

I explained I was a private detective working for the family of a missing young woman. Carter was a suspect back then and still was.

'Day after tomorrow I'm off to Timor, and tomorrow I'll be pretty busy but I've got an hour or two now.'

That suited me fine.

'You know Carter is dead, don't you?'

I said I'd heard that but would still like to see him. He was up in the hills, Parkerville way. I arranged to meet him at the Tavern. For some reason the hills east of Perth had always fostered a few arty types and a lot of fleecy check shirts and large dogs. It must have been low on dentists though, judging from the clientele of the tavern this night. The wind had kicked up. It was a few degrees cooler up on the escarpment and a log fire was going in the bar. Whitmore hadn't changed at all from his Facebook photo. I bought us each a dark beer and we moved closer to the fire. It was a bit too warm for Whitmore who stripped off his jacket and sat in a t-shirt. I remembered when I had a taut body like that.

'You'd be pleased,' I said, nodding at the Eagles tattoo. Down to the last four now, they could win the whole thing.

He smiled. 'I grew up in New South Wales. I'm still a rugby man at heart but I thought I should fit in.'

'You settled here?'

'Met a local girl. I wasn't into a long-term relationship when I was in the army. Not fair on your woman. I did two tours of Afghanistan then I'd had enough. I quit, was going to go back east but met Karen. We shacked up. It lasted eleven years before it turned to shit.'

'So you're going to Timor?'

'I always liked the place. I applied to an NGO. Anyway, Mathew Carter. I heard he was bashed to death. I hate to say it but it's no surprise.'

'Did he stay in touch with you?'

'Briefly, after we left the army. He went back to Victoria. We weren't close in Afghanistan but we were still connected. He emailed me a few times. He called me up once or twice from a phone box. I think he was lonely, lost. I heard he got in with a biker crowd. You think he might have killed this girl?'

'There are some indications he may have, nothing concrete though, which is where I thought you might be able to rule him out, or in.'

He told me to fire away. I asked him about the Northam camp in August of 2000. His shoulders slumped.

'That's so long ago.'

I asked him to try and remember. 'It was just before the Olympic Games.'

That brought him back. Everybody seemed to remember where they were when Cathy Freeman won. This was just a bit before of course.

'I don't recall a lot. We were doing a lot of training at that time because of Timor.'

I asked him if he could recall if there would have been any opportunity for Carter to leave the camp and get to the city and back undetected. He let out a low whistle.

'That's a real stretch. We did occasionally have bivouacs where you'd be out a couple of nights but there was always somebody nearby. We might be in three-man or six-man teams ...' He shook his head. 'I just think, well, it's not impossible if you had a car standing by, but ...'

He let his doubt smother my hope.

'Is there any chance Carter didn't go on that camp?'

'Well, if he was sick or copped an injury. That's possible. The girl, you got a photo? That might help.'

Maybe I shouldn't have shown him, but he was going in two days. I'd brought my case folder. I showed him a photo of Jessica Scanlan without any identification.

'She's familiar.' Then I saw it in his eyes. 'Isn't she ...?'

'Yeah.'

I let it sink in.

'I never saw him with her. To be honest, she's way out of his class. Any of us for that matter. What about the other girls?'

'Your squad was in Perth. You remember what you did the weekend after Australia Day that year?'

'Probably beach cricket. I'm sorry, it's so long ago. I don't think Carter could have done it though.'

'He was violent.'

'But not that smart. If he pulled it off, I don't think he could have kept it a secret.'

I asked Whitmore to please keep my inquiry confidential for the families' sake. He said the Taliban had helped him learn to keep a low profile. I wished him well in his new job.

I drove back down along the slumbering backbone of the city. It had been a while since I'd been up here at night. The lights seemed brighter, the city much bigger. But we're still just a big hole, I thought, and we're not done with digging yet.

...

Like a PSA reading that tells you you're off for another visit to the urologist, my meeting with Luke Whitmore was far from what I wished. Even so, I wasn't without hope. Yes, it might have been extremely hard for Carter to have got to the city from a training exercise in Northam some hundred k away, abducted and killed Jessica Scanlan and then got back without being detected, but it wasn't impossible. And his memory wasn't exactly sharp. Maybe Carter was off on some special exercise. Then again, maybe Carter never made the camp, maybe the army records we'd got the first time were wrong. I wanted to view an actual roll before I conceded Carter was not my guy. Clement called for the bad news. The task force guys were still interviewing Plaistowe. He was maintaining his innocence.

'Maybe Plaistowe just made up that bit about the station wagon. Perhaps there was one nearby and he just improvised a story we'd swallow.'

What Clement said could be true but I wanted to be certain I had tried every door before I declared the castle empty.

'The DNA result won't be in for a few more days. And the army records are still "in the pipeline".'

My guess was that pipeline could make the Perth to Kalgoorlie pipe look like a popper straw.

...

The next two days I pottered, dividing my time between home repairs and office work. Two jobs came in but I palmed them off, my heart wasn't in it. Tash and Grace skyped and I felt better hearing their adventures. I even took myself off for a swim at North Cott. On the Friday, eve of the big knock-out final, Barry Dunn sauntered in and planted himself in the seat opposite me.

'I hear you did good work for Nelson Feister.'

His macchiato arrived promptly.

'Not from any moral perspective.' I was sulky, I admit it.

'Maybe Feister's guy is telling the truth.'

I deadpanned him. He sipped.

'They're talking sixteen billion dollars, Snowy. For that kind of money they'd gloss over Mother Teresa being killed.'

I pointed out she was long dead.

'And that's my point, Snowy,' he said, and finished off his cup.

...

'No dice, Snow, it's no match.'

I stood rooted to the spot, a bad sense of déjà vu about this. Clement waited on the line.

'Snow?'

'I'm processing,' I lied. My processing machinery was busted and smashed and waiting by the bin. Clement went on.

'I even had them compare the DNA you took from the hairbrush back in two thousand with the sample from the Vic police. It was Carter's. He didn't rape Carmel Younger.'

'Maybe he was there?'

'It's possible. We're still waiting on the army to come back with exactly what the training exercises were but it's looking more like Plaistowe is our guy. Thanks to you.'

I told him I appreciated the pep talk, but I didn't.

'I've suggested they run Plaistowe's DNA against the DNA on the Carmel Younger kit.'

'The Commissioner is going to break a leg on that ... not.'

'Sit back and enjoy the footy.'

As if. I hung up and mooched. The game passed before me in a fuzz, like I was disconnected from my body. At half-time I turned it off and cracked a bottle of white. My phone buzzed. James Feruggi had accepted me as a Facebook friend. What the hell. I messaged him, said I was an investigator in Perth and I wanted to call him about Mathew Carter. To my surprise, he messaged me straight back with a Skype contact. I skyped immediately.

He was early forties, thick dark hair, tanned and lined face, serious. He was wearing some kind of work shirt like maybe he worked ground staff for an airline. The room was bare, a spare computer room, I guessed. I got through the formalities.

'Look, James,' I said, tired of circumvention, 'I've been on the Autostrada case for years.' He knew what I was talking about. 'I red-flagged Mathew Carter as a prime suspect back in two thousand. There was a girl raped near Karrakatta Cemetery.' I ran him through video vision, the SAS tattoo. I told him how a number of people had fingered Carter. 'Luke Whitmore told me about the Timor tour and what went on. I know Carter owned a maroon station wagon back in ninety-nine.' I watched him reach for a smoke and light up. I was guessing he might be single because he grabbed a soft-drink tin for an ashtray. 'I was wondering if you remember by any chance a Northam training bivouac in August of two thousand, the weekend Jessica Scanlan went missing. I know it's a long time ago.'

He nodded slowly. 'I remember.'

'You remember if Mathew Carter was there?'

He took a long draw on his smoke. My hopes lifted.

'He was there. We talked football. It was near the finals.'

My hopes crashed and burned.

'What did Whitmore tell you about Timor?'

I ran him through the story, how Carter had possibly assaulted the woman. He raised an eyebrow.

'That's not how I remember it.'

'How did you remember it?'

'The three of us were there. Whitmore and Carter took the suspect woman into this little hut. I stood guard. I heard a woman sobbing. I yelled at them what's going on? There were eyes on us, the men of the village weren't there but the women and kids were. Carter came out, agitated. Carter was an arsehole but Carter was a puppet. Then Whitmore came out looking, I don't know how you'd describe it, like, beaming. I think he said "sweet" or something like that.'

I was riveted, I couldn't move as he talked.

'I said something like I was going to report it. Whitmore said it was two against one. Carter got some balls then and told me I might find my rifle going off accidentally. Some shit like that. I never reported it because I figured in the end they were right. It would be their word against mine. I'll tell you something else. That August camp was just before we went away again, to the Middle-East. Carter was there but Whitmore wasn't. He was playing rugby against Navy the weekend before, and hurt his ankle. If you're looking for a stone-cold psycho, Whitmore's your man.'

CHAPTER 38

Clement sat there with the receiver in his hand, cursing. What did Lane think he was playing at going after Whitmore by himself? Lane had obviously waited to the last minute to call. Clement had heard the boarding call in the background. It was only an hour flight from Darwin to Dili and Lane knew it would take Clement hours to organise himself from Broome. And even if he could get to Darwin, Lane had told him that was the only flight out today. He'd called 'out of courtesy', he had said. Clement had barked at him.

'This is effing courtesy?'

Lane told him he was sorry, but it was for Clement's own sake.

'It's much better I'm deniable.'

Of course Lane might be wrong about Whitmore. He'd been wrong about Crossland, and sure, he'd held off on declaring Plaistowe a killer, but he'd been dead certain it was Carter. In baseball parlance he was batting three for none.

'What proof have you got?' Clement had demanded that at least from him.

All he'd said was he was certain this time.

'Don't worry about me,' Lane had said. 'I have backup.'

And that's where he apologised and said he had to go and terminated the call. Leaving Clement to stew because there was no flight to Dili now even if he wanted to ...

Clement stopped, reversed.

No *commercial* flight. The Feds owed him a favour. They were flying to and from Dili all the time. Clement yelled for Mal Gross. Clement's phone pinged as Mal Gross stuck his head in the doorway.

'Can you see if the Feds can fly me to Timor asap?'

Gross didn't ask why. He disappeared quick smart. Clement checked his phone, a pithy 'Sorry, mate' and an attachment. Clement clicked on the attachment and a photo bloomed. It showed Mathew Carter and Luke Whitmore in SAS gear in what might have been Dili. They both proudly displayed an SAS tattoo in the same place on their right arm.

...

Whitmore must have had his tattoo doctored later to look like an Eagles tattoo. I thought about him, sprawling on his chair in front of the fire at the Parky pub, deliberately taking off his jacket, taunting me in his own private joke. 'I'm the gingerbread man, you can't catch me.' I didn't remember seeing a tattoo the previous time we met. I guessed he was wearing a jumper or windcheater. From that first interview he must have known I was looking at the Autostrada case. He'd probably gone the next day and had the tattoo altered just in case, knowing something had led me to think SAS. Or maybe Cornelius had innocently mentioned it when he set us up for a meet. Such a cocky bastard, he even told me he wasn't really into footy, giving me a clue. He must have enjoyed life on the edge.

Maybe it was combat high, maybe that was what drove him to abduct and kill. Or more likely he'd always been like that and the army was a perfect profession. I know they do tests for that kind of thing but there was always somebody could beat the system.

'They got them the same time. Whitmore's idea. I took the photo.'

Feruggi sat next to me on the plane. At Perth airport I'd been heading out as the Eagles supporters rolled in. I still hadn't seen the game. Sunday had been all about logistics, booking flights and hotels. On Skype Feruggi's arms had looked tatt-free but I double-checked when we met at Darwin airport. He'd insisted on coming.

'You're going to need backup. Do you know where you're going to get the gun?'

This was a reference to my carefully thought out plan. I was going to meet up with Luke Whitmore, somewhere; I wasn't sure where; I was going to tell him it was all over and ask Whitmore what had happened to Emily Virtue and Caitlin O'Grady. If he refused, I would threaten him with the gun, which I didn't have yet but was going to get from someone who I hadn't yet identified. If he continued to refuse, I was going to beat him, then shoot him, somewhere like a thigh, not lethal. This was why I could not have Dan Clement along. He was still young enough to have a career. In the blink of an eye I would be sixty. Close to a third of my life I had been tracking a phantom, and now that phantom had flesh, blood and a name. What I was prepared to do was not in any sense smart, or considered, but dealing with these monsters you cannot be smart or considered. They'll laugh in your face and cut your throat, I've seen it before. If things went awry, if I had to shoot him, I guessed they would stick me in jail in Dili.

Or maybe they wouldn't.

Maybe they'd think that having a serial killer in their midst where he could go back to his old ways with impunity was not such a good thing. And maybe I would convince them that, regardless of what this lying killer said, the fact was I was trying to bring him in peacefully when he jumped me and I had to shoot him. Fact is, I didn't want to think that far ahead, I didn't want images of Tash and Grace visiting me in a Dili prison to cloud the judgement I knew I must not have.

'I know where we can get a gun,' said Feruggi, bringing me back to the present.

He told me he had a girlfriend but nothing serious. He was divorced with two kids. He had convinced me he had nothing to do with the abductions – don't worry, the thought had crossed my mind that all three of them could be in on it. I'd made him scan his passport and send it to me to prove that when Caitlin disappeared he had been in Thailand.

···

We reached Dili quicker than a below-quota parking inspector writes a ticket. I was nervous approaching passport control. What if I read Clement wrong and he'd alerted them about me? I was gambling that deep in his heart Clement knew this was the best way, that stuffing around with extradition and lawyers would only buy a smart sociopath more time to find a way out. I was gambling he was smart enough to know he needed a stalking horse and Snowy Lane was dumb enough to be it. My heart was in my mouth and poking out my nostrils as I waited. The official glanced at my passport then waved me through. I floated all the way to the taxi. An Immigration contact of mine had slipped me the details of Whitmore's NGO, an aid-distribution organisation backed by good people who would have had seizures had they known the background of the person driving their truck. Feruggi didn't have any doubt why Whitmore had come here.

'He got away with it before. The police won't have a clue.'

'You never suspected him?' I had to ask.

'No. I didn't, but when you told me why you thought it was Carter, it all just fitted into place.'

We drove into town. It was reminiscent of Geraldton, Denpasar and Saigon all blended: sparse bush, eucalypts, white concrete houses, palms and pagoda shapes. It was still early in the build-up season but stickier than date pudding and the taxi had no air con. The driver smelled like he'd been lying in a urinal. He dropped us at the hotel, a two-storey concrete affair, The Lux, that sported plastic chairs and tables in an undercroft area, rated 7 on TripAdvisor, and was the second cheapest I could find online. Feruggi had offered to pay his own way but I'd nixed that and booked him his own room.

The reception area had the feel of a youth-hostel canteen. The girl on the desk wore immaculately clean clothes but they looked a few years old and had the thinness caused by repeated washing.

It was moving on towards 4.30 by the time we opened the doors of our rooms. My reminiscence of Geraldton was rekindled. It could have been a room I stayed in back in the early '80s. Feruggi said he was going out to get the 'you know what'.

'If the guy is still alive and in the same place it should take me less than an hour. If he's not, I'll have to ask around.'

There was an old fashioned air-cooler, one of those that I can never get to work. This was no exception. I wished in vain for a fan and had to make do with opening the windows, aluminium sliding style. A sea breeze entered but it didn't have the weight to shift the boulder of humidity that had taken up residence. I decided I'd be better off outside, headed downstairs and out, walking the main drag, trying not to think too hard because sooner or later I'd begin to dwell on Tash and Grace and everything I stood to lose. Traffic was scant. I found myself in some kind of market that evoked those early days in Bali when you'd wander past brightly coloured mats and tie-dye t-shirts, clutching the little plastic travel bag the airlines used to give you to prove you were an international traveller. I'd hoped by the time I got back to The Lux that Feruggi would have returned but there was still no sign of him and it was well into an hour since he'd left. That meant he was having trouble getting a gun. Something else I didn't want to have to think about. I bought a beer from the receptionist who doubled as bartender. She poured it daintily so as not to chip her nails. The beer glass was frosted on the outside and I felt better just looking at it. The only trouble was it was xxxx, but it would do. I plonked myself on top of a stool that was losing stuffing, right in the path of a big fan. I sipped slowly and began to feel human. There was one other person in the place, an old guy, some sort of local, maybe the owner. He was playing a solo card game at the table. The girl disappeared behind a cloth curtain. It was then I realised I only had Australian dollars. Feruggi had told me they took US dollars but he was the only one of us with any. I guessed they would just bill my room and I could burn it off plastic. After I finished my beer I waited a few moments in case the girl returned but there was no sign of her so I took the tiny elevator back up, thinking a shower might help revive me.

I keyed the door, no fancy plastic magnetic keys here, and walked in to see Whitmore standing in front of me. Then something that felt like a swarm of bees hit me. My muscles went liquid and I dropped. Whitmore had tasered me. I opened my mouth to speak but all I saw was a bunch of knuckles heading my way. I felt pain and left the earth.

···

It was rare that Clement felt Fate favoured him. In that, he wondered if he was different or alike to most people. He couldn't actually conceive anybody thought they were naturally lucky but he guessed somebody must. Anyway this time he was lucky. The Feds had a plane in Broome, a Learjet, and were prepared to help. It was Risely who made the plea via Nikki Sutton. Clement and Graeme Earle grabbed their passports. At this stage there were no charges against Whitmore but the Dili police had been requested to detain him. He'd then be asked to accompany the police back to WA and if he refused they would determine whether to bring charges or not. Clement was still pissed off with Snowy Lane. He understood Lane's thinking: he was protecting him from unpleasant things, things being a cop wouldn't allow him to do to Whitmore. And Clement might almost let him get away with that, except that he wasn't sure Lane could handle Whitmore.

The direct route and the Feds hitting the gas meant he was in Dili in around three hours. From Immigration he knew Lane was staying at The Lux so they made straight for it in their taxi. Lane should have only a ninety-minute headstart, hopefully not long enough for him to do too much damage. He and Earle buttonholed the receptionist who was busy tending happy hour to half-a-dozen expats. She gave them Lane's room number and they scuttled up. The door was open. A guy was sitting on the bed.

'Who are you?" asked Clement.

'I was going to ask the same question.'

Clement flashed ID. 'What's your name?'

'James Feruggi.'

Now he saw it. 'You're Lane's backup.'

'Don't know what you're talking about.'

'Where is he?'

Feruggi looked from Earle to Clement. 'You don't have jurisdiction.'

Earle could look mean when he wanted. 'Dili police are working with us.'

Clement saw doubt creep into Feruggi's face.

'Is he with Whitmore? We know everything.'

Feruggi gave it up. 'I don't know where he is. I went out for a while, when I came back he was gone. He was supposed to stay here.'

Earle was already on one knee looking at something on the dressing table, a little speck. He caught Clement's eye. 'Blood,' he said.

...

I was in the back of a vehicle, on the floor behind the front seat, covered in what smelled like a tarp rather than a blanket. My hands were bound behind my back, my feet tied. My head throbbed. I didn't remember anything at first except for Whitmore being in my room. I was guessing he'd slugged me but I felt weird, my muscles weak. Had he drugged me? It started coming at me then in fractured flickers: the bastard had tasered me, then hit me when I was down. I remembered the hallway, elevator, a knife in my ribs. He must have dragged me into the lift before he rolled me out into a back lane. It was twilight when we'd emerged. He'd slipped prepared ties over me, pulled them tight, then dragged me into the car, some kind of four-wheel drive. It did not escape me that this was most likely how Caitlin and the other girls had felt, assaulted, in shock, terrified. I guessed he jumped them in the dark. I doubt tasers were around back then but he could have stunned them with his fists, pulled a knife. His training had prepared him for exactly this role: silent, efficient abduction, and death. I'm a big man and he'd handled me like a toy. All the theories about the girls knowing their abductor became straw when you saw this kind of man-machine in action.

My spine told me when we left smooth road for some kind of track. I felt the pull as the car went uphill. When he stopped I figured we must have driven for forty minutes to an hour. The door at the rear of the car was pulled open. I heard something metallic yanked out and then the blade of a spade bit dirt.

He was digging my grave.

My brain ran wild. What did I have to defend myself? Nothing. Could I jump him before he dragged me out? Once I was out of the car I was dead meat. I saw Natasha and Grace in my head and bile rose in my mouth at what I was going to lose. Maybe Feruggi had seen us leave? It was a weak hope anyway; he had no vehicle, how could he follow? And through all this the spade drove down into the earth, duller as the sand got richer and the hole deeper. I can't tell you how long this took. It seemed like an hour or longer, maybe it was, or maybe it was twenty minutes. Then I heard a final grunt and the spade blade was driven down for the last time. I tensed as I felt him approach.

...

Earle had gone to get to the police. Clement felt his blood pumping too fast. Think. He grabbed Feruggi.

'There might be somewhere he'd take him. Somewhere he used to hang out. Come on!'

Feruggi was trying. Clement urged him, aware it was probably useless but unable to help himself.

'Somewhere he would go that he thought was connected to him.'

'There was a hill on the way to Maubisse. We'd drink beers. He used to say, this wouldn't be a bad place to be buried.'

Clement told himself that had to be it. There was no time for second-guessing.

How far?'

'Forty-five minutes?'

Clement started moving. 'Let's go.'

The lift was already occupied and heading down. Clement pressed and re-pressed the button. No exit stairs. He saw the lift had hit the ground floor, and heard it start back up.

'Come on,' he urged. It seemed to take forever. Not for the first time he cursed Lane. Finally the lift clicked in. He pulled open the door and Feruggi and he jumped in. Another eternity going down. Maybe Snowy could talk his way out of whatever Whitmore had planned but he thought the odds were all the other way. Whitmore was used to beating the police. He was probably too arrogant to think he'd ever be caught.

They ran out of the hotel onto the street. There had been no time to organise phones that worked here. Earle came running towards them. He started calling out ten metres off.

'Police are scrambling. They're checking on Whitmore's vehicle. He left work early and nobody has seen him.'

'We're going south towards Maubisse,' yelled Clement. 'It could be where Whitmore's taken him. You wait here.'

Feruggi had waved down a four-wheel drive and had the back door open.

'He'll take us.'

Clement followed him into the rear seat. 'Thank you.'

The driver, a local by the look of him, waved and smiled. It made Clement feel worse. He did not want a Good Samaritan hurt but that did not stop him shouting.

'Faster! Vite.'

'I hope I can remember the way,' said Feruggi as night rushed by outside.

...

I was still jammed between the back of the front seats and rear seats. I knew Whitmore was above me now. I could feel him there. I held my breath, I made my eyes lose focus, played dead. I heard and felt the tarp ripped away.

'Ready, arsehole?' he said.

I didn't blink, didn't breathe. You're dead, you're dead, I told myself. I imagined him thinking: Have I killed him? Did his heart give out?

I felt him lean in ...

With all the force I could muster I lifted my body and rammed my head into his face. I heard a crack of cartilage, a stifled cry. I tried to push myself backwards and out but remained stuck in the gully between front and back seats. This time he grunted from anger and effort and brought both hands down like a hammer on my face. The pain was exquisite.

'Fucking arsehole.'

He pulled me out of the car by my shoulders. I tasted blood down the back of my throat from my smashed nose. My head and shoulders hit rough earth, my arse and legs were still in the car. Another heave and I was out under stars I could not appreciate. We were on a hill, wooded. I saw him close up. I'd done some damage to his face, maybe broken his nose. He kicked me in the ribs, twice. A drop of his blood fell beside me. It gave me a stupid sense of achievement. I had to get him talking, hope he'd make a mistake.

'This is pointless. The police are onto you.'

'No, the police have that vet. They're dumb. They'll set him up if the facts don't fit.'

'You think I would come here without letting them know?'

'Probably. You are pretty damn stupid, "Snowy".'

He liked to think he did good snide.

'I've been working with Inspector Dan Clement in Broome and Superintendent Nikki Sutton.'

'Bullshit. Nobody believes in you Snowy, except me, and I don't count.'

'No, you're the most important person of all.'

People usually want to be flattered. Maybe I could string out time. He looked down at me, his lips twisted. He half-realised I was trying to play him but his arrogance knew no bounds.

'If you say so,' he said.

'Why did you do it, Luke? You were abused by your father? Your mother was a prostitute? Come on, you're not going to get this chance again.'

The moon was pale as an Irish track star but his narcissism was luminescent.

'Because I could. Anybody can, they just don't know it. I didn't know it until I came here that first time. We were called into a village on the border with the West. The men were supposedly out in the fields but we knew they were on patrol against us. I went into a hut. The woman had a knife hidden. She pulled it when I had my back to her. She might have killed me but something warned me. I turned, grabbed her hand. It was like a switch went off then and I understood: there's no good or bad, there's just life and death and an instant where that's in your power. Maybe it's the only time anything in our lives is in our power, wholly.

'I disarmed her. I smacked her and her mouth bled and I ... felt totally alive. Every knot in every piece of wood, I could see. Every scent I could separate and smell. She understood then that whether she lived or died was up to me. She was ... forthcoming.'

'Why did you dob in Carter?'

'I knew she wouldn't say anything, but Feruggi was a problem. Be prepared, Scout's motto. Be prepared if somebody talks, create doubt. Carter was an arsehole, people wanted to believe he was guilty. So I quietly shopped him. Insurance, I guess you could call it. The dumb bastard never realised. But after that, going back to Perth was like ... sepia. And those girls at the OBH and Autostrada didn't even look at you, like you were a clear space, a blurred face at the end of a pool cue. It was insulting. Those shallow little bitches had no clue that I'd been on that thin skin of ice, life, death, On, Off. They'd laugh at jokes with their stupid college boys with their fringes and designer singlets, without any idea the one who could suck their life from them was right there. But you get it, Snowy Lane. I've read about you. Life, death. You get it.' His turn to flatter me. 'I could let you go, but I won't. Because then it would be me that would suffer, right?'

'You kill me, there's no way you get out of the corner. It's an admission. With a good lawyer you could still walk. Like you said, there are alternative suspects. There's mitigating circumstances.'

'PTSD?' He laughed. 'That's a *good* thing. That's a great thing. I'm not going to say I killed because action fucked me up. The opposite, it liberated me. And what about this? How do I explain all this? I brought you up here to ... dance?'

'You were angry. You thought I had some agenda against you. You wanted to know why I was hounding you.'

He reached behind him. When his hands returned pointed in front of him they were holding a pistol. I think it was a Beretta but I'm no gun expert. I didn't care what killed me to be honest, I just did not want it to happen. But it seemed my appeal had fallen on deaf ears.

'So long, Snowy Lane.' He aimed. I think I wet myself.

'You killed Carter, didn't you?'

He cocked his head. 'Carter was a liability. I thought I could trust him. He was dumb, he was loyal, but finally the dumbness outstripped the loyalty. Soon as he left the SAS he blew his dough. He demanded money from me. I flew over. I paid him out.'

'Why did you stop? Did you stop?'

He regarded me seriously. 'If you really want to prove you are God, that you hold life and death in your palm, you have to be stronger than all those who have gone before you. You have to be strong enough to say, I can stop, I can do whatever I want. I can take life, I can choose to not take life. Combat helped. Afghanistan, shit, man, that was the peak. Intense. But, you stay there too long, you fucking die. I'm not that stupid.' He tapped his head. 'I could visit up here whenever I wanted. But you know how it is, old habits die hard. Sometimes you take a nibble here and there, to keep your hand in.'

He chuckled. I kept pushing.

'So you have killed since?'

'You're boring me.'

'What did you do with the girls? You're still just as smart if you tell me.'

'No point telling you is there?'

'So what have you got to lose?'

'I'm bored, bored, bored with this, Snowy.' He raised the pistol again.

'At least tell the parents. Hurting them, that's not being strong.'

I'd pushed too far. I saw his eyes go dead.

'Shut the fuck ... up.'

The shot rang out.

I thought I was dead. Then I thought he'd missed. Then I thought ... No, he *didn't* fire! Another shot rang out. A piece of branch flew. I heard him yelp in pain. I dared to look. A piece of wood the size of a pencil had speared his skin just under his eye. He clawed at it, gun grip loose for an instant. I mule-kicked his knee as best I could, the pistol dropped. Another shot went high. We both dived for the gun. Hostage training, six hundred and sixty bucks worth: seizing a gun with hands tied behind your back. My hands closed on it. He drove his chest into me. I pulled the trigger. His weight knocked us both forward, we went rolling in one ball for a few metres, the gun dropping from my grip. Then suddenly I was lighter. Voices like arrows in the dark. One sounded like Clement.

It couldn't be.

I'd come to rest kind of on my side with my left arm sprawled down the hill. I twisted my head to look back up the hill. Whitmore was on his back a metre away. From him came a sucking sound. I wriggled towards him. This is what I experienced in a late-'60s experimental-film montage: ink spilling from him, I guessed blood; gaping chest cavity; that constant sucking sound growing weaker, while footsteps grew stronger.

Clement and Feruggi ran in. Feruggi pointed a pistol.

'Call an ambulance,' I said without thinking.

'We don't have a phone,' said Clement, 'or a knife.' A reference to them being unable to do anything about me being trussed.

'He's ex-SAS,' said Feruggi, who felt down Whitmore's leg, pulled out a serious blade and sliced through the plastic ties binding me. Clement had

DAVE WARNER

some keyring torch. He shone it in Whitmore's face. His eyes were glazed but there was still a whiff of life.

'His car,' Clement said, ripping off his shirt and shoving it in the chest cavity.

I'd been through this before with Craig Drummond, the switch poised between on and off. We picked Whitmore up – actually, they picked him up, my circulation was still a ghost – and carried him towards the back seat. Just as we were about to lay Whitmore down, he expelled a gasp. By the interior light of the car I saw life had vanished from his eyes. We all knew it at the same instant. There was no longer any rush.

'He wouldn't tell me where they were,' I said, 'even though he was going to kill me.'

And as I said it I felt a terrible shame. I had survived but the misery of Whitmore's victims' families continued.

CHAPTER 39

Later Clement told me it was 'sheer arse', but from what I heard he was selling himself short. Feruggi had remembered the track that led up to the hill. They'd caught the shape of a vehicle in a clearing between trees, abandoned their ride lest it alert Whitmore, and closed on foot under the low moon. Feruggi had secured an old Glock. They were trying to get closer when they saw Whitmore draw down on me. Feruggi aimed but was scared of hitting me. The pistol hadn't even been tested. Clement told him to fire. He missed but without it I was deader than the wicket in a Sheffield Shield final. Not for the first time Clement was furious with me. I don't blame him but I still think, deep down, he knew I did him a favour. Whitmore would have told him nothing. It took a week for Whitmore's DNA to come through. It matched the Carmel Younger rape. They ran airline records and found that Whitmore had flown from Perth to Melbourne the day Carter was bashed to death. Army records confirmed Feruggi's assertion that Whitmore was not at Northam when Jessica Scanlan disappeared. They searched anywhere and everywhere that Whitmore had lived in Australia. The Dili police searched there. No physical evidence of the girls was found. Without Plaistowe breaking that pendant chain and keeping it for a reason he probably couldn't even explain himself, we would never have got a sniff. The huge weight of evidence against Whitmore mitigated the political fallout of foreigners running around Dili with guns. We were all questioned. Feruggi was deported but otherwise not chastised. I think they had a fair idea of what Whitmore might have got up to under the guise of his aid work, especially after Sutton's people traced his movements post-Autostrada looking for unexplained disappearances. Whitmore had indicated that combat in Afghanistan had satisfied his death lust for a time. He'd returned to Perth but the fever inside him had remained dormant and there had been no similar disappearances. He settled down with his girl, Karen, still nothing. Then that relationship had fallen apart. According to the ex, she had no idea about the monster he was, but found him 'like a mirage'. There was a point beyond which you never got closer. He had not threatened her. He had told her she had been a 'disappointment' and that he had given up a lot for her. In retrospect that was a chilling reference.

After they busted up he'd spent six months travelling through Thailand. Two female tourists and a number of local girls disappeared during his time. Most had simply vanished but the body of one of the locals had been found. The police were looking into Whitmore as a suspect.

The media had a field day. This time we couldn't keep my name out of it. I suppose I got written up again as some kind of master hunter of psychos. I ignored the constantly ringing phone, hid as best I could, but skyped Tash and Grace daily. Tash urged me to join them. I was tempted but somehow it felt like running away. I wasn't going to let Luke Whitmore get that satisfaction, even if he was dead, so I kept my head down and swept leaves.

There were repercussions against my old pal Tregilgas who had refused to take my leads seriously back in 2000. A 'source' – I suspected George Tacich – had dropped a bucket on the Commissioner. He had 'arrogantly dismissed my suspicions regarding an SAS suspect while hounding an innocent man to suicide'. The Commissioner came out swinging, justifying his actions, pointing out I'd wasted their time on Crossland but the media had nailed him with the fact that his own team had also interviewed Crossland at length just recently. After that, Tregilgas kept his mouth shut but according to Clement, the Minister was already involved and Nikki Sutton had been tapped for the job. Once a face-saving amount of time had passed, Tregilgas would retire and plead having to leave 'to spend more time with his family'.

My nose was indeed broken but it excused me from having to visit the O'Gradys right off. I knew they must have been desperate for every detail. Carmel Younger called me and thanked me on behalf of herself and her mother who was still alive, now in a retirement village. After that I felt a lot better.

Nikki Sutton personally briefed all the victims' families but I owed the O'Gradys a firsthand account. Grand Final eve I found myself back at the O'Grady house in the same lounge room where I had first sat nearly twenty years earlier, this time my nose in a splint, my eyes black. The house had been remodelled, given that more open look that Australians were crazy over now. It was a different sofa with different colours. Soupy had long since moved on to the great field in the sky but a new model had taken his place, some little bitsa. It had not been that long since I had seen Michelle and Gerry at Craig Drummond's funeral so there was no shock in how they looked but nobody was more aware than me that all of us were on the same ride. The pubs and clubs of our youth were now waiting rooms and MRI machines. Caitlin's photo was displayed as before, forever young, as Neil Young sang and never did it ring in my head more poignantly. I imagined she could be sitting alongside her parents, the same age, just back from walking Soupy, listening in with curiosity.

Gerry made the tea, he had semi-retired, he said. I asked after Nellie, the younger daughter. She was still overseas. I sipped my tea and ate a fancier biscuit than I had back in the day, and then I told them everything germane that had happened from the time I walked into a Broome police station and recognised the pendant of Jessica Scanlan. I jumped back and forth in time, shaded some stuff and highlighted other business. I explained what I had learnt from Feruggi, that Whitmore often took Carter's car. Carter had a habit of getting blind drunk in the afternoon and Whitmore would just take the car and go out. The police couldn't rule out Carter being a party to the abductions of Emily or Caitlin but thought it unlikely given he was involved in neither Carmel's rape or Jessica's death. Eventually my account meandered its way to the Timor hillside. I told them what had transpired,

'That bastard.' Michelle was shaking her head. 'He was never going to tell, never going to give us that satisfaction.'

And then the tears started. Not hers, mine, out of nowhere. I felt them running down my face. I was sobbing but I had no control. It was weird. I could taste my own tears and yet it was as if I might have been in somebody else's body. I'd had nearly twenty years to get it right, I still couldn't manage it. I had risked hurting Tash and Grace, risked losing them all for nothing. Gerry O'Grady put down his cup and walked over to me and hugged me. And that made me weep even more.

...

Initially Clement had planned to wear the same suit he always did, the one he'd last worn in the meeting with the Feister lawyers. It had originally been bought for Phoebe's christening because Geraldine had pressured Marilyn that he shouldn't be in some disgusting old work-suit, as if he were likely to turn up covered in bloodstains and fingerprint powder. It still fitted fine but wearing it would feel like an admission of defeat, that his life had stalled for eight years. So, while back in Perth tying up the Whitmore business, he strolled up St George's Terrace to a menswear shop and asked the assistant to fit him out. Clement was lucky. He had not put on weight, in fact he'd lost weight these last couple of years, and he could pretty much buy off the rack. The shop owner – a tailor, Clement presumed, because he was balding and wore a tape measure around his neck, with the chain to which his glasses were attached – was insistent however on measuring him up.

'These days everybody except you is carrying too much weight so they make the waist a fraction too large.' He pointed to a couple of other areas he could improve on the standard model. 'It's a service. It won't cost you anything.' Clement produced the plastic magic.

'I need it by tomorrow,' he cautioned.

'It will be ready by five this afternoon. Wedding?' asked the tailor as he wrote left-handed.

'Yes.'

'Not yours?'

No, thought Clement, the exact opposite.

...

He sat in his little flat now, the brown paper package wrapped in string in front of him like some message from the past. It made him think of Olive Pickering. Perhaps he should have gone to her? Or would that have seemed patronising? He opened the parcel and took out the suit. It looked good, it smelled good. He was almost vain enough to think that it would so impress Louise he should invite her as his guest after all but he dismissed that idea as quickly as it arrived. He hated that people might think he was showing what's good for the goose was good for the gander. He'd been to functions where the ex-married couple were both squiring new partners. Phoebe wouldn't like it. And it was Marilyn's day. Plus he wanted to savour the terrible hollowness that he would inevitably feel, all by himself, without the solace of a companion. He pressed the suit; the shirt he had already ironed, his shoes he had polished to an impressive sheen. He wondered if this new state of affairs would increase pressure from Louise. They were sleeping together more regularly yet he had still not stayed over.

He showered and dressed. Time was on drugs, inching forward. The wedding was for 2.00 pm on the lawns overlooking the ocean at Geraldine's house. The day was almost perfect. This time of the year you felt the air growing progressively humid but it was a long way off being oppressive just yet. His choice of aftershave was telling, the sort she always liked best, also the only one in his tiny cabinet.

What's Snowy Lane doing this minute? he thought idly as he straightened his tie in a mirror he'd salvaged from out the back of Traffic. He guessed he'd be sitting back to watch the big game. They'd not really ever had the chance to celebrate their case, too much to and fro with the East Timorese cops, the Commissioner, the media. But they'd cracked it, Lane and him – okay, more Lane than him. The memory of sharing beers and pizza on Cable Beach returned. If only life could be like that all the time.

The Waifs accompanied him out of town and along the road north to the homestead property Marilyn's father had selected and built off the proceeds from natural pearls. At the foot of the long driveway were tied satin bows and white balloons. 1.56, perfect, he'd judged his run so as to have no time to mingle. They'd have somebody valet parking. He'd get to the back of the crowd as Marilyn stepped out of the house seven minutes late. He knew it would be seven minutes, not six, not eight. He took his foot off the accelerator and let the car glide until it could no longer match the gravity caused by the incline, then he pulled the wheel so the car slid to the side of the driveway.

Did he really want to do this?

No.

Phoebe would be disappointed.

But Phoebe would get over it.

He could not.

'You can't, can you?' he asked himself there on the side of the road. 1.57 now. No. He didn't want to give her up. If he had to, he certainly did not want to witness it like some POW forced to watch their flag torched. He did not want to see Brian beaming with happiness, or shake his hand over a delicious canapé and French champagne. He did not want to be a good sport, an honourable ex-husband, a considerate father, not in that moment. 1.58. Be honest, some part of you wants her to stop the ceremony, to look over at you and say, 'This is a mistake, this is the only man I ever loved and I'm sorry about your cancer, Brian, but no can do,' and then run into his arms. Yes, yes, yes. Part of him wanted that. The rest, the great bulk of Daniel Clement, knew it would not happen, that she would gaze into the eyes of Brian and say 'I do' under a cloudless sky to a ripple of applause and that everything from then on would be changed, and he would be an interloper.

1.59.

He turned around his car. Three point – textbook – and sped out the way he came.

CHAPTER 40

After the O'Gradys, I went into some kind of fugue state. I couldn't be bothered to watch the footy. Everything seemed trivial and indulgent. Instead I sat and played my stereo, old LPs, bands I'd worshipped. It was like floating on my back in an ocean of music, my youth drifting above me: friends long forgotten, old cars distinguished by overheating radiators or cracked windshields, smoky pubs, street posters. Somewhere during The Angels' 'Marseilles', it hit me. I called James Feruggi in Darwin and fluked him right away. There were no polite catch-ups.

'Did you guys ever do manoeuvres or bivouacs at Jarrahdale?'

'Let me think. Yes, yes we did.'

Jarrahdale, where Jessica's body had been dumped. The police had thoroughly searched that area after the body had been found, and intermittently since.

'Where else did you do exercises?'

'There were a lot.'

I thought of where Whitmore had been going to bury me: on a hill with a view. Not dissimilar to where Jessica had been found.

'Hills, slopes, anywhere like that?'

He said he'd need time to think.

'Do that. Write them down, better still, mark them on a map if you can.'

It took around four hours for him to come back to me. He'd nominated six sites.

The next day, first thing, I put a call into Nikki Sutton. She accepted right away.

'Thanks for taking my call,' I said.

'Your call will always be accepted here,' she replied.

I asked if they'd found anything new that might give a location for where Emily and Caitlin might be found.

'Not yet, but there's a lot to check. He has a half-brother in country Victoria, we're only just getting to him now.'

'I have an idea, could be dumb.'

'I like dumb ideas if they come from you.'

Like Whitmore, I enjoyed the flattery. I told her there were some places I thought might be worth checking out.

*

It was raining. I don't know where that came from. You don't expect rain mid-October. The first two places they'd tried had produced a duck egg. James Feruggi had been good enough to come down for a couple of days and drive around to the sites of the training exercises, pointing out where they had camped. This place near Gidgegannup had a sloping hill, wooded with a clearing or two. I thought about where Whitmore was going to bury me on that hillside, near the base of the highest ring of trees in the clearing.

'Try there,' I suggested.

They had some X-ray machine where they could fly overhead and look for buried objects. I was told the bikie gangs buried guns or money or drugs in containers and they could find them from the plane, but they didn't need a plane here. I was hanging with the tech team personally appointed by Sutton. They drove their machine over in a van. I don't know how it worked, kind of like a glass-bottomed boat I think, that's how it seemed from where I was watching a few hundred metres away, sipping thermos coffee, as rain pattered on my hoodie. They drove up and back, up and back. Then, brakelights. They stopped and jumped out and somebody, I think it was one of the female techs, Bernie, was waving and shouting and the secondary team, who were huddled with me, ditched their coffees and started running. The rain stopped all of a sudden and I looked up at the sky; a few drops were spilling from leaves onto my face, but the clouds just vanished and sun beamed out like the smile of a beautiful, innocent girl.

Four hours later as they carefully extracted remains believed to be those of Caitlin, her parents were huddled close to the gravesite, tightly holding one another's hand just the way they must have that very first night when Caitlin had not returned home, their love and courage through the darkness undiminished.

EPILOGUE

Emily Virtue, the first of the young women to vanish, was the last to be yielded up. Fortunately for her family she was buried at the very next site on the list.

Closure, finally. Luke Whitmore had not won after all.

Tash came back with Grace, and my life too once more became complete. I found myself standing on the water's edge at North Cottesloe just as I had almost eighteen years ago to the day, recalling that spring, the drone of planes overhead, the ships on the horizon. I wondered about invisible connections: if Timor had never happened would Whitmore's sociopathy have ever been forged, would Caitlin O'Grady now be standing looking at this horizon with her own young children? I contemplated what Whitmore had said to me as he prepared to kill me: we were on the frailest of ice every day of our lives. Sidney Turner, Ian Bontillo were dead because of a crack in the ice started all those years ago by Whitmore. Robert Plaistowe's life was in tatters. Kelly Davies had fallen through the ice and perished in an ancient desert. Maybe Whitmore was right, we had such little power in the scheme of things, but here's where I disagreed with him: the little we did have was critical and what gave us humanity. I thought about the goodness of Craig Drummond who so few would ever know, and about the evil of Whitmore, which would be embossed on the psyche of Western Australia for generations.

And what of Snowy Lane, the celebrated psycho-hunter? What did he think of himself? My summary: he'd done what he could with what he had. He'd made mistakes, he'd been dogged in equal proportions to stupid. Ultimately a life was no more enduring than the impression we leave on a leather sofa but, maybe in my time, I had made a difference. I hoped so.

Gruesome had been a long time ago and whatever gift I had then had languished. Drummond had brought me into the maze and, helpless, I had watched him bleed to death. I'd started my second tilt at this case looking for a daughter who was feared dead but was never missing, and found a daughter who was.

I eased myself into the water. It was still a little cold. My arms and feet began moving, and before long I was just a small splash in the distance.

ACKNOWLEDGEMENTS

I wish to thank my editor Georgia Richter for her assiduous work on the manuscript, and all those at Fremantle Press who transition the book from an idea into a living reality. Professor Ian Dadour I thank for his insight into many things forensic but especially the effect of desert location on human remains. A big thank you also to Murray Kimber for the benefit of his description of the Bay View Terrace area in the late '90s and Peter Burke who knows the Kimberley far better than me and gave me his insights.

While the novel uses the infamous Claremont Serial Killings as a prototype for the 'Autostrada' killings of the story, this is only to provide a vehicle to explore the psychological impact of such crimes on a community, victims' families and investigators. There is no sense in which this is a true crime work. This novel is a work of fiction, all characters are fictitious and any resemblance to real people living or dead is coincidental. The geography of most places in the novel, including Bay View Terrace and the streets of Broome, may be recognised in general structure but micro details, such as shops and street names, and the actual layout of lanes, streets and carparks have been altered to assist a work of fiction.

First published 2017 by
FREMANTLE PRESS
25 Quarry Street, Fremantle WA 6160
(PO Box 158, North Fremantle WA 6159)
www.fremantlepress.com.au

Front cover photograph: Orien Harvey, 'A storm rolls in over Cottesloe Beach'
Back cover: Todd Quakenbush (swimmer) and Jeremy Bishop (ocean),
www.unsplash.com

Printed by Everbest Printing Company, China

National Library of Australia
Cataloguing-in-Publication entry

Warner, Dave, 1953–, author
Clear to the horizon
ISBN 9781925164459 (pbk)
Detective and mystery stories
Australian fiction.

Government of **Western Australia**
Department of **Culture and the Arts**

Fremantle Press is supported by the State Government through the Department
of Culture and the Arts.

Australian Government · Australia Council for the Arts

Publication of this title was assisted by the Commonwealth Government
through the Australia Council, its arts funding and advisory body